CONTENTS

Acknowledgments

Editors' Preface:

This book collects the previously published stories that Rod Serling bought for THE TWILIGHT ZONE; with one exception. Permissions difficulties prevented us from including "The Chaser" by John Collier, which was adapted by screenwriter Robert Presnell, Jr., and aired under that name on May 13, 1960, starring George Grizzard and John McIntire.

The editors would like to thank Kathy Vought and Geoff Cohen of Avon Books for their good advice; Roberta Pryor of International Creative Management and Don Congdon of Don Congdon Associates for their help and cooperation; and most of all, Carol Serling, for giving us the permission to compile the book you are about to read.

Preface

by Carol Serling

Rod Serling freely admitted that he was unabashedly a great devotee of tales of horror, fantasy, and the supernatural. He grew up reading Poe and Lovecraft, so that when CBS gave the green light to the new series—*The Twilight Zone*—he sought out the master fantasy storytellers of the day, many of whom you will meet in this book.

Several years later, when an Emmy Award was presented to Rod for the series, he said, "Come on over, fellas, we'll carve it up like a turkey." He was really speaking to two "fellas": Richard Matheson and Chuck Beaumont. In collaboration, the three of them produced over ninety-nine percent of the work for the early years of *The Twilight Zone*. It was only natural that Rod would turn to Beaumont, who, as someone once said, actually lived in the Twilight Zone. Chuck, in his enthusiasm at the time, said that if the series was successful, "the dream of every green-blooded fan would come true and for the first time we'll have decent science fiction and fantasy available on a regular basis." And natural, too, that Rod would call upon Matheson, a writer of great variety and strong plots whose excursions in the genre were well known. Dick remembers his years of working on the series as some of the most enjoyable writing assignments of his career. Each man's work was different, but the chemistry was right and from this alliance came one of the most successful and creative series ever to hit television.

As you read these stories, you'll journey through inner

1

space, where man's primal fears, hopes, dreams, and nightmares lie. You'll find a strange beauty, fanciful humor, and chilling terror. Hopefully, too, you'll find some of the caring and concern and commitment to the human condition that was such an integral part of *The Twilight Zone*. Here, then, you can read the inspirations of some of the most memorable and best-remembered *TZs*. This brilliant collection, *The Twilight Zone: The Original Stories*, is a tribute to the fine writers whose imaginative ideas and talent made *TZ* a reality. And remember . . . as you begin your journey through the following pages . . . the ordinary laws of the universe do not apply; no luggage is required for the trip. All you need bring is your imagination.

Introduction

by Richard Matheson

Time is, to say the least, a tricky business. The future is the trickiest; unless one is a skillful futurist, in which case one can extrapolate and make some educated guesses regarding times to come. Or unless one is an authentic psychic with the gift of precognition, in which case one can probably approximate the same percentage of hits versus misses regarding the future.

The past, while less tricky, has its own integral perils. One of these is the undependability of memory. Do we recall past occurrences with accuracy? Most often, not. Such is the vulnerability of the aging and the consequent plight of the young who must listen to the waning recollections of their elders. *Things were different in my day. When I was a boy I had to. When I was a girl we never had.* And on and on, children groaning inwardly and praying for surcease.

The truth is, of course, that we see past events through lenses which, if not entirely murky, are tinted with that much-referred-to color of rose. Even general history errs more often than not. A writer friend has told me that his preference in research sources is old newspapers. They, too, may get things awry but, at worst, they do it only at the remove of a day or a week. A history book, on the other hand, may be based on another history book, which is based on another history book, and so on back through time to an original source that may well have gotten the facts wrong in the first

3

place, thus misleading generations of trusting researchers into repeating falsehoods *ad infinitum*.

What, then, can one do to avoid the pitfalls of aberrant memory? In personal life, the only evidence to verify statements made in recollection is letters, diaries, journals, photographs. This kind of evidence is also used by historians. None of it is wholly dependable.

Fortunately, with the advent of motion-picture film, memory became more a matter of visible proof than vague remembrance. If a picture cannot lie, a motion picture (assuming that it was not originally intended to be a lie such as fraud and/or propaganda) is positively trapped in the snare of What Really Was. This can, in short order, end an argument as to past veracity. It can, also, verify for all time (assuming that long a life for film stock) the quality of past endeavors.

The Twilight Zone program is, happily, a beneficiary of this permanent verification. It is *there;* on the screen, all moving, all sound, no tricks. What you see is what it was. And a good many people like what they see—and see—and see. Having first appeared on television in 1959, *The Twilight Zone* is still rolling along at a good clip *twenty-five years later.* An incredible longevity for a television show.

True, this evidence, created from 1959 to 1963, has its negative aspects. I happen to be one of those who feel that it is a mistake to revive shows from the so-called Golden Age of Television. I believe that they were created for and were superlative in that Age. Today, the seams show. They are, by and large, "revived": brought back to consciousness, their production values well below the standard of what we now see customarily on television. All of which gives these shows, in 1984, a certain primitive quality which, in the 1950s and '60s, they most definitely did not possess. This is less true of *The Twilight Zone* than of most other shows from that period, but, despite its more viable genre, even that show has not (could not possibly have) escaped this inevitable point of recession.

What keeps *The Twilight Zone* so popular, of course, are the stories. The STORIES. The concepts, which intrigue and excite and amuse and terrify and half a dozen other wonderful emotions. The story was all in *The Twilight Zone*—which makes this collection of stories more than appropriate for this or any time. The criticism regarding possible primitivism in *The Twilight Zone* programs does not apply to these stories. They are completely pure in the sense that the influences of time have never subjected them to any possible diminishing effect. No producer or director or actor or editor or composer or cameraman or lighting man ever touched them. They are pristine, exactly (word for word) as they appeared from their creators' minds. That is the charm (and, to the writer, the blessing) of the printed word. These stories do not depend on anyone's interpretation. They are words on paper, and so long as paper and print exist, the *original* thoughts will remain unaltered.

A long way around to praise the stories in this collection. Omitting mention of my own—even nearing the age of sixty, I find it difficult to tout myself or my work—the stories can be seen for what they (purely) are: enormously original and effective. Little wonder that they were purchased by *The Twilight Zone* to be adapted into scripts. Charles Beaumont did his own adaptations, as I did except for my stories "Disappearing Act" and "Third from the Sun," which were adapted by Rod Serling, and Beaumont's "The Beautiful People," adapted by John Tomerlin. Serling also adapted the other stories in this book with the exceptions of "I Sing the Body Electric!," adapted by its author, Ray Bradbury, and "The Self-Improvement of Salvadore Ross," which was adapted by Jerry McNeely. Ambrose Bierce's "An Occurrence at Owl Creek Bridge" was adapted and directed by Robert Enrico and was, as a point of information, not made specifically for *The Twilight Zone* but acquired for it after the film won in the short-subject category at the Cannes Film Festival.

Early in 1959, Charles (Chuck) Beaumont and I were invited to see the pilot film for a new CBS series to be entitled

The Twilight Zone. Chuck and I were, naturally, aware of Rod Serling and his outstanding writing accomplishments in television (''Patterns,'' ''Requiem for a Heavyweight,'' etc.). What we didn't know was how very nice a man he was and how pleasant it was going to be to work with him and his producers for the next five years, first Buck Houghton, then Herb Hirschman, then Bert Granet. And what we could not possibly have foreseen was how successful the show was going to be, what a cult phenomenon it was destined to become.

Not that all was smooth sailing for *The Twilight Zone.* My recollection is that the show was more a survivor than a glowing success. I speak, of course, in terms of ratings, not creative output. In the latter category, the show proved itself again and again—and is still proving itself a quarter of a century later.

How did I, personally, feel about the transition of my stories from prose to film? Of the eight in this collection, my favorites, in general order of preference, are ''Steel,'' ''Death Ship,'' ''Nightmare at 20,000 Feet,'' ''Night Call,'' ''Little Girl Lost,'' ''Mute,'' then the two Rod adapted. Pure ego at work on these last two, although I certainly appreciate the problem Rod faced in expanding what is essentially a short-short story (''Third from the Sun'') into a full half-hour program; and, as a matter of fact, ''Disappearing Act'' was not really adapted at all, only the smallest aspect of its premise being used.

Recollections of the shows made from these stories:

''Steel'': Lee Marvin, during rehearsal, simulating crowd noises in order to psych himself into feeling the reality of what he was doing.

''Death Ship'': One of the two hour-long scripts I wrote for *The Twilight Zone,* the other being ''Mute.'' I liked this one very much, thought the direction by Don Medford fine, the three lead performances by Jack Klugman, Ross Martin and Frederick Beir excellent, emotionally moving.

''Nightmare at 20,000 Feet'': The irony of the fact that the man inside the "panda" suit (which was the monster on the wing) looked exactly like the creature on the wing as I visualized him in my story. Well, with apologies to Nick Cravat, not *exactly* but so close that a minimal amount of makeup would have easily completed the resemblance—something I have always wished they'd done.

"Night Call": The only *Twilight Zone* helmed by that master director of the genre, Jacques Tourneur; my doing, I am happy to say. At least, I forcefully suggested the idea to Bert Granet and he hired Tourneur. A wondrous talent, Jacques Tourneur. He should have been hired to do far more than he was able to do in his lifetime. Also, who could ask for a better performer than Gladys Cooper?

"Little Girl Lost": Paul Stewart's excellent direction and Charles Aidman's superlative performance. And the amusement of watching, transferred to film, an incident that—at least until the fourth dimension came into play—was a literal reenactment of something that had happened to my older daughter, also named Tina.

"Mute": The second hour-long *Twilight Zone* I wrote. In the story, the young telepath is a boy; in the script, she became a girl, I don't recall why. And that little girl has become, in real life, the most-exotic Ann Jillian, who has lately played a ghost and Mae West on television. A far cry.

And a final recollection: of Rod Serling and my good friend Charles Beaumont. Rod, as noted, could not have been a nicer man. To me, he was always kind and thoughtful, supportive, helpful, and a joy to know and work with—not to mention his awesome talent. And Chuck Beaumont was a scintillating light in my existence during his all-too-brief a span. Funny, charming, a challenging delight to be with—and also an awesome talent. I miss him. I miss his lovely, wonderfully good-natured wife, Helen. I admire, to this moment, the talent and resourceful courage of their four children—Chris, Cathy, Elizabeth, and Greg—who were left, far too early, with the need to grow into maturity without their parents.

* * *

What remains to be said? Only this: to reemphasize what I firmly believe—that in all writing media—stage, screen, television, and printed word—the *story* is all. If, when I move on, I am remembered as a good storyteller, my soul will be content.

Accordingly, to those of you who are devotees of *The Twilight Zone* reruns, enjoy here the reading of the original stories for these particular segments. And for those of you who regard television as the Idiot Box and/or Satan's Abomination, read these stories anyway. Exclusive of what they became on television, they stand up just fine by themselves: *good stories*. Enjoy them as such.

Richard Matheson
June, 1984

One for the Angels

Adapted by Anne Serling-Sutton

TELEPLAY BY ROD SERLING

AIRED OCTOBER 9, 1959

STARRING ED WYNN

WHEN LEW BOOKMAN'S ALARM CLOCK WENT OFF AT six-thirty, he was already awake and sitting by the window. He'd been sitting there for quite some time, watching the chipped and peeling paint grow more visible in the growing light. He pulled himself out of the ancient brown chair, causing yet another spring to bounce loose, and shut the alarm off. He walked back to the window, peering through the dirty glass at the street below. The sidewalks were already steaming from the heat, the traffic was growing, the dogs barking. Summers on the East Side were always the same. Days began early and didn't end until absolutely forced to. And although Lew spent the whole day, each day, behind a pitch stand hawking his goods, summers were special to him. And Lew Bookman though a minor component, was a fixture of the summer.

At seven A.M. prompt, he was behind his pitch stand, with everything set up and a few children already surrounding him. They loved him—this dumpy, shabby little man in the mangled seersucker suit with his pants invariably too short and his coat too long. A flamboyant tie hung askew at his

9

neck with a misshapen knot, and a summer porkpie tilted rakishly and idiotically at an angle on his head. These set off the odd, bizarre quality of the little man and made him even more endearing in the children's eyes.

On the pitch stand were perhaps two dozen items. Everything from toys to needle and thread, cheap ties, can openers, TV tubes, puzzles, and tennis balls. Lew began a pitch. "Here you go, ladies and gentlemen . . . nice things for the home . . . wearing apparel, toys . . . everything. Special July cleanup sale!" No one but the children paid attention.

Too early. Too hot, he thought to himself. Lew was a walking rebuttal to the American dream that success can be carved, gouged, and grubbed out of log cabins and tenements. He had not even a nodding acquaintance with success, and his dreams extended only from the curb to the sidewalk.

Lew continued through the day, calling out to anyone who passed by, his voice beginning to grow hoarse. He lost himself, temporarily, watching the children down the street play kick the can. Leaning over his stand to see them more closely, he yelled, his voice cracking, "Go get it, Paul!" And then, a little embarrassed and self-conscious, he looked around to see if anyone had heard him. A dark-coated man was standing about five feet away, staring at him. In his hand was a small ledger. Lew looked at him a little warily and turned back to his pitch stand, fondled some of the items nervously, mopped his forehead for perhaps the hundredth time that day, and then glanced back at the children's game. Sensing the growing shadows of the day's aging, he heaved a couple of extremely deep sighs and with a slight shrug began to close up the pitch. Automatically he put things into their places, retrieved samples, and buttoned the whole thing up. Every now and then he compulsively looked up to see the man in the dark suit still staring at him. Finally he had the whole pitch put away. He hoisted it under his arm and walked down the long, hot sidewalk toward home. Just once, he turned back to look at the man and then continued on his way.

The children, playing in the water by the fire hydrants, saw him coming and called out and waved to him. "Hi, Lew!" "How ya doin', Lew?" "How'd she go today, Lew?" A few of them pushed their way to grab his free hand.

Lew responded to every call. On occasion, he'd stop and cup a child's face in his hands. Maggie, a little seven-year-old with an infectious grin displaying two missing teeth, ran excitedly toward him. He put down his bundle, swooped her into his arms, and sat down on the steps. He breathed deeply, took out his handkerchief, and again mopped his forehead. "Hot one today, huh, guys?"

The children gathered around him asking questions in unison. "What ya sellin' today, Lew? Toys, Lew? Were ya sellin' toys?"

Lew shook his head pontifically and held up a protesting hand. "They may look like toys. But they are not just toys. Just toys, anyone can sell. These, my young friends, are the toy wonders of the world."

The children were wide-eyed now, and Maggie said breathlessly, "Go ahead, Lew. Give us the pitch!"

Lew cleared his throat, looked down at the starry-eyed kids, and the words came easily, effectively, with import and meaning. "Young ladies and gentlemen, the toys you now hold in your hand come from a remote corner of the mysterious Tibetan mountain country. They are patterned, shaped, and forged by strange little men who work underground. And in their final operation—"

Maggie, twisting her hair, unable to hold back, blurted out, "They are subject to the strange life-force!"

A small boy disappointedly said, "Aw, come on. Let Lew tell it."

Lew laughed and hugged them both to him. "You all know it by heart." He rose very slowly and picked up his satchel. "Now don't forget. Bookman social and ice cream hour after supper at the usual time. See you then." He

winked and waved and continued up the steps and into the
foyer and up to the third floor. He leaned against his door
and fumbled for his key. "Gotcha!" he said upon retrieving
it. He walked into the room and opened the threadbare curtains he had closed earlier to keep out the stifling heat. He
hummed a little song and crossed the room to the sink. After
filling a small watering can, he took it over to a row of flowers
that were blooming heroically on the windowsill. Still humming, he put the can down, started to take off his coat and, in
the process of turning, saw the man in the dark suit sitting in
a chair staring at him.

Lew jumped back, startled, and almost knocked one of the
flower pots to the floor. "You're—you're the man from the
sidewalk. I saw you today writing things in your book." He
craned his neck to look over on the man's lap and saw the
ledger.

The stranger uncrossed his legs, and both men were very
quiet for a moment. The sounds from the street became very
audible, and Lew could hear the children laughing over the
impatient traffic.

Finally the stranger said, "You are Lew Bookman, aren't
you?"

Lew's anxiety visibly decreased as he began to think
maybe this man had come to buy something. "That's right.
Lewis J. Bookman. Something I can show you?" In a half-
hearted hope he added, "Something in collar stays,
maybe?"

"Mr. Bookman. I'm not here to buy anything."

Lew hunched down on a kitchen chair and tapped his fingers nervously on the small, scratched tabletop beside him.

The stranger looked down at the ledger. "Now, let's get
to business, shall we? Lewis J. Bookman, age sixty-nine,
right?"

Lew continued to tap the table with trembling fingers.
"Seventy in September."

"Occupation—pitchman. Right?"

Lew nodded. "That's right. Are you a census taker?"

The stranger disregarded him. "Born in New York City, 1910?"

Lew tried to concentrate on the voices from beneath the window. His agitation and anxiety were increasing. He got up and walked to the flowers, touched them lightly in an absentminded gesture, and then walked back to the chair, where he sat crossing and uncrossing his legs. Taking a deep breath, he said, "That's right. 1910."

"Mother—Flora Bookman. Father—Jacob Bookman. Mother's place of birth—Syracuse, New York. Father's place of birth—Detroit, Michigan. Right?"

Lew rose and looked down at the ledger. "That's right. My, you have it all down."

The stranger nodded, bored. "We have to keep these things efficient. Now, today is the 19th of July. And your departure is at midnight tonight."

Lew started to rise. "My departure? I have—" At that moment he heard the sound of footsteps running up several flights of stairs and then a knock on the door.

"Excuse me." He opened the door. Maggie was standing there with tears brimming in her eyes.

Lew touched her face. "Hey, Maggie. What's the matter?"

She held up a toy. "The key's bent, Lew. Can you fix it?"

Lew took the toy and studied it. "Here's your trouble right here, little one. See this little cogwheel? You've pushed down on the key when you've been winding it." They both leaned over the toy. Lew, remembering the man, said, "Oh! I'd introduce you two, only I don't know your name, sir."

The stranger smiled. "No need."

Maggie looked up at Lew with adoration. "I think I got it now, Lew."

Lew looked back at the man. "This gentleman here has come to ask me a lot of questions." He scratched his chin and as a frightened afterthought said, "You're not the police, are you?"

The stranger shook his head. "Hardly."

Lew turned back to the little girl. "Kind of gave me a turn.

I'm glad he's not the police. I've got my vendor's license here someplace. I thought maybe I'd forgotten to renew it or something.''

The little girl was still intent on the toy. ''Who's the police, Lew?''

Lew pointed and said, ''This gentleman here.''

Maggie looked up briefly and pushed the hair out of her face. ''What gentleman?''

Lew pointed to the chair. ''That gentleman.''

The little girl stretched her head inside the door, and again asked, ''What gentleman?''

With growing confusion, Lew looked around at the stranger sitting in the chair.

The stranger placed his hands behind his head. ''Mr. Bookman, she can't see me or hear me.''

Lew looked from the man to Maggie. ''Why not?''

Maggie asked, ''Why not what, Lew?''

''Why can't you see him or hear him?''

Maggie smiled, sensing that Lew was playing a game. ''See who, Lew?'' And then, delighted that the toy was fixed, she said, ''It works great now, Lew. Thanks an awful lot. See you after supper, huh?''

She started out the door.

Lew gently touched her arm. ''Hey, Maggie, wait a minute. Aren't you going to say goodbye?''

Maggie smiled her toothless grin and held the toy tightly. ''Oh yeah! Goodbye, Lew. Thanks a lot.''

''Maggie, I meant to the gentleman.''

Maggie again looked at the empty chair, and she laughed. ''Oh, it's a game! The invisible man. Goodbye, invisible man. See you after supper, Lew.''

She gamboled out of the apartment and ran down the stairs, two at a time.

Lew closed the door very, very thoughtfully and turned toward the man. ''I can see you . . . yet she can't.''

''Mr. Bookman. Only those who are to accompany me can

see me. Understand, Mr. Bookman? Now, don't you think you'd better start making your arrangements?''

Lew said softly, ''Arrangements for what?''

''For your departure.''

''My departure where?''

The stranger rose and stared at him. Taking a deep breath, he said, ''You still don't get it! I just never will understand you people! You get this idiotic notion that life goes on forever, and of course it doesn't. Everyone has to go sometime.''

Lew shook his head back and forth. ''Go? You mean . . . ?''

The stranger nodded, walked around the room, and surveyed things. ''That's right.'' He stopped and looked down at the flowers on the windowsill.

Lew, momentarily forgetting the frighteningly insane conversation, said proudly, ''I won second prize last year at the YMHA flower show. Wisteria, open class.''

The stranger said, ''How nice.'' He turned and looked at Lew. ''And what I further don't understand is how little you appreciate the nature of your departure. Think of the poor souls who go in violent accidents. Those are the non-precognition victims. We're not permitted to forewarn them. You, Mr. Bookman, fall into the category of—natural causes.'' He cleared his throat and looked intently at Lew.

Lew took a step toward him. ''Natural causes?'' He pointed a slightly wavering finger at the stranger. ''I find you a very devious sort. This is not to say dishonest. Why don't you say what you mean?''

''Mr. Bookman, I have done everything but phone your own undertaker. How much clearer do you want it? If you still don't know who I am''—he turned toward the flowers—''then you are the most dense man I've come up against.'' He touched one of the flowers. It wilted under his touch, fell forward on its stem, and died.

Lew opened his mouth in astonishment. ''You're . . . death?''

The stranger took another deep sigh. ''Exactly, Mr. Bookman. Now shall we get down to business? Time of departure is midnight tonight. I trust that will suit you. The preordination is for death during sleep. I presume this too will meet with your approval. You'll find this a relatively simple and painless and barely noticeable—''

Lew, with nervous fingers, beat a tattoo all over his face, and finally he shouted, ''Please! I don't want to go!''

The stranger said, to himself, ''They never do.''

''But I can't go yet! There's nothing wrong with me. I'm a healthy man. Outside of a cold last winter and an infected liver, I don't think I've been sick a day in the last twenty years.''

''Mr. Bookman. That's as it may be, but departure time is set for midnight and departure time will be at midnight.''

Lew pushed his hands deep into his pockets. ''Hey! Don't I have anything to say about that?''

The stranger nodded and opened his ledger. ''We do listen to appeals, but frankly, Mr. Bookman, I must tell you that there's very little here in the way of an extenuating circumstance. There are three major categories of appeals. One is hardship cases. Now, do you have a wife or family who might suffer by your demise beyond a reasonable point?''

Lew shook his head. ''No—no family.'' He picked up the old photograph album and turned a few of the pages, very gently and very carefully. He studied a browning picture of his mother and father's wedding and then cleared his throat and carefully put the book back in its place.

The stranger watched this but didn't acknowledge it openly. ''Second category is priority cases. Statesmen, scientists, men on the verge of discoveries.'' He looked up at Lew and then over to the pitchman's satchel. ''I take it you're not working on any major scientific pursuit at this moment.''

Lew said, in a whisper, ''No, I'm not. What—what about the third category?''

''Well, Mr. Bookman, that would be unfinished business of a major nature.''

Lew turned to the stranger. ''I've—I've never made a truly

successful pitch. I mean . . . I mean a big pitch. I mean a pitch for the angels!'' He turned away and very quietly said, ''I guess that wouldn't mean much to you. But it would mean a great deal to me. It would mean that—'' His face was very soft and reflective. ''That I could have one moment in my whole life when I was successful at something. Just one moment when the children would be able to . . . would be able to feel proud of me.''

The stranger displayed no emotion at all. ''The children?''

Lew nodded. His face suddenly carried a peculiar brightness. ''I've always had rather a fondness for children.''

The stranger said dispassionately, ''That's in the record here.'' Then his face began, just barely perceptibly, to soften as he stared intently at Lew. ''Problem here, Mr. Bookman, is that you'd require a delay until—''

Lew's face began to relax. The tense muscles began to release. ''Until I could make a pitch! I mean, the kind of pitch I told you about!''

The stranger half smiled. ''One for the angels, you mean? I'm terribly sorry, Mr. Bookman. You see, these categories are fairly specific, and when reference is made to unfinished business of a major nature, well, the only interpretation to be made here is simply that . . . what I mean is that unfortunately, Mr. Bookman, the ability to achieve success in a given professional venture is really hardly of a major—'' He stopped abruptly, conscious of the face of Lewis J. Bookman. Suddenly he was aware of the poignance of it, the pathos of it, the infinite sadness, and with it the infinite gentleness and kindness. The stranger cleared his throat, looked away, and drummed with his fingers on the ledger. ''Mr. Bookman, mean a great deal to you, does it?''

Lew, with growing intensity, sputtered, ''A—a great deal!''

The stranger pursed his lips, drummed again with his fingers, walked over to the window, and then turned back to Lew. ''All right, Mr. Bookman. Under the circumstances, I believe we could grant you a delay.''

Lew looked up at him. His eyes were bright with a strange relief. "Until?"

The stranger responded pettishly. "What do you mean, 'until'? Until you've made this . . . this pitch you're talking about."

Lew felt like a child talking to his parent—very small, very vulnerable, and very innocent. "I—I can stay alive until then?"

The stranger nodded. "That's the agreement."

Lew began to feel better. His eyes narrowed and a very wise, rather cat-got-canary look covered his face. Then he smiled. "I think that's a fine bargain. It's been awfully nice talking to you, Mr. . . . I didn't get your name." He opened the door and motioned. Two children were playing jacks on the stairway. He stretched his neck out into the hall and called, "Hi, guys!"

The stranger headed for the door and looked at Lew. "Now, about this pitch, Mr. Bookman. When might we expect it?"

Lew, turning his attention from the children, giggled and said, "When? Oh, soon, soon. Maybe not this year. Maybe not next year, but soon."

The stranger put a large hand on the door. "Mr. Bookman, I have an odd feeling that you're taking advantage of us."

Lew smiled at him. "Do you really? Well now, that's a pity." He giggled again and slammed the door shut and shouted, "Because I am!" He turned from the door, looked at his flowers, and rubbed his hands together. His face conveyed a sense of relief, a sense of mischief, and a desperate desire to live. "I just won't make any pitches at all. I won't even hardly open my mouth. Think you'll get me, huh? Well, I just won't—" He stopped dead, staring toward the mirror over the sink. There he saw the reflection of the stranger back in the room.

"Mr. Bookman, really, this is much more serious than you imagine."

Lew went to the door in a rush, flung it open, and hurried

out. The hall was cast with late-afternoon shadows and had an eerie, lonely feeling.

The stranger waved a reproving finger at Lew as he passed him. "It's much more complex than you realize—what you've just done."

Lew stared at him, then shut his eyes, hoping he would disappear. He ran down one flight of stairs and stood on the landing. He looked up and the stranger was also there, casting an ominous shadow.

"Mr. Bookman, here we have gone out of our way to help you, and this is the way you repay us!"

Lew took a long, shuddering breath as he waved the stranger off and ran down another flight of the old, battered stairway, finally arriving in the foyer. He looked around, waiting, and the stranger stepped out of the shadows and faced him.

"Mr. Bookman, it won't just end here, you understand. There'll be consequences, you see!"

Lew shook his head back and forth in a gesture of disdain. He pointed a wavery finger at the man and in a voice fairly dripping with contempt and with power said, "F.Y.I.—that means 'for your information'—you have made your bed and you shall now sleep in it! You say I won't go until I make the pitch—well, all right! You'll have to wait until I make the pitch! And, young man, this I can say to you without fear of contradiction: You have got a long wait!"

The stranger's eyes narrowed thoughtfully. "That may well be, Mr. Bookman, but since you won't come with me—we have been forced to select an alternative."

At that moment there was the sound of shrieking brakes from outside. A woman screamed, and then a jumble of excited, frightened, horrified voices could be heard. Lew ran to the door and pushed it open. He saw a truck with blinking lights and people crying and holding on to each other. He ran through the crowd and finally reached a little knot of people on the curb. They parted for him and revealed the body of a little girl lying on the sidewalk. The truck driver, his face ashen, kneeled beside her, wringing his hands, and said, "I swear I didn't see her. She just jumped off the curb and I didn't have no chance to stop! I swear to you, I never had no chance to stop."

Lew looked at the child, at the blond curls framing her face, tinted with blood. Very quietly, very slowly, he leaned down beside her and stroked her face. "Oh, Maggie. Oh, baby." Still touching and looking at the child, he said, "Has anyone gone for a doctor? The ambulance coming?"

There was a chorus of accents as a few people backed off to give the child and the old man some room.

Lew pushed a wisp of hair off the tortured little face and kissed the child's cheek. "You're gonna be all right, Maggie darling. You're gonna be just fine."

The little girl opened her eyes and smiled wanly. "Hi, Lew!" Then her eyes traveled past Lew as a shadow crossed over her face. She looked frightened. "Lew—Lew, who's that man?"

Lew turned, and over his shoulder he saw the dark stranger. Terrified, he pressed his hands to the ground for support, and in a voice that trembled with intensity, he said, "You can't take her. No siree—you can't take her! I'll go. I'll go as planned. Never mind the pitch. I'll go right now. I don't want to wait, even. I want to go right now!"

The stranger began to walk away and Lew raced after him. "Mr. Death? Mr. Death—I'll go. You mustn't take the little girl. I'll go. Please, Mr. Death." He dropped his head in his hands and shuddered. The overwhelming emotion could no longer be contained, and he dropped to his knees and sobbed. "Please, please, listen to me. I'll go."

The doctor came and they carried Maggie inside.

The neighbors crowded around the door, somber and silent. Finally the doctor came out, and pulling his sleeves down, he walked through the crowd at the door. There were hushed questions. "How is she?" "Is she gonna be all right?" "How's the little girl, Doc?" On the front stoop, Lew stood waiting.

He was shaking. "Doctor?"

The doctor took out a cigarette, lit it, and inhaled deeply. "I don't know. She was hurt mighty bad and I don't want to move her, but we'll know by midnight."

Lew looked up at him. "By midnight?"

The doctor nodded. "I think by then."

Lew looked out at the street. The traffic flow had returned to normal. The crowd had dispersed and gone home. He looked up at the streetlights and at the yellow glow they cast, throwing ominous shadows on the pavement. His face was grim. "He won't come in! *I won't let him come in!*" He backed his way into the building, surveying every movement around him, and walked into the child's room.

Maggie was in bed beside the window. She was unconscious, her blond curls still matted with blood. Her eyes were closed, and beside her, on the table by the bed, was a cheap alarm clock ticking clangorously, reading 11:40. Lew peered at her, pulled her blanket up, and kissed her on the forehead; then he left, looking back once to check on her. Very quietly, he closed the door, picked up his pitch stand and walked back to the front stoop. The traffic had died down, and he sat there completely alone. His figure cast a long shadow as he sat there, guarding. He looked at his pitch stand briefly, then at his watch, and intermittently scanned the street. Suddenly the light from the streetlamp was momentarily eclipsed by a large black shadow. Lew looked up quickly, his fists clenched, his brow damp. Out of the shadows and into the periphery of light around the streetlamp came the stranger. He walked very slowly across the street and stood a few feet away from Lew.

Lew peered at him and said curtly, "You got business in there?"

The stranger nodded. "I certainly do." He took out a pocket watch, snapped it open, looked at it, snapped it shut, and then put it back into his pocket. "It's a quarter to twelve. In fifteen minutes—midnight. That's my appointment."

Lew stood up, attempting to swell his body, and stood before the entrance. ''Mr. Death . . . the little girl is only seven years old.'' Hysteria began to creep into his voice once again. He took a step down toward the stranger. ''Please—please, I'm ready now.''

The stranger said, firmly but not urgently, ''I'm sorry, Mr. Bookman. We had to make other arrangements. It's impossible to change it now. She's to come with me at midnight. So I must be in there at midnight.'' He made a somewhat resigned and hopeless gesture.

Lew thought about the child. He remembered her holding out the toy to him, arms outstretched, smile big and wide. Pretty, tiny face. This memory collided harshly with the image he'd just left behind. The little girl curled up in bed, in pain. He looked back at the stranger. His voice was strained and tight. ''And if you're not in there by midnight?''

The stranger laughed. ''That would be pretty much unheard of. If I didn't get there at precisely midnight then the whole timetable would be upset. Oh my, no . . . it's unheard of.''

Very slowly, Lew started to walk back up toward his pitch stand. He picked it up, carried it down to the sidewalk, opened it up, and started to arrange the merchandise.

''Mr. Bookman, what are you doing?''

Lew said, over his shoulder, ''What am I doing? Oh, nothing. Just setting up a pitch is all.''

''At this time of night?''

Lew coughed. ''Oh, I very often have a late-night sale. Very often.''

The stranger looked up and down the street. ''Not many customers.''

''They come. They show up.'' He turned and stood behind the pitch stand, which was all set up. He looked very closely at the stranger. ''You're here, anyway.''

The stranger laughed softly. ''Oh, I'm not much of a customer.''

Lew, with his eyes still fixed on him in deep concentration, said, "How do you know? Have you ever seen my stock? Now—now you take a tie like this right here—"

The stranger looked at him quizzically. "Like what?"

Lew looked down. In his shaking hand, he was holding a toy walking man. "Excuse me. Right here." He picked up the tie and held it out. "See this? What's it look like to you?"

The stranger smiled. "It looks like a tie."

Lew held it closer. "Feel it."

The stranger felt it and shrugged. "So?"

Lew began to talk very quickly, and the stranger moved close to the pitch stand. His mouth hung open as he became more and more enthralled, more and more captivated. Others began to gather and surround the two of them as Lew gained speed and strength.

"If you'll feast your eyes on this, my good man. Probably one of the most exciting inventions since atomic energy. A simulated silk so fabulously conceived as to mystify even the ancient Chinese silk manufacturers. A perfection of detail . . . an almost unbelievable attention to detail. A piquant interweaving of gossamer softness."

He continued to talk, the words spewing out on top of one another, and the stranger stood there, still openmouthed, almost mesmerized by the pitch. Lew handed him various items to examine and then quickly checked his watch. It was now 11:50.

Under his arm, the stranger now had several boxes of ties and Lew was still talking. Lew held up a piece of thread. "Witness, if you will, a demonstration of tensile strength. Feel this, if you will, sir."

The stranger tentatively touched the thread and then Lew yanked it away.

"Unbelievable, isn't it, sir? As strong as steel and yet as delicate as shantung silk. Picture, if you will, three hundred years of backbreaking research and labor to develop this, the absolute ultimate in thread. And what will you pay for this fabulous—I say fabulous—incredible and amazing development of the tailor's art? Will you pay twenty dollars, or ten dollars? Or even five? You might indeed if you were trying to purchase this at a store. But this fantastic thread is unavailable in stores. It is smuggled in by Oriental birds specially trained for ocean travel, each carrying a minute quantity in a small satchel underneath its ruby throat. It takes eight hundred and thirty-two crossings to supply enough thread to go around one spool, and tonight, as my special get-acquainted, introductory, mid-July, hot-summer sale, I offer you this thread not at thirty dollars. Not at twenty or ten, but for the ridiculously low price of twenty-five cents a spool.''

The stranger had moved even closer. His shirt was open, his tie askew, and he looked punchy. ''I'll take all you have.'' While he was looking at more of the items, Lew again stole a look at his watch: 11:55.

The night had grown darker. The sole light was from the streetlamps, and beneath them, Lew continued his pitch.

The stranger was loaded down with boxes and bags. Behind him and flanking him were other people, also holding on to things they had bought. From a distance, the scene looked like a Macy's sale. As Lew rummaged through his goods and held them up, people yanked them out of his hands. All the time he kept up a constant, steady stream of chatter.

''Sewing needles. Yarn. Simulated cashmere socks. Odd lots of leather. Marvelous plastic shoelaces. Genuine static eradicator, fits in any standard radio or clothes dryer. Suntan oil. Eczema powder. Athlete's-foot destroyer. How about nice shantung scarves?''

Sweat rolled down his face. The merchandise came in and out of his hands as he grabbed at other things while he talked.

The stranger was only semiconscious now. His mouth hung open and his eyes rolled. Lew stole another glance at his watch: 11:57.

''And now for the *pièce de résistance*. The bargain of the evening. An item never before offered in this or any other country." He waited a dramatic beat. "One guaranteed, live, human, genuine manservant."

The stranger held heavy eyes up to him and weakly said, "How's that?"

Lew ran the back of his hand over his forehead. "For what I ask, you, sir, receive a willing, capable, worldly, highly sophisticated, wonderfully loyal right-hand man to be used in any capacity you see fit."

The stranger was mystified. "How's that?"

Lew, without missing a beat, continued, "Me. Lewis J. Bookman. The first model of his kind. He comes to you with an absolute guarantee. All parts interchangeable. A certificate of four years' serviceability. Eats little. Sleeps little. Rests only a fraction of the time, and there he is at your elbow. At your beck and call whenever needed."

The stranger shook his head as if coming out of a trance and smiled. "Mr. Bookman, you are a persuasive man—"

Lew continued, "I challenge any other store, industry, or wholesale house to even come close to matching what I offer you here. Because, my dear man, I offer you . . ." And then, for the first time, his voice began to fade. "I offer you here . . ." His features suddenly went lax. His eyes half closed. The sweat poured down his face. Suddenly his hands fell to his sides. His head went down and he had to support himself on the railing. He stood there for a long, silent moment and then looked up as he heard the sound of a child crying and, concurrent with this, the sound of distant chimes that rang twelve times. He listened very closely, and then he looked at his watch.

The stranger wailed, "It's midnight. I've missed the appointment!"

Lew's eyes closed in massive relief. He turned when he heard the door of the building open. The doctor, holding his black case, was saying to the child's mother, "Just give her the sedatives. All she needs now is rest. But she's going to be all right!" He winked, smiled, and went down the steps past Lew to the sidewalk.

The stranger slowly shut his watch and put it back in his pocket. "One minute past twelve, Mr. Bookman, and you made me miss my appointment."

Lew nodded and softly said, "Thank God."

Slowly, as if in a dream, Lew shuffled over to the pitch stand and started to shut it up. He paused and then sat down and buried his face in his hands. After a moment, he was aware of the stranger standing very close to him, and he looked up.

"Mr. Bookman, a most persuasive pitch. An excellent pitch. It had to be to . . . to make me miss my appointment."

Lew nodded and smiled. "Yes, quite a pitch. Very effective. Best I've ever done. That's the kind of pitch I've always wanted to make. A big one. A pitch so big . . . so big the sky would open up." He smiled and looked off a little dreamily.

The stranger smiled at him. "A pitch for the angels."

Lew nodded. "That's right. A pitch for the angels." Suddenly his smile faded, his eyes looked down, and he turned away. "I guess . . . I guess it's time for *me* now."

The stranger sighed a deep sigh. "As per our agreement."

Lew tilted his hat on the back of his head. "Well, I'm ready."

The stranger gestured and said, "After you, Mr. Bookman."

The two men started to walk down the steps to the sidewalk. Suddenly Lew stopped and turned around. "You'll excuse me for a moment? I forgot something."

Lew walked back to the stoop, folded up the pitch stand, hoisted it under his arm, and then walked back down the steps toward the waiting stranger.

Lew patted the stand. "You never know who might need something up there!" Then he paused as his face took on a questioning look. "Up there?"

The stranger nodded and smiled. "Up there, Mr. Bookman. You made it!"

Lew smiled, and the two men walked slowly down the sidewalk away from the building. The street was quiet, save for the sounds of summer—distant crickets and a gentle wind. Lew thought of Maggie and smiled.

Perchance to Dream

Charles Beaumont

TELEPLAY BY CHARLES BEAUMONT

AIRED NOVEMBER 27, 1959

STARRING RICHARD CONTE, JOHN LARCH, AND
SUZANNE LLOYD

"PLEASE SIT DOWN," THE PSYCHIATRIST SAID, IN-
dicating a somewhat worn leather couch.

Automatically, Hall sat down. Instinctively, he leaned
back. Dizziness flooded through him, his eyelids fell like
sashweights, the blackness came. He jumped up quickly and
slapped his right cheek, then he slapped his left cheek, hard.

"I'm sorry, Doctor," he said.

The psychiatrist, who was tall and young and not in the
least Viennese, nodded. "You prefer to stand?" he asked,
gently.

"Prefer?" Hall threw his head back and laughed. "That's
good," he said. "*Prefer!*"

"I'm afraid I don't quite understand."

"Neither do I, Doctor." He pinched the flesh of his left
hand until it hurt. "No, no: that isn't true. I do understand.
That's the whole trouble, I do."

"You—want to tell me about it?"

"Yes. No." It's silly, he thought. You can't help me. No one
can. I'm alone! "Forget it," he said, and started for the door.

27

The psychiatrist said, "Wait a minute." His voice was friendly, concerned; but not patronizing. "Running away won't do you much good, will it?"

Hall hesitated.

"Forgive the cliché. Actually, running away is often the best answer. But I don't know yet that yours is that sort of problem."

"Did Dr. Jackson tell you about me?"

"No. Jim said he was sending you over, but he thought you'd do a better job on the details. I only know that your name is Philip Hall, you're thirty-one, and you haven't been able to sleep for a long time."

"Yes. A long time . . ." To be exact, seventy-two hours, Hall thought, glancing at the clock. Seventy-two horrible hours . . .

The psychiatrist tapped out a cigarette. "Aren't you—" he began.

"Tired? God yes. I'm the tiredest man on Earth! I could sleep forever. But that's just it, you see: I would. I'd never wake up."

"Please," the psychiatrist said.

Hall bit his lip. There wasn't, he supposed, much point to it. But, after all, what *else* was there for him to do? Where would he go? "You mind if I pace?"

"Stand on your head, if you like."

"Okay. I'll take one of your cigarettes." He drew the smoke into his lungs and walked over to the window. Fourteen floors below, the toy people and the toy cars moved. He watched them and thought, this guy's all right. Sharp. Intelligent. Nothing like what I expected. Who can say—*maybe* it'll do some good. "I'm not sure where to begin."

"It doesn't matter. The beginning might be easier for you."

Hall shook his head, violently. The beginning, he thought. Was there such a thing?

"Just take it easy."

After a lengthy pause, Hall said: "I first found out about

the power of the human mind when I was ten. Close to that time, anyway. We had a tapestry in the bedroom. It was a great big thing, the size of a rug, with fringe on the edges. It showed a group of soldiers Napoleonic soldiers—on horses. They were at the brink of some kind of a cliff, and the first horse was reared up. My mother told me something. She told me that if I stared at the tapestry long enough, the horses would start to move. They'd go right over the cliff, she said. I tried it, but nothing happened. She said, 'You've got to take time. You've got to *think* about it.' So, every night, before I went to bed, I'd sit up and stare at that damn tapestry. And finally, it happened. Over they went, all the horses, all the men, over the edge of the cliff . . .'' Hall stubbed out the cigarette and began to pace. ''Scared hell out of me,'' he said. ''When I looked again, they were all back. It got to be a game with me. Later on, I tried it with pictures in magazines, and pretty soon I was able to move locomotives and send balloons flying and make dogs open their mouths: everything, anything I wanted.''

He paused, ran a hand through his hair. ''Not too unusual, you're thinking,'' he said. ''Every kid does it. Like standing in a closet and shining a flashlight through your finger, or sewing up the heel of your palm . . . common stuff?''

The psychiatrist shrugged.

''There was a difference,'' Hall said. ''One day it got out of control. I was looking at a coloring book. One of the pictures showed a knight and a dragon fighting. For fun I decided to make the knight drop his lance. He did. The dragon started after him, breathing fire. In another second the dragon's mouth was open and he was getting ready to eat the knight. I blinked and shook my head, like always, only—nothing happened. I mean, the picture didn't 'go back.' Not even when I closed the book and opened it again. But I didn't think too much about it, even then.''

He walked to the desk and took another cigarette. It slipped from his hands.

"You've been on Dexedrine," the psychiatrist said, watching as Hall tried to pick up the cigarette.

"Yes."

"How many grains a day?"

"Thirty, thirty-five, I don't know."

"Potent. Knocks out your co-ordination. I suppose Jim warned you?"

"Yes, he warned me."

"Well, let's get along. What happened then?"

"Nothing." Hall allowed the psychiatrist to light his cigarette. "For a while, I forgot about the 'game' almost completely. Then, when I turned thirteen, I got sick. Rheumatic heart—"

The psychiatrist leaned forward and frowned. "And Jim let you have thirty-five—"

"Don't interrupt!" He decided not to mention that he had gotten the drug from his aunt, that Dr. Jackson knew nothing about it. "I had to stay in bed a lot. No activity; might kill me. So I read books and listened to the radio. One night I heard a ghost story. 'Hermit's Cave' it was called. All about a man who gets drowned and comes back to haunt his wife. My parents were gone, at a movie. I was alone. And I kept thinking about that story, imagining the ghost. Maybe, I thought to myself, he's in that closet. I knew he wasn't; I knew there wasn't any such thing as a ghost, really. But there was a little part of my mind that kept saying, 'Look at the closet. Watch the door. He's in there, Philip, and he's going to come out.' I picked up a book and tried to read, but I couldn't help glancing at the closet door. It was open a crack. Everything dark behind it. Everything dark and quiet."

"And the door moved."

"That's right."

"You understand that there's nothing terribly unusual in anything you've said so far?"

"I know," Hall said. "It was my imagination. It *was*, and I realized it even then. But—I got just as scared. Just as scared as if a ghost actually *had* opened that door! And that's the whole point. The mind, Doctor. It's everything. If you *think* you have a pain in your arm and there's no physical reason for it, you don't hurt any less . . . My mother died because she thought she had a fatal disease. The autopsy showed malnutrition, nothing else. But she died just the same!''

''I won't dispute the point.''

''All right. I just don't want you to tell me it's all in my mind. I *know* it is.''

''Go on.''

''They told me I'd never really get well, I'd have to take it easy the rest of my life. Because of the heart. No strenuous exercise, no stairs, no long walks. No shocks. Shock produces excessive adrenaline, they said. Bad. So that's the way it was. When I got out of school, I grabbed a soft desk job. Unexciting: numbers, adding numbers, that's all. Things went okay for a few years. Then it started again. I read about where some woman got into her car at night and happened to check for something in the back seat and found a man hidden there. Waiting. It stuck with me; I started dreaming about it. So every night, when I got into my car, I automatically patted the rear seat and floorboards. It satisfied me for a while, until I started thinking, 'What if I forget to check?' Or, 'What if there's something back there that isn't human?' I had to drive across Laurel Canyon to get home, and you know how twisty that stretch is. Thirty-fifty-foot drops, straight down. I'd get this feeling halfway across. 'There's someone . . . something . . . in the back of the car!' Hidden, in darkness. Fat and shiny. I'll look in the rear-view mirror and I'll see his hands ready to circle my throat . . . Again, Doctor: understand me. *I knew it was my imagination.* I had no doubt at all that the back seat was empty—hell, I kept the car locked and I double-checked! But, I told myself, you keep thinking this way, Hall, and you'll see those hands. It'll be a reflection, or somebody's headlights, or nothing at all—but you'll see them! Finally one night, I did see them! The car lurched a couple of times and went down the embankment.''

The psychiatrist said, "Wait a minute," rose, and switched the tape on a small machine.

⟡ "I knew how powerful the mind was, then," Hall continued. "I know that ghosts and demons did exist, they did, if you only thought about them long enough and hard enough. After all, one of them almost killed me!" He pressed the lighted end of the cigarette against his flesh; the fog lifted instantly. "Dr. Jackson told me afterwards that one more serious shock like that would finish me. And that's when I started having the dream."

There was a silence in the room, compounded of distant automobile horns, the ticking of the ship's-wheel clock, the insectival tapping of the receptionist's typewriter. Hall's own tortured breathing.

"They say dreams last only a couple of seconds," he said. "I don't know whether that's true or not. It doesn't matter. They *seem* to last longer. Sometimes I've dreamed a whole lifetime; sometimes generations have passed. Once in a while, time stops completely; it's a frozen moment, lasting forever. When I was a kid I saw the Flash Gordon serials; you remember? I loved them, and when the last episode was over, I went home and started dreaming more. Each night, another episode. They were vivid, too, and I remembered them when I woke up. I even wrote them down, to make sure I wouldn't forget. Crazy?"

"No," said the psychiatrist.

"I did, anyway. The same thing happened with the Oz books and the Burroughs books. I'd keep them going. But after the age of fifteen, or so, I didn't dream much. Only once in a while. Then, a week ago—" Hall stopped talking. He asked the location of the bathroom and went there and splashed cold water on his face. Then he returned and stood by the window.

"A week ago?" the psychiatrist said, flipping the tape machine back on.

"I went to bed around eleven-thirty. I wasn't too tired, but I needed the rest, on account of my heart. Right away the dream started. I was walking along Venice Pier. It was close to midnight. The place was crowded, people everywhere; you know the kind they used to get there. Sailors, dumpy-looking dames, kids in leather jackets. The pitchmen were going through their routines. You could hear the roller coasters thundering along the tracks, the people inside the roller coasters, screaming; you could hear the bells and the guns cracking and the crazy songs they play on calliopes. And, far away, the ocean, moving. Everything was bright and gaudy and cheap. I walked for a while, stepping on gum and candy apples, wondering why I was there." Hall's eyes closed. He opened them quickly and rubbed them. "Halfway to the end, passing the penny arcade, I saw a girl. She was about twenty-two or -three. White dress, very thin and tight, and a funny white hat. Her legs were bare, nicely muscled and tan. She was alone. I stopped and watched her, and I remembered thinking, 'She *must* have a boy friend. He *must* be here somewhere.' But she didn't seem to be waiting for anyone, or looking. Unconsciously, I began to follow her. At a distance.

"She walked past a couple of concessions, then she stopped at one called The Whip and strolled in and went for a ride. The air was hot. It caught her dress as she went around and sent it whirling. It didn't bother her at all. She just held onto the bar and closed her eyes, and—I don't know, a kind of ecstasy seemed to come over her. She began to laugh. A high-pitched, musical sound. I stood by the fence and watched her, wondering why such a beautiful girl should be laughing in a cheap carnival ride, in the middle of the night, all by herself. Then my hands *froze* on the fence, because suddenly I saw that she was looking at me. Every time the car would whip around, she'd be looking. And there was something in her eyes, something that said, Don't go away, don't leave, don't move . . .

"The ride stopped and she got out and walked over to me. As naturally as if we'd known each other for years, she put her arm in mine, and said, 'We've been expecting you, Mr.

Hall.' Her voice was deep and soft, and her face, close up, was even more beautiful than it had seemed. Full, rich lips, a little wet; dark, flashing eyes; a warm gleam to her flesh. I didn't answer. She laughed again and tugged at my sleeve. 'Come on, darling,' she said. 'We haven't much time.' And we walked, almost running, to The Silver Flash—a roller coaster, the highest on the pier. I knew I shouldn't go on it because of my heart condition, but she wouldn't listen. She said I had to, for her. So we bought our tickets and got into the first seat of the car . . .''

Hall held his breath for a moment, then let it out, slowly. As he relived the episode, he found that it was easier to stay awake. Much easier.

"That," he said, "was the end of the first dream. I woke up sweating and trembling, and thought about it most of the day, wondering where it had all come from. I'd only been to Venice Pier once in my life, with my mother. Years ago. But that night, just as it'd happened with the serials, the dream picked up exactly where it had left off. We were settling into the seat. Rough leather, cracked and peeling, I recall. The grab bar iron, painted black, the paint rubbed away in the center.

"I tried to get out, thinking, Now's the time to do it; do it now or you'll be too late! But the girl held me, and whispered to me. We'd be together, she said. Close together. If I'd do this one thing for her, she'd belong to me. 'Please! Please!' Then the car started. A little jerk; the kids beginning to yell and scream; the *clack-clack* of the chain pulling up; and up, slowly, too late now, too late for anything, up the steep wooden hill . . .

"A third of the way to the top, with her holding me, pressing herself against me, I woke up again. Next night, we went up a little farther. Next night, a little farther. Foot by foot, slowly, up the hill. At the halfway point, the girl began kissing me. And laughing. 'Look down!' she told me. 'Look down, Philip!' And I did and saw the little people and little cars and everything tiny and unreal.

"Finally we were within a few feet of the crest. The night was black and the wind was fast and cold now, and I was scared, so scared that I couldn't move. The girl laughed louder than ever, and a strange expression came into her eyes. I remembered then how no one else had noticed her. How the ticket-taker had taken the two stubs and looked around questioningly.

" 'Who are you?' I screamed. And she said, 'Don't you know?' And she stood up and pulled the grab bar out of my hands. I leaned forward to get it.

"Then we reached the top. And I saw her face and I knew what she was going to do, instantly: I knew. I tried to get back into the seat, but I felt her hands on me then and I heard her voice, laughing, high, laughing and shrieking with delight, and—"

Hall smashed his fist against the wall, stopped and waited for calm to return.

When it did, he said, "That's the whole thing, Doctor. Now you know why I don't dare go to sleep. When I do—and I'll have to, eventually; I realize that!—the dream will go on. And my heart won't take it!"

The psychiatrist pressed a button on his desk.

"Whoever she is," Hall went on, "she'll push me. And I'll fall. Hundreds of feet. I'll see the cement rushing up in a blur to meet me and I'll feel the first horrible pain of contact—"

There was a click.

The office door opened.

A girl walked in.

"Miss Thomas," the psychiatrist began, "I'd like you to—"

Philip Hall screamed. He stared at the girl in the white nurse's uniform and took a step backward. "Oh, Christ! No!"

"Mr. Hall, this is my receptionist, Miss Thomas."

"No," Hall cried. "It's her. It is. And I know who she is now, God save me! I know who she is!"

The girl in the white uniform took a tentative step into the room.

Hall screamed again, threw his hands over his face, turned and tried to run.

A voice called, "Stop him!"

Hall felt the sharp pain of the sill against his knee, realized in one hideous moment what was happening. Blindly he reached out, grasping. But it was too late. As if drawn by a giant force, he tumbled through the open window, out into the cold clear air.

"Hall!"

All the way down, all the long and endless way down past the thirteen floors to the gray, unyielding, hard concrete, his mind worked; and his eyes never closed . . .

"I'm afraid he's dead," the psychiatrist said, removing his fingers from Hall's wrist.

The girl in the white uniform made a little gasping sound. "But," she said, "only a minute ago, I saw him and he was—"

"I know. It's funny; when he came in, I told him to sit down. He did. And in less than two seconds he was asleep. Then he gave that yell you heard and . . ."

"Heart attack?"

"Yes." The psychiatrist rubbed his cheek thoughtfully. "Well," he said, "I guess there are worse ways to go. At least he died peacefully."

Disappearing Act

Richard Matheson

Teleplay by Rod Serling

Aired December 11, 1959, as ''And When the Sky Was Opened''

Starring Rod Taylor, Charles Aidman, and James Hutton

SATURDAY MORNING EARLY:

I shouldn't be writing this. What if Mary found it? Then what? The end, that's what, five years out the window.

But I have to put it down. I've been writing too long. There's no peace unless I put things on paper. I have to get them out and simplify my mind. But it's so hard to make things simple and so easy to make them complicated.

Thinking back through the months.

Where did it start? An argument of course. There must have been a thousand of them since we married. And always the same one, that's the horror.

Money.

''It's not a question of confidence in your writing,'' Mary will say. ''It's a question of bills and are we or aren't we going to pay them?''

''Bills for what?'' I'll say. ''For necessities? No. For things we don't even need.''

''Don't need!'' And off we go. God, how impossible life is

without money. Nothing can overcome it, it's everything when it's anything. How can I write in peace with endless worries of money, money, money? The television set, the refrigerator, the washer—none of them paid for yet. And the bed she wants . . .

But despite all, I—I with wide-eyed idiocy—keep making it even worse.

❡Why did I have to storm out of the apartment that first time? We'd argued, sure, but we'd argued before. Vanity, that's all. After seven years—*seven!*—of writing I've made only $316 from it. And I'm still working nights at the lousy part-time job typing. And Mary has to keep working at the same place with me. Lord knows she has a perfect right to doubt. A perfect right to keep insisting I take that full-time job Jim keeps offering me on his magazine.

All up to me. An admission of lack, a right move and everything would be solved. No more night work. Mary could stay home the way she wants to, the way she should. The right move, that's all.

So, I've been making the wrong one. God, it makes me sick.

Me, going out with Mike. Both of us glassy-eyed imbeciles meeting Jean and Sally. For months now pushing aside the obvious knowledge that we were being fools. Losing ourselves in a new experience. Playing the ass to perfection.

And, last night, both of us married men, going with them to their club apartment and . . .

Can't I say it? Am I afraid, too weak? Fool!

Adulterer.

How can things get so mixed up? I love Mary. Very much. And yet, even loving her, I did this thing.

And to make it all even more complicated, I enjoyed it. Jean is sweet and understanding, passionate, a sort of symbol of lost things. It was wonderful. I can't say it wasn't.

But how can wrong be wonderful? How can cruelty be exhilarating? It's all perverse, it's jumbled and confused and enraging.

* * *

Saturday afternoon:

She's forgiven me, thank God. I'll never see Jean again. Everything will be all right.

This morning I went and sat on the bed and Mary woke up. She stared up at me, then looked at the clock. She'd been crying.

"Where have you been?" she asked in that thin little girl voice she gets when she's scared.

"With Mike," I told her. "We drank and talked all night."

She stared a second more. Then she took my hand slowly and pressed it against her cheek.

"I'm sorry," she said, and tears came to her eyes.

I had to put my head next to hers so she wouldn't see my face. "Oh, Mary," I said. "I'm sorry too."

I'll never tell her. She means too much to me. I *can't* lose her.

Saturday night:

We went down to Mandel's Furniture Mart this afternoon and got a new bed.

"We can't afford it, honey," Mary said.

"Never mind," I said. "You know how lumpy the old one is. I want my baby to sleep in style."

She kissed my cheek happily. She bounced on the bed like an excited kid. "Oh, feel how soft!" she said.

Everything is all right. Everything except the new batch of bills in today's mail. Everything except for my latest story which won't get started. Everything except for my novel which has bounced five times. Burney House *has* to take it. They've held it long enough. I'm counting on it. Things are coming to a head with my writing. With everything. More and more I get the feeling that I'm a wound-up spring.

Well, Mary's all right.

* * *

Sunday night:

More trouble. Another argument. I don't even know what it was about. She's sulking. I'm burning. I can't write when I'm upset. She knows that.

I feel like calling Jean. At least *she* was interested in my writing. I feel like saying the hell with everything. Getting drunk, jumping off a bridge, something. No wonder babies are happy. Life is simple for them. Some hunger, some cold, a little fear of darkness. That's all. Why bother growing up? Life gets too complicated.

Mary just called me for supper. I don't feel like eating. I don't even feel like staying in the house. Maybe I'll call up Jean later. Just to say hello.

Monday morning:

Damn, damn, damn!

Not only to hold the book for over three months. That's not bad enough, oh no! They had to spill coffee all over the manuscript and send me a *printed* rejection slip to boot. I could kill them! I wonder if they think they know what they're doing?

Mary saw the slip. "Well, what *now?*" she said disgustedly.

"Now?" I said. I tried not to explode.

"Still think you can write?" she asked.

I exploded. "Oh, they're the last judge and jury, aren't they?" I raged. "They're the final word on my writing, aren't they?"

"You've been writing for seven years," she said. "Nothing's happened."

"And I'll write seven more," I said. "A hundred, a *thousand!*"

"You won't take that job on Jim's magazine?"

"No, I will not."

"You said you would if the book failed."

"I *have* a job," I said, "and you have a job and that's the way it is and that's the way it's going to stay."

"It's not the way I'm going to stay!" she snapped.

She may leave me. Who cares! I'm sick of it all anyway. Bill, bills. Writing, writing. Failures, failures, *failures!* And little old life dribbling on, building up its beautiful, brain-busting complexities like an idiot with blocks.

You! Who run the world, who spin the universe. If there's anybody listening to me, make the world simpler! I don't believe in anything but I'd give . . . *anything!* If only . . .

Oh, what's the use? I don't care anymore.

I'm calling Jean tonight.

Monday afternoon:

I just went down to call up Jean about Saturday night. Mary is going to her sister's house that night. She hasn't mentioned me going with her so I'm certainly not going to mention it.

I called Jean last night but the switchboard operator at the Club Stanley said she was out. I figured I'd be able to reach her today at her office.

So I went to the corner candy store to look up the number. I probably should have memorized it by now. I've called her enough. But somehow, I never bothered. What the hell, there are always telephone books.

She works for a magazine called *Design Handbook* or *Designer's Handbook* or something like that. Odd, I can't remember that either. Guess I never gave it much thought.

I do remember where the office is though. I called for her there a few months ago and took her to lunch. I think I told Mary I was going to the library that day.

Now, as I recall, the telephone number of Jean's office was in the upper right-hand corner of the right page in the directory. I've looked it up dozens of times and that's where it always was.

Today it wasn't.

I found the word *Design* and different business names starting with that word. But they were in the lower left-hand corner of the left page, just the opposite. And I couldn't seem to find any name that clicked. Usually as soon as I see the name of the magazine I think: *there it is.* Then I look up the number. Today it wasn't like that.

I looked and looked and thumbed around but I couldn't find anything like *Design Handbook.* Finally I settled for the number of *Design Magazine* but I had the feeling it wasn't the one I was searching for.

I . . . I'll have to finish this later. Mary just called me for lunch, dinner, what have you? The big meal of the day anyway since we both work at night.

Later:

It was a good meal. Mary can certainly cook. If only there weren't those arguments. I wonder if Jean can cook.

At any rate the meal steadied me a little. I needed it. I was a little nervous about that telephone call.

I dialed the number. A woman answered.

"*Design Magazine,*" she said.

"I'd like to talk to Miss Lane," I told her.

"Who?"

"Miss Lane."

"One moment," she said. And I knew it was the wrong number. Every other time I'd called the woman who answered had said, "All right," immediately and connected me with Jean.

"What was that name again?" she asked.

"Miss Lane. If you don't know her, I must have the wrong number."

"You might mean Mr. Payne."

"No, no. Before, the secretary who answered always knew right away who I wanted. I have the wrong number. Excuse me."

I hung up. I was pretty irritated. I've looked that number up so many times it isn't funny.

Now, I can't find it.

Of course I didn't let it get me at first. I thought maybe the phone book in the candy store was an old one. So I went down the street to the drugstore. It had the same book.

Well, I'll just have to call her from work tonight. But I wanted to get her this afternoon so I'd be sure she'd save Saturday night for me.

I just thought of something. That secretary. Her voice. It was the same one who used to answer for *Design Handbook.*

But . . . Oh, I'm dreaming.

Monday night:

I called the club while Mary was out of the office getting us some coffee.

I told the switchboard operator the same way I've told her dozens of times. "I'd like to speak to Miss Lane, please."

"Yessir, one moment," she said.

There was silence a long time. I got impatient. Then the phone clicked again.

"What was that name?" the operator asked.

"Miss Lane, Miss *Lane,*" I said. "I've called her any number of times."

"I'll look at the list again," she said.

I waited some more. Then I heard her voice again.

"I'm sorry. No one by that name is listed here."

"But I've called her any number of times there."

"Are you sure you have the right number?"

"Yes, yes, I'm sure. This is the Club Stanley, isn't it?"

"Yes, it is."

"Well, that's where I'm calling."

"I don't know what to say," she said. "All I can tell you is that I'm certain there isn't anyone by that name living here."

"But I just called *last night!* You said she wasn't in."

"I'm sorry, I don't remember."

"Are you sure? Absolutely sure?"

"Well, if you want, I'll look at the list again. But no one by that name is on it, I'm positive."

"And no one by that name moved out within the last few days?"

"We haven't had a vacancy for a year. Rooms are hard to get in New York, you know."

"I know," I said, and hung up.

I went back to my desk. Mary was back from the drugstore. She told me my coffee was getting cold. I said I was calling Jim in regard to that job. That was an ill-chosen lie. Now she'll start in on that again.

I drank my coffee and typed a while. But I didn't know what I was doing. I was trying hard to settle my mind.

She has to be somewhere, I thought. I know I didn't dream all those moments together. I know I didn't imagine all the trouble I had keeping it a secret from Mary. And I know that Mike and Sally didn't . . .

Sally! Sally lived at the Club Stanley too.

I told Mary I had a headache and was going out for an aspirin. She said there must be some in the men's room. I told her they were a kind I didn't like. I get involved in the flimsiest lies!

I half ran to the nearby drugstore. Naturally I didn't want to use the phone at work again.

The same operator answered my ring.

"Is Miss Sally Norton there?" I asked.

"One moment please," she said, and I felt a sinking sensation in my stomach. She always knew the regular members right away. And Sally and Jean had been living there for at least *two years*.

"I'm sorry," she said. "No one by that name is listed here."

I groaned. "Oh my God."

"Is something wrong?" she asked.

"No Jean Lane and no Sally Norton live there?"

"Are you the same party who called a little while ago?"

"Yes."

"Now look. If this is a joke . . ."

"A joke! Last night I called you and you told me Miss Lane was out and would I like to leave a message. I said no. Then I call tonight and you tell me there's nobody there by that name."

"I'm sorry. I don't know what to say. I was on the board last night but I don't recall what you say. If you like I'll connect you with the house manager."

"No, never mind," I said, and hung up.

Then I dialed Mike's number. But he wasn't home. His wife Gladys answered, told me Mike had gone bowling.

I was a little nervous or I wouldn't have slipped up.

"With the boys?" I asked her.

She sounded kind of slighted. "Well, I *hope* so," she said.
I'm getting scared.

Tuesday night:

I called Mike again tonight. I asked him about Sally.

"Who?"

"Sally."

"Sally who?" he asked.

"You know damn well Sally who, you hypocrite!"

"What is this, a gag?" he asked.

"Maybe it is," I said. "How about cutting it out?"

"Let's start all over," he said. "Who the hell is Sally?"

"You don't know Sally Norton?"

"No. Who is she?"

"You never went on a date with her and Jean Lane and me?"

"Jean Lane! What are you talking about?"

"You don't know Jean Lane either?"

"No, I *don't* and this is getting very unfunny. I don't know what you're trying to pull but cut it out. As two married men we . . ."

"Listen!" I almost shouted into the phone. "Where were you three weeks ago Saturday night?"

He was silent a moment.

"Wasn't that the night you and I bached while Mary and Glad went to see the fashion show at . . ."

"Bached! There was no one with us?"

"Who?"

"No girls? Sally? Jean?"

"Oh, here we go again," he groaned. "Look, pal, what's eating you? Anything I can do?"

I slumped against the wall of the telephone booth.

"No," I said weakly. "No."

"Are you sure you're all right? You sound upset as hell."

I hung up. I *am* upset. I have a feeling as though I were starving and there wasn't a scrap of food in the whole world to feed me.

What's wrong?

Wednesday afternoon:

There was only one way to find out if Sally and Jean had really disappeared.

I had met Jean through a friend I knew at college. Her home is in Chicago and so is my friend Dave's. He was the one who gave me her New York address, the Club Stanley. Naturally I didn't tell Dave I was married.

So I'd looked up Jean and I went out with her and Mike went out with her friend Sally. That's the way it was, I *know* it happened.

So today I wrote a letter to Dave. I told him what had happened. I begged him to check up at her home and write quickly and tell me it was a joke or some amazing set of coincidences. Then I got out my address book.

Dave's name is gone from the book.

Am I really going crazy? I know perfectly well that the address was in there. I can remember the night, years ago, when I carefully wrote it down because I didn't want to lose contact with him after we graduated from college. I can even remember the ink blot I made when I wrote it because my pen leaked.

The page is blank.

I remember his name, how he looked, how he talked, the things we did, the classes we took together.

I even had a letter of his he sent me one Easter vacation

while I was at school. I remember Mike was over at my room. Since we lived in New York there wasn't time to get home because the vacation was only for a few days.

But Dave had gone home to Chicago and, from there, sent us a very funny letter, special delivery. I remember how he sealed it with wax and stamped it with his ring for a gag.

The letter is gone from the drawer where I always kept it.

And I had three pictures of Dave taken on graduation day. Two of them I kept in my picture album. They're still there . . .

But he's not on them.

They're just pictures of the campus with buildings in the background.

I'm afraid to go on looking. I could write the college or call them and ask if Dave ever went there.

But I'm afraid to try.

Thursday afternoon:

Today I went out to Hempstead to see Jim. I went to his office. He was surprised when I walked in. He wanted to know why I'd traveled so far just to see him.

"Don't tell me you've decided to take that job offer," he said.

I asked him, "Jim, did you ever hear me talking about a girl named Jean in New York?"

"Jean? No, I don't think so."

"Come on, Jim. I did mention her to you. Don't you remember the last time you and I and Mike played poker? I told you about her then."

"I don't remember, Bob," he said. "What about her?"

"I can't find her. And I can't find the girl Mike went out with. And Mike denies that he ever knew either of them."

He looked confused so I told him again. Then he said, "What's this? Two old married men gallivanting around with . . ."

"They were just friends," I cut in. "I met them through a fellow I knew at college. Don't get any bright ideas."

"All right, all right, skip it. Where do I fit in?"

"I can't *find* them. They're gone. I can't even prove they existed."

He shrugged. "So what?" Then he asked me if Mary knew about it. I brushed that off.

"Didn't I mention Jean in any of my letters?" I asked him.

"Couldn't say. I never keep letters."

I left soon after that. He was getting too curious. I can see it now. He tells his wife, his wife tells Mary—fireworks.

When I rode to work late this afternoon I had the most awful feeling that I was something temporary. When I sat down it was like resting on air.

I guess I must be cracking. Because I bumped into an old man deliberately to find out if he saw me or felt me. He snarled and called me a clumsy idiot.

I was grateful for that.

Thursday night:

Tonight at work I called up Mike again to see if he remembered Dave from college.

The phone rang, then it clicked off. The operator cut in and asked, "What number are you calling, sir?"

A chill covered me. I gave her the number. She told me there wasn't any such number.

The phone fell out of my hand and clattered on the floor. Mary stood up at her desk and looked over. The operator was saying, "Hello, hello, hello . . ." I hurriedly put the phone back in the cradle.

"What happened?" Mary asked when I came back to my desk.

"I dropped the phone," I said.

I sat and worked and shivered with cold.

I'm afraid to tell Mary about Mike and his wife, Gladys.

I'm afraid she'll say she never heard of them.

* * *

Friday:

Today I checked up on *Design Handbook*. Information told me there was no such publication listed. But I went over to the city anyway. Mary was angry about me going. But I had to go.

I went to the building. I looked at the directory in the lobby. And even though I knew I wouldn't find the magazine listed there, it was still a shock that made me feel sick and hollow.

I was dizzy as I rode up the elevator. I felt as if I were drifting away from everything.

I got off at the third floor at the exact spot where I'd called for Jean that afternoon.

There was a textile company there.

"There never was a magazine here?" I asked the receptionist.

"Not as long as I can remember," she said. "Of course, I've only been here three years."

I went home. I told Mary I was sick and didn't want to go to work tonight. She said all right she wouldn't go either. I went into the bedroom to be alone. I stood in the place where we're going to put the new bed when it's delivered next week.

Mary came in. She stood in the doorway restively.

"Bob, what's the matter?" she asked. "Don't I have a right to know?"

"Nothing," I told her.

"Oh, please don't tell me that," she said. "I know there is."

I started toward her. Then I turned away.

"I . . . I have to write a letter," I said.

"Who to?"

I flared up. "That's my business," I said. Then I told her to Jim.

She turned away. "I wish I could believe you," she said.

"What does *that* mean?" I asked. She looked at me for a long moment and then turned away again.

"Give *Jim* my best," she said, and her voice shook. The way she said it made me shudder.

I sat down and wrote the letter to Jim. I decided he might help. Things were too desperate for secrecy. I told him that Mike was gone. I asked him if he remembered Mike.

Funny. My hand hardly shook at all. Maybe that's the way it is when you're almost gone.

Saturday:

Mary had to work on some special typing today. She left early.

After I had breakfast I got the bank book out of the metal box in the bedroom closet. I was going down to the bank to get the money for the bed.

At the bank I filled out a withdrawal slip for $97. Then I waited in line and finally handed the slip and the book to the teller.

He opened it and looked up with a frown.

"This supposed to be funny?" he asked.

"What do you mean, funny?"

He pushed the book across to me. "Next," he said.

I guess I shouted. "What's the matter with you!"

Out of the corner of my eye I saw one of the men at the front desks jump up and hurry over. A woman behind me said, "Let me at the window, if you please."

The man came fussing up.

"What seems to be the trouble, sir?" he asked me.

"The teller refuses to honor my bank book," I told him.

He asked for the book and I handed it to him. He opened it. Then he looked up in surprise. He spoke quietly.

"This book is blank," he said.

I grabbed it and stared at it, my heart pounding.

It was completely unused.

"Oh, my God," I moaned.

"Perhaps we can check on the number of the book," the man said. "Why don't you step over to my desk?"

But there wasn't any number on the book. I saw that. And I felt tears coming into my eyes.

"No," I said. "No." I walked past him and started toward the doorway.

"One moment, sir," he called after me.

I ran out and ran all the way home.

I waited in the front room for Mary to come home. I'm waiting now. I'm looking at the bank book. At the line where we both signed our names. At the spaces where we had made our deposits. Fifty dollars from her parents on our first anniversary. Two hundred and thirty dollars from my veteran's insurance dividend. Twenty dollars. Ten dollars.

All blank.

Everything is going. Jean. Sally. Mike. Names fluttering away and the people with them.

Now this. What's next?

Later:

I know.

Mary hasn't come home.

I called up the office. I heard Sam answer and I asked him if Mary was there. He said I must have the wrong number, no Mary works there. I told him who I was. I asked him if *I* worked there.

"Stop kidding around," he said. "See you Monday night."

I called up my cousin, my sister, her cousin, her sister, her parents. No answer. Not even ringing. None of the numbers work. Then they're all gone.

Sunday:

I don't know what to do. All day I've been sitting in the livingroom looking out at the street. I've been watching to see if anybody I know comes by the house. But they don't. They're all strangers.

I'm afraid to leave the house. That's all there is left. Our furniture and our clothes.

I mean *my* clothes. Her closet is empty. I looked into it

this morning when I woke up and there wasn't a scrap of clothing left. It's like a magic act, everything disappearing, it's like . . .

I just laughed. I must be . . .

I called the furniture store. It's open Sunday afternoons. They said they had no record of us buying a bed. Would I like to come in and check?

I hung up and looked out the window some more.

I thought of calling up my aunt in Detroit. But I can't remember the number. And it isn't in my address book any more. The entire book is blank. Except for my name on the cover stamped in gold.

My name. Only my name. What can I say? What can I do? Everything is so simple. There's *nothing* to do.

I've been looking at my photograph album. Almost all the pictures are different. There aren't any people on them.

Mary is gone and all of our friends and our relatives.

It's funny.

In the wedding picture I sit all by myself at a huge table covered with food. My left arm is out and bent as though I were embracing my bride. And all along the table are glasses floating in the air.

Toasting me.

Monday morning:

I just got back the letter I sent Jim. It has NO SUCH ADDRESS stamped on the envelope.

I tried to catch the mailman but I couldn't. He was gone before I woke up.

I went down to the grocer before. He knew me. But when I asked him about Mary he said stop kidding, I'd die a bachelor and we both knew it.

I have only one more idea. It's a risk, but I'll have to take it. I'll have to leave the house and go downtown to the Veterans Administration. I want to see if my records are there. If they are, they'll have something about my schooling and about my marriage and the people who were in my life.

I'm taking this book with me. I don't want to lose it. If I lost it, then I wouldn't have a thing in the world to remind me that I'm not insane.

Monday night:

The house is gone.

I'm sitting in the corner candy store.

When I got back from the V.A. I found an empty lot there. I asked some of the boys playing there if they knew me. They said they didn't. I asked them what happened to the house. They said they'd been playing in that empty lot since they were babies.

The V.A. didn't have any records about me. Not a thing.

That means I'm not even a person now. All I have is all I am, my body and the clothes on it. All the identification papers are gone from my wallet.

My watch is gone too. Just like that. From my wrist.

It had an inscription on the back. I remember it.

To my own darling with all my love. Mary.

I'm having a cup of cof

Time Enough at Last

Lynn A. Venable

Teleplay by Rod Serling

Aired December 20, 1959

Starring Burgess Meredith and Vaughn Taylor

FOR A LONG TIME, HENRY BEMIS HAD HAD AN AMBItion. To read a book. Not just the title or the preface, or a page somewhere in the middle. He wanted to read the whole thing, all the way through from beginning to end. A simple ambition perhaps, but in the cluttered life of Henry Bemis, an impossibility.

Henry had no time of his own. There was his wife, Agnes, who owned that part of it that his employer, Mr. Carsville, did not buy. Henry was allowed enough to get to and from work—that in itself being quite a concession on Agnes' part.

Also, nature had conspired against Henry by handing him a pair of hopelessly myopic eyes. Poor Henry literally couldn't see his hand in front of his face. For a while, when he was very young, his parents had thought him an idiot. When they realized it was his eyes, they got glasses for him. He was never quite able to catch up. There was never enough time. It looked as though Henry's ambition would never be realized. Then something happened which changed all that.

Henry was down in the vault of the Eastside Bank & Trust

when it happened. He had stolen a few moments from the duties of his teller's cage to try to read a few pages of the magazine he had bought that morning. He'd made an excuse to Mr. Carsville about needing bills in large denominations for a certain customer, and then, safe inside the dim recesses of the vault he had pulled from inside his coat the pocket-size magazine.

He had just started a picture article cheerfully entitled "The New Weapons and What They'll Do to YOU," when all the noise in the world crashed in upon his eardrums. It seemed to be inside of him and outside of him all at once. Then the concrete floor was rising up at him and the ceiling came slanting down toward him, and for a fleeting second Henry thought of a story he had started to read once called "The Pit and the Pendulum." He regretted in that insane moment that he had never had time to finish that story to see how it came out. Then all was darkness and quiet and uncon-sciousness.

When Henry came to, he knew that something was des-perately wrong with the Eastside Bank & Trust. The heavy steel door of the vault was buckled and twisted and the floor tilted up at a dizzy angle, while the ceiling dipped crazily to-ward it. Henry gingerly got to his feet, moving arms and legs experimentally. Assured that nothing was broken, he ten-derly raised a hand to his eyes. His precious glasses were in-tact, thank God! He would never have been able to find his way out of the shattered vault without them.

He made a mental note to write Dr. Torrance to have a spare pair made and mailed to him. Blasted nuisance not having his prescription on file locally, but Henry trusted no-one but Dr. Torrance to grind those thick lenses into his own complicated prescription. Henry removed the heavy glasses from his face. Instantly the room dissolved into a neutral blur. Henry saw a pink splash that he knew was his hand, and a white blob come up to meet the pink as he withdrew his pocket handkerchief and carefully dusted the lenses. As he replaced the glasses, they slipped down on the bridge of his nose a little. He had been meaning to have them tightened for some time.

He suddenly realized, without the realization actually entering his conscious thoughts, that something momentous had happened, something worse than the boiler blowing up, something worse than a gas main exploding, something worse than anything that had ever happened before. He felt that way because it was so quiet. There was no whine of sirens, no shouting, no running, just an ominous and all-pervading silence.

Henry walked across the slanting floor. Slipping and stumbling on the uneven surface, he made his way to the elevator. The car lay crumpled at the foot of the shaft like a discarded accordion. There was something inside of it that Henry could not look at, something that had once been a person, or perhaps several people, it was impossible to tell now.

Feeling sick, Henry staggered toward the stairway. The steps were still there, but so jumbled and piled back upon one another that it was more like climbing the side of a mountain than mounting a stairway. It was quiet in the huge chamber that had been the lobby of the bank. It looked strangely cheerful with the sunlight shining through the girders where the ceiling had fallen. The dappled sunlight glinted across the silent lobby, and everywhere there were huddled lumps of unpleasantness that made Henry sick as he tried not to look at them.

"Mr. Carsville," he called. It was very quiet. Something had to be done, of course. This was terrible, right in the middle of a Monday, too. Mr. Carsville would know what to do. He called again, more loudly, and his voice cracked hoarsely, "Mr. Carrrrsville!" And then he saw an arm and shoulder extending out from under a huge fallen block of marble ceiling. In the buttonhole was the white carnation Mr. Carsville had worn to work that morning, and on the third finger of that hand was a massive signet ring, also belonging to Mr.

Carsville. Numbly, Henry realized that the rest of Mr. Carsville was under that block of marble.

Henry felt a pang of real sorrow. Mr. Carsville was gone, and so was the rest of the staff—Mr. Wilkinson and Mr. Emory and Mr. Prithard, and the same with Pete and Ralph and Jenkins and Hunter and Pat the guard and Willie the doorman. There was no one to say what was to be done about the Eastside Bank & Trust except Henry Bemis, and Henry wasn't worried about the bank, there was something he wanted to do.

He climbed carefully over piles of fallen masonry. Once he stepped down into something that crunched and squashed beneath his feet and he set his teeth on edge to keep from retching. The street was not much different from the inside, bright sunlight and so much concrete to crawl over, but the unpleasantness was much, much worse. Everywhere there were strange, motionless lumps that Henry could not look at.

Suddenly, he remembered Agnes. He should be trying to get to Agnes, shouldn't he? He remembered a poster he had seen that said, "In event of emergency do not use the telephone; your loved ones are as safe as you." He wondered about Agnes. He looked at the smashed automobiles, some with their four wheels pointing skyward like the stiffened legs of dead animals. He couldn't get to Agnes now anyway, if she was safe, then, she was safe, otherwise . . . of course, Henry knew Agnes wasn't safe. He had a feeling that there wasn't anyone safe for a long, long way, maybe not in the whole state or the whole country, or the whole world. No, that was a thought Henry didn't want to think, he forced it from his mind and turned his thoughts back to Agnes.

She had been a pretty good wife, now that it was all said and done. It wasn't exactly her fault if people didn't have time to read nowadays. It was just that there was the house, and the bank, and the yard. There were the Joneses for bridge and the Graysons for canasta and charades with the Bryants. And the television, the television Agnes loved to watch, but would never watch alone. He never had time to read even a newspaper. He started thinking about last night, that business about the newspaper.

Henry had settled into his chair, quietly, afraid that a creaking spring might call to Agnes' attention the fact that he was momentarily unoccupied. He had unfolded the newspaper slowly and carefully, the sharp crackle of the paper would have been a clarion call to Agnes. He had glanced at the headlines of the first page. "Collapse Of Conference Imminent." He didn't have time to read the article. He turned to the second page. "Solon Predicts War Only Days Away." He flipped through the pages faster, reading brief snatches here and there, afraid to spend too much time on any one item. On a back page was a brief article entitled, "Prehistoric Artifacts Unearthed in Yucatan." Henry smiled to himself and carefully folded the sheet of paper into fourths. That would be interesting, he would read all of it. Then it came, Agnes' voice. "Henrrreee!" And then she was upon him. She lightly flicked the paper out of his hands and into the fireplace. He saw the flames lick up and curl possessively around the unread article. Agnes continued, "Henry, tonight is the Joneses' bridge night. They'll be here in thirty minutes and I'm not dressed yet, and here you are . . . *reading*." She had emphasized the last word as though it were an unclean act. "Hurry and shave, you know how smooth Jasper Jones' chin always looks, and then straighten up this room." She glanced regretfully toward the fireplace. "Oh dear, that paper, the television schedule . . . oh well, after the Joneses leave there won't be time for anything but the late-late movie and . . . Don't just sit there, Henry, hurrreeee!"

Henry was hurrying now, but hurrying too much. He cut his leg on a twisted piece of metal that had once been an automobile fender. He thought about things like lockjaw and gangrene and his hand trembled as he tied his pocket-handkerchief around the wound. In his mind, he saw the fire again, licking across the face of last night's newspaper. He thought that now he would have time to read all the newspapers he wanted to, only now there wouldn't be any more. That heap of rubble across the street had been the Gazette Building. It was terrible to think there would never be another up-to-date newspaper. Agnes would have been very upset, no television schedule. But then, of course, no television. He wanted to laugh but he didn't. That wouldn't have been fitting, not at all.

He could see the building he was looking for now, but the silhouette was strangely changed. The great circular dome was now a ragged semi-circle, half of it gone, and one of the great wings of the building had fallen in upon itself. A sudden panic gripped Henry Bemis. What if they were all ruined, destroyed, every one of them? What if there wasn't a single one left? Tears of helplessness welled in his eyes as he painfully fought his way over and through the twisted fragments of the city.

He thought of the building when it had been whole. He remembered the many nights he had paused outside its wide and welcoming doors. He thought of the warm nights when the doors had been thrown open and he could see the people inside, see them sitting at the plain wooden tables with the stacks of books beside them. He used to think then, what a wonderful thing a public library was, a place where anybody, anybody at all could go in and read.

He had been tempted to enter many times. He had watched the people through the open doors, the man in greasy work clothes who sat near the door, night after night, laboriously studying, a technical journal perhaps, difficult for him, but promising a brighter future. There had been an aged, scholarly gentleman who sat on the other side of the door, leisurely paging, moving his lips a little as he did so, a man having little time left, but rich in time because he could do with it as he chose.

Henry had never gone in. He had started up the steps once, got almost to the door, but then he remembered

Agnes, her questions and shouting, and he had turned away.

He was going in now though, almost crawling, his breath coming in stabbing gasps, his hands torn and bleeding. His trouser leg was sticky red where the wound in his leg had soaked through the handkerchief. It was throbbing badly but Henry didn't care. He had reached his destination.

Part of the inscription was still there, over the now door-less entrance. P-U-B—C L-I-B-R—. The rest had been torn away. The place was in shambles. The shelves were over-turned, broken, smashed, tilted, their precious contents spilled in disorder upon the floor. A lot of the books, Henry noted gleefully, were still intact, still whole, still readable. He was literally knee deep in them, he wallowed in books. He picked one up. The title was "Collected Works of William Shakespeare." Yes, he must read that, sometime. He laid it aside carefully. He picked up another. Spinoza. He tossed it away, seized another, and another, and still another. Which to read first . . . there were so many.

He had been conducting himself a little like a starving man in a delicatessen—grabbing a little of this and a little of that in a frenzy of enjoyment.

But now he steadied away. From the pile about him, he selected one volume, sat comfortably down on an overturned shelf, and opened the book.

Henry Bemis smiled.

There was the rumble of complaining stone. Minute in comparison with the epic complaints following the fall of the bomb. This one occurred under one corner of the shelf upon which Henry sat. The shelf moved; threw him off balance. The glasses slipped from his nose and fell with a tinkle.

He bent down, clawing blindly, and found, finally, their smashed remains. A minor, indirect destruction stemming from the sudden, wholesale smashing of a city. But the only one that greatly interested Henry Bemis.

He stared down at the blurred page before him.

He began to cry.

What You Need

Lewis Padgett (Henry Kuttner and C. L. Moore)

TELEPLAY BY ROD SERLING

AIRED DECEMBER 25, 1959

STARRING STEVE COCHRAN

WE HAVE WHAT YOU NEED

THAT'S WHAT THE SIGN SAID. TIM CARMICHAEL, who worked for a trade paper that specialized in economics, and eked out a meager salary by selling sensational and untrue articles to the tabloids, failed to sense a story in the reversed sign. He thought it was a cheap publicity gag, something one seldom encounters on Park Avenue, where the shop fronts are noted for their classic dignity. And he was irritated.

He growled silently, walked on, then suddenly turned and came back. He wasn't quite strong enough to resist the temptation to unscramble the sentence, though his annoyance grew. He stood before the window, staring up, and said to himself, '' 'We have what you need.' Yeah?''

The sign was in prim, small letters on a black painted ribbon that stretched across a narrow glass pane. Below it was

61

one of those curved, invisible-glass windows. Through the window Carmichael could see an expanse of white velvet, with a few objects carefully arranged there. A rusty nail, a snowshoe, and a diamond tiara. It looked like a Dali décor for Cartier or Tiffany.

"Jewelers?" Carmichael asked silently. "But why *what you need?*" He pictured millionaires miserably despondent for lack of a matched pearl necklace, heiresses weeping inconsolably because they needed a few star sapphires. The principle of luxury merchandising was to deal with the whipped cream of supply and demand; few people needed diamonds. They merely wanted them and could afford them.

"Or the place might sell jinni-flasks," Carmichael decided. "Or magic wands. Same principle as a Coney carny, though. A sucker trap. Bill the Whatzit outside and people will pay their dimes and flock in. For two cents—"

He was dyspeptic this morning, and generally disliked the world. Prospect of a scapegoat was attractive, and his press card gave him a certain advantage. He opened the door and walked into the shop.

It was Park Avenue, all right. There were no showcases or counters. It might be an art gallery, for a few good oils were displayed on the walls. An air of overpowering luxury, with the bleakness of an unlived-in place, struck Carmichael.

Through a curtain at the back came a very tall man with carefully combed white hair, a ruddy, healthy face, and sharp blue eyes. He might have been sixty. He wore expensive but careless tweeds, which somehow jarred with the décor.

"Good morning," the man said, with a quick glance at Carmichael's clothes. He seemed slightly surprised. "May I help you?"

"Maybe." Carmichael introduced himself and showed his press card.

"Oh? My name is Talley. Peter Talley."

"I saw your sign."

"Oh?"

"Our paper is always on the lookout for possible write-ups. I've never noticed your shop before—"

"I've been here for years," Talley said.

"This is an art gallery?"

"Well—no."

The door opened. A florid man came in and greeted Talley cordially. Carmichael, recognizing the client, felt his opinion of the shop swing rapidly upward. The florid man was a Name—a big one.

"It's a bit early, Mr. Talley," he said, "but I didn't want to delay. Have you had time to get—what I needed?"

"Oh, yes. I have it. One moment." Talley hurried through the draperies and returned with a small, neatly wrapped parcel, which he gave to the florid man. The latter forked over a check—Carmichael caught a glimpse of the amount and gulped—and departed. His town car was at the curb outside.

Carmichael moved toward the door, where he could watch. The florid man seemed anxious. His chauffeur waited stolidly as the parcel was unwrapped with hurried fingers.

"I'm not sure I'd want publicity, Mr. Carmichael," Talley said. "I've a select clientele—carefully chosen."

"Perhaps our weekly economic bulletins might interest you."

Talley tried not to laugh. "Oh, I don't think so. It really isn't in my line."

The florid man had finally unwrapped the parcel and taken out an egg. As far as Carmichael could see from his post near the door, it was merely an ordinary egg. But its possessor regarded it almost with awe. Had Earth's last hen died ten years before, the man could have been no more pleased. Something like deep relief showed on the Florida-tanned face.

He said something to the chauffeur, and the car rolled smoothly forward and was gone.

"Are you in the dairy business?" Carmichael asked abruptly.

"No."

"Do you mind telling me what your business is?"

"I'm afraid I do, rather," Talley said.

Carmichael was beginning to scent a story. "Of course, I could find out through the Better Business Bureau—"

"You couldn't."

"No? They might be interested in knowing why an egg is worth five thousand dollars to one of your customers."

Talley said, "My clientele is so small I must charge high fees. You—ah—know that a Chinese mandarin has been known to pay thousands of taels for eggs of proved antiquity."

"That guy wasn't a Chinese mandarin," Carmichael said.

"Oh, well. As I say, I don't welcome publicity—"

"I think you do. I was in the advertising game for a while. Spelling your sign backward is an obvious baited hook."

"Then you're no psychologist," Talley said. "It's just that I can afford to indulge my whims. For five years I looked at that window every day and read the sign backward—from inside my shop. It annoyed me. You know how a word will begin to look funny if you keep staring at it? Any word. It turns into something in no human tongue. Well, I discovered I was getting a neurosis about that sign. It makes no sense backward, but I kept finding myself trying to read sense into it. When I started to say 'Deen uoy tahw evah ew' to myself and looking for philological derivations, I called in a sign-painter. People who are interested enough still drop in."

"Not many," Carmichael said shrewdly. "This is Park Avenue. And you've got the place fixed up too expensively. Nobody in the low-income brackets—or the middle brackets—would come in here. So you run an upper-bracket business."

"Well," Talley said, "yes, I do."

"And you won't tell me what it is?"

"I'd rather not."

"I can find out, you know. It might be dope, pornography, high-class fencing—"

"Very likely," Mr. Talley said smoothly. "I buy stolen

jewels, conceal them in eggs, and sell them to my customers.
Or perhaps that egg was loaded with microscopic French
postcards. Good morning, Mr. Carmichael."

"Good morning," Carmichael said, and went out. He was
overdue at the office, but annoyance was the stronger moti-
vation. He played sleuth for a while, keeping an eye on Talley's shop, and the results were thoroughly satisfactory—to a
certain extent. He learned everything but why.

Late in the afternoon, he sought out Mr. Talley again.

"Wait a minute," he said, at sight of the proprietor's dis-
couraging face. "For all you know, I may be a customer."

Talley laughed.

"Well, why not?" Carmichael compressed his lips. "How
do you know the size of my bank account? Or maybe you've
got a restricted clientele?"

"No. But—"

Carmichael said quickly, "I've been doing some investi-
gating. I've been noticing your customers. In fact, following
them. And finding out what they buy from you."

Talley's face changed. "Indeed?"

"In*deed*. They're all in a hurry to unwrap their little bundles. So that gave me my chance to find out. I missed a few,
but—I saw enough to apply a couple of rules of logic, Mr. Talley. *Item:* your customers don't know what they're buying
from you. It's a sort of grab bag. A couple of times they were
plenty surprised. The man who opened his parcel and found
an old newspaper clipping. What about the sunglasses? And
the revolver? Probably illegal, by the way—no license. And
the diamond—it must have been paste, it was so big."

"M-mmm," Mr. Talley said.

"I'm no smart apple, but I can smell a screwy set-up. Most
of your clients are big shots, in one way or another. And why
didn't any of 'em pay you, like the first man—the guy who
came in when I was here this morning?"

"It's chiefly a credit business," Talley said. "I've my eth-
ics. I have to, for my own conscience. It's responsibility. You

see, I sell—my goods—with a guarantee. Payment is made only if the product proves satisfactory."

"So. An egg. Sunglasses. A pair of asbestos gloves—I think they were. A newspaper clipping. A gun and a diamond. How do you take inventory?"

Talley said nothing.

Carmichael grinned. "You've an errand boy. You send him out and he comes back with bundles. Maybe he goes to a grocery on Madison and buys an egg. Or a pawnshop on Sixth for a revolver. Or—well, anyhow, I told you I'd find out what your business is."

"And have you?" Talley asked.

" 'We have what you need,' " Carmichael said. "But how do you *know*?"

"You're jumping to conclusions."

"I've got a headache—I didn't have sunglasses!—and I don't believe in magic. Listen, Mr. Talley, I'm fed up to the eyebrows and way beyond on queer little shops that sell peculiar things. I know too much about 'em—I've written about 'em. A guy walks along the street and sees a funny sort of store and the proprietor won't serve him—he sells only to pixies—or else he *does* sell him a magic charm with a double edge. Well—*pfui!*"

"Mph," Talley said.

" 'Mph' as much as you like. But you can't get away from logic. Either you've got a sound, sensible racket here, or else it's one of those funny, magic-shop set-ups—and I don't believe that. For it isn't logical."

"Why not?"

"Because of economics," Carmichael said flatly. "Grant the idea that you've got certain mysterious powers—let's say you can make telepathic gadgets. All right. Why the devil would you start a business so you could sell the gadgets so you could make money so you could live? You'd simply put on one of your gadgets, read a stockbroker's mind, and buy the right stocks. That's the intrinsic fallacy in these crazy-shop things—if you've got enough stuff on the ball to be able to stock and run such a shop, you wouldn't need a business in the first place. Why go round Robin Hood's barn?''

Talley said nothing.

Carmichael smiled crookedly. '' 'I often wonder what the vintners buy one half so precious as the stuff they sell,' '' he quoted. ''Well—what do *you* buy? I know what you sell— eggs and sunglasses.''

''You're an inquisitive man, Mr. Carmichael,'' Talley murmured. ''Has it ever occurred to you that this is none of your business?''

''I may be a customer,'' Carmichael repeated. ''How about that?''

Talley's cool blue eyes were intent. A new light dawned in them; Talley pursed his lips and scowled. ''I hadn't thought of that,'' he admitted. ''You might be. Under the circumstances. Will you excuse me for a moment?''

''Sure,'' Carmichael said. Talley went through the curtains.

Outside, traffic drifted idly along Park. As the sun slid down beyond the Hudson, the street lay in a blue shadow that crept imperceptibly up the barricades of the buildings. Carmichael stared at the sign—''WE HAVE WHAT YOU NEED''—and smiled.

In a back room, Talley put his eye to a binocular plate and moved a calibrated dial. He did this several times. Then, biting his lip—for he was a gentle man—he called his errand boy and gave him directions. After that he returned to Carmichael.

''You're a customer,'' he said. ''Under certain conditions.''

''The condition of my bank account, you mean?''

''No,'' Talley said. ''I'll give you reduced rates. Understand one thing. I really do have what you need. You don't *know* what you need, but I know. And as it happens—well, I'll sell you what you need for, let's say, five dollars.''

Carmichael reached for his wallet. Talley held up a hand. ''Pay me after you're satisfied. And the money's the nominal part of the fee. There's another part. If you're satisfied, I want you to promise that you'll never come near this shop again and never mention it to anyone."

"I see," Carmichael said slowly. His theories had changed slightly.

"It won't be long before—ah, here he is now." A buzzing from the back indicated the return of the errand boy. Talley said, "Excuse me," and vanished. Soon he returned with a neatly wrapped parcel, which he thrust into Carmichael's hands.

"Keep this on your person," Talley said. "Good afternoon."

Carmichael nodded, pocketed the parcel, and went out. Feeling affluent, he hailed a taxi and went to a cocktail bar he knew. There, in the dim light of a booth, he unwrapped the bundle.

Protection money, he decided. Talley was paying him off to keep his mouth shut about the racket, whatever it was. O.K., live and let live. How much would be—

Ten thousand? Fifty thousand? How big was the racket?

He opened an oblong cardboard box. Within, nesting upon tissue paper, was a pair of shears, the blades protected by a sheath of folded, glued cardboard.

Carmichael said something softly. He drank his highball and ordered another, but left it untasted. Glancing at his wrist watch, he decided that the Park Avenue shop would be closed by now and Mr. Peter Talley gone.

" '. . . one half so precious as the stuff they sell,' " Carmichael said. "Maybe it's the scissors of Atropos. Blah." He unsheathed the blades and snipped experimentally at the air. Nothing happened. Slightly crimson around the cheekbones, Carmichael reholstered the shears and dropped them into the side pocket of his topcoat. Quite a gag!

He decided to call on Peter Talley tomorrow.

Meanwhile, what? He remembered he had a dinner date with one of the girls at the office, and hastily paid his bill and left. The streets were darkening, and a cold wind blew southward from the park. Carmichael wound his scarf tighter around his throat and made gestures toward passing taxis.

He was considerably annoyed.

Half an hour later a thin man with sad eyes—Jerry Worth, one of the copy writers from his office—greeted him at the bar where Carmichael was killing time. "Waiting for Betsy?" Worth said, nodding toward the restaurant annex. "She sent me to tell you she couldn't make it. A rush deadline. Apologies and stuff. Where were you today? Things got gummed up a bit. Have a drink with me."

They worked on a rye. Carmichael was already slightly stiff. The dull crimson around his cheekbones had deepened, and his frown had become set. "What you need," he remarked. "Double-crossing little—"

"Huh?" Worth said.

"Nothing. Drink up. I've just decided to get a guy in trouble. If I can."

"You almost got in trouble yourself today. That trend analysis of ores—"

"Eggs. Sunglasses!"

"I got you out of a jam—"

"Shut up," Carmichael said, and ordered another round. Every time he felt the weight of the shears in his pocket he found his lips moving.

Five shots later Worth said plaintively, "I don't mind doing good deeds, but I do like to mention them. And you won't let me. All I want is a little gratitude."

"All right, mention them," Carmichael said. "Brag your head off. Who cares?"

Worth showed satisfaction. "That ore analysis—it was that. You weren't at the office today, but I caught it. I checked with our records and you had Trans-Steel all wrong. If I hadn't altered the figures, it would have gone down to the printer—"

"What?"

"The Trans-Steel. They—"

"Oh, you fool," Carmichael groaned. "I know it didn't

check with the office figures. I meant to put in a notice to have them changed. I got my dope from the source. Why don't you mind your own business?''

Worth blinked. "I was trying to help."

"It would have been good for a five-buck raise," Carmichael said. "After all the research I did to uncover the real dope— Listen, has the stuff gone to bed yet?''

"I dunno. Maybe not. Croft was still checking the copy—''

"O.K.!'' Carmichael said. "Next time—'' He jerked at his scarf, jumped off the stool, and headed for the door, trailed by the protesting Worth. Ten minutes later he was at the office, listening to Croft's bland explanation that the copy had already been dispatched to the printer.

"Does it matter? Was there— Incidentally, where were you today?''

"Dancing on the rainbow," Carmichael snapped, and departed. He had switched over from rye to whiskey sours, and the cold night air naturally did not sober him. Swaying slightly, watching the sidewalk move a little as he blinked at it, he stood on the curb and pondered.

"I'm sorry, Tim," Worth said. "It's too late now, though. There won't be any trouble. You've got a right to go by our office records.''

"Stop me now," Carmichael said. "Lousy little—" He was angry and drunk. On impulse he got another taxi and sped to the printer's, still trailing a somewhat confused Jerry Worth.

There was rhythmic thunder in the building. The swift movement of the taxi had given Carmichael a slight nausea; his head ached, and alcohol was in solution in his blood. The hot, inky air was unpleasant. The great Linotypes thumped and growled. Men were moving about. It was all slightly nightmarish, and Carmichael doggedly hunched his shoulders and lurched on until something jerked him back and began to strangle him.

Worth started yelling. His face showed drunken terror. He made ineffectual gestures.

But this was all part of the nightmare. Carmichael saw what had happened. The ends of his scarf had caught in the moving gears somewhere and he was being drawn inexorably into meshing metal cogs. Men were running. The clanking, thumping, rolling sounds were deafening. He pulled at the scarf.

Worth screamed, ". . . knife! Cut it!"

The warping of relative values that intoxication gives saved Carmichael. Sober, he would have been helpless with panic. As it was, each thought was hard to capture, but clear and lucid when he finally got it. He remembered the shears, and he put his hand in his pocket. The blades slipped out of their cardboard sheath, and he snipped through the scarf with fumbling, hasty movements.

The white silk disappeared. Carmichael fingered the ragged edge at his throat and smiled stiffly.

Mr. Peter Talley had been hoping that Carmichael would not come back. The probability lines had shown two possible variants; in one, all was well; in the other . . .

Carmichael walked into the shop the next morning and held out a five-dollar bill. Talley took it.

"Thank you. But you could have mailed me a check."

"I could have. Only that wouldn't have told me what I wanted to know."

"No," Talley said, and sighed. "You've decided, haven't you?"

"Do you blame me?" Carmichael asked. "Last night—do you know what happened?"

"Yes."

"How?"

"I might as well tell you," Talley said. "You'd find out anyway. That's certain, anyhow."

Carmichael sat down, lit a cigarette, and nodded. "Logic. You couldn't have arranged that little accident, by any manner of means. Betsy Hoag decided to break our date early yesterday morning. Before I saw you. That was the beginning of the chain of incidents that led up to the accident. *Ergo,* you must have known what was going to happen.''

"I did know.''

"Prescience?''

"Mechanical. I saw that you would be crushed in the machine—''

"Which implies an alterable future.''

"Certainly,'' Talley said, his shoulders slumping. "There are innumerable possible variants to the future. Different lines of probability. All depending on the outcome of various crises as they arise. I happen to be skilled in certain branches of electronics. Some years ago, almost by accident, I stumbled on the principle of seeing the future.''

"How?''

"Chiefly it involves a personal focus on the individual. The moment you enter this place''—he gestured—"you're in the beam of my scanner. In my back room I have the machine itself. By turning a calibrated dial, I check the possible futures. Sometimes there are many. Sometimes only a few. As though at times certain stations weren't broadcasting. I look into my scanner and see what you need—and supply it.''

Carmichael let smoke drift from his nostrils. He watched the blue coils through narrowed eyes.

"You follow a man's whole life—in triplicate or quadruplicate or whatever?''

"No,'' Talley said. "I've got my device focused so it's sensitive to crisis curves. When those occur, I follow them farther and see what probability paths involve the man's safe and happy survival.''

"The sunglasses, the egg, and the gloves—''

Talley said, "Mr.—uh—Smith is one of my regular clients. Whenever he passes a crisis successfully, with my aid, he comes back for another checkup. I locate his next crisis and supply him with what he needs to meet it. I gave him the asbestos gloves. In about a month, a situation will arise where he must—under the circumstances—move a red-hot bar of metal. He's an artist. His hands—''

"I see. So it isn't always saving a man's life."

"Of course not," Talley said. "Life isn't the only vital factor. An apparently minor crisis may lead to—well, a divorce, a neurosis, a wrong decision, and the loss of hundreds of lives indirectly. I insure life, health, and happiness."

"You're an altruist. Only why doesn't the world storm your doors? Why limit your trade to a few?"

"I haven't got the time or the equipment."

"More machines could be built."

"Well," Talley said, "most of my customers are wealthy. I must live."

"You could read tomorrow's stock-market reports if you wanted dough," Carmichael said. "We get back to that old question. If a guy has miraculous powers, why is he satisfied to run a hole-in-the-wall store?"

"Economic reasons. I—ah—I'm averse to gambling."

"It wouldn't be gambling," Carmichael pointed out. " 'I often wonder what the vintners buy . . .' Just what *do* you get out of this?"

"Satisfaction," Talley said. "Call it that."

But Carmichael wasn't satisfied. His mind veered from the question and turned to the possibilities. Insurance, eh? Life, health, and happiness.

"What about me? Won't there be another crisis in my life sometime?"

"Probably. Not necessarily one involving personal danger."

"Then I'm a permanent customer."

"I—don't—"

"Listen," Carmichael said, "I'm not trying to shake you down. I'll pay. I'll pay plenty. I'm not rich, but I know exactly what a service like this would be worth to me. No worries—"

"It couldn't be—"

"Oh, come off it. I'm not a blackmailer or anything. I'm not threatening you with publicity, if that's what you're afraid of. I'm an ordinary guy, not a melodramatic villain. Do I look dangerous? What are you afraid of?''

"You're an ordinary guy, yes," Talley admitted. "Only—"

"Why not?" Camichael argued. "I won't bother you. I passed one crisis successfully, with your help. There'll be another one due sometime. Give me what I need for that. Charge me anything you like. I'll get the dough somehow. Borrow it, if necessary. I won't disturb you at all. All I ask is that you let me come in whenever I've passed a crisis, and get ammunition for the next one. What's wrong with that?''

"Nothing," Talley said soberly.

"Well, then. I'm an ordinary guy. There's a girl—it's Betsy Hoag. I want to marry her. Settle down somewhere in the country, raise kids, and have security. There's nothing wrong with that either, is there?''

Talley said, "It was too late the moment you entered this shop today.''

Carmichael looked up. "Why?" he asked sharply.

A buzzer rang in the back. Talley went through the curtains and came back almost immediately with a wrapped parcel. He gave it to Carmichael.

Carmichael smiled. "Thanks," he said. "Thanks a lot. Do you have any idea when my next crisis will come?''

"In a week.''

"Mind if I—" Carmichael was unwrapping the package. He took out a pair of plastic-soled shoes and looked at Talley, bewildered.

"Like that, eh? I'll need—shoes?''

"Yes.''

"I suppose—" Carmichael hesitated. "I guess you wouldn't tell me why?''

"No, I won't do that. But be sure to wear them whenever you go out.''

"Don't worry about that. And—I'll mail you a check. It may take me a few days to scrape up the dough, but I'll do it. How much?''

"Five hundred dollars.''

"I'll mail a check today."

"I prefer not to accept a fee until the client has been satisfied," Talley said. He had grown more reserved, his blue eyes cool and withdrawn.

"Suit yourself," Carmichael said. "I'm going out and celebrate. You—don't drink?"

"I can't leave the shop."

"Well, good-by. And thanks again. I won't be any trouble to you, you know. I promise that!" He turned away.

Looking after him, Talley smiled a wry, unhappy smile. He did not answer Carmichael's good-by. Not then.

When the door had closed behind him, Talley turned to the back of his shop and went through the door where the scanner was.

The lapse of ten years can cover a multitude of changes. A man with the possibility of tremendous power almost within his grasp can alter, in that time, from a man who will not reach for it to a man who will—and moral values be damned.

The change did not come quickly to Carmichael. It speaks well for his integrity that it took ten years to work such an alteration in all he had been taught. On the day he first went into Talley's shop there was little evil in him. But the temptation grew stronger week by week, visit by visit. Talley, for reasons of his own, was content to sit idly by, waiting for customers, smothering the inconceivable potentialities of his machine under a blanket of trivial functions. But Carmichael was not content.

It took him ten years to reach the day, but the day came at last.

Talley sat in the inner room, his back to the door. He was slumped low in an ancient rocker, facing the machine. It had changed little in the space of a decade. It still covered most of the two walls, and the eyepiece of its scanner glittered under amber fluorescents.

Carmichael looked covetously at the eyepiece. It was window and doorway to a power beyond any man's dreams.

Wealth beyond imagining lay just within that tiny opening. The rights over the life and death of every man alive. And nothing between that fabulous future and himself except the man who sat looking at the machine.

Talley did not seem to hear the careful footsteps or the creak of the door behind him. He did not stir as Carmichael lifted the gun slowly. One might think that he never guessed what was coming, or why, or from whom, as Carmichael shot him through the head.

Talley sighed and shivered a little, and twisted the scanner dial. It was not the first time that the eyepiece had shown him his own lifeless body, glimpsed down some vista of probability, but he never saw the slumping of that familiar figure without feeling a breath of indescribable coolness blow backward upon him out of the future.

He straightened from the eyepiece and sat back in his chair, looking thoughtfully at a pair of rough-soled shoes lying beside him on a table. He sat quietly for a while, his eyes upon the shoes, his mind following Carmichael down the street and into the evening, and the morrow, and on toward that coming crisis which would depend on his secure footing on a subway platform as a train thundered by the place where Carmichael would be standing one day next week.

Talley had sent his messenger boy out this time for two pairs of shoes. He had hesitated long, an hour ago, between the rough-soled pair and the smooth. For Talley was a humane man, and there were many times when his job was distasteful to him. But in the end, this time, it had been the smooth-soled pair he had wrapped for Carmichael.

Now he sighed and bent to the scanner again, twisting the dial to bring into view a scene he had watched before.

Carmichael, standing on a crowded subway platform, glittering with oily wetness from some overflow. Carmichael, in the slick-soled shoes Talley had chosen for him. A commotion in the crowd, a surge toward the platform edge. Carmichael's feet slipping frantically as the train roared by.

"Good-by, Mr. Carmichael," Talley murmured. It was the farewell he had not spoken when Carmichael left the shop. He spoke it regretfully, and the regret was for the Carmichael of today, who did not yet deserve that end. He was not now a melodramatic villain whose death one could watch unmoved. But the Tim Carmichael of today had atonement to make for the Carmichael of ten years ahead, and the payment must be exacted.

It is not a good thing to have the power of life and death over one's fellow humans. Peter Talley knew it was not a good thing—but the power had been put into his hands. He had not sought it. It seemed to him that the machine had grown almost by accident to its tremendous completion under his trained fingers and trained mind.

At first it had puzzled him. How ought such a device to be used? What dangers, what terrible potentialities, lay in that Eye that could see through the veil of tomorrow? His was the responsibility, and it had weighed heavily upon him until the answer came. And after he knew the answer—well, the weight was heavier still. For Talley was a mild man.

He could not have told anyone the real reason why he was a shopkeeper. Satisfaction, he had said to Carmichael. And sometimes, indeed, there was deep satisfaction. But at other times—at times like this—there was only dismay and humility. Especially humility.

We have what you need. Only Talley knew that message was not for the individuals who came to his shop. The pronoun was plural, not singular. It was a message for the world—the world whose future was being carefully, lovingly reshaped under Peter Talley's guidance.

The main line of the future was not easy to alter. The future is a pyramid shaping slowly, brick by brick, and brick by brick Talley had to change it. There were some men who were necessary—men who would create and build—men who should be saved.

Talley gave them what they needed.

But inevitably there were others whose ends were evil. Talley gave them, too, what the world needed—death.

Peter Talley had not asked for this terrible power. But the key had been put in his hands, and he dared not delegate such authority as this to any other man alive. Sometimes he made mistakes.

He had felt a little surer since the simile of the key had occurred to him. The key to the future. A key that had been laid in his hands.

Remembering that, he leaned back in his chair and reached for an old and well-worn book. It fell open easily at a familiar passage. Peter Talley's lips moved as he read the passage once again, in his room behind the shop on Park Avenue.

"And I say also unto thee, that thou art Peter. . . . And I will give unto thee the keys of the Kingdom of Heaven. . . ."

Third from the Sun

Richard Matheson

Teleplay by Rod Serling

Aired January 8, 1960

Starring Fritz Weaver and Edward Andrews

HIS EYES WERE OPEN FIVE SECONDS BEFORE THE alarm was set to go off. There was no effort in waking. It was sudden. Coldly conscious, he reached out his left hand in the dark and pushed in the stop. The alarm glowed a second, then faded.

At his side, his wife put her hand on his arm.

"Did you sleep?" he asked.

"No, did you?"

"A little," he said. "Not much."

She was silent for a few seconds. He heard her throat contract. She shivered. He knew what she was going to say.

"We're still going?" she asked.

He twisted his shoulders on the bed and took a deep breath.

"Yes," he said, and he felt her fingers tighten on his arm.

"What time is it?" she asked.

"About five."

"We'd better get ready."

"Yes, we'd better."

They made no move.

''You're sure we can get on the ship without anyone noticing?'' she asked.

''They think it's just another test flight. Nobody will be checking.''

She didn't say anything. She moved a little closer to him. He felt how cold her skin was.

''I'm afraid,'' she said.

He took her hand and held it in a tight grip. ''Don't be,'' he said. ''We'll be safe.''

''It's the children I'm worried about.''

''We'll be safe,'' he repeated.

She lifted his hand to her lips and kissed it gently.

''All right,'' she said.

They both sat up in the darkness. He heard her stand. Her night garment rustled to the floor. She didn't pick it up. She stood still, shivering in the cold morning air.

''You're sure we don't need anything else with us?'' she asked.

''No, nothing. I have all the supplies we need in the ship. Anyway . . .''

''What?''

''We can't carry anything past the guard,'' he said. ''He has to think you and the kids are just coming to see me off.''

She began dressing. He threw off the covering and got up. He went across the cold floor to the closet and dressed.

''I'll get the children up,'' she said.

He grunted, pulling clothes over his head. At the door she stopped. ''Are you sure . . .'' she began.

''What?''

''Won't the guard think it's funny that . . . that our neighbors are coming down to see you off, too?''

He sank down on the bed and fumbled for the clasps on his shoes.

''We'll have to take that chance,'' he said. ''We need them with us.''

She sighed. ''It seems so cold. So calculating.''

He straightened up and saw her silhouette in the doorway.

"What else can we do?" he asked intensely. "We can't interbreed our own children."

"No," she said. "It's just . . ."

"Just what?"

"Nothing, darling. I'm sorry."

She closed the door. Her footsteps disappeared down the hall. The door to the children's room opened. He heard their two voices. A cheerless smile raised his lips. You'd think it was a holiday, he thought.

He pulled on his shoes. At least the kids didn't know what was happening. They thought they were going to take him down to the field. They thought they'd come back and tell all their schoolmates about it. They didn't know they'd never come back.

He finished clasping his shoes and stood up. He shuffled over to the bureau and turned on the light. It was odd, such an undistinguished-looking man planning this.

Cold. Calculating. Her words filled his mind again. Well, there was no other way. In a few years, probably less, the whole planet would go up with a blinding flash. This was the only way out. Escaping, starting all over again with a few people on a new planet.

He stared at the reflection.

"There's no other way," he said.

He glanced around the bedroom. Good-bye this part of my life. Turning off the lamp was like turning off a light in his mind. He closed the door gently behind him and slid his fingers off the worn handle.

His son and daughter were going down the ramp. They were talking in mysterious whispers. He shook his head in slight amusement.

His wife waited for him. They went down together, holding hands.

"I'm not afraid, darling," she said. "It'll be all right."

"Sure," he said. "Sure it will."

They all went in to eat. He sat down with his children. His

wife poured out juice for them. Then she went to get the food.

"Help your mother, doll," he told his daughter. She got up.

"Pretty soon, haah, pop?" his son said. "Pretty soon, haah?"

"Take it easy," he cautioned. "Remember what I told you. If you say a word of it to anybody I'll have to leave you behind."

A dish shattered on the floor. He darted a glance at his wife. She was staring at him, her lips trembling.

She averted her eyes and bent down. She fumbled at the pieces, picked up a few. Then she dropped them all, stood up and pushed them against the wall with her shoe.

"As if it mattered," she said nervously. "As if it mattered whether the place is clean or not."

The children were watching her in surprise.

"What is it?" asked the daughter.

"Nothing, darling, nothing," she said. "I'm just nervous. Go back to the table. Drink your juice. We have to eat quickly. The neighbors will be here soon."

"Pop, why are the neighbors coming with us?" asked his son.

"Because," he said vaguely, "they want to. Now forget it. Don't talk about it so much."

The room was quiet. His wife brought their food and set it down. Only her footsteps broke the silence. The children kept glancing at each other, at their father. He kept his eyes on the plate. The food tasted flat and thick in his mouth and he felt his heart thudding against the wall of his chest. Last day. This is the last day.

"You'd better eat," he told his wife.

She sat down to eat. As she lifted the eating utensil the door buzzer sounded. The utensil skidded out of her nerveless fingers and clattered on the floor. He reached out quickly and put his hand on hers.

"All right, darling," he said. "It's all right." He turned to the children. "Go answer the door," he told them.

"Both of us?" his daughter asked.

"Both of you."

"But . . ."

"Do as I say."

They slid off their chairs and left the room, glancing back at their parents.

When the sliding door shut off their view, he turned back to his wife. Her face was pale and tight; she had her lips pressed together.

"Darling, please," he said. "Please. You know I wouldn't take you if I wasn't sure it was safe. You know how many times I've flown the ship before. And I know just where we're going. It's safe. Believe me it's safe."

She pressed his hand against her cheek. She closed her eyes and large tears ran out under her lids and down her cheeks.

"It's not that so m-much," she said. "It's just . . . leaving, never coming back. We've been here all our lives. It isn't like . . . like moving. We can't come back. Ever."

"Listen, darling." His voice was tense and hurried. "You know as well as I do. In a matter of years, maybe less, there's going to be another war, a terrible one. There won't be a thing left. We have to leave. For our children, for ourselves . . ."

He paused, testing the words in his mind.

"For the future of life itself," he finished weakly. He was sorry he said it. Early in the morning over prosaic food, that kind of talk didn't sound right. Even if it was true.

"Just don't be afraid," he said. "We'll be all right."

She squeezed his hand.

"I know," she said quietly. "I know."

There were footsteps coming toward them. He pulled out a tissue and gave it to her. She hastily dabbed at her face.

The door slid open. The neighbors and their son and

daughter came in. The children were excited. They had trouble keeping it down.

"Good morning," the neighbor said.

The neighbor's wife went to his wife and the two of them went over to the window and talked in low voices. The children stood around, fidgeted and looked nervously at each other.

"You've eaten?" he asked his neighbor.

"Yes," his neighbor said. "Don't you think we'd better be going?"

"I suppose so," he said.

They left all the dishes on the table. His wife went upstairs and got garments for the family.

He and his wife stayed on the porch a moment while the rest went out to the ground car.

"Should we lock the door?" he asked.

She smiled helplessly and ran a hand through her hair. She shrugged. "Does it matter?" she said, and turned away.

He locked the door and followed her down the walk. She turned as he came up to her.

"It's a nice house," she murmured.

"Don't think about it," he said.

They turned their backs on their home and got in the ground car.

"Did you lock it?" asked the neighbor.

"Yes."

The neighbor smiled wryly. "So did we," he said. "I tried not to, but then I had to go back."

They moved through the quiet streets. The edges of the sky were beginning to redden. The neighbor's wife and the four children were in back. His wife and the neighbor were in front with him.

"Going to be a nice day," said the neighbor.

"I suppose so," he said.

"Have you told your children?" the neighbor asked softly.

"Of course not."

"I haven't, I haven't," insisted his neighbor, "I was just asking."

"Oh."

They rode in silence a while.

"Do you ever get the feeling that we're . . . running out?" asked the neighbor.

He tightened. "No," he said. His lips pressed together. "No."

"I guess it's better not to talk about it," his neighbor said hastily.

"Much better," he said.

As they drove up to the guardhouse at the gate, he turned to the back.

"Remember," he said. "Not a word from any of you."

The guard was sleepy and didn't care. The guard recognized him right away as the chief test pilot for the new ship. That was enough. The family was coming down to watch him off, he told the guard. That was all right. The guard let them drive to the ship's platform.

The car stopped under the huge columns. They all got out and stared up.

Far above them, its nose pointed toward the sky, the great metal ship was beginning to reflect the early morning glow.

"Let's go," he said. "Quickly."

As they hurried toward the ship's elevator, he stopped for a moment to look back. The guardhouse looked deserted. He looked around at everything and tried to fix it all in his memory.

He bent over and picked up some dirt. He put it in his pocket.

"Good-bye," he whispered.

He ran to the elevator.

The doors shut in front of them. There was no sound in the rising cubicle but the hum of the motor and a few self-conscious coughs from the children. He looked at them. To be taken so young, he thought, without a chance to help.

He closed his eyes. His wife's arm rested on his arm. He looked at her. Their eyes met and she smiled at him.

"It's all right," she whispered.

The elevator shuddered to a stop. The doors slid open and they went out. It was getting lighter. He hurried them along the enclosed platform.

They all climbed through the narrow doorway in the ship's side. He hesitated before following them. He wanted to say something fitting the moment. It burned in him to say something fitting the moment.

He couldn't. He swung in and grunted as he pulled the door shut and turned the wheel tight.

"That's it," he said. "Come on, everybody."

Their footsteps echoed on the metal decks and ladders as they went up to the control room.

The children ran to the ports and looked out. They gasped when they saw how high they were. Their mothers stood behind them, looking down at the ground with frightened eyes.

He went up to them.

"So high," said his daughter.

He patted her head gently. "So high," he repeated.

Then he turned abruptly and went over to the instrument panel. He stood there hesitantly. He heard someone come up behind him.

"Shouldn't we tell the children?" asked his wife. "Shouldn't we let them know it's their last look?"

"Go ahead," he said. "Tell them."

He waited to hear her footsteps. There were none. He turned. She kissed him on the cheek. Then she went to tell the children.

He threw over the switch. Deep in the belly of the ship, a spark ignited the fuel. A concentrated rush of gas flooded from the vents. The bulkheads began to shake.

He heard his daughter crying. He tried not to listen. He extended a trembling hand toward the lever, then glanced back suddenly. They were all staring at him. He put his hand on the lever and threw it over.

The ship quivered a brief second and then they felt it rush along the smooth incline. It flashed up into the air, faster and faster. They all heard the wind rushing past.

He watched the children turn to the ports and look out again.

"Good-bye," they said. "Good-bye."

He sank down wearily at the control panel. Out of the corner of his eyes he saw his neighbor sit down next to him.

"You know just where we're going?" his neighbor asked.

"On that chart there."

His neighbor looked at the chart. His eyebrows raised.

"In another solar system," he said.

"That's right. It has an atmosphere like ours. We'll be safe there."

"The race will be safe," said his neighbor.

He nodded once and looked back at his and his neighbor's families. They were still looking out the ports.

"What?" he asked.

"I said," the neighbor repeated, "which one of these planets is it?"

He leaned over the chart, pointed.

"That small one over there," he said. "Near that moon."

"This one, third from the sun?"

"That's right," he said. "That one. Third from the sun."

Elegy

Charles Beaumont

Teleplay by Charles Beaumont

Aired February 19, 1960

Starring Cecil Kellaway and Jeff Morrow

Port: Asteroid K7.

THE FIERY METAL LEG FELL INTO THE COOL AIR,
heating it; burnt into the green grass and licked a craterous
hole. There were fire flags and fire sparks, hisses and explosions and the weary groaning sound of a great beast.

The rocket grumbled and muttered for a while on its finny
tripod, then was silent; soon the heat vanished also.

"Are you all right, sir?"

"Yes. The rest?"

"Fine, sir."

Captain Webber swung himself erect and tested his limbs.
"Well, then, Lieutenant, has the atmosphere been checked?"

"The air is pure and fit to breathe, sir."

"Instruct the others to drop the ladder."

A door in the side of the rocket opened and men began
climbing out: "Look!" said crewman Milton, pointing.
"Trees and grass and—little wooden bridges going over the
water."

Beyond the trees a brick lodge extended over a rivulet

which foamed and bubbled. Fishing poles protruded from the lodge windows.

"And there, to the right!"

A steel building thirty stories high with a pink cloud near the top. And, separated by a hedge, a brown tent with a barbecue pit before it, smoke rising in a rigid ribbon from the chimney.

Crewman Chitterwick blinked and squinted his eyes. "Where are we?"

Distant and near, houses of stone and brick and wood, painted all colors, small, large; and further, golden fields of wheat, each blown by a different breeze in a different direction.

"I don't believe it," said Captain Webber. "It's a *park*—millions of miles away from where a park could possibly be."

"Damned strange," said Lieutenant Peterson, picking up a rock. "We're on an asteroid not shown on *any* chart, in the middle of a place that belongs in history records."

A little man with thin hair stepped briskly from a tree clump. "Well, well, I hadn't been expecting you gentlemen, to be perfectly honest," the little man chuckled, then, "Oh dear, see what you've done to the property of Mr. Bellefont. I do hope you haven't hurt *him*—no, I see that he is all right."

An old man with red hair was seated at the base of a tree, apparently reading a book.

"We are from Earth," said Captain Webber.

"Yes, yes."

"My name is Webber, these are my men."

"Of course," said the little man.

"Who are you?" asked Webber.

"Who—Greypoole, Mr. Greypoole. Didn't *they* tell you?"

"Then you are *also* from Earth?"

"Heavens, yes! But let us go where we can chat more comfortably. Follow me." Mr. Greypoole struck out down a small path past scorched trees and underbrush.

They walked onto a wooden porch and through a door with

a wire screen; Lieutenant Peterson first, then Captain Webber, Mr. Friden and the rest of the crew. Greypoole followed.

"You must forgive me—it's been a while. Take chairs, there—there. Please be comfortable."

Captain Webber glanced around the room at the lace curtains, the needle-point tapestries and the lavender wallpaper.

"Mr. Greypoole, I'd like to ask some questions."

"Certainly, certainly. But first, this being an occasion—" the little man stared at each of them, then shook his head, "ah, do you all like wine? Good wine? I shall be back soon. Forgive me, gentlemen."

He ducked through a small door.

Captain Webber exhaled. "Friden, you stay here; you others see what you can find. Scout around. We'll wait."

The men left the room.

Crewman Chitterwick made his way along a hedgerow, feeling cautiously, maintaining a delicate balance. When he came to a doorway he stopped, looked about, then entered.

The room was dark and quiet and odorous. Mr. Chitterwick groped a few steps, put out his hand and encountered what seemed to be raw flesh; he swiftly withdrew his hand. "Excuse," he said, then "Uh!" as his face came against a slab of moist red meat.

Mr. Chitterwick began to tremble and he blinked furiously, reaching out and finding flesh, cold and hard.

When he stepped upon the toe of a large man with a walrus mustache, he wheeled, located the sunlight, and ran from the butcher shop . . .

The door of the temple opened with difficulty, which caused crewman Milton to breathe unnaturally. Once inside, he gasped.

Row upon row of people, their fingers outstretched, lips open but immobile and silent, their bodies prostrate on the floor. And upon a strange black altar, a tiny woman with silver hair and a long thyrsus in her right hand.

Nothing stirred but the mosaic squares in the walls. The colors danced here; otherwise, everything was frozen, everything was solid.

Even the air hung suspended, stationary.

Mr. Milton left the temple . . .

There was a table and a woman on the table and people all around the woman on the table. Crewman Goeblin rubbed his eyes and stared.

It was an operating room. There were masked men and women with shining scissors and glistening saws in their hands. And up above, the students' aperture: filled seats, filled aisles.

A large man stood over the recumbent figure, his lusterless eyes regarding the crimson-puce incision, but he did not move. The nurses did not move, nor the students. No one moved, especially the smiling middle-aged woman on the table.

Mr. Goeblin moved . . .

"Hello!" said Lieutenant Peterson, after he had searched through eight long aisles of books. "Hello!"

He pointed his gun menacingly.

There were many books with many titles and they all had a fine gray dust about them. Lieutenant Peterson paused to examine a bulky volume, when he happened to look upward.

"Who are *you*?" he demanded.

The mottled, angular man perched atop the ladder did not respond. He clutched a book and looked at the book and not at Lieutenant Peterson.

Peterson climbed up the ladder, scowling; he reached the man and drew in a breath. He looked into the eyes of the reading man and descended hastily . . .

Mr. Greypoole re-entered the living room with a tray of glasses. "This is apricot wine," he announced, distributing the glasses. "But—where are the others? Out for a walk? Ah well, they can drink theirs later. Incidentally, Captain, how many Guests did you bring? Last time it was only twelve. Not an extraordinary shipment either; they all preferred ordinary things. All but Mrs. Dominguez—dear me, she was worth the carload herself. Wanted a zoo, can you imagine? —a regular zoo, with her put right in the birdhouse. Oh, they had a time putting that one up!"

Mr. Greypoole chuckled and sipped at his drink. He leaned back in his chair and crossed a leg. "Ah," he continued, "you have no idea how good this is. Once in a while it does get lonely for me here—why, I can remember when Mr. Waldmeyer first told me of this idea. 'A grave responsibility,' he said, 'a *grave* responsibility.' Mr. Waldmeyer has a keen sense of humor, needless to say."

Captain Webber put down his glass. Outside, a small child on roller skates stood unmoving on the sidewalk.

"Finished your wine? Good. Perhaps you'd care to join me in a brief turn about the premises?"

Webber sighed, stood up. "Friden, you stay here and wait for the men." He followed Greypoole out onto the porch and down the steps.

Crewman Friden drummed his fingers upon the arm of a chair, surveyed his empty glass and hiccoughed softly.

"I *do* wish you had landed your ship elsewhere, Captain. Mr. Bellefont was quite particular and, as you can see, his park is hopelessly disfigured."

"We were given no choice. Our fuel was running out."

"Indeed? Well, then, that explains everything. A beautiful day, don't you find, sir? Fortunately, with the exception of Professor Carling, all the Guests preferred good weather. Plenty of sunshine, they said. It helps."

When they passed a statue-still woman on a bicycle, Captain Webber stopped walking.

"Mr. Greypoole, we've *got* to have a talk."

The little man shrugged and pointed and they went into an

office building which was crowded with motionless men, women and children.

"Since I'm so mixed up myself," Webber said, "maybe I'd better ask—just who do you think *we* are?"

"The men from the Glades, of course."

"I don't know what you're talking about. We're from Earth. They were on the verge of another war—the 'Last War'—and we escaped and started off for Mars. But something went wrong—crewman named Appleton pulled a gun, others just didn't like the Martians—we needn't go into it; Mars didn't work out. We were forced to leave. Then, more trouble. We ended up lost with only a little store of fuel and supplies. Friden noticed this city or whatever it is and we had just enough fuel to land."

Mr. Greypoole nodded his head slowly. "I see . . . You say there was a war on Earth?"

"They were going to set off the X-Bomb."

"What dreadful news! May I inquire, Captain, as to what you intend to do now?"

"Why, live here, of course!"

"No, no—that's quite impossible."

Captain Webber glanced at the motionless people. "Why not? What *is* this place? Where *are* we?"

Mr. Greypoole smiled.

"Captain, we are in a cemetery."

At that moment, Friden and the other crewmen arrived. Chitterwick blinked.

"I heard what he said, sir. The man's insane."

"What about *this?*" Friden asked. "Take a look, Captain." He handed Webber a pamphlet.

In the center of the first page was a photograph, untinted and solemn; it depicted a white cherub delicately poised on a granite slab. Beneath the photograph were the words: HAPPY GLADES.

"It's one of those old level cemeteries!" said Webber. "I remember seeing pictures of them."

He began to read the pamphlet:

For fifty years, an outstanding cultural and spiritual asset to this community, HAPPY GLADES is proud to announce yet another innovation in its program of post-benefits. Now you can enjoy the afterlife in surroundings which suggest the here-and-now. For those who prefer that their late departed have really permanent eternal happiness, for those who are dismayed by the fragility of all things mortal, we of HAPPY GLADES are proud to offer:
1. The duplication of physical conditions identical to those enjoyed by the departed on Earth. Park, playground, lodge, office building, hotel or house, etc., may be secured at varying prices. All workmanship and materials attuned to conditions on ASTEROID K, and guaranteed for permanence.
2. Permanent conditioning of late beloved so that, in the midst of surroundings he favored, a genuine Eternity may be assured.

Webber swung toward Greypoole. "You mean *all* these people are dead?"
The little fellow proceeded to straighten the coat of a middle-aged man with a cigar.
"No, no," laughed Mr. Greypoole, "only the main Guests. The others are imitations. Mr. Conklin upstairs was head of a large firm; absolutely in love with his work, you know—that kind of thing. So we had to duplicate not only the office, but the building—and even provide replicas of all the people *in* the building. Mr. Conklin himself is in an easy chair on the twentieth story."
"And?"
"Well, gentlemen, what with the constant exploration of planets and moons, our Mr. Waldmeyer hit upon this scheme: seeking to extend the ideal hereafter to our Guests, he bought this little asteroid. With the vast volume and the tremendous turnover, as it were, HAPPY GLADES offered this plan—to duplicate the exact surroundings which the

Guest most enjoyed in Life, assure him privacy, permanence.''

''But why here? Why cart bodies off a million miles or more when the same thing could have been done on Earth?''

''My communications system went bad, I fear, so I haven't heard from the offices in some while—but you tell me there *is* a war beginning? That is the idea, Captain; one could never really be sure of one's self down there, what with all the new bombs and things being discovered.''

''And where do you fit in, Mr. Greypoole?''

The little man lowered his eyes. ''I was head caretaker, you see. But I wasn't well—gastric complaints, liver, heart palpitations, this and that, so I decided to allow them to—change me. By the time I got here, why, I was almost, you might say, a machine. Now, whenever the film is punctured, I wake to do my prescribed duties.''

''The film?''

''The asteroid covering that seals in the conditioning. Nothing can get out, nothing get in—except rockets. Then, it's self-sealing. They threw up the film and coated us with their preservative, or Eternifier, and—well, with the exception of my communications system, everything's worked perfectly. Until now . . .''

Captain Webber spoke slowly. ''We're tired men, Mr. Greypoole. There are lakes and farms here, all we need to make a new start—more than we'd hoped for . . . Will you help us?''

Mr. Greypoole clucked his tongue. Then he smiled. ''Yes, Captain, I will. But, first, let us go back to your rocket. You'll need supplies.''

Captain Webber nodded. They left the building.

They passed a garden with little spotted trees and flowers, a brown desert of shifting sands and a striped tent. They walked by strawberry fields and airplane hangars and coal mines; past tiny yellow cottages, cramped apartments, fluted houses, past rock pools and a great zoo full of animals that stared out of vacant eyes; and everywhere, the seasons changing gently: crisp autumn, cottony summer, windy spring and winters cool and white . . .

The six men in uniform followed the little man with thin hair. They did not speak as they walked, but looked, stared, craned, wondered . . .

And the old, young, middle-aged, white, brown, yellow people around them did not move.

"You can see, Captain, the success of Mr. Waldmeyer's plan, the perfection here, the quality of Eternal Happiness. Here we have brotherhood; no wars or hatreds or prejudices. And now you who left Earth to escape war and hatred, you want to begin life here?"

Cross-breezes ruffled the men's hair.

As they neared the rocket, Greypoole turned to them. "By your own admission, from the moment of your departure, you had personal wars of your own, and killed, and hurled prejudice against a race of people not like you, a race who rejected and cast you out into space again! From your *own* account! Gentlemen, I am truly sorry. You may mean well, after all—I *am* sorry." Mr. Greypoole sighed.

"What do you mean, you're sorry?" demanded Webber.

"Well . . ."

"Captain—" cried Chitterwick, blinking.

"Yes, yes?"

"I feel terrible."

Mr. Goeblin clutched at his stomach.

"So do I!"

"And me!"

Captain Webber looked at Greypoole. His mouth twitched in sudden pain.

"I'm sorry, gentlemen. Into your ship, quickly." Mr. Greypoole motioned them forward.

Crewman Milton staggered, groping for balance. "We—we shouldn't have drunk that wine. It was—poisoned!"

Greypoole produced a weapon. "*Tell* them, Captain, tell them to climb the ladder. Or they'll die here and now."

"Go on. Up!"

The crew climbed into the ship.

Captain Webber ascended jerkily. When he reached the open lock, he coughed and pulled himself into the rocket.

Greypoole followed.

"You don't dislike this ship, do you—that is, the surroundings are not offensive? If only I had been allowed more latitude! But everything functions automatically here; no real choice in the matter, actually. The men mustn't writhe about on the floor like that. Get them to their stations—the stations they would most prefer. And hurry!"

Dully, Captain Webber ordered Mr. Chitterwick to the galley, Mr. Goeblin to the engineering chair, Mr. Friden to the navigator's room . . .

"Sir, what's going to happen?"

Mr. Milton to the pilot's chair . . .

"The pain will last only another moment or so—it's unfortunately part of the Eternifier," said Mr. Greypoole. "There, all in order? Good, good. Now, Captain, I see understanding in your face; that pleases me more than I can say. My position is so difficult! But a machine *is* geared to its job—which, in this case, is to retain permanence."

Captain Webber leaned on the arm of the little man. He tried to speak, then slumped into his control seat.

"You *do* understand?" asked Mr. Greypoole, putting away the weapon.

Captain Webber's head nodded halfway down, then stopped, and his eyes froze forever.

"Fine. Fine."

The little man with the thin hair walked about the cabins and rooms, straightening, arranging; he climbed down the ladder, and returned to the wooden house, humming to himself.

When he had washed all the empty wineglasses and replaced them, he sat down in the large leather chair and adjusted himself into the most comfortable position.

His eyes stared in waxen contentment at the homely interior, with its lavender wallpaper, needle-point tapestries . . .

He did not move.

Brothers Beyond the Void

Paul Fairman

Teleplay by Rod Serling

Aired March 25, 1960, as "People Are Alike All Over"

Starring Roddy McDowall and Susan Oliver

IT WAS A MATTER OF GREAT SATISFACTION TO MARcusson that he could be with Sam Conrad upon the eve of his great adventure. Marcusson's day had been full; the final briefing during the morning hours at the Foundation headquarters; the many handshakes and well-wishes—these carried over into the afternoon cocktail party given in his honor.

The party had been a boring affair because Marcusson did not care for liquor, the fevered enthusiasm which always went with it, nor the brittle garden variety of compliment:

"Oh, Mr. Marcusson! You've no idea how thrilled I am to shake your hand!"

"You'll make it, boy—make it and come back again. A little thing like space won't stop you!"

"Would you just give me one little old autograph, Mr. Marcusson? Here on my scarf. I'd be so thrilled."

Boring.

So Marcusson had left at the earliest opportunity and hastened away to spend his last evening on Earth—for a time at least—with Sam Conrad. They sat on Conrad's vine-covered porch and there was lemonade in a pitcher filled with tinkling cubes of ice; that, the fragrant night, and the quiet restful aura of a true friend.

Wonderful.

Marcusson lay back in his chair and closed his eyes. "I'll remember this," he said.

Sam Conrad puffed on his pipe. "I'm honored. The world's most currently famous man comes to visit me."

"Cut it out. My head's crammed full with that kind of rot. It's also full of exact science and cold mathematical calculations. Facts and figures haunt my dreams. I want some good steadying conjecture—some of your tobacco-stained philosophy to wet down the indigestible mass."

"Are you afraid, Charles?"

"No—no, I don't think so." Marcusson leaned suddenly forward in his chair. "Sam—what do you think I'll find?"

Conrad shrugged. "Your men at the Foundation would know more about that than I. Mars is really beyond the abstract and restful philosophies—"

"Let's not kid ourselves. They know nothing at all—I know nothing."

"Nor do I. But let's project a bit from what solid ground we have. We'll look at it this way: you are a lone Earthman hoping to set your feet on the planet Mars. Therefore, your instinctive interest is in your own safety. What sort of people will you find there—if any? Will they haul you from your ship and kick the life out of you? Will they find pleasure in tearing you to pieces?"

"What do you think, Sam?"

The older man poured two leisurely glasses of lemonade. "We can project with a fair chance of being right. Mars is an old planet. There will certainly be no newly evolved lifeforms there. So, if you find living creatures, they will certainly have every right to be called *people*."

"I'll go along with that."

"And *people*, Charles, are the same everywhere."

"I don't know—"

"There is absolutely no reason why they shouldn't be. In constructing humankind, Nature invented a fixed formula —a pattern of behavior built upon basic instincts to meet certain physical needs and spiritual conditions. Those conditions, so far as a *humanoid* is concerned, are the same here on Earth as they would be in the furthest reaches of space. Physical characteristics, of course, are changeable to meet changed geographical and geological conditions. But such things are only trappings; outer garments, so to speak. The spiritual and emotional care of the *humanoid* is as fixed as the stars."

"Then you believe people are the same everywhere?"

"People—wherever they are able to exist—are all the same."

Marcusson left an hour later. He shook hands with Conrad at the gate and pointed to a certain spot in the heavens. "Tomorrow night about this time, look just—there. You may not see me, but don't forget to look."

"I certainly shall. Good luck."

As Marcusson drove home, he thought again of Conrad's words and found a comfort in them. Not that he was afraid, he assured himself.

Then he refuted that assertion and admitted the truth. Of course he was afraid. Any man in his position would know fear whether he admitted it or not. So the words of his friend were a comfort.

People—wherever they are able to exist—are all the same. And as he went to sleep, the thought was still there: *People are all the same.*

Everything went off as scheduled—as smoothly and efficiently as Foundation know-how and money could make it. And Marcusson was struck, later, by how swiftly it all slithered into the past and found a storage-niche in his memory. He thought of this when he was far out in space and there was time to think.

He also thought of Sam Conrad.

But the schedule ran true, and before too long there were other things to think about. A planet rearing up out of the void to seemingly snatch at his little craft and bring it into strange port.

Here, the mathematics failed to some extent. Marcusson was supposed to have set down in daylight, but as he arced in out of his orbit, the moons of Mars were racing through the sky. This was a bit disappointing, but he set down safely, so the mathematics could not really be charged with failure. He left the ship, cautiously removed his oxygen mask, and found he could breathe. Also, that he was exhausted to a point of physical weakness. He sat down on the cool ground for a moment's rest. He slept.

He awakened. Daylight was blazing down. He blinked.

And saw the Martians.

There were two of them—males, Marcusson decided. One was about three inches shorter than the other and the taller stood roughly four feet five inches. They wore clothing of a loose, comfortable sort. The garments were dyed in the brightest hues imaginable and, while they hung to body contour, they seemed to be starched or impregnated with some similar substance.

The Martians were not ugly or especially beautiful from the standpoint of an Earthman's eye. Nor was the land striking in any manner whatsoever. There was a gray spired city off to the left, but the only Martians in sight were the two males who stood at a safe distance regarding him.

One of them was obviously armed. He carried a small stick with a butt set into it at right angles. He gripped the butt tightly in his small fist, but made no motion to use the weapon.

But Marcusson paid scant attention to all this. These were merely the outer trappings—the superficial structure-work in which these people existed.

He was interested basically and tensely in—the Martians.

He got slowly to his feet, careful to make no sudden movements. They were alert, wary, but not afraid. They had eyes of a particularly clear sea-green, and behind these eyes was intelligence. They paid no attention to the ship, having evidently inspected it to their satisfaction while he slept. They watched Marcusson and discussed him between themselves in a musical language—a pleasant, bird-like warble that gave off most ably the nuances of mood, thought, and inflection for which anyone unfamiliar with a language always listens.

Marcusson tentatively extended a hand, thinking, with elation, that all was well. People were the same everywhere. These could be two Earthmen inspecting an interplanetary arrival on Terra. Their reactions, their natural caution, their instincts, were of the same pattern exactly.

One of them was eyeing the gun on Marcusson's hip. Quite obviously, the Martian knew what it was. Marcusson made no motion toward it. Rather, he smiled and raised his hand, palm outward.

"I am Charles Marcusson. I come from Earth. I come in peace and with a spirit of brotherhood." He didn't expect them to understand, but he had invented that speech during the long hours in void and wanted to get it off his chest.

The Martians glanced at each other with bright interest. They did not speak to Marcusson but discussed something between themselves, glancing now and again at the spires of the city beyond the rolling hills.

It was obvious to Marcusson that they were attempting to arrive at some decision. A moment later he knew this had been accomplished because they nodded in agreement and turned their attention to the Earthman.

But cautiously and with ever-present alertness. The one with the weapon motioned—a beckoning motion—after which he pointed across the hills toward a spot somewhat to the right of the city.

Then, both Martians invited Marcusson to walk in that direction by doing so themselves. They stopped, glanced back expectantly, and both of them smiled.

Marcusson chuckled inwardly at these hospitable and

kindly gestures. Without hesitation, he moved in the indicated direction. The Martians registered, between themselves, a marked satisfaction. An almost childlike elation, Marcusson thought, at getting their simple ideas across to him. They did not come close, but moved to a point on either side of him and well out of harm's way if he made a quick movement. The armed one kept his weapon ever at ready, but his smile mirrored the friendliness in his mind.

Marcusson estimated they had traveled about four miles when they moved over a low hill and came to the house. Obviously it was a house, but it was like nothing Marcusson had ever seen in the way of a dwelling.

It was a perfect square and no attempt had been made to achieve beauty. Each side ran about twenty feet, and beside it was a smaller square, identical in every respect except size. Grayish windowless walls about ten feet high. Marcusson got the impression of a stockade with a roof, and a tool shed hard by.

The door was merely a section of the wall that pushed inward. Marcusson would have had trouble locating it. One of the Martians opened the door and then both of them stepped back, a careful distance away, and indicated. Marcusson was being invited to precede them.

This he did and was struck immediately by the lighting system inside; or rather, by the apparent absence of a lighting system. He could not discover from whence came the illumination; yet, through some indirect means, there was shadowless light throughout the single room of the house.

Swiftly he took the place in, and marveled at the entirely different manner in which another race on another planet could arrive at the same objective as the inhabitants of Earth. While the contents of the great room bore no similarity to the furnishings of a Terran home, yet there was no doubt that people could live here comfortably and adequately.

They'll be surprised, he thought, *when I tell them about this back in New York.*

The Martians entered behind him, closed the door and looked at each other in complete understanding.

Never in his life had Marcusson had such a feeling of contentment, well-being, and achievement. At times he thought to marvel at how smoothly everything had gone. Time slipped by and he felt no sense of urgency, because each day brought accomplishment in increased knowledge of these people.

He did not see any Martians other than the two in whose house he lived. And he got the idea he was being jealously guarded by these two; sort of an honored guest they didn't care to share with their world.

This amused him and he made no protest because he felt all that could be taken care of in due time. Besides, he was learning a great deal about the Martians. He discovered they were far ahead of Earthlings in many facets of science. The lighting, for instance. He was never able to discover from whence it came. Yet he knew that it was artificial.

The small shed next to the house seemed to contain a great many things they needed. He was never invited to enter it and did not press the point, but he felt sure the lighting, the refrigeration, the water supply, and all the Martians' conveniences of living originated in that small building.

He was somewhat surprised that, while the two Martians were unfailingly attentive and courteous, they continued to mistrust him. They never came close to him in a pair. Always one stood back on the alert, ready to use the small weapon if necessary.

He discarded his own weapon the first night, as a gesture of friendship. He was disappointed, but not discouraged, when they did not reciprocate.

Yet he had no complaint. It was a little like having two excellent servants to do his bidding night and day.

And he was puzzled at the continual air of anticipation between them. They had long discussions in the soft liquid language and, though he couldn't understand it, he felt it was all of a tenor, always relative to the same subject.

Then came the day he'd hoped for—the day they definitely became more intimate with him. The taller of the two took the initiative in the missionary work, and after a little time Marcusson found out what he was driving at. He wanted to know about the place Marcusson had come from.

Their intercourse took on varied forms. Marcusson printed the word *Earth* on a metal writing plate and the Martian swifly understood. He put down some spidery hieroglyphics of his own and Marcusson picked up a smattering of the language. But not much. It was very difficult.

Most of the communications were by way of drawings. When Marcusson indicated the Martian domicile with a wave of his arm and then sketched a Terran cottage, the Martian was highly elated and went into conference with his partner.

The Martian evinced a tremendous interest in the sketch and Marcusson elaborated upon it greatly, sketching out the rooms, the furnishings, and several outside angles until the Martian appeared satisfied.

On the day following the final sketching of a Terran dwelling place, Marcusson awoke to find what he rated as almost a miracle. The Martians alertly invited him outside and over the brow of the nearest hill. Marcusson gasped.

They had built him a house.

They watched him closely for his reaction, and were pleased when it was favorable. Marcusson moved forward in a daze, entered the cottage and felt himself to be back on Earth. Every detail of his sketches had been carried out with amazing accuracy. The furniture, the floor coverings, the wallpaper—even the light fixtures were in place. And when Marcusson snapped a wall switch, the bulbs gave forth the yellow radiance he had known on Terra.

He was astounded. *They are far ahead of us,* he thought. *Beside them, we are children. Here advanced science is commonplace. Science of which we have not even dreamed.*

But Conrad was right, he thought warmly. *They are people. Basically they are no different from us.*

Marcusson moved into his new home that night, much to

the delight of the Martians. He ate his dinner at a table which could have come from any Terran furniture store. He lay down in a bed any Terran would have been proud to own.

The Martians did not dine with him. Instead they stood by, conversing in their soothing musical language, happiness mirrored in every syllable.

When darkness fell, they left him alone in his house.

Marcusson filled the early evening hours studying the written Martian language. He had made quite a little progress with the words and could now pick out phrases and whole sentences from the long, narrow books the two Martians had given him.

It was about time, he decided, to widen his areas of research. Tomorrow he would insist upon visiting the gray city across the hills.

But the people of the city came to visit him. He arose the next morning and found breakfast awaiting him. But as he sat down to the table, something caught his eye through the window. He arose and went outside.

The Martians were there—hundreds of them—and more coming over the hills from the spired city.

A chill such as he had never known swept through Marcusson. He saw the bars in which he was imprisoned—the cage erected around his house—the sign in Martian lettering he interpreted into his own language and read with horror:

EARTH CREATURE—IN ITS
NATURAL HABITAT

He saw the staring eyes of the Martians and realized the full, ghastly truth of Conrad's words: *People are the same everywhere.*

He gripped the cage bars in his fists.

And screamed.

The Howling Man

Charles Beaumont

TELEPLAY BY CHARLES BEAUMONT

AIRED NOVEMBER 4, 1960

STARRING H. M. WYNANT AND JOHN CARRADINE

THE GERMANY OF THAT TIME WAS A LAND OF VAL-
leys and mountains and swift dark rivers, a green and fertile
land where everything grew tall and straight out of the earth.
There was no other country like it. Stepping across the border from Belgium, where the rain-caped, mustached guards
saluted, grinning, like operetta soldiers, you entered a different world entirely. Here the grass became as rich and smooth
as velvet; deep, thick woods appeared; the air itself, which
had been heavy with the French perfume of wines and
sauces, changed: the clean, fresh smell of lakes and pines
and boulders came into your lungs. You stood a moment,
then, at the border, watching the circling hawks above and
wondering, a little fearfully, how such a thing could happen.
In less than a minute you had passed from a musty, ancient
room, through an invisible door, into a kingdom of winds
and light. Unbelievable! But there, at your heels, clearly in
view, is Belgium, like all the rest of Europe, a faded tapestry
from some forgotten mansion.

In that time, before I had heard of St. Wulfran's, of the
wretch who clawed the stones of a locked cell, wailing in the

midnight hours, or of the daft Brothers and their mad Abbot, I had strong legs and a mind on its last search, and I preferred to be alone. A while and I'll come back to this spot. We will ride and feel the sickness, fall, and hover on the edge of death, together. But I am not a writer, only one who loves wild, unhousebroken words; I must have a real beginning.

Paris beckoned in my youth. I heeded, for the reason most young men just out of college heed, although they would never admit it: to lie with mysterious beautiful women. A solid, traditional upbringing among the corseted ruins of Boston had succeeded, as such upbringings generally do, in honing the urge to a keen edge. My nightly dreams of beaded bagnios and dusky writhing houris, skilled beyond imagining, reached, finally, the unbearable stage beyond which lies either madness or respectability. Fancying neither, I managed to convince my parents that a year abroad would add exactly the right amount of seasoning to my maturity, like a dash of curry in an otherwise bland, if not altogether tasteless, chowder. I'm afraid that Father caught the hot glint in my eye, but he was kind. Describing, in detail, and with immense effect, the hideous consequences of profligacy, telling of men he knew who'd gone to Europe, innocently, and fallen into dissolutions so profound they'd not been heard of since, he begged me at all times to remember that I was an Ellington and turned me loose. Paris, of course, was enchanting and terrifying, as a jungle must be to a zoo-born monkey. Out of respect to the honored dead, and Dad, I did a quick trot through the Tuileries, the Louvre, and down the Champs-Elysées to the Arc de Triomphe; then, with the fall of night, I cannoned off to Montmartre and the Rue Pigalle, embarking on the Grand Adventure. Synoptically, it did not prove to be so grand as I'd imagined; nor was it, after the fourth week, so terribly adventurous. Still: important to what followed, for what followed doubtless wouldn't have but for the sweet complaisant girls.

Boston's Straights and Narrows don't, I fear, prepare one—except psychologically—for the Wild Life. My health broke in due course and, as my thirst had been well and truly slaked, I was not awfully discontent to sink back into the contemplative cocoon to which I was, apparently, more suited. Abed for a month I lay, in celibate silence and almost total inactivity. Then, no doubt as a final gesture of rebellion, I got my idea—got? or had my concentrated sins received it, like a signal from a failing tower?—and I made my strange, un-Ellingtonian decision. I would explore Europe. But not as a tourist, safe and fat in his fat, safe bus, insulated against the beauty and the ugliness of changing cultures by a pane of glass and a room at the English-speaking hotel. No. I would go like an unprotected wind, a seven-league-booted leaf, a nestless bird, and I would see this dark strange land with the vision of a boy on the last legs of his dreams. I would go by bicycle, poor and lonely and questing—as poor and lonely and questing, anyway, as one can be with a hundred thousand in the bank and a partnership in Ellington, Carruthers & Blake waiting.

So it was. New England blood and muscles wilted on that first day's pumping, but New England spirit toughened as the miles dropped back. Like an ant crawling over a once-lovely, now decayed and somewhat seedy Duchess, I rode over the body of Europe. I dined at restaurants where boars' heads hung, all vicious-tusked and blind; I slept at country inns and breathed the musty age, and sometimes girls came to the door and knocked and asked if I had everything I needed ("Well . . .") and they were better than the girls in Paris, though I can't imagine why. No matter. Out of France I pedaled, into Belgium, out, and to the place of cows and forests, mountains, brooks, and laughing people: Germany. (I've rhapsodized on purpose for I feel it's quite important to remember how completely Paradisical the land was then, at that time.)

I looked odd, standing there. The border guard asked what was loose with me, I answered Nothing—grateful for the German, and the French, Miss Finch had drummed into me—and set off along the smallest, darkest path. It serpentined through forests, cities, towns, villages, and always I followed its least likely appendages. Unreasonably, I pedaled as if toward a destination: into the Moselle Valley country, up into the desolate hills of emerald.

By a ferry, fallen to desuetude, the reptile drew me through a bosky wood. The trees closed in at once. I drank the fragrant air and pumped and kept on pumping, but a heat began to grow inside my body. My head began to ache. I felt weak. Two more miles and I was obliged to stop, for perspiration filmed my skin. You know the signs of pneumonia: a sapping of the strength, a trembling, flashes of heat and of cold; visions. I lay in the bed of damp leaves for a time, then forced myself onto the bicycle and rode for what seemed an endless time. At last a village came to view. A thirteenth-century village, gray and narrow-streeted, cobbled to the hidden store fronts. A number of old people in peasant costumes looked up as I bumped along, and I recall one ancient tallow-colored fellow—nothing more. Only the weakness, like acid, burning off my nerves and muscles. And an intervening blackness to pillow my fall.

I awoke to the smells of urine and hay. The fever had passed, but my arms and legs lay heavy as logs, my head throbbed horribly, and there was an empty shoveled-out hole inside my stomach somewhere. For a long while I did not move or open my eyes. Breathing was a major effort. But consciousness came, eventually.

I was in a tiny room. The walls and ceiling were of rough gray stone, the single glassless window was arch-shaped, the floor was uncombed dirt. My bed was not a bed at all but a blanket thrown across a disorderly pile of crinkly straw. Beside me, a crude table; upon it, a pitcher; beneath it, a bucket. Next to the table, a stool. And seated there, asleep, his tonsured head adangle from an Everest of robe, a monk.

I must have groaned, for the shorn pate bobbed up precipitately. Two silver trails gleamed down the corners of the suddenly exposed mouth, which drooped into a frown. The slumbrous eyes blinked.

"It is God's infinite mercy," sighed the gnomelike little man. "You have recovered."

"Not as yet," I told him. Unsuccessfully, I tried to remember what had happened; then I asked questions.

"I am Brother Christophorus. This is the Abbey of St. Wulfran's. The Burgermeister of Schwartzhof, Herr Barth, brought you to us nine days ago. Father Jerome said that you would die and he sent me to watch, for I have never seen a man die, and Father Jerome holds that it is beneficial for a Brother to have seen a man die. But now I suppose that you will not die." He shook his head ruefully.

"Your disappointment," I said, "cuts me to the quick. However, don't abandon hope. The way I feel now, it's touch and go."

"No," said Brother Christophorus sadly. "You will get well. It will take time. But you will get well."

"Such ingratitude, and after all you've done. How can I express my apologies?"

He blinked again. With the innocence of a child, he said, "I beg your pardon?"

"Nothing." I grumbled about blankets, a fire, some food to eat, and then slipped back into the well of sleep. A fever dream of forests full of giant two-headed beasts came, then the sound of screaming.

I awoke. The scream shrilled on—Klaxon-loud, high, cutting, like a cry for help.

"What is that sound?" I asked.

The monk smiled. "Sound? I hear no sound," he said.

It stopped. I nodded. "Dreaming. Probably I'll hear a good deal more before I'm through. I shouldn't have left Paris in such poor condition."

"No," he said. "You shouldn't have left Paris."

Kindly now, resigned to my recovery, Brother Christophorus became attentive to a fault. Nurselike, he spooned thick soups into me, applied compresses, chanted soothing prayers, and emptied the bucket out the window. Time passed slowly. As I fought the sickness, the dreams grew less

vivid—but the nightly cries did not diminish. They were as
full of terror and loneliness as before, strong, real in my ears.
I tried to shut them out, but they would not be shut out. Still,
how could they be strong and real except in my vanishing delirium? Brother Christophorus did not hear them. I watched
him closely when the sunlight faded to the gray of dusk and
the screams began, but he was deaf to them—if they existed.
If they existed!

"Be still, my son. It is the fever that makes you hear these
noises. That is quite natural. Is that not quite natural?
Sleep."

"But the fever is gone! I'm sitting up now. Listen! Do you
mean to tell me you don't hear *that?*"

"I hear only you, my son."

The screams, that fourteenth night, continued until dawn.
They were totally unlike any sounds in my experience. Impossible to believe they could be uttered and sustained by a
human, yet they did not seem to be animal. I listened, there
in the gloom, my hands balled into fists, and knew, suddenly, that one of two things must be true. Either someone or
something was making these ghastly sounds, and Brother
Christophorus was lying, or—I was going mad. Hearing-
voices mad, climbing-walls and frothing mad. I'd have to
find the answer: that I knew. And by myself.

I listened with a new ear to the howls. Razoring under the
door, they rose to operatic pitch, subsided, resumed, like the
cries of a surly, hysterical child. To test their reality, I
hummed beneath my breath, I covered my head with a blan-
keting, scratched at the straw, coughed. No difference. The
quality of substance, of existence, was there. I tried, then, to
localize the screams; and, on the fifteenth night, felt sure that
they were coming from a spot not far along the hall.

"The sounds that maniacs hear seem quite real to them."

I know. I know!

The monk was by my side, he had not left it from the start,
keeping steady vigil even through Matins. He joined his
tremulous soprano to the distant chants, and prayed exces-

sively. But nothing could tempt him away. The food we ate was brought to us, as were all other needs. I'd see the Abbot, Father Jerome, once I was recovered. Meanwhile . . .

"I'm feeling better, Brother. Perhaps you'd care to show me about the grounds. I've seen nothing of St. Wulfran's except this little room."

"There is only this little room multiplied. Ours is a rigorous order. The Franciscans, now, they permit themselves esthetic pleasure; we do not. It is, for us, a luxury. We have a single, most unusual job. There is nothing to see."

"But surely the Abbey is very old."

"Yes, that is true."

"As an antiquarian—"

"Mr. Ellington—"

"What is it you don't want me to see? What are you afraid of, Brother?"

"Mr. Ellington? I do not have the authority to grant your request. When you are well enough to leave, Father Jerome will no doubt be happy to accommodate you."

"Will he also be happy to explain the screams I've heard each night since I've been here?"

"Rest, my son. Rest."

The unholy, hackle-raising shriek burst loose and bounded off the hard stone walls. Brother Christophorus crossed himself, apropos of nothing, and sat like an ancient Indian on the weary stool. I knew he liked me. Especially, perhaps. We'd got along quite well in all our talks. But this—*verboten*.

I closed my eyes. I counted to three hundred. I opened my eyes.

The good monk was asleep. I blasphemed, softly, but he did not stir, so I swung my legs over the side of the straw bed and made my way across the dirt floor to the heavy wooden door. I rested there a time, in the candleless dark, listening to the howls; then, with Bostonian discretion, raised the bolt. The rusted hinges creaked, but Brother Christophorus was deep in celestial marble: his head drooped low upon his chest.

Panting, weak as a landlocked fish, I stumbled out into the corridor. The screams became impossibly loud. I put my hands to my ears, instinctively, and wondered how anyone could sleep with such a furor going on. It *was* a furor. In my mind? No. Real. The monastery shook with these shrill cries. You could feel their realness with your teeth.

I passed a Brother's cell and listened, then another; then I paused. A thick door, made of oak or pine, was locked before me. Behind it were the screams.

A chill went through me on the edge of those unutterable shrieks of hopeless, helpless anguish, and for a moment I considered turning back—not to my room, not to my bed of straw, but back into the open world. But duty held me. I took a breath and walked up to the narrow bar-crossed window and looked in.

A man was in the cell. On all fours, circling like a beast, his head thrown back, a man. The moonlight showed his face. It cannot be described—not, at least, by me. A man past death might look like this, a victim of the Inquisition rack, the stake, the pincers: not a human in the third decade of the twentieth century, surely. I had never seen such suffering within two eyes, such lost, mad suffering. Naked, he crawled about the dirt, cried, leaped up to his feet and clawed the hard stone walls in fury.

Then he saw me.

The screaming ceased. He huddled, blinking, in the corner of his cell. And then, as though unsure of what he saw, he walked right to the door.

In German, hissing: "Who are you?"

"David Ellington," I said. "Are you locked in? Why have they locked you in?"

He shook his head. "Be still, be still. You are not German?"

"No." I told him how I came to be at St. Wulfran's.

"Ah!" Trembling, his horny fingers closing on the bars, the naked man said: "Listen to me, we have only moments. They are mad. You hear? All mad. I was in the village, lying with my woman, when their crazy Abbot burst into the house and hit me with his heavy cross. I woke up here. They flogged me. I asked for food, they would not give it to me. They took my clothes. They threw me in this filthy room. They locked the door.''

''Why?''

''Why?'' He moaned. ''I wish I knew. That's been the worst of it. Five years imprisoned, beaten, tortured, starved, and not a reason given, not a word to guess from—Mr. Ellington! I have sinned, but who has not? With my woman, quietly, alone with my woman, my love. And this God-drunk lunatic, Jerome, cannot stand it. Help me!''

His breath splashed on my face. I took a backward step and tried to think. I couldn't quite believe that in this century a thing so frightening could happen. Yet, the Abbey was secluded, above the world, timeless. What could not transpire here, secretly?

''I'll speak to the Abbot.''

''No! I tell you, he's the maddest of them all. Say nothing to him.''

''Then how can I help you?''

He pressed his mouth against the bars. ''In one way only. Around Jerome's neck, there is a key. It fits this lock. If—''

''Mr. Ellington!''

I turned and faced a fierce El Greco painting of a man. White-bearded, prow-nosed, regal as an Emperor beneath the gray peaked robe, he came out of the darkness. ''Mr. Ellington, I did not know that you were well enough to walk. Come with me, please.''

The naked man began to weep hysterically. I felt a grip of steel about my arm. Through corridors, past snore-filled cells, the echoes of the weeping dying, we continued to a room.

''I must ask you to leave St. Wulfran's,'' the Abbot said. ''We lack the proper facilities for care of the ill. Arrangements will be made in Schwartzhof—''

''One moment,'' I said. ''While it's probably true that

Brother Christophorus's ministrations saved my life—and certainly true that I owe you all a debt of gratitude—I've got to ask for an explanation of that man in the cell."

"What man?" the Abbot said softly.

"The one we just left, the one who's screamed all night long every night."

"No man has been screaming, Mr. Ellington."

Feeling suddenly very weak, I sat down and rested a few breaths' worth. Then I said, "Father Jerome—you are he? I am not necessarily an irreligious person, but neither could I be considered particularly religious. I know nothing of monasteries, what is permitted, what isn't. But I seriously doubt that you have the authority to imprison a man against his will."

"That is quite true. We have no such authority."

"Then why have you done so?"

The Abbot looked at me steadily. In a firm, inflexible voice, he said: "No man has been imprisoned at St. Wulfran's."

"He claims otherwise."

"Who claims otherwise?"

"The man in the cell at the end of the corridor."

"There is no man in the cell at the end of the corridor."

"I was talking with him!"

"You were talking with no man."

The conviction in his voice shocked me into momentary silence. I gripped the arms of the chair.

"You are ill, Mr. Ellington," the bearded holy man said. "You have suffered from delirium. You have heard and seen things which do not exist."

"That's true," I said. "But the man in the cell—whose voice I can hear now!—is not one of those things."

The Abbot shrugged. "Dreams can seem very real, my son."

I glanced at the leather thong about his turkey-gobbler neck, all but hidden beneath the beard. "Honest men make unconvincing liars," I lied convincingly. "Brother Christophorus has a way of looking at the floor whenever he denies the cries in the night. You look at me, but your voice loses its command. I can't imagine why, but you are both very intent upon keeping me away from the truth. Which is not only poor Christianity, but also poor psychology. For now I am quite curious indeed. You might as well tell me, Father; I'll find out eventually."

"What do you mean?"

"Only that. I'm sure the police will be interested to hear of a man imprisoned at the Abbey."

"I tell you, *there is no man!*"

"Very well. Let's forget the matter."

"Mr. Ellington—" The Abbot put his hands behind him. "The person in the cell is, ah, one of the Brothers. Yes. He is subject to . . . seizures, fits. You know fits? At these times, he becomes intractable. Violent. Dangerous! We're obliged to lock him in his cell, which you can surely understand."

"I understand," I said, "that you're still lying to me. If the answer were as simple as that, you'd not have gone through the elaborate business of pretending I was delirious. There'd have been no need. There's something more to it, but I can wait. Shall we go on to Schwartzhof?"

Father Jerome tugged at his beard viciously, as if it were some feathered demon come to taunt him. "Would you truly go to the police?" he asked.

"Would you?" I said. "In my position?"

He considered that for a long time, tugging the beard, nodding the prowed head; and the screams went on, so distant, so real. I thought of the naked man clawing in his filth.

"Well, Father?"

"Mr. Ellington, I see that I shall have to be honest with you—which is a great pity," he said. "Had I followed my original instinct and refused to allow you in the Abbey to begin with . . . but, I had no choice. You were near death. No physician was available. You would have perished. Still, perhaps that would have been better."

"My recovery seems to have disappointed a lot of people," I commented. "I assure you it was inadvertent."

The old man took no notice of this remark. Stuffing his mandarin hands into the sleeves of his robe, he spoke with great deliberation. "When I said that there was no man in the cell at the end of the corridor, I was telling the truth. Sit down, sir! Please! Now." He closed his eyes. "There is much to the story, much that you will not understand or believe. You are sophisticated, or feel that you are. You regard our life here, no doubt, as primitive—"

"In fact, I—"

"In fact, you do. I know the current theories. Monks are misfits, neurotics, sexual frustrates, and aberrants. They retreat from the world because they cannot cope with the world. Et cetera. You are surprised I know these things? My son, I was told by the one who began the theories!" He raised his head upward, revealing more of the leather thong. "Five years ago, Mr. Ellington, there were no screams at St. Wulfran's. This was an undistinguished little Abbey in the wild Black Mountain region, and its inmates' job was quite simply to serve God, to save what souls they could by constant prayer. At that time, not very long after the great war, the world was in chaos. Schwartzhof was not the happy village you see now. It was, my son, a resort for the sinful, a hive of vice and corruption, a pit for the unwary—and the wary also, if they had not strength. A Godless place! Forsaken, fornicators paraded the streets. Gambling was done. Robbery and murder, drunkenness, and evils so profound I cannot put them into words. In all the universe you could not have found a fouler pesthole, Mr. Ellington! The Abbots and the Brothers at St. Wulfran's succumbed for years to Schwartzhof, I regret to say. Good men, lovers of God, chaste good men came here and fought but could not win against the black temptations. Finally it was decided that the Abbey should be closed. I heard of this and argued. 'Is that not surrender?' I said. 'Are we to bow before the strength of evil? Let me try, I beg you. Let me try to amplify the word of God that all in Schwartzhof shall hear and see their dark transgressions and repent!' "

The old man stood at the window, a trembling shade. His hands were now clutched together in a fervency of remembrance. "They asked," he said, "if I considered myself more virtuous than my predecessors that I should hope for success where they had failed. I answered that I did not, but that I had an advantage. I was a convert. Earlier I had walked with evil, and knew its face. My wish was granted. For a year. One year only. Rejoicing, Mr. Ellington, I came here; and one night, incognito, walked the streets of the village. The smell of evil was strong. Too strong, I thought—and I had reveled in the alleys of Morocco, I had seen the dens of Hong Kong, Paris, Spain. The orgies were too wild, the drunkards much too drunk, the profanities a great deal too profane. It was as if the evil of the world had been distilled and centered here, as if a pagan tribal chief, in hiding, had assembled all his rituals about him . . ." The Abbot nodded his head. "I thought of Rome, in her last days; of Byzantium; of—Eden. That was the first of many hints to come. No matter what they were. I returned to the Abbey and donned my holy robes and went back into Schwartzhof. I made myself conspicuous. Some jeered, some shrank away, a voice cried, 'Damn your foolish God!' And then a hand thrust out from darkness, touched my shoulder, and I heard: 'Now, Father, are you lost?' "

The Abbot brought his tightly clenched hands to his forehead and tapped his forehead.

"Mr. Ellington, I have some poor wine here. Please have some."

I drank, gratefully. Then the priest continued.

"I faced a man of average appearance. So average, indeed, that I felt I knew, then. 'No,' I told him, 'but you are lost!' He laughed a foul laugh. 'Are we not all, Father?' Then he said a most peculiar thing. He said his wife was dying and begged me to give her Extreme Unction. 'Please,' he said, 'in God's sweet name!' I was confused. We hurried to his house. A woman lay upon a bed, her body nude. 'It is a different Extreme Unction that I have in mind,' he whispered, laughing. 'It's the only kind, dear Father, that she understands. No other will have her! Pity! Pity on the poor soul lying there in all her suffering. Give her your Sceptre!' And the woman's arms came snaking, supplicating toward me, round and sensuous and hot . . .''

Father Jerome shuddered and paused. The shrieks, I thought, were growing louder from the hall. ''Enough of that,'' he said. ''I was quite sure then. I raised my cross and told the words I'd learned, and it was over. He screamed—as he's doing now—and fell upon his knees. He had not expected to be recognized, nor should he have been normally. But in my life, I'd seen him many times, in many guises. I brought him to the Abbey. I locked him in the cell. We chant his chains each day. And so, my son, you see why you must not speak of the things you've seen and heard?''

I shook my head, as if afraid the dream would end, as if reality would suddenly explode upon me. ''Father Jerome,'' I said, ''I haven't the vaguest idea of what you're talking about. Who is the man?''

''Are you such a fool, Mr. Ellington? That you must be told?''

''Yes!''

''Very well,'' said the Abbot. ''He is Satan. Otherwise known as the Dark Angel, Asmodeus, Belial, Ahriman, Diabolus—the Devil.''

I opened my mouth.

''I see you doubt me. That is bad. Think, Mr. Ellington, of the peace of the world in these five years. Of the prosperity, of the happiness. Think of this country, Germany, now. Is there another country like it? Since we caught the Devil and locked him up here, there have been no great wars, no overwhelming pestilences: only the sufferings man was meant to endure. Believe what I say, my son: I beg you. Try very hard to believe that the creature you spoke with is Satan himself. Fight your cynicism, for it is born of him; he is the father of cynicism, Mr. Ellington! His plan was to defeat God by implanting doubt in the minds of Heaven's subjects!'' The Abbot cleared his throat. ''Of course,'' he said, ''we could never release anyone from St. Wulfran's who had any part of the Devil in him.''

I stared at the old fanatic and thought of him prowling the streets, looking for sin; saw him standing outraged at the bold fornicator's bed, wheedling him into an invitation to the Abbey, closing that heavy door and locking it, and, because of the world's temporary postwar peace, clinging to his fantasy. What greater dream for a holy man than actually capturing the Devil!

''I believe you,'' I said.

''Truly?''

''Yes. I hesitated only because it seemed a trifle odd that Satan should have picked a little German village for his home.''

''He moves around,'' the Abbot said. ''Schwartzhof attracted him as lovely virgins attract perverts.''

''I see.''

''Do you? My son, do you?''

''Yes. I swear it. As a matter of fact, I thought he looked familiar, but I simply couldn't place him.''

''Are you lying?''

''Father, I am a Bostonian.''

''And you promise not to mention this to anyone?''

''I promise.''

''Very well.'' The old man sighed. ''I suppose,'' he said, ''that you would not consider joining us as a Brother at the Abbey?''

''Believe me, Father, no one could admire the vocation more than I. But I am not worthy. No; it's quite out of the question. However, you have my word that your secret is safe with me.''

He was very tired. Sound had, in these years, reversed for him: the screams had become silence, the sudden cessation of them, noise. The prisoner's quiet talk with me had awakened him from deep slumber. Now he nodded wearily, and I saw that what I had to do would not be difficult after all. Indeed, no more difficult than fetching the authorities.

I walked back to my cell, where Brother Christophorus still slept, and lay down. Two hours passed. I rose again and returned to the Abbot's quarters.

The door was closed but unlocked.

I eased it open, timing the creaks of the hinges with the screams of the prisoner. I tiptoed in. Father Jerome lay snoring in his bed.

Slowly, cautiously, I lifted out the leather thong, and was a bit astounded at my technique. No Ellington had ever burgled. Yet a force, not like experience, but like it, ruled my fingers. I found the knot. I worked it loose.

The warm iron key slid off into my hand.

The Abbot stirred, then settled, and I made my way into the hall.

The prisoner, when he saw me, rushed the bars. "He's told you lies, I'm sure of that!" he whispered hoarsely. "Disregard the filthy madman!"

"Don't stop screaming," I said.

"What?" He saw the key and nodded, then, and made his awful sounds. I thought at first the lock had rusted, but I worked the metal slowly and in time the key turned over.

Howling still, in a most dreadful way, the man stepped out into the corridor. I felt a momentary fright as his clawed hand reached up and touched my shoulder; but it passed. "Come on!" We ran insanely to the outer door, across the frosted ground, down toward the village.

The night was very black.

A terrible aching came into my legs. My throat went dry. I thought my heart would tear loose from its moorings. But I ran on.

"Wait."

Now the heat began.

"Wait."

By a row of shops I fell. My chest was full of pain, my head of fear: I knew the madmen would come swooping from their dark asylum on the hill. I cried out to the naked hairy man: "Stop! Help me!"

"Help you?" He laughed once, a high-pitched sound more awful than the screams had been; and then he turned and vanished in the moonless night.

I found a door, somehow.

The pounding brought a rifled burgher. Policemen came at last and listened to my story. But of course it was denied by Father Jerome and the Brothers of the Abbey.

"This poor traveler has suffered from the visions of pneumonia. There was no howling man at St. Wulfran's. No, no, certainly not. Absurd! Now, if Mr. Ellington would care to stay with us, we'd happily—no? Very well. I fear that you will be delirious a while, my son. The things you see will be quite real. Most real. You'll think—how quaint!—that you have loosed the Devil on the world and that the war to come—what war? But aren't there always wars? Of course!—you'll think that it's your fault"—those old eyes burning condemnation! Beak-nosed, bearded head atremble, rage in every word!—"that you'll have caused the misery and suffering and death. And nights you'll spend, awake, unsure, afraid. How foolish!"

Gnome of God, Christophorus, looked terrified and sad. He said to me, when Father Jerome swept furiously out: "My son, don't blame yourself. Your weakness was *his* lever. Doubt unlocked that door. Be comforted: we'll hunt *him* with our nets, and one day . . ."

One day, what?

I looked up at the Abbey of St. Wulfran's, framed by dawn, and started wondering, as I have wondered since ten thousand times, if it weren't true. Pneumonia breeds delirium; delirium breeds visions. Was it possible that I'd imagined all of this?

No. Not even back in Boston, growing dewlaps, paunches, wrinkles, sacks and money, at Ellington, Carruthers & Blake, could I accept that answer.

The monks were mad, I thought. Or: The howling man was mad. Or: The whole thing was a joke.

I went about my daily work, as every man must do, if sane,

although he may have seen the dead rise up or freed a bottled djinn or fought a dragon, once, quite long ago.

But I could not forget. When the pictures of the carpenter from Braunau-am-Inn began to appear in all the papers, I grew uneasy; for I felt I'd seen this man before. When the carpenter invaded Poland, I was sure. And when the world was plunged into war and cities had their entrails blown asunder and that pleasant land I'd visited became a place of hate and death, I dreamed each night.

Each night I dreamed, until this week.

A card arrived. From Germany. A picture of the Moselle Valley is on one side, showing mountains fat with grapes and the dark Moselle, wine of these grapes.

On the other side of the card is a message. It is signed *"Brother Christophorus"* and reads (and reads and reads!):

"Rest now, my son. We have him back with us again."

It's a **Good** Life

Jerome Bixby

TELEPLAY BY ROD SERLING

AIRED NOVEMBER 3, 1961

STARRING BILLY MUMY, JOHN LARCH, AND
CLORIS LEACHMAN

AUNT AMY WAS OUT ON THE FRONT PORCH, ROCK-
ing back and forth in the highbacked chair and fanning herself, when Bill Soames rode his bicycle up the road and
stopped in front of the house.

Perspiring under the afternoon "sun," Bill lifted the box of
groceries out of the big basket over the front wheel of the
bike, and came up the front walk.

Little Anthony was sitting on the lawn, playing with a rat.
He had caught the rat down in the basement—he had made it
think that it smelled cheese, the most rich-smelling and
crumbly-delicious cheese a rat had ever thought it smelled,
and it had come out of its hole, and now Anthony had hold of
it with his mind and was making it do tricks.

When the rat saw Bill Soames coming, it tried to run, but
Anthony thought at it, and it turned a flip-flop on the grass,
and lay trembling, its eyes gleaming in small black terror.

Bill Soames hurried past Anthony and reached the front
steps, mumbling. He always mumbled when he came to the
Fremont house, or passed by it, or even thought of it. Every-

125

body did. They thought about silly things, things that didn't mean very much, like two-and-two-is-four-and-twice-is-eight and so on; they tried to jumble up their thoughts and keep them skipping back and forth, so Anthony couldn't read their minds. The mumbling helped. Because if Anthony got anything strong out of your thoughts, he might take a notion to do something about it—like curing your wife's sick headaches or your kid's mumps, or getting your old milk cow back on schedule, or fixing the privy. And while Anthony mightn't actually mean any harm, he couldn't be expected to have much notion of what was the right thing to do in such cases.

That was if he liked you. He might try to help you, in his way. And that could be pretty horrible.

If he didn't like you . . . well, that could be worse.

Bill Soames set the box of groceries on the porch railing, and stopped his mumbling long enough to say, "Everythin' you wanted, Miss Amy."

"Oh, fine, William," Amy Fremont said lightly. "My, ain't it terrible hot today?"

Bill Soames almost cringed. His eyes pleaded with her. He shook his head violently *no*, and then interrupted his mumbling again, though obviously he didn't want to: "Oh, don't say that, Miss Amy . . . it's fine, just fine. A real *good* day!"

Amy Fremont got up from the rocking chair, and came across the porch. She was a tall woman, thin, a smiling vacancy in her eyes. About a year ago, Anthony had gotten mad at her, because she'd told him he shouldn't have turned the cat into a cat-rug, and although he had always obeyed her more than anyone else, which was hardly at all, this time he'd snapped at her. With his mind. And that had been the end of Amy Fremont's bright eyes, and the end of Amy Fremont as everyone had known her. And that was when word got around in Peaksville (population: 46) that even the members of Anthony's own family weren't safe. After that, everyone was twice as careful.

Someday Anthony might undo what he'd done to Aunt

Amy. Anthony's Mom and Pop hoped he would. When he
was older, and maybe sorry. If it was possible, that is. Because Aunt Amy had changed a lot, and besides, now
Anthony wouldn't obey anyone.

"Land alive, William," Aunt Amy said, "you don't have
to mumble like that. Anthony wouldn't hurt you. My goodness, Anthony likes you!" She raised her voice and called to
Anthony, who had tired of the rat and was making it eat itself. "Don't you, dear? Don't you like Mr. Soames?"

Anthony looked across the lawn at the grocery man—a
bright, wet, purple gaze. He didn't say anything. Bill Soames
tried to smile at him. After a second Anthony returned his attention to the rat. It had already devoured its tail, or at least
chewed it off—for Anthony had made it bite faster than it
could swallow, and little pink and red furry pieces lay around
it on the green grass. Now the rat was having trouble reaching its hindquarters.

Mumbling silently, thinking of nothing in particular as
hard as he could, Bill Soames went stiff-legged down the
walk, mounted his bicycle and pedaled off.

"We'll see you tonight, William," Aunt Amy called after
him.

As Bill Soames pumped the pedals, he was wishing deep
down that he could pump twice as fast, to get away from
Anthony all the faster, and away from Aunt Amy, who
sometimes just forgot how _careful_ you had to be. And he
shouldn't have thought that. Because Anthony caught it. He
caught the desire to get away from the Fremont house as if it
was something _bad_, and his purple gaze blinked, and he
snapped a small, sulky thought after Bill Soames—just a
small one, because he was in a good mood today, and besides, he liked Bill Soames, or at least didn't dislike him, at
least today. Bill Soames wanted to go away—so, petulantly,
Anthony helped him.

Pedaling with superhuman speed—or rather, appearing
to, because in reality the bicycle was pedaling _him_—Bill

Soames vanished down the road in a cloud of dust, his thin, terrified wail drifting back across the summerlike heat.

Anthony looked at the rat. It had devoured half its belly, and had died from pain. He thought it into a grave out deep in the cornfield—his father had once said, smiling, that he might as well do that with the things he killed—and went around the house, casting his odd shadow in the hot, brassy light from above.

In the kitchen, Aunt Amy was unpacking the groceries. She put the Mason-jarred goods on the shelves, and the meat and milk in the icebox, and the beet sugar and coarse flour in big cans under the sink. She put the cardboard box in the corner, by the door, for Mr. Soames to pick up next time he came. It was stained and battered and torn and worn fuzzy, but it was one of the few left in Peaksville. In faded red letters it said *Campbell's Soup.* The last cans of soup, or of anything else, had been eaten long ago, except for a small communal hoard which the villagers dipped into for special occasions—but the box lingered on, like a coffin, and when it and the other boxes were gone, the men would have to make some out of wood.

Aunt Amy went out in back, where Anthony's Mom—Aunt Amy's sister—sat in the shade of the house, shelling peas. The peas, every time Mom ran a finger along a pod, went *lollop-lollop-lollop* into the pan on her lap.

"William brought the groceries," Aunt Amy said. She sat down wearily in the straightbacked chair beside Mom, and began fanning herself again. She wasn't really old; but ever since Anthony had snapped at her with his mind, something had seemed to be wrong with her body as well as her mind, and she was tired all the time.

"Oh, good," said Mom. *Lollop* went the fat peas into the pan.

Everybody in Peaksville always said "Oh, fine," or "Good," or "Say, that's swell!" when almost anything happened or was mentioned—even unhappy things like accidents or even deaths. They'd always say "Good," because if they didn't try to cover up how they really felt, Anthony might overhear with his mind, and then nobody knew what might happen. Like the time Mrs. Kent's husband, Sam, had come walking back from the graveyard, because Anthony liked Mrs. Kent and had heard her mourning.

Lollop.

"Tonight's television night," said Aunt Amy. "I'm glad. I look forward to it so much every week. I wonder what we'll see tonight?"

"Did Bill bring the meat?" asked Mom.

"Yes." Aunt Amy fanned herself, looking up at the featureless brassy glare of the sky. "Goodness, it's so hot! I wish Anthony would make it just a little cooler——"

"*Amy!*"

"Oh!" Mom's sharp tone had penetrated, where Bill Soames's agonized expression had failed. Aunt Amy put one thin hand to her mouth in exaggerated alarm. "Oh . . . I'm sorry, dear." Her pale blue eyes shuttled around, right and left, to see if Anthony was in sight. Not that it would make any difference if he was or wasn't—he didn't have to be near you to know what you were thinking. Usually, though, unless he had his attention on somebody, he would be occupied with thoughts of his own.

But some things attracted his attention—you could never be sure just what.

"This weather's just *fine*," Mom said.

Lollop.

"Oh, yes," Aunt Amy said. "It's a wonderful day. I wouldn't want it changed for the world!"

Lollop.

Lollop.

"What time is it?" Mom asked.

Aunt Amy was sitting where she could see through the kitchen window to the alarm clock on the shelf above the stove. "Four-thirty," she said.

Lollop.

"I want tonight to be something special," Mom said. "Did Bill bring a good lean roast?"

"Good and lean, dear. They butchered just today, you know, and sent us over the best piece."

"Dan Hollis will be *so* surprised when he finds out that tonight's television party is a birthday party for him too!"

"Oh *I* think he will! Are you sure nobody's told him?"

"Everybody swore they wouldn't."

"That'll be real nice," Aunt Amy nodded, looking off across the cornfield. "A birthday party."

"Well——" Mom put the pan of peas down beside her, stood up and brushed her apron. "I'd better get the roast on. Then we can set the table." She picked up the peas.

Anthony came around the corner of the house. He didn't look at them, but continued on down through the carefully kept garden—*all* the gardens in Peaksville were carefully kept, very carefully kept—and went past the rusting, useless hulk that had been the Fremont family car, and went smoothly over the fence and out into the cornfield.

"Isn't this a lovely day!" said Mom, a little loudly, as they went toward the back door.

Aunt Amy fanned herself. "A beautiful day, dear. Just *fine!*"

Out in the cornfield, Anthony walked between the tall, rustling rows of green stalks. He liked to smell the corn. The alive corn overhead, and the old dead corn underfoot. Rich Ohio earth, thick with weeds and brown, dry-rotting ears of corn, pressed between his bare toes with every step—he had made it rain last night so everything would smell and feel nice today.

He walked clear to the edge of the cornfield, and over to where a grove of shadowy green trees covered cool, moist, dark ground, and lots of leafy undergrowth, and jumbled moss-covered rocks, and a small spring that made a clear, clean pool. Here Anthony liked to rest and watch the birds and insects and small animals that rustled and scampered and chirped about. He liked to lie on the cool ground and look up through the moving greenness overhead, and watch the insects flit in the hazy soft sunbeams that stood like slanting, glowing bars between ground and treetops. Somehow, he liked the thoughts of the little creatures in this place better than the thoughts outside; and while the thoughts he picked up here weren't very strong or very clear, he could get enough out of them to know what the little creatures liked and wanted, and he spent a lot of time making the grove more like what they wanted it to be. The spring hadn't always been here; but one time he had found thirst in one small furry mind, and had brought subterranean water to the surface in a clear cold flow, and had watched blinking as the creature drank, feeling its pleasure. Later he had made the pool, when he found a small urge to swim.

He had made rocks and trees and bushes and caves, and sunlight here and shadows there, because he had felt in all the tiny minds around him the desire—or the instinctive want—for this kind of resting place, and that kind of mating place, and this kind of place to play, and that kind of home.

And somehow the creatures from all the fields and pastures around the grove had seemed to know that this was a good place, for there were always more of them coming in—every time Anthony came out here there were more creatures than the last time, and more desires and needs to be tended to. Every time there would be some kind of creature he had never seen before, and he would find its mind, and see what it wanted, and then give it to it.

He liked to help them. He liked to feel their simple gratification.

Today, he rested beneath a thick elm, and lifted his purple gaze to a red and black bird that had just come to the grove. It twittered on a branch over his head, and hopped back and forth, and thought its tiny thoughts, and Anthony made a big, soft nest for it, and pretty soon it hopped in.

A long, brown, sleek-furred animal was drinking at the pool. Anthony found its mind next. The animal was thinking about a smaller creature that was scurrying along the ground on the other side of the pool, grubbing for insects. The little creature didn't know that it was in danger. The long, brown animal finished drinking and tensed its legs to leap, and Anthony thought it into a grave in the cornfield.

He didn't like those kinds of thoughts. They reminded him of the thoughts outside the grove. A long time ago some of the people outside had thought that way about *him,* and one night they'd hidden and waited for him to come back from the grove—and he'd just thought them all into the cornfield. Since then, the rest of the people hadn't thought that way—at least, very clearly. Now their thoughts were all mixed up and confusing whenever they thought about him or near him, so he didn't pay much attention.

He liked to help them too, sometimes—but it wasn't simple, or very gratifying either. They never thought happy thoughts when he did—just the jumble. So he spent more time out here.

He watched all the birds and insects and furry creatures for a while, and played with a bird, making it soar and dip and streak madly around tree trunks until, accidentally, when another bird caught his attention for a moment, he ran it into a rock. Petulantly, he thought the rock into a grave in the cornfield; but he couldn't do anything more with the bird. Not because it was dead, though it was; but because it had a broken wing. So he went back to the house. He didn't feel like walking back through the cornfield, so he just *went* to the house, right down into the basement.

It was nice down here. Nice and dark and damp and sort of fragrant, because once Mom had been making preserves in a rack along the far wall, and then she'd stopped coming down ever since Anthony had started spending time here, and the preserves had spoiled and leaked down and spread over the dirt floor, and Anthony liked the smell.

He caught another rat, making it smell cheese, and after he played with it, he thought it into a grave right beside the long animal he'd killed in the grove. Aunt Amy hated rats, and so he killed a lot of them, because he liked Aunt Amy most of all and sometimes did things that Aunt Amy wanted. Her mind was more like the little furry minds out in the grove. She hadn't thought anything bad at all about him for a long time.

After the rat, he played with a big black spider in the corner under the stairs, making it run back and forth until its web shook and shimmered in the light from the cellar window like a reflection in silvery water. Then he drove fruit flies into the web until the spider was frantic trying to wind them all up. The spider liked flies, and its thoughts were stronger than theirs, so he did it. There was something bad in the way it liked flies, but it wasn't clear—and besides, Aunt Amy hated flies too.

He heard footsteps overhead—Mom moving around in the kitchen. He blinked his purple gaze, and almost decided to make her hold still—but instead he *went* up to the attic, and, after looking out the circular window at the front end of the long V-roofed room for a while at the front lawn and the dusty road and Henderson's tip-waving wheatfield beyond, he curled into an unlikely shape and went partly to sleep.

Soon people would be coming for television, he heard Mom think.

He went more to sleep. He liked television night. Aunt Amy had always liked television a lot, so one time he had thought some for her, and a few other people had been there at the time, and Aunt Amy had felt disappointed when they wanted to leave. He'd done something to them for that—and now everybody came to television.

He liked all the attention he got when they did.

Anthony's father came home around six-thirty, looking tired and dirty and bloody. He'd been over in Dunn's pasture with the other men, helping pick out the cow to be slaughtered this month and doing the job, and then butchering the meat and salting it away in Soames's icehouse. Not a job he cared for, but every man had his turn. Yesterday, he had helped scythe down old McIntyre's wheat. Tomorrow, they would start threshing. By hand. Everything in Peaksville had to be done by hand.

He kissed his wife on the cheek and sat down at the kitchen table. He smiled and said, "Where's Anthony?"

"Around someplace," Mom said.

Aunt Amy was over at the wood-burning stove, stirring the big pot of peas. Mom went back to the oven and opened it and basted the roast.

"Well, it's been a *good* day," Dad said. By rote. Then he looked at the mixing bowl and breadboard on the table. He sniffed at the dough. "M'm," he said. "I could eat a loaf all by myself, I'm so hungry."

"No one told Dan Hollis about its being a birthday party, did they?" his wife asked.

"Nope. We kept as quiet as mummies."

"We've fixed up such a lovely surprise!"

"Um? What?"

"Well . . . you know how much Dan likes music. Well, last week Thelma Dunn found a *record* in her attic!"

"No!"

"Yes! And we had Ethel sort of ask—you know, without really *asking*—if he had that one. And he said no. Isn't that a wonderful surprise?"

"Well, now, it sure is. A record, imagine! That's a real nice thing to find! What record is it?"

"Perry Como, singing *You Are My Sunshine.*"

"Well, I'll be darned. I always liked that tune." Some raw carrots were lying on the table. Dad picked up a small one, scrubbed it on his chest, and took a bite. "How did Thelma happen to find it?"

"Oh, you know—just looking around for new things."

"M'm." Dad chewed the carrot. "Say, who has that picture we found a while back? I kind of liked it—that old clipper sailing along——"

"The Smiths. Next week the Sipichs get it, and they give the Smiths old McIntyre's music-box, and we give the Sipichs——" and she went down the tentative order of things that would exchange hands among the women at church this Sunday.

He nodded. "Looks like we can't have the picture for a while, I guess. Look, honey, you might try to get that detective book back from the Reillys. I was so busy the week we had it, I never got to finish all the stories——"

"I'll try," his wife said doubtfully. "But I hear the van Husens have a stereoscope they found in the cellar." Her voice was just a little accusing. "They had it two whole months before they told anybody about it——"

"Say," Dad said, looking interested. "That'd be nice, too. Lots of pictures?"

"I suppose so. I'll see on Sunday. I'd like to have it—but we still owe the van Husens for their canary. I don't know why that bird had to pick *our* house to die . . . it must have been sick when we got it. Now there's just no satisfying Betty van Husen—she even hinted she'd like our *piano* for a while!"

"Well, honey, you try for the stereoscope—or just anything you think we'll like." At last he swallowed the carrot. It had been a little young and tough. Anthony's whims about the weather made it so that people never knew what crops would come up, or what shape they'd be in if they did. All they could do was plant a lot; and always enough of something came up any one season to live on. Just once there had been a grain surplus; tons of it had been hauled to the edge of Peaksville and dumped off into the nothingness. Otherwise, nobody could have breathed, when it started to spoil.

"You know," Dad went on. "It's nice to have the new things around. It's nice to think that there's probably still a lot of stuff nobody's found yet, in cellars and attics and barns and down behind things. They help, somehow. As much as anything can help——"

"Sh-h!" Mom glanced nervously around.

"Oh," Dad said, smiling hastily. "It's all right! The new things are *good*! It's *nice* to be able to have something around you've never seen before, and know that something you've given somebody else is making them happy . . . that's a real *good* thing.''

''A good thing,'' his wife echoed.

''Pretty soon,'' Aunt Amy said, from the stove, ''there won't be any more new things. We'll have found everything there is to find. Goodness, that'll be too bad——''

''*Amy!*''

''Well——''her pale eyes were shallow and fixed, a sign of her recurrent vagueness. ''It will be kind of a shame—no new things——''

''Don't *talk* like that,'' Mom said, trembling. ''Amy, be *quiet!*''

''It's *good*,'' said Dad, in the loud, wanting-to-be-over-heard tone of voice. ''Such talk is *good*. It's okay, honey—don't you see? It's good for Amy to talk any way she wants. It's good for her to feel bad. Everything's good. Everything *has* to be good . . .''

Anthony's mother was pale. And so was Aunt Amy—the peril of the moment had suddenly penetrated the clouds surrounding her mind. Sometimes it was difficult to handle words so that they might not prove disastrous. You just never *knew*. There were so many things it was wise not to say, or even think—but remonstration for saying or thinking them might be just as bad, if Anthony heard and decided to do anything about it. You could just never tell what Anthony was liable to do.

Everything had to be good. Had to be fine just as it was, even if it wasn't. Always. Because any change might be worse. So terribly much worse.

''Oh, my goodness, yes, of course it's good,'' Mom said. ''You talk any way you want to, Amy, and it's just fine. Of course, you want to remember that some ways are *better* than others . . .''

Aunt Amy stirred the peas, fright in her pale eyes.

''Oh, yes,'' she said. ''But I don't feel like talking right now. It . . . it's *good* that I don't feel like talking.''

Dad said tiredly, smiling, ''I'm going out and wash up.''

* * *

They started arriving around eight o'clock. By that time, Mom and Aunt Amy had the big table in the dining room set, and two more tables off to the side. The candles were burning, and the chairs situated, and Dad had a big fire going in the fireplace.

The first to arrive were the Sipichs, John and Mary. John wore his best suit, and was well-scrubbed and pink-faced after his day in McIntyre's pasture. The suit was neatly pressed, but getting threadbare at elbows and cuffs. Old McIntyre was working on a loom, designing it out of school-books, but so far it was slow going. McIntyre was a capable man with wood and tools, but a loom was a big order when you couldn't get metal parts. McIntyre had been one of the ones who, at first, had wanted to try to get Anthony to make things the villagers needed, like clothes and canned goods and medical supplies and gasoline. Since then, he felt that what had happened to the whole Terrance family and Joe Kinney was his fault, and he worked hard trying to make it up to the rest of them. And since then, no one had tried to get Anthony to do anything.

Mary Sipich was a small, cheerful woman in a simple dress. She immediately set about helping Mom and Aunt Amy put the finishing touches on the dinner.

The next arrivals were the Smiths and the Dunns, who lived right next to each other down the road, only a few yards from the nothingness. They drove up in the Smiths' wagon, drawn by their old horse.

Then the Reillys showed up, from across the darkened wheatfield, and the evening really began. Pat Reilly sat down at the big upright in the front room, and began to play from the popular sheet music on the rack. He played softly, as expressively as he could—and nobody sang. Anthony liked piano playing a whole lot, but not singing; often he would come up from the basement, or down from the attic, or just *come*, and sit on top of the piano, nodding his head as Pat played *Lover* or *Boulevard of Broken Dreams* or *Night and Day.*

He seemed to prefer ballads, sweet-sounding songs—but the one time somebody had started to sing, Anthony had looked over from the top of the piano and done something that made everybody afraid of singing from then on. Later, they'd decided that the piano was what Anthony had heard first, before anybody had ever tried to sing, and now anything else added to it didn't sound right and distracted him from his pleasure.

So, every television night, Pat would play the piano, and that was the beginning of the evening. Wherever Anthony was, the music would make him happy, and put him in a good mood, and he would know that they were gathering for television and waiting for him.

By eight-thirty everybody had shown up, except for the seventeen children and Mrs. Soames, who was off watching them in the schoolhouse at the far end of town. The children of Peaksville were never, never allowed near the Fremont house—not since little Fred Smith had tried to play with Anthony on a dare. The younger children weren't even told about Anthony. The others had mostly forgotten about him, or were told that he was a nice, nice goblin but they must never go near him.

Dan and Ethel Hollis came late, and Dan walked in not suspecting a thing. Pat Reilly had played the piano until his hands ached—he'd worked pretty hard with them today—and now he got up, and everybody gathered around to wish Dan Hollis a happy birthday.

"Well, I'll be darned," Dan grinned. "This is swell. I wasn't expecting this at all . . . gosh, this is *swell!*"

They gave him his presents—mostly things they had made by hand, though some were things that people had possessed as their own and now gave him as his. John Sipich gave him a watch charm, hand-carved out of a piece of hickory wood. Dan's watch had broken down a year or so ago, and there was nobody in the village who knew how to fix it, but he still carried it around because it had been his grandfather's and was a fine old heavy thing of gold and silver. He attached the charm to the chain, while everybody laughed and said John had done a nice job of carving. Then Mary Sipich gave him a knitted necktie, which he put on, removing the one he'd worn.

The Reillys gave him a little box they had made, to keep things in. They didn't say what things, but Dan said he'd keep his personal jewelry in it. The Reillys had made it out of a cigar box, carefully peeled of its paper and lined on the inside with velvet. The outside had been polished, and carefully if not expertly carved by Pat—but his carving got complimented too. Dan Hollis received many other gifts—a pipe, a pair of shoelaces, a tie pin, a knit pair of socks, some fudge, a pair of garters made from old suspenders.

He unwrapped each gift with vast pleasure, and wore as many of them as he could right there, even the garters. He lit up the pipe, and said he'd never had a better smoke; which wasn't quite true, because the pipe wasn't broken in yet. Pete Manners had had it lying around ever since he'd received it as a gift four years ago from an out-of-town relative who hadn't known he'd stopped smoking.

Dan put the tobacco into the bowl very carefully. Tobacco was precious. It was only pure luck that Pat Reilly had decided to try to grow some in his backyard just before what had happened to Peaksville had happened. It didn't grow very well, and then they had to cure it and shred it and all, and it was just precious stuff. Everybody in town used wooden holders old McIntyre had made, to save on butts.

Last of all, Thelma Dunn gave Dan Hollis the record she had found.

Dan's eyes misted even before he opened the package. He knew it was a record.

"Gosh," he said softly. "What one is it? I'm almost afraid to look . . ."

"You haven't got it, darling," Ethel Hollis smiled. "Don't you remember, I asked about *You Are My Sunshine*?"

"Oh, gosh," Dan said again. Carefully he removed the wrapping and stood there fondling the record, running his big hands over the worn grooves with their tiny, dulling crosswise scratches. He looked around the room, eyes shining, and they all smiled back, knowing how delighted he was.

"Happy birthday, darling!" Ethel said, throwing her arms around him and kissing him.

He clutched the record in both hands, holding it off to one side as she pressed against him. "Hey," he laughed, pulling back his head. "Be careful . . . I'm holding a priceless object!" He looked around again, over his wife's arms, which were still around his neck. His eyes were hungry. "Look . . . do you think we could play it? Lord, what I'd give to hear some new music . . . just the first part, the orchestra part, before Como sings?"

Faces sobered. After a minute, John Sipich said, "I don't think we'd better, Dan. After all, we don't know just where the singer comes in—it'd be taking too much of a chance. Better wait till you get home."

Dan Hollis reluctantly put the record on the buffet with all his other presents. "It's *good*," he said automatically, but disappointedly, "that I can't play it here."

"Oh, yes," said Sipich. "It's good." To compensate for Dan's disappointed tone, he repeated, "It's *good*."

They ate dinner, the candles lighting their smiling faces, and ate it all right down to the last delicious drop of gravy. They complimented Mom and Aunt Amy on the roast beef, and the peas and carrots, and the tender corn on the cob. The corn hadn't come from the Fremonts' cornfield, naturally— everybody knew what was out there; and the field was going to weeds.

Then they polished off the dessert—homemade ice cream and cookies. And then they sat back, in the flickering light of the candles, and chatted, waiting for television.

There never was a lot of mumbling on television night— everybody came and had a good dinner at the Fremonts', and that was nice, and afterward there was television, and nobody really thought much about that—it just had to be put up with. So it was a pleasant enough get-together, aside from your having to watch what you said just as carefully as you always did everyplace. If a dangerous thought came into your mind, you just started mumbling, even right in the middle of a sentence. When you did that, the others just ignored you until you felt happier again and stopped.

Anthony liked television night. He had done only two or three awful things on television night in the whole past year.

Mom had put a bottle of brandy on the table, and they each had a tiny glass of it. Liquor was even more precious than tobacco. The villagers could make wine, but the grapes weren't right, and certainly the techniques weren't, and it wasn't very good wine. There were only a few bottles of real liquor left in the village—four rye, three Scotch, three brandy, nine real wine and half a bottle of Drambuie belonging to old McIntyre (only for marriages)—and when those were gone, that was it.

Afterward, everybody wished that the brandy hadn't been brought out. Because Dan Hollis drank more of it than he should have, and mixed it with a lot of the homemade wine. Nobody thought anything about it at first, because he didn't show it much outside, and it was his birthday party and a happy party, and Anthony liked these get-togethers and shouldn't see any reason to do anything even if he was listening.

But Dan Hollis got high, and did a fool thing. If they'd seen it coming, they'd have taken him outside and walked him around.

The first thing they knew, Dan stopped laughing right in the middle of the story about how Thelma Dunn had found the Perry Como record and dropped it and it hadn't broken because she'd moved faster than she ever had before in her life and caught it. He was fondling the record again, and looking longingly at the Fremonts' gramophone over in the corner, and suddenly he stopped laughing and his face got slack, and then it got ugly, and he said, "Oh, *Christ!*"

Immediately the room was still. So still they could hear the whirring movement of the grandfather's clock out in the hall. Pat Reilly had been playing the piano, softly. He stopped, his hands poised over the yellowed keys.

The candles on the dining-room table flickered in a cool breeze that blew through the lace curtains over the bay window.

"Keep playing, Pat," Anthony's father said softly.

Pat started again. He played *Night and Day*, but his eyes were sidewise on Dan Hollis, and he missed notes.

Dan stood in the middle of the room, holding the record. In his other hand he held a glass of brandy so hard his hand shook.

They were all looking at him.

"*Christ*," he said again, and he made it sound like a dirty word.

Reverend Younger, who had been talking with Mom and Aunt Amy by the dining-room door, said "Christ" too—but he was using it in a prayer. His hands were clasped, and his eyes were closed.

John Sipich moved forward. "Now, Dan . . . it's *good* for you to talk that way. But you don't want to talk too much, you know."

Dan shook off the hand Sipich put on his arm.

"Can't even play my record," he said loudly. He looked down at the record, and then around at their faces. "Oh, my God . . ."

He threw the glassful of brandy against the wall. It splattered and ran down the wallpaper in streaks.

Some of the women gasped.

"Dan," Sipich said in a whisper. "Dan, cut it out——"

Pat Reilly was playing *Night and Day* louder, to cover up the sounds of the talk. It wouldn't do any good, though, if Anthony was listening.

Dan Hollis went over to the piano and stood by Pat's shoulder, swaying a little.

"Pat," he said. "Don't play *that*. Play *this*." And he began

to sing. Softly, hoarsely, miserably: "Happy birthday to me
. . . Happy birthday to me . . ."

"*Dan!*" Ethel Hollis screamed. She tried to run across the
room to him. Mary Sipich grabbed her arm and held her
back. "Dan," Ethel screamed again. "Stop——"

"My God, be quiet!" hissed Mary Sipich, and pushed her
toward one of the men, who put his hand over her mouth
and held her still.

"——Happy birthday, dear Danny," Dan sang. "Happy
birthday to me!" He stopped and looked down at Pat Reilly.
"Play it, Pat. Play it, so I can sing right . . . you know I can't
carry a tune unless somebody plays it!"

Pat Reilly put his hands on the keys and began *Lover*—in a
slow waltz tempo, the way Anthony liked it. Pat's face was
white. His hands fumbled.

Dan Hollis stared over at the dining-room door. At
Anthony's mother, and at Anthony's father who had gone to
join her.

"*You* had him," he said. Tears gleamed on his cheeks
as the candlelight caught them. "*You* had to go and *have*
him . . ."

He closed his eyes, and the tears squeezed out. He sang
loudly, "You are my sunshine . . . my only sunshine . . .
you make me happy . . . when I am blue . . ."

Anthony *came* into the room.

Pat stopped playing. He froze. Everybody froze. The
breeze rippled the curtains. Ethel Hollis couldn't even try to
scream—she had fainted.

"Please don't take my sunshine . . . away . . ." Dan's
voice faltered into silence. His eyes widened. He put both
hands out in front of him, the empty glass in one, the record
in the other. He hiccupped, and said, "*No*——"

"Bad man," Anthony said, and thought Dan Hollis into
something like nothing anyone would have believed possible, and then he thought the thing into a grave deep, deep in
the cornfield.

The glass and record thumped on the rug. Neither broke.

Anthony's purple gaze went around the room.

Some of the people began mumbling. They all tried to smile. The sound of mumbling filled the room like a far-off approval. Out of the murmuring came one or two clear voices:

"Oh, it's a very *good* thing," said John Sipich.

"A good thing," said Anthony's father, smiling. He'd had more practice in smiling than most of them. "A wonderful thing."

"It's swell . . . just swell," said Pat Reilly, tears leaking from eyes and nose, and he began to play the piano again, softly, his trembling hands feeling for *Night and Day*.

Anthony climbed up on top of the piano, and Pat played for two hours.

Afterward, they watched television. They all went into the front room, and lit just a few candles, and pulled up chairs around the set. It was a small-screen set, and they couldn't all sit close enough to it to see, but that didn't matter. They didn't even turn the set on. It wouldn't have worked anyway, there being no electricity in Peaksville.

They just sat silently, and watched the twisting, writhing shapes on the screen, and listened to the sounds that came out of the speaker, and none of them had any idea of what it was all about. They never did. It was always the same.

"It's real nice," Aunt Amy said once, her pale eyes on the meaningless flickers and shadows. "But I liked it a little better when there were cities outside and we could get real——"

"Why, Amy!" said Mom. "It's good for you to say such a thing. Very good. But how can you mean it? Why, this television is *much* better than anything we ever used to get!"

"Yes," chimed in John Sipich. "It's fine. It's the best show we've ever seen!"

He sat on the couch, with two other men, holding Ethel Hollis flat against the cushions, holding her arms and legs and putting their hands over her mouth, so she couldn't start screaming again.

"It's really *good!*" he said again.

Mom looked out of the front window, across the darkened road, across Henderson's darkened wheatfield to the vast, endless, gray nothingness in which the little village of Peaksville floated like a soul—the huge nothingness that was most evident at night, when Anthony's brassy day had gone.

It did no good to wonder where they were . . . no good at all. Peaksville was just someplace. Someplace away from the world. It was wherever it had been since that day three years ago when Anthony had crept from her womb and old Doc Bates—God rest him—had screamed and dropped him and tried to kill him, and Anthony had whined and done the thing. Had taken the village someplace. Or had destroyed the world and left only the village, nobody knew which.

It did no good to wonder about it. Nothing at all did any good—except to live as they must live. Must always, always live, if Anthony would let them.

These thoughts were dangerous, she thought.

She began to mumble. The others started mumbling too. They had all been thinking, evidently.

The men on the couch whispered and whispered to Ethel Hollis, and when they took their hands away, she mumbled too.

While Anthony sat on top of the set and made television, they sat around and mumbled and watched the meaningless, flickering shapes far into the night.

Next day it snowed, and killed off half the crops—but it was a *good* day.

The Valley Was Still

Manly Wade Wellman

Teleplay by Rod Serling

Aired November 24, 1961, as "Still Valley"

Starring Gary Merrill

WIND TOUCHED THE PINES ON THE RIDGE, AND stirred the thicker forest on the hills opposite; but the grassy valley between, with its red and white houses at the bottom, was as still as a painted backdrop in a theater. Not even a grasshopper sang in it.

Two cavalrymen sat their mounts at the edge of the pines. The one in the torn butternut blouse hawked and spat, and the sound was strangely loud at the brink of that silence.

"I'd reckoned the Yanks was down in that there little town," he said. "Channow, it's called. Joe, you look like a Yank yourself in them clothes."

His mate, who wore half-weathered blue, did not appear complimented. The garments had been stripped from an outraged sergeant of Pennsylvania Lancers, taken prisoner at the Seven Days. They fitted their new wearer's lean body nicely, except across the shoulders. His boots were likewise trophies of war—from the Second Manassas, where the Union Army had learned that lightning can strike twice in the same place; and his saddle-cloth, with its U. S. stamp, had also been unwillingly furnished by the Federal army. But the gray horse had come from his father's Virginia farm, and had lived through a year of fierce fighting and fiercer toil. The rider's name was Joseph Paradine, and he had recently declined, with thanks, the offer of General J. E. B. Stuart to recommend him for a commission.

He preferred to serve as a common trooper. He was a chivalric idealist, and a peerless scout.

"You'd better steal some Yankee blues yourself, Dauger," he advised. "Those homespun pants would drop off of you if you stood up in your stirrups. . . . Yes, the enemy's expected to take up a position in Channow Valley. But if he had done so, we'd have run into his videttes by now, and that town would be as noisy as a county fair."

He rode from among the pines and into the open on the lower slope.

"You're plumb exposin' yourself, Joe," warned Dauger anxiously.

"And I'm going to expose myself more," returned Paradine, his eyes on the valley. "We've been told to find the Yankees, establish their whereabouts. Then our people will tackle them." He spoke with the confidence of triumph that in the summer of 1862 possessed Confederates who had driven the Union's bravest and best all through Virginia. "I'm going all the way down."

"There'll be Yanks hidin'," suggested Dauger pessimistically. "They'll plug you plumb full of lead."

"If they do," called Paradine, "ride back and tell the boys, because then you'll know the Yankees actually are in Channow." He put his horse to the slope, feeling actually happy at the thought that he might suffer for the sake of his cause. It is worthy of repetition that he was a chivalric idealist.

Dauger, quite as brave but more practical, bode where he was. Paradine, riding downhill, passed out of reach of any more warnings.

Paradine's eyes were kept on the village as he descended deep into silence as into water. He had never known such silence, not even at the frequent prayings of his very devout regiment. It made him nervous, a different nervousness from the tingling elation brought by battle thunders, and it fairly daunted his seasoned and intelligent horse. The beast tossed its head, sniffed, danced precariously, and had to be urged to the slope's foot and the trail that ran there.

From the bottom of the slope, the village was a scant two miles away. Its chimneys did not smoke, nor did its trees stir in the windless air. Nor was there sign or motion upon its streets and among its houses of red brick and white wood —no enemy soldiers, or anything else.

Was this a trap? But Paradine smiled at the thought of a whole Yankee brigade or more, lying low to capture one lone Southerner.

More likely they thought him a friend, wearing blue as he did; but why silence in that case, either?

He determined to make noise. If there were hostile forces in and among the houses of Channow, he would draw their attention, perhaps their musket fire. Spurring the gray so that it whickered and plunged, he forced it to canter at an angle toward the nearest houses. At the same time he drew his saber, whetted to a razor-edge contrary to regulations, and waved it over his head. He gave the rebel yell, high and fierce.

"Yee-hee!"

Paradine's voice was a strong one, and it could ring from end to end of a brigade in line; but, even as he yelled, that yell perished—dropped from his lips, as though cut away.

He could not have been heard ten yards. Had his throat dried up? Then, suddenly, he knew. There was no echo here, for all the ridge lay behind, and the hills in front to the north. Even the galloping hoofs of the gray sounded muffled, as if in cotton. Strange . . . there was no response to his defiance.

That was more surprising still. If there were no enemy troops, what about the people of the town? Paradine felt his brown neck-hair, which needed cutting badly, rise and stiffen. Something sinister lay yonder, and warned him away. But he had ridden into this valley to gather intelligence for his officers. He could not turn back, and respect himself thereafter, as a gentleman and a soldier. Has it been noted that Paradine was a chivalric idealist?

But his horse, whatever its blood and character, lacked such selfless devotion to the cause of States' Rights. It faltered in its gallop, tried first to turn back, and then to throw Paradine. He cursed it feelingly, fought it with bit, knee and spur, and finally pulled up and dismounted. He drew the reins forward over the tossing gray head, thrust his left arm through the loop, and with his left hand drew the big cap-and-ball revolver from his holster. Thus ready, with shot or saber, he proceeded on foot, and the gray followed him protestingly.

"Come on," he scolded, very loudly—he was sick of the silence. "I don't know what I'm getting into here. If I have to retreat, it won't be on foot."

Half a mile more, at a brisk walk. A quarter-mile beyond that, more slowly; for still there was no sound or movement from the village. Then the trail joined a wagon track, and Paradine came to the foot of the single street of Channow.

He looked along it, and came to an abrupt halt.

The street, with its shaded yards on either side, was littered with slack blue lumps, each the size of a human body.

The Yankee army, or its advance guard, was there—but fallen and stony still.

"Dead!" muttered Paradine, under his breath.

But who could have killed them? Not his comrades, who had not known where the enemy was. Plague, then? But the most withering plague takes hours, at least, and these had plainly fallen all in the same instant.

Paradine studied the scene. Here had been a proper entry of a strange settlement—first a patrol, watchful and suspicious; then a larger advance party, in two single files, each file hugging one side of the street with eyes and weapons commanding the other side; and, finally, the main body—men, horses and guns, with a baggage train—all as it should be; but now prone and still, like tin soldiers strewn on a floor after a game.

The house at the foot of the street had a hitching-post, cast from iron to represent a Negro boy with a ring in one lifted hand. To that ring Paradine tethered the now almost unmanageable gray. He heard a throbbing roll, as of drums, which he identified as the blood beating in his ears. The saber-hilt was slippery with the sweat of his palm.

He knew that he was afraid, and did not relish the knowledge. Stubbornly he turned his boot-toes forward, and approached the fallen ranks of the enemy. The drums in his ears beat a cadence for his lone march.

He reached and stood over the nearest of the bodies. A blue-bloused infantryman this, melted over on his face, his hands slack upon the musket lying crosswise beneath him. The peaked forage cap had fallen from rumpled, bright hair. The cheek, what Paradine could see of it, was as downy as a peach. Only a kid, young to die; but was he dead?

There was no sign of a wound. Too, a certain waxy finality was lacking in that slumped posture. Paradine extended the point of his saber and gingerly prodded a sun-reddened wrist.

No response. Paradine increased the pressure. A red drop appeared under the point, and grew. Paradine scowled. The boy could bleed. He must be alive, after all.

"Wake up, Yankee," said Joseph Paradine, and stirred the blue flank with his foot. The flesh yielded, but did not stir otherwise. He turned the body over. A vacant pink face stared up out of eyes that were fixed, but bright. Not death—and not sleep.

Paradine had seen men in a swoon who looked like that. Yet even swooners breathed, and there was not a hair's line of motion under the dimmed brass buttons.

"Funny," thought Paradine, not meaning that he was amused. He walked on because there was nothing left to do. Just beyond that first fallen lad lay the rest of the patrol, still in the diamond-shaped formation they must have held when awake and erect. One man lay at the right side of the street, another opposite him at the left. The corporal was in the center and, to his rear, another private.

The corporal was, or had been, an excitable man. His hands clutched his musket firmly, his lips drew back from gritted teeth, his eyes were narrow instead of staring. A bit of awareness seemed to remain upon the set, stubbly face. Paradine forbore to prod him with the saber, but stooped and twitched up an eyelid. It snapped back into its squint. The corporal, too, lived but did not move.

"Wake up," Paradine urged him, as he had urged the boy. "You aren't dead." He straightened up, and stared at the more distant and numerous blue bodies in their fallen ranks. "None of you are dead!" he protested at the top of his lungs, unable to beat down his hysteria. "Wake up, Yankees!"

He was pleading with them to rise, even though he would be doomed if they did.

"*Yee-hee!*" he yelled. "You're all my prisoners! Up on your feet!"

"Yo're wastin' yore breath, son."

Paradine whirled like a top to face this sudden quiet rebuke.

A man stood in the front yard of a shabby house opposite, leaning on a picket fence. Paradine's first impression was of noble and vigorous old age, for a mighty cascade of white beard covered the speaker's chest, and his brow was fringed with thick cottony hair. But next moment Paradine saw that the brow was strangely narrow and sunken, that the mouth in the midst of its hoary ambush hung wryly slack, and that the eyes were bright but empty, like cheap imitation jewels.

The stranger moved slowly along the fence until he came to a gate. He pushed it creakily open, and moved across the dusty road toward Paradine. His body and legs were meager, even for an old man, and he shook and shuffled as though extremely feeble. His clothing was a hodgepodge of filthy tatters.

At any rate, he was no soldier foe. Paradine holstered his

revolver, and leaned on his saber. The bearded one came close, making slow circuit of two fallen soldiers that lay in his path. Close at hand, he appeared as tall and gaunt as a flag-staff, and his beard was a fluttering white flag, but not for truce.

"I spoke to 'em," he said, quietly but definitely, "an' they dozed off like they was drunk."

"You mean these troops?"

"Who else, son? They come marchin' from them hills to the north. The folks scattered outa here like rabbits—all but me. I waited. An'—I put these here Yanks to sleep."

He reached under his veil of beard, apparently fumbling in the bosom of his ruined shirt. His brown old fork of a hand produced a dingy book, bound in gray paper.

"This does it," he said.

Paradine looked at the front cover. It bore the woodcut of an owl against a round moon.

The title was in black capitals:

JOHN GEORGE HOHMAN'S
POW-WOWS
OR
LONG LOST FRIEND

"Got it a long time back, from a Pennsylvany witch-man."

Paradine did not understand, and was not sure that he wanted to. He still wondered how so many fighting-men could lie stunned.

"I thought ye was a Yank, an' I'd missed ye somehow," the quiet old voice informed him. "That's a Yank sojer suit, hain't it? I was goin' to read ye some sleep words, but ye give the yell, an' I knew ye was secesh."

Paradine made a gesture, as though to brush away a trou-blesome fly. He must investigate further. Up the street he walked, among the prone soldiers.

It took him half an hour to complete his survey, walking from end to end of that unconscious host. He saw infantry, men and officers sprawling together in slack comradeship; three batteries of Parrott guns, still coupled to their limbers, with horses slumped in their harness and riders and drivers fallen in the dust beneath the wheels; a body of cavalry—it should have been scouting out front, thought Paradine professionally—all down and still, like a whole parkful of equestrian statues overturned; wagons; and finally, last of the procession save for a prudently placed rearguard, a little clutter of men in gold braid. He approached the oldest and stoutest of these, noting the two stars on the shoulder straps—a major general.

Paradine knelt, unbuttoned the frock coat, and felt in the pockets. Here were papers. The first he unfolded was the copy of an order:

General T. F. Kottler,
Commanding —— Division, USA.

General:
    You will move immediately, with your entire force, taking up a strong defensive position in the Channow Valley. . . .

This, then, was Kottler's Division. Paradine estimated the force as five thousand bluecoats, all veterans by the look of them, but nothing that his own comrades would have feared. He studied the wagon-train hungrily. It was packed with food and clothing, badly needed by the Confederacy. He would do well to get back and report his find. He turned, and saw that the old man with the white beard had followed him along the street.

"I reckon," he said to Paradine, in tones of mild reproach, "ye think I'm a-lyin' about puttin' these here Yanks to sleep."

Paradine smiled at him, as he might have smiled at an importunate child. "I didn't call you a liar," he temporized, "and the Yankees are certainly in dreamland. But I think there must be some natural explanation for—"

"Happen I kin show ye better'n tell ye," cut in the dotard. His paper-bound book was open in his scrawny hands. Stooping close to it, he began rapidly to mumble something. His voice suddenly rose, sounded almost young:

"Now, stand there till I tell ye to move!"

Paradine, standing, fought for explanations. What was happening to him could be believed, was even logical. Mesmerism, scholars called it, or a newer name, hypnotism.

As a boy he, Paradine, had amused himself by holding a hen's beak to the floor and drawing a chalk line therefrom. The hen could never move until he lifted it away from that mock tether. That was what now befell him, he was sure. His muscles were slack, or perhaps tense; he could not say by the feel. In any case, they were immovable. He could not move an eye. He could not loosen grip on his saber-hilt. Yes, hypnotism. If only he rationalized it, he could break the spell.

But he remained motionless, as though he were the little iron figure to which his horse was tethered, yonder at the foot of the street.

The old man surveyed him with a flicker of shrewdness in those bright eyes that had seemed foolish.

"I used only half power. Happen ye kin still hear me. So listen:

"My name's Teague. I live down yon by the crick. I'm a witch-man, an' my pappy was a witch-man afore me. He was the seventh son of a seventh son—an' I was *his* seventh son. I know conjer stuff—black an' white, forrard an' back'ard. It's my livin'.

"Folks in Channow make fun o' me, like they did o' my pappy when he was livin', but they buy my charms. Things to bring love or hate, if they hanker fer 'em. Cures fer sick hogs an' calves. Sayin's to drive away fever. All them things. I done it fer Channow folks all my life."

It was a proud pronouncement, Paradine realized. Here was the man diligent in business, who could stand before kings. So might speak a statesman who had long served his constituency, or the editor of a paper that had built respectful traditions, or a doctor who guarded a town's health for decades, or a blacksmith who took pride in his lifetime of skilled toil. This gaffer who called himself a witch-man considered that he had done service, and was entitled to respect and gratitude. The narrator went on, more grimly:

"Sometimes I been laffed at, an' told to mind my own bizness. Young 'uns has hooted, an' throwed stones. I coulda cursed 'em—but I didn't. Nossir. They's my friends an' neighbors—Channow folks. I kep' back evil from 'em."

The old figure straightened, the white beard jutted forward. An exultant note crept in.

"But when the Yanks come an' everybody run afore 'em but me, I didn't have no scruples! Invaders! Tyrants! Thievin' skunks in blue!" Teague sounded like a recruiting officer for a Texas regiment. "I didn't owe them nothin'—an' here in the street I faced 'em. I dug out this here little book, an' I read the sleep words to 'em. See," and the old hands gestured sweepingly, "they sleep till I tell 'em to wake. *If* I ever tell 'em!"

Paradine had to believe this tale of occult patriotism. There was nothing else to believe in its place. The old man who called himself Teague smiled twinklingly.

"Yo're secesh. Ye fight the Yanks. If ye'll be good, an' not gimme no argyments, blink yore left eye."

Power of blinking returned to that lid, and Paradine lowered it submissively.

"Now ye kin move again—I'll say the words."

He leafed through the book once more, and read out: "Ye horsemen an' footmen, conjured here at this time, ye may pass on in the name of . . ." Paradine did not catch the name, but it had a sound that chilled him. Next instant, motion was restored to his arms and legs. The blood tingled sharply in them, as if they had been asleep.

Teague offered him a hand, and Paradine took it. That hand was froggy cold and soft, for all its boniness.

"After this," decreed Teague, "do what I tell ye, or I'll read ye somethin' ye'll like less." And he held out the open book significantly.

Paradine saw the page—it bore the number 60 in one corner, and at its top was a heading in capitals: TO RELEASE SPELLBOUND PERSONS. Beneath were the lines with which Teague had set him in motion again, and among them were smudged inky marks.

"You've crossed out some words," Paradine said at once.

"Yep. An' wrote in others." Teague held the book closer to him.

Paradine felt yet another chill, and beat down a desire to turn away. He spoke again, because he felt that he should.

"It's the name of God that you've cut out, Teague. Not once, but three times. Isn't that blasphemy? And you've written in—"

"The name of somebody else." Teague's beard ruffled into a grin. "Young feller, ye don't understand. This book was wrote full of the name of God. That name is good—fer some things. But fer curses an' deaths an' overthrows, sech as this 'un—well, I changed the names an' spells by puttin' in that other name ye saw. An' it works fine." He grinned wider as he surveyed the tumbled thousands around them, then shut the book and put it away.

Paradine had been well educated. He had read Marlowe's *Dr. Faustus*, at the University of Virginia, and some accounts of the New England witchcraft cases. He could grasp, though he had never been called upon to consider, the idea of an alliance with evil. All he could reply was:

"I don't see more than five thousand Yankees in this town. Our boys can whip that many and more, without any spells."

Teague shook his old head. "Come on, let's go an' set on them steps," he invited, pointing.

The two walked back down the street, entered a yard and dropped down upon a porch. The shady leaves above them hung as silent as chips of stone. Through the fence-pickets showed the blue lumps of quiet that had been a fighting division of Federals. There was no voice, except Teague's.

"Ye don't grasp what war means, young feller. Sure, the South is winnin' now—but to win, men must die. Powder must burn. An' the South hain't got men an' powder enough to keep it up."

If Paradine had never thought of that before, neither had his superiors, except possibly General Lee. Yet it was plainly true.

Teague extended the argument:

"But if every Yank army was put to sleep, fast's it got in reach—what then? How'd ye like to lead yore own army into Washington an' grab ole Abe Lincoln right outen the White House? How'd ye like to be the second greatest man o' the South?"

"Second greatest man?" echoed Paradine breathlessly, forgetting to fear. He was being tempted as few chivalric idealists can endure. "Second only to—Robert E. Lee!"

The name of his general trembled on his lips. It trembles to this day, on the lips of those who remember. But Teague only snickered, and combed his beard with fingers like skinny sticks.

"Ye don't ketch on yet. Second man, not to Lee, but to—me, Teague! Fer I'd be a-runnin' things!"

Paradine, who had seen and heard so much to amaze him during the past hour, had yet the capacity to gasp. His saber was between his knees, and his hands tightened on the hilt until the knuckles turned pale. Teague gave no sign. He went on:

"I hain't never got no respect here in Channow. Happen it's time I showed 'em what I can do." His eyes studied the windrows of men he had caused to drop down like sickled wheat. Creases of proud triumph deepened around his eyes. "We'll do all the Yanks this way, son. Yore gen'rals hain't never done nothing like it, have they?"

His generals—Paradine had seen them on occasion. Jackson, named Stonewall for invincibility, kneeling in unashamed public prayer; Jeb Stuart, with his plume and his brown beard, listening to the clang of Sweeney's banjo; Hood, who outcharged even his wild Texans; Polk blessing the soldiers in the dawn before battle, like a prophet of brave old days; and Lee, the gray knight, at whom Teague had laughed. No, they had never done anything like it. And, if they could, they would not.

"Teague," said Paradine, "this isn't right."

"Not right? Oh, I know what ye mean. Ye don't like them names I wrote into the *Pow-Wows*, do ye? But ain't everything fair in love an' war?"

Teague laid a persuasive claw on the sleeve of Paradine's looted jacket. "Listen this oncet. Yore idee is to win with sword an' gun. Mine's to win by conjurin'. Which is the quickest way? The easiest way? The only way?"

"To my way of thinking, the only way is by fair fight. God," pronounced Paradine, as stiffly as Leonidas Polk himself, "watches armies."

"An' so does somebody else," responded Teague. "Watches —an' listens. Happen he's listenin' this minit. Well, lad, I need a sojer to figger army things fer me. You joinin' me?"

Not only Teague waited for Paradine's answer. . . . The young trooper remembered, from *Pilgrim's Progress*, what sort of dealings might be fatal. Slowly he got to his feet.

"The South doesn't need that kind of help," he said flatly.

"Too late to back out," Teague told him.

"What do you mean?"

"The help's been asked fer already, son. An' it's been given. A contract, ye might call it. If the contract's broke— well, happen the other party'll get mad. They can be worse enemies 'n Yanks."

Teague, too, rose to his feet. "Too late," he said again. "That power can sweep armies away fer us. But if we say no—well, it's been roused up, it'll still sweep away armies— Southern armies. Ye think I shouldn't have started sech a thing? But I've started it. Can't turn back now."

Victory through evil—what would it become in the end?

Faust's story told, and so did the legend of Gilles de Retz, and the play about Macbeth. But there was also the tale of the sorcerer's apprentice, and of what befell him when he tried to reject the force he had thoughtlessly evoked.

"What do you want me to do?" he asked, through lips that muddled the words.

"Good lad, I thought ye'd see sense. First off, I want yore name to the bargain. Then me 'n' you can lick the Yanks."

Lick the Yankees! Paradine remembered a gayly profane catch-phrase of the Confederate camp: "Don't say Yankee, say damned Yankee." But what about a damned Confederacy? Teague spoke of the day of victory; what of the day of reckoning?

What payment would this ally ask in the end?

Again Faust popped into his mind. He imagined the Confederacy as a Faust among the nations, devil-lifted, devil-nurtured—and devil-doomed, by the connivance of one Joseph Paradine.

Better disaster, in the way of man's warfare.

The bargain was offered him for all the South. For all the South he must reject, completely and finally.

Aloud he said: "My name? Signed to something?"

"Right here'll do."

Once more Teague brought forth the *Pow-Wows* book which he had edited so strangely. "Here, son, on this back page—in blood."

Paradine bowed his head. It was to conceal the look in his eyes, and he hoped to look as though he acquiesced. He drew his saber, passed it to his left hand. Upon its tip he pressed his right forefinger. A spot of dull pain, and a drop of blood creeping forth, as had appeared on the wrist of the ensorcelled boy lying yonder among the Yankees in the street.

"That'll be enough to sign with," approved Teague.

He flattened out the book, exposing the rear flyleaf. Paradine extended his reddened forefinger. It stained the rough white paper.

"J for Joseph," dictated Teague. "Yep, like that—"

Paradine galvanized into action. His bloody right hand seized the book, wrenching it from the trembling fingers. With the saber in his left hand, he struck.

A pretty stroke for even a practiced swordsman; the honed edge of the steel found the shaggy side of Teague's scrawny neck. Paradine felt bone impeding his powerful drawing slash. Then he felt it no longer. The neck had sliced in two, and for a moment Teague's head hung free in the air, like a lantern on a wire.

The bright eyes fixed Paradine's, the mouth fell open in the midst of the beard, trying to speak a word that would not come. Then it fell, bounced like a ball, and rolled away. The headless trunk stood on braced feet, crumpling slowly. Paradine stepped away from it, and it collapsed upon the steps of the house.

Again there was utter silence in the town and valley of Channow. The blue soldiers did not budge where they lay, Paradine knew that he alone moved and breathed and saw—no, not entirely alone. His horse was tethered at the end of the street.

He flung away his saber and ran, ashamed no more of his dread. Reaching the gray, he found his fingers shaky, but he wrenched loose the knotted reins. Flinging himself into the saddle, he rode away across the level and up the slope.

The pines sighed gently, and that sound gave him comfort after so much soundlessness.

He dismounted, his knees swaying as though their tendons had been cut, and studied the earth. Here were the footprints of Dauger's horse. Here also was a cleft stick, and in it a folded scrap of paper, a note. He lifted it, and read the penciled scrawl:

Dear frend Joe, you ant come back so I left like you said to bring up the boys. I hope your alright N if the Yankies have got you well get you back.

L. DAUGER

His comrades were coming, then, with gun and sword. They expected to meet Union soldiers. Paradine gazed back into the silence-brimmed valley, then at what he still held in his right hand. It was the *Pow-Wows* book, marked with a wet capital J in his own blood.

What had Teague insisted? The one whose name had been invoked would be fatally angry if his help were refused. But Paradine was going to refuse it.

He turned to Page 60. His voice was shaky, but he managed to read aloud:

"Ye horsemen and footmen, conjured here at this time, ye may pass on in the name of"—he faltered, but disregarded the ink-blotting, and the substituted names—"of Jesus Christ, and through the word of God."

Again he gulped, and finished. "Ye may now ride on and pass."

From under his feet burst a dry, startling thunder of sound, a partridge rising to the sky. Farther down the slope a crow took wing, cawing querulously. Wind wakened in the Channow Valley; Paradine saw the distant trees of the town stir with it. Then a confused din came to his ears, as though something besides wind was wakening.

After a moment he heard the notes of a bugle, shrill and tremulous, sounding an alarm.

Paradine struck fire, and built it up with fallen twigs. Into the hottest heart of it he thrust Teague's book of charms. The flame gnawed eagerly at it, the pages crumpled and fanned and blackened with the heat. For a moment he saw, standing out among charred fragments, a blood-red J, his writing, as though it fought for life. Then it, too, was consumed, and there were only ashes. Before the last red tongue subsided, his ears picked up a faint rebel yell, and afar into the valley rode Confederate cavalry.

He put his gray to the gallop, got down the slope and joined his regiment before it reached the town. On the street a Union line was forming. There was hot, fierce fighting, such as had scattered and routed many a Northern force.

But, at the end of it, the Southerners ran like foxes before hounds, and those who escaped counted themselves lucky.

In his later garrulous years, Joseph Paradine was apt to say that the war was lost, not at Antietam or Gettysburg, but at a little valley hamlet called Channow. Refusal of a certain alliance, he would insist, was the cause; that offered ally fought thenceforth against the South.

But nobody paid attention, except to laugh or to pity. So many veterans go crazy.

The Jungle

Charles Beaumont

TELEPLAY BY CHARLES BEAUMONT

AIRED DECEMBER 1, 1961

STARRING JOHN DEHNER AND EMILY McLAUGHLIN

SUDDENLY IT WAS THERE. ON FOXFEET, INVISIBLY, it had crept, past all the fences and traps he had laid, past all the barriers. And now it sat inside his mind, a part of him, like his pulse, like the steady beat of his heart.

Richard Austin became rigid in the chair. He closed his eyes and strained the muscles in his body until they were silent and unmoving as granite; and he listened to the thing that had come again, taking him by surprise even while he had been waiting. He listened to it grow—it *seemed* to grow; he couldn't be sure: perhaps he was merely bringing it into sharper focus by filtering out the other constant sounds: the winds that whispered through the foliage of balloon-topped trees, the murmurous insect-drone of all the machines that produced this wind and pumped blood through the city from their stations far beneath the night-heavy streets. Or, perhaps, it was because he was searching, trying to lay hands on it that the thing seemed to be different tonight, stronger, surer. Or—what did it matter?

He sat in the darkened room and listened to the drums; to the even, steady throb that really neither rose nor diminished, but held to that slow dignified tempo with which he'd become so familiar.

Then quickly he rose from the chair and shook his head. The sounds died and became an indistinguishable part of the silence. It was only concentration, he thought, and the desire to hear them that gave them life . . .

Richard Austin released a jagged breath from his swollen lungs, painfully. He walked to the bar and poured some whiskey into a glass and drank most of it in a single swallow: it went down his dry throat like knives, forcing the salivary glands back into action.

He shook his head again, turned and walked back across the living room to the far door. It swung out noiselessly as his hand touched the ornamented circle of hammered brass.

The figure of his wife lay perfectly still under the black light, still and pale, as she had lain three hours before. He walked toward her, feeling his nostrils dilate at the acrid medicine smells, harshly bitter and new to his senses. He blinked away the hot tears that had rushed, stinging, to his eyes; and stood for a time, quietly, trying not to think of the drums.

Then he whispered: ''Mag . . . Mag, don't die tonight!''

Imbecile words! He clenched his fists and stared down at the face that was so full of pain, so twisted with defeat, that now you could not believe it had once been different, a young face, full of laughter and innocence and courage.

The color had gone completely. From the burning splotchy scarlet of last week to this stiff white mask, lifeless, brittle as drying paste. And covered over with perspiration that glistened above her mouth in cold wet buttons and over her face like oil on white stone. The bedding under and around her was drenched gray.

Austin looked at the bandage that covered his wife's head, and forced away the memory, brutally. The memory of her long silver hair and how it had fallen away in clumps in his hands within a week after she had been stricken . . .

But the thoughts danced out of control, and he found himself remembering all the terrible steps in this nightmare.

The scientists had thought it malaria, judging from the symptoms, which were identical. But that was difficult to accept, for malaria had been effectively conquered—powerful new discoveries in vaccines having been administered first, and then the primary cause of the disease itself—the Anopheles mosquito—destroyed completely. And the liquid alloys which formed the foundations for this new city eliminated all the likely breeding places, the bogs and marshlands and rivers. No instance of re-occurrence of the disease had been reported for half a century. Yet—malarial parasites were discovered in the bloodstreams of those first victims, unmistakable parasites that multiplied at a swift rate and worked their destruction of the red corpuscles. And the chemists immediately had to go about the business of mixing medicines from now ancient prescriptions, frantically working against time. A disquieting, even a frightening thing; but without terror for the builders of the new city; not sufficient to make them abandon their work or to spark mass evacuations. Panic was by now so forgotten by most that it had become a new emotion, to be learned all over again.

It had not taken very long to relearn, Austin recalled. Terror had come soon enough. The stricken—some thirty husky workmen, engineers, planners—had rallied under the drugs and seemed to be out of critical condition when, one night, they had all suffered relapses, fallen into fevered comas and proceeded to alternate between unconsciousness and delirium. The scientists were baffled. They tried frenziedly to arrest the parasites, but without success. Their medicines were useless, their drugs and radium treatments and inoculations—all, useless. Finally, they could only look on as the disease took new turns, developed strange characteristics, changed altogether from what they had taken to be malaria to something utterly foreign. It began to assume a horrible regular pattern: from prolonged delirium to catatonia, whereby the victim's respiratory system and heartbeat

diminished to a condition only barely distinguishable from
death. And then, the most hideous part: the swift decompo-
sition of the body cells, the destruction of the tissues . . .

Richard Austin carefully controlled a shudder as he thought
of those weeks that had been the beginning. He fingered out
a cigarette from his pocket, started to strike it, then broke the
cylinder and ground its bright red flakes into his palms.

No other real hint had been given then: only the disease.
Someone had nicknamed it "Jungle Rot"—cruel, but apt.
The victims *were* rotting alive, the flesh falling from them
like rain-soaked rags; and they did not die wholly, ever,
until they had been transformed into almost unrecognizable
mounds of putrescence . . .

He put out a hand and laid it gently against his wife's
cheek. The perspiration was chill and greasy to his touch, like
the stagnant water of slew banks. Instinctively his fingers recoiled and balled back into fists. He forced them open again
and stared at the tiny dottles of flesh that clung to them.

"Mag!" It had started already! Wildly, he touched her
arm, applying very slight pressure. The outer skin crumbled
away, leaving a small wet gray patch. Austin's heart raced;
an involuntary movement caused his fingers to pinch his
own wrists, hard. A wrinkled spot appeared and disappeared, a small, fading red line.

She's dying, he thought. Very surely, very slowly, she's
begun to die—Mag. Soon her body will turn gray and then it
will come loose; the weight of the sheet will be enough to tear
big strips of it away . . . She'll begin to rot, and her brain will
know it—they had discovered that much: the victims were
never completely comatose, could not be adequately drugged
—she will know that she is mouldering even while she lives
and thinks . . .

And why? His head ached, throbbed. *Why?*

The years, these past months, the room with its stink of
decay—everything rushed up, suddenly, filling Austin's
mind.

If I had agreed to leave with the rest, he thought, to run

away, then Mag would be well and full of life. But—I didn't agree . . .

He had stayed on to fight. And Mag would not leave without him. Now she was dying and that was the end of it.

Or—he turned slowly—was it? He walked out to the balcony. The forced air was soft and cool; it moved in little patches through the streets of the city. Mbarara, *his* city; the one he'd dreamed about and then planned and designed and pushed into existence; the place built to pamper five hundred thousand people.

Empty, now, and deserted as a gigantic churchyard . . .

Dimly he recognized the sound of the drums, with their slow muffled rhythm, directionless as always, seeming to come from everywhere and from nowhere. Speaking to him. Whispering.

Austin lit a cigarette and sucked the calming smoke into his lungs. He remained motionless until the cigarette was down to the cork.

Then he walked back into the bedroom, opened a cabinet and took a heavy silver pistol.

He loaded it carefully.

Mag lay still; almost, it seemed to Austin, expectant, waiting. So very still and pale.

He pointed the barrel of the pistol at his wife's forehead and curled his finger around the trigger. Another slight pressure and it would be over. Her suffering would be over. Just a slight pressure!

The drums droned louder until they were exploding in the quiet room.

Austin tensed and fought the trembling, gripped the pistol with his other hand to steady it.

But his finger refused to move on the curved trigger.

After a long moment, he lowered his arm and dropped the gun into his pocket.

"No." He said it quietly, undramatically. The word hit a barrier of mucus and came out high-pitched and childlike.

He coughed.

That was what they wanted him to do—he could tell, from the drums. That's what so many of the others had done. Panicked.

"No."

He walked quickly out of the room, through the hall, to the elevator. It lowered instantly but he did not wait for it to reach bottom before he leapt off and ran across the floor to the barricaded front door.

He tore at the locks. Then the door swung open and he was outside; for the first time in three weeks—outside, alone, in the city.

He paused, fascinated by the strangeness of it. Impossible to believe that he was the only white man left in the entire city.

He stode to a high-speed walkway, halted it and stepped on. Setting the power at half with his passkey, he pressed the control button and sagged against the rail as the belt whispered into movement.

He knew where he was going. Perhaps he even knew why. But he didn't think about that; instead, he looked at the buildings that slid by silently, the vast rolling spheres and columns of colored stone, the balanced shapes that existed now and that had once existed only in his mind. And he listened to the drums, wondering why the sound of them seemed natural and his buildings suddenly so unnatural, so strange and disjointed.

Like green balloons on yellow sticks, the cultured Grant Wood trees slipped by, uniform and straight, arranged in aesthetically pleasing designs on the stone islands between belts. Austin smiled: The touch of nature. Toy trees, ruffling in artificial winds . . . It all looked, now, like the model he had presented to the Senators. About as real and lifelike.

Austin moved like a carefully carved and painted figurine, incredibly small and lonely-looking on the empty walkway. He thought about the years of preparation; the endless red tape and paper work that had preceded the actual job. Then of the natives, how they had protested and petitioned to influence the Five-Power governments and how that had slowed them down. The problem of money, whipped only by pounding at the point of over-population, again and again, never letting up for a moment. The problems, problems . . .

He could not recall when the work itself had actually begun—it was all so joined. Laying the first railroad could certainly not have been a particle as beset with difficulty. Because the tribes of the Kenya territory numbered into the millions; and they were all filled with hatred and fury, opposing the city at every turn.

No explanation had satisfied them. They saw it as the destruction of their world and so they fought. With guns and spears and arrows and darts, with every resource at their disposal, refusing to capitulate, hunting like an army of mad ants scattered over the land.

And, since they could not be controlled, they had to be destroyed. Like their forests and rivers and mountains, destroyed, to make room for the city.

Though not, Austin remembered grimly, without loss. The white men had fine weapons, but none more fatal than machetes biting deep into neck flesh or sharp wooden shafts coated with strange poisons. And they did not all escape. Some would wander too far, unused to this green world where a man could become hopelessly lost within three minutes. Others would forget their weapons. And a few were too brave.

Austin thought of Joseph Fava, the engineer, who had been reported missing. And of how Fava had come running back to the camp after two days, running and screaming, a bright crimson nearly dead creature out of the worst dreams. He had been cleanly stripped of all his skin, except for the face, hands, and feet . . .

But, the city had grown, implacably, spreading its concrete and alloy fingers wider every day over the dark and feral country. Nothing could stop it. Mountains were stamped flat. Rivers were dammed off or drained or put elsewhere.

The marshes were filled. The animals shot from the trees and then the trees cut down. And the big gray machines moved forward, gobbling up the jungle with their iron teeth, chewing it clean of its life and all its living things.

Until it was no more.

Leveled, smoothed as a highway is smoothed, its centuries choked beneath millions and millions of tons of hardened stone.

The birth of a city . . . It had become the death of a world.

And Richard Austin was its murderer.

As he traveled, he thought of the shaman, the half-naked, toothless Bantu medicine man who had spoken for most of the tribes. *"You have killed us, and we could not stop you. So now we will wait, until you have made your city and others come to live here. Then* YOU *will know what it is to die."* Bokawah, who lived in superstition and fear, whom civilization had passed, along with the rest of his people. Who never spoke again after those words, and allowed himself to be moved to the wide iron plateau that had been built for the surviving natives.

Bokawah, the ignorant shaman, with his eternal smile . . . How distinct that smile was now!

The walkway shuddered, suddenly, and jarred to a noisy grinding stop. Austin pitched forward and grasped the railing in order to break his fall.

Awareness of the silence came first. The eerie dead silence that hung like a pall. It meant that the central machines had ceased functioning. They had been designed to operate automatically and perpetually; it was unthinkable that these power sources could break down!

As unthinkable as the drums that murmured to life again beyond the stainless towers, so loud now in the silence, so real.

Austin gripped his pistol tightly and shook away the panic that had bubbled up like acid in his chest. It was merely that the power had gone off. Strike out impossible, insert improbable. Improbabilities happen. The evil spirits do not summon them, they *happen*. Like strange diseases.

I am fighting, he thought, *a statistical paradox. That's all. A storage pile of coincidences. If I wait*—he walked close to the sides of the buildings—*and fight, the graph will change. The curve will* . . .

The drums roared out a wave of scattered sound, stopped, began again . . .

He thought a bit further of charts; then the picture of Mag materialized, blocking out the thick ink lines, ascending and descending on their giant graphs.

Thinking wasn't going to help . . .

He walked on.

Presently, at the end of a curve in the city maze, the "village" came into view, suspended overhead like a gigantic jeweled spider. It thrust out cold light. It was silent.

Austin breathed deeply. By belt, his destination was only minutes away. But the minutes grew as he walked through the city, and when he had reached the lift, hot pains wrenched at his muscles. He stood by the crystal platform, working action back into numbed limbs.

Then he remembered the silence, the dead machines. If they were not functioning, then the elevator—

His finger touched a button, experimentally.

A glass door slid open with a pneumatic hiss.

He walked inside, and tried not to think as the door closed and the bullet-shaped lift began to rise.

Below, Mbarara grew small. The treated metals glowed in a dimming lace of light. And the city looked even more like the little clay model he had built with his hands.

At last movement ceased. Austin waited for the door to slide open again, then he strode out onto the smooth floor.

It was very dark. The artificial torches did not even smolder: their stubs, he noticed, were blackened and cold.

But the gates to the village lay open.

He looked past the entrance into the frozen shadows. He heard the drums, throbbing from within, loud and distinct.

But—ordinary drums, whose sound-waves would dissipate before ever reaching the city below.

He walked into the village.

The huts, like glass blisters on smooth flesh, sat silent. Somehow, they were obscene in the dark, to Austin. Built to incorporate the feel and the atmosphere of their originals and yet to include the civilized conveniences; planned from an artistic as well as a scientific standpoint—they were suddenly obscene.

Perhaps, Austin thought, as he walked, perhaps there was something to what Barney had been saying . . . No—these people had elected to stay of their own free will. It would have been impossible to duplicate *exactly* the monstrous conditions under which they had lived. If not impossible, certainly wrong.

Let them wallow in their backward filth? In their disease and corruption, let them die—merely because their culture had failed to absorb scientific progress? No. You do not permit a man to leap off the top of a hundred-story building just because he has been trained to believe it is the only way to get to the ground floor—even though you insult him and blaspheme against his gods through your intervention. You restrain him, at any cost. Then, much later, you show him the elevator. And because he is a man, with a brain no smaller than yours, he will understand. He will understand that a crushed superstition is better than a crushed head. And he will thank you, eventually.

That is logic.

Austin walked, letting these thoughts form a thick crust. He felt the slap of the pistol against his thigh and this, also, was comforting.

Where were they now? Inside the huts, asleep? All of them? Or had they, too, contracted the disease and begun to die of it? . . .

Far ahead, at the clearing which represented the tip of the design, a glow of light appeared. As he approached, the drums grew louder, and other sounds—voices. How many voices? The air was at once murmurous and alive.

He stopped before the clearing and leaned on the darkness and watched.

Nearby a young woman was dancing. Her eyes were closed, tightly, and her arms were straight at her sides like black roots. She was in a state of possession, dancing in rhythm to the nearest drum. Her feet moved so fast they had become a blur, and her naked body wore a slick coat of perspiration.

Beyond the dancing woman, Austin could see the crowd, squatted and standing, swaying; over a thousand of them— surely every native in the village!

A clot of brown skin and bright white paint and brilliant feathers, hunched in the firelight.

An inner line of men sat over drums and hollow logs, beating these with their palms and with short sticks of wood. The sounds blended strangely into one—the one Austin had been hearing, it seemed, all his life.

He watched, fascinated, even though he had witnessed Bantu ceremonies countless times in the past, even though he was perfectly familiar with the symbols. The little leather bags of hex-magic: nail-filings, photographs, specks of flesh; the rubbing boards stained with fruit-skins; the piles of bones at the feet of the men—old bones, very brittle and dry and old.

Then he looked beyond the natives to the sensible clean crystal walls that rose majestically, cupping the area, giving it form.

It sent a chill over him.

He walked into the open.

The throng quieted, instantly, like a scream cut off. The dancers caught their balance, blinked, drew in breath. The others lifted their heads, stared.

All were turned to dark unmoving wax.

Austin went past the gauntlet of eyes, to one of the painted men.

"Where is Bokawah?" he said loudly, in precise Swahili. His voice regained its accustomed authority. "Bokawah. Take me to him."

No one moved. Hands lay on the air inches above drums, petrified.

"I have come to talk!"

From the corner of his eyes, Austin felt the slight disturbance. He waited a moment, then turned.

A figure crouched beside him. A man, unbelievably old and tiny, sharp little bones jutting into loose flesh like pins, skin cross-hatched with a pattern of white paint, chalky as the substance some widows of the tribes wore for a year after the death of their mates. His mouth was pulled into a shape not quite a smile, but resembling a smile. It revealed hardened toothless gums.

The old man laughed, suddenly. The amulet around his chicken-neck bobbled. Then he stopped laughing and stared at Austin.

"We have been waiting," he said, softly. Austin started at the perfect English. He had not heard English for a long time; and now, coming from this little man . . . Perhaps Bokawah had learned it. Why not? "Walk with me, Mr. Austin."

He followed the ancient shaman, dumbly, not having the slightest idea why he was doing so, to a square of moist soil. It was surrounded by natives.

Bokawah looked once at Austin, then reached down and dipped his hands into the soil. The horny fingers scratched away the top-dirt, burrowed in like thin, nervous animals, and emerged, finally, holding something.

Austin gasped. It was a doll.

It was Mag.

He wanted to laugh, but it caught in his throat. He knew how the primitives would try to inflict evil upon an enemy by burying his effigy. As the effigy rotted, symbolically, so would . . .

He snatched the doll away from the old man. It crumbled in his hands.

"Mr. Austin," Bokawah said, "I'm very sorry you did not come for this talk long ago." The old man's lips did not move. The voice was his and yet not his.

Austin knew, suddenly, that he had not come to this place of his own accord. He had been summoned.

The old man held a hyena's tail in his right hand. He waved this and a slight wind seemed to come up, throwing the flames of the fire into a neurotic dance.

"You are not convinced, even now, Mr. Austin. Aiii. You have seen suffering and death, but you are not convinced." Bokawah sighed. "I will try one last time." He squatted on the smooth floor. "When you first came to our country, and spoke your plans, I told you—even then—what must happen. I told you that this city must not be. I told you that my people would fight, as *your* people would fight if *we* were to come to your land and build jungles. But you understood nothing of what I said." He did not accuse; the voice was expressionless. "Now Mbarara lies silent and dead beneath you and still you do not wish to understand. What must we do, Mr. Austin? How shall we go about proving to you that this Mbarara of yours will *always* be silent and dead, that your people will never walk through it?"

Austin thought of his old college friend Barney—and of what Barney had once told him. Staring at Bokawah, at this scrawny, painted savage, he saw the big Texan clearly, and he remembered his wild undergraduate theories—exhuming the antique view of primitives and their religions, their magics.

"*Go on, pal, laugh at their tabus,*" Barney, who was an anthropologist, used to be fond of saying, "*sneer, while you throw salt over your shoulder. Laugh at their manas, while you blab about our own 'geniuses'!*"

He had even gone beyond the point of believing that magic was important because it held together the fabric of culture among these natives, because it—and their religious superstitions—gave them a rule for behavior, therefore, in most cases, happiness. He had even come to believe that native magic was just another method of arriving at physical truths.

Of course, it was all semantic nonsense. It suggested that primitive magic could lift a ship into space or destroy disease or . . .

That had been the trouble with Barney. You could never tell when he was serious. Even a social anthropologist wouldn't go so far as to think there was more than one law of gravity.

"Mr. Austin, we have brought you here for a purpose. Do you know what that purpose is?"

"I don't know and I don't—"

"Have you wondered why you, alone, of all your people, have been spared? Then—listen to me, very carefully. Because if you do not, then what has happened in your new city is merely the beginning. The winds of death will blow over Mbarara and it will be far more awful than what has been." The medicine man stared down at the scattered piles of bones. Panther bones, Austin knew—a divination device. Their position on the ground told Bokawah much about the white people.

"Go back to your chiefs. Tell them that they must forget this city. Tell them that death walks here and that it will always walk, and that their magic is powerful but not powerful enough. It cannot stand against the spirits from time who have been summoned to fight. Go and talk to your chiefs and tell them these things. Make them believe you. *Force* them to understand that if they come to Mbarara, they will die, in ways they never dreamed, of sickness, in pain, slowly. Forever."

The old man's eyes were closed. His mouth did not move at all and the voice was mechanical.

"Tell them, Mr. Austin, that at first you thought it was a strange new disease that struck the workers. But then remind them that your greatest doctors were powerless against the contagion, that it spread and was not conquered. Say these things. And, perhaps, they will believe you. And be saved.''

Bokawah studied the panther bones carefully, tracing their arrangement.

Austin's voice was mechanical, also. ''You are forgetting something,'' he said. He refused to let the thoughts creep in. He refused to wonder about the voice that came through closed lips, about where the natives could have found soil or fresh panther bones or . . . ''No one,'' he said to the old man, ''has fought back—yet.''

''But why would you do that, Mr. Austin, since you do not believe in the existence of your enemy? Whom shall you fight?'' Bokawah smiled.

The crowd of natives remained quiet, unmoving, in the dying firelight.

''The only fear you hold for us,'' Austin said, ''is the fear that you may prove psychologically harmful.'' He looked at the crushed doll at his feet. The face was whole; otherwise, it lay hideously disfigured.

''Yes?''

''Right now, Bokawah, my government is sending men. They will arrive soon. When they do, they will study what has happened. If it is agreed that your rites—however harmless in themselves—cause currents of fear—are in *any way* responsible for the disease—you will be given the opportunity to go elsewhere or—''

''Or, Mr. Austin?''

''—you will be eliminated.''

''Then people will come to Mbarara. Despite the warnings and the death, they will come?''

''Your magic sticks aren't going to scare away five hundred thousand men and women.''

''Five hundred thousand . . .'' The old man looked at the bones, sighed, nodded his head. ''You know your people very well,'' he murmured.

Austin smiled. ''Yes, I do.''

''Then I think there is little left for us to talk about.''

Austin wanted to say, No, you're wrong. We must talk about Mag! She's dying and I want to keep her from dying. But he knew what these words would mean. They would sketch his real feelings, his fears and doubts. And everything would be lost. He could not admit that the doll was anything more than a doll. He must not!

The old man picked up a calabash and ran water over his hands. "I am sorry," he said, "that you must learn the way you must."

A slow chant rose from the natives. It sounded to Austin like Swahili, yet it was indistinct. He could recognize none of the words, except *gonga* and *bagana*. Medicine? The man with the medicine? It was a litany, not unlike the Gregorian chants he had once heard, full of overpowering melancholy. Calm and ethereal and sad as only the human voice can be sad. It rode on the stale air, swelling, diminishing, cutting through the stench of decay and rot with profound dignity.

Austin felt the heaviness of his clothes. The broken machines had stopped pumping fresh breezes, so the air was like oil, opening the pores of his body, running coldly down his arms and legs.

Bokawah made a motion with his hand and sank back onto the smooth floor. He breathed wrackingly, and groaned as if in pain. Then he straightened and looked at Austin and hobbled quickly away.

The drums began. Movement eased back into the throng and soon the dancers were up, working themselves back into their possessed states.

Austin turned and walked quickly away from the ceremony. When he had reached the shadows, he ran. He did not stop running until he had reached the lift, even while his muscles, long dormant, unaccustomed to this activity, turned to stone, numb and throbbing stone.

He stabbed the button and closed his eyes, while his heart pumped and roared sound into his ears and colored fire into his mind. The platform descended slowly, unemotional and calm as its parts.

Austin ran out and fell against a building, where he tried to push away the image of the black magic ceremony, and what he had felt there.

He swallowed needles of pain into his parched throat.

And the fear mounted and mounted, strangling him slowly . . .

The Towers of Mbarara loomed, suddenly, to Austin, more unreal and anachronistic than the tribal rites from which he had just come. Stalagmites of crystal pushing up to the night sky that bent above them; little squares and diamonds and circles of metal and stone. Office buildings; apartments; housing units; hat stores and machine factories and restaurants; and, cobwebbing among them, all these blind and empty shells, the walkways, like colored ribbons, like infinitely long reptiles, sleeping now, dead, still.

Or, were they only waiting, as he wanted to believe?

Of course they're waiting, he thought. People who know the answers will come to Mbarara tomorrow. Clear-headed scientists who have not been terrorized by a tribe of beaten primitives. And the scientists will find out what killed the workers, correct it, and people will follow. Five hundred thousand people, from all over the closet-crowded world, happy to have air to breathe once more—air that hasn't had to travel down two hundred feet—happy to know the Earth can yet sustain them. No more talk, then, of "population decreases"—murder was a better word—; no more government warnings screaming "depopulation" at you . . .

The dream would come true, Austin told himself. Because it must. Because he'd promised Mag and they'd lived it all together, endless years, hoped and planned and fought for the city. With Mbarara, it would begin: the dark age of a sardine can world would end, and life would begin. It would be many years before the worry would begin all over—for half the earth lay fallow, wasted. Australia, Greenland, Iceland, Africa, the Poles . . . And perhaps then the population graph would change, as it had always changed before. And men would come out of their caverns and rat-holes and live as men.

Yes. But only if Mbarara worked. If he could show them his success here . . .

Austin cursed the men who had gone back and screamed the story of what had happened to the other engineers. God knew there were few enough available, few who had been odd enough to study a field for which there seemed little further use.

If they'd only kept still about the disease! Then others would have come and . . .

Died. The word came out instantly, uncalled, and vanished.

Austin passed the Emperor, the playhouse he had thought of that night with Mag, ten years before. As he passed, he tried to visualize the foyer jammed with people in soup-and-fish and jeweled gowns, talking of whether the play had meat or not. Now, its marbled front putting out yellow glow, it looked foolish and pathetic. The placard case shone through newly gathered dust, empty.

Austin tried to think of what had been on this spot originally. Thick jungle growth alone. Or had there been a native village—with monkeys climbing the trees and swinging on vines and white widows mourning under straw roofs?

Now playing: JULIUS CAESAR. Admission: Three coconuts.

Be still. You've stayed together all this time, he thought, you can hold out until tomorrow. Tcheletchew will be here, sputtering under his beard, and they'll fly Mag to a hospital and make her well and clear up this nonsense in a hurry.

Just get home. Don't think and get home and it will be all right.

The city was actually without formal streets. Its plan did not include the antiquated groundcars that survived here and there in old families. Therefore, Mbarara was literally a maze. A very pretty maze. Like an English estate—Austin had admired these touches of vanished gentility—the areas were sometimes framed by green stone hedges, carved into functional shapes.

He had no difficulty finding his way. It was all too fresh, even now, the hours of planning every small curve and design, carefully leaving no artistic "holes" or useless places. He could have walked it blindfolded.

But when he passed the food dispensary and turned the corner, he found that it did not lead to the 'copter-park, as it should have. There were buildings there, but they were not the ones they ought to have been.

Or else he'd turned the wrong— He retraced his steps to the point where he had gone left. The food dispensary was nowhere in sight. Instead he found himself looking at the general chemistry building. Austin paused and wiped his forehead. The excitement, of course. It had clouded his mind for a moment, making him lose his way.

He began walking. Warm perspiration coursed across his body, turning his suit dark-wet, staining his jacket.

He passed the food dispensary.

Austin clenched his fists. It was impossible that he could have made a complete circle. He had built this city, he knew it intimately. He had walked through it without even thinking of direction, in the half-stages of construction, and never taken a wrong step.

How could he be lost?

Nerves. Nothing strange in it. Certainly enough had happened to jar loose his sense of direction.

Calmly, now. Calmly.

The air hung fetid and heavy. He had to pull it into his lungs, push it out. Of course, he could go below and open the valves—at least *they* could be operated by hand. He could, but why? It would mean hunching down in a dark shaft—damn, should have made that shaft larger! And, there were, after all, enough openings in the sealing-bubble to keep a breathable flow of oxygen in circulation. If the air was heavy and still outside the bubble, he could scarcely expect it to be different within . . .

He looked up at the half-minaretted tower that was one of the 'copter repair centers. It was located in exactly the opposite direction to the one he thought he'd taken.

Austin sank onto a stone bench. Images floated through his mind. He was lost; precisely as lost as if he had wandered into the jungle that had stood here before the building of Mbarara, and then tried to find his way back.

He closed his eyes and saw a picture, startlingly clear, of himself, running through the matted growths of dark green foliage, stumbling across roots, bumping trees, face grotesque with fear, and screaming . . .

He opened his eyes quickly, shook away the vision. His brain was tired; that was why he saw such a picture. He must keep his eyes open.

The city was unchanged. The park, designed for housewives who might wish to pause and rest or chat, perhaps feed squirrels, surrounded him.

Across the boating lake was the university.

Behind the university was home.

Austin rose, weakly, and made his way down the grassy slope to the edge of the artificial lake. Cultured city trees dotted the banks: the lake threw back a geometrically perfect reflection.

He knelt and splashed water into his face. Then he gulped some of it down and paused until the ripples spread to the center of the lake.

He studied his image in the water carefully. White skin, smooth cheeks, iron-colored hair. Good clothes. A dolichocephalic head evenly spaced, the head of a twenty-second-century civilized . . .

Above his reflection, Austin detected movement. He froze and blinked his eyes. As the water smoothed, the image of an animal appeared on the surface, wavering slightly. A small animal, something like a monkey. Like a monkey hanging from the branches of a tree.

Austin whirled around.

There was only the darkness, the golfing-green lawn, the cultured trees—smooth-barked, empty.

He passed a hand through his hair. It was a trick of the lights. His subconscious fear, the shimmering water . . .

He walked quickly to the darkened boathouse, across its floor, his footsteps ringing against the stone, echoing loudly.

At the end of the miniature pier, he untied a small battery boat and jumped into it. He pulled a switch at the side, waited, forced himself to look back at the deserted bank.

The boat moved slowly, with only a whisper of sound, through the water. *Hurry*, Austin thought. *Hurry— Oh God, why are they so slow!*

The boat, whose tin flag proclaimed its name to be Lucy, sliced the calm lake with its toy prow, and, after many minutes, reached the center.

The glow was insufficient to make the approaching bank distinct. It lay wrapped in darkness, a darkness that hid even the buildings.

Austin narrowed his eyes and stared. He blinked. It was the fuzziness of the luminescence, of course, that gave movement to the bank. That made it seem to seethe with unseen life.

It was only that his position to the shadows kept changing that made them turn into dark and feral shapes; trees, where buildings surely were, dense growth . . .

It was the milky phosphorescence of the metals that rose like marsh-steam from the nearing water . . .

He thought of stepping off the boat into a jungle, a magical forest, alive and waiting for him.

He closed his eyes and gripped the sides of the boat.

There was a scraping. Austin felt the cement guard, sighed, switched off the battery and leapt from the little boat.

There was no jungle. Only the lime-colored city trees and the smooth lawn.

The university sat ahead like a string of dropped pearls:

blister-shaped, connected by elevated tunnels, twisting, delicate strands of metal and alloy.

Austin scrambled up the embankment. It must be very late now. Perhaps nearly morning. In a few hours, the others would arrive. And—

He halted, every muscle straining.

He listened.

There were the drums. But not only the drums, now.

Other sounds.

He closed his eyes. The airless night pressed against him. He heard a rustling noise. Like something traveling through dense brush. He heard, far away, tiny sounds, whistlings, chitterings. Like monkeys and birds.

He tore open his eyes. Only the park, the city.

He went on. Now his feet were on stone and the park was behind him. He walked through the canyons of the city again, the high buildings, metal and crystal and alloy and stone.

The rustling noises did not cease, however. They were behind him, growing nearer. Bodies, moving through leaves and tall grass.

Austin suddenly remembered where he'd heard the sound before. Years ago, when he'd first visited this land. They had taken him on a hunting expedition, deep into the wild country. They were going to bag something—he forgot exactly what. Something strange. Yes; it was a wild pig. They had walked all day, searching, through the high tan grass, and then they had heard the rustling sounds.

Exactly like the sound he heard now.

Austin recalled the unbelievable fury of the boar, how it had disemboweled two dogs with a couple of swipes of those razor-sharp fangs. He recalled clearly the angry black snout, curled over yellow teeth.

He turned and stared into the darkness. The noises grew steadily louder, and were broken by yet another sound. Deep and guttural, like a cough.

As the sound behind him came closer, he ran, stumbled

and fell, pulled himself from the stone and ran until he had reached a flight of steps.

The coughing noise was a fast, high-pitched scream now, a grunting, snorting, a rush of tiny feet galloping across tamped earth, through dry grass. Austin stared blindly, covered his face with his arms and sank back until the sound was almost upon him.

His nostrils quivered at the animal smell.

His breath stopped.

He waited.

It was gone. Fading in the distance, the rustling, the coughing, and then there was the silence of the drums again.

Austin pressed the bones of his wrist into his throbbing skull to quiet the ache.

The panic drained off slowly. He rose, climbed the steps and walked through the shadowed courtyard onto the campus.

It was a vast green plain, smooth and grassy.

Across from it, in sight, was Austin's home.

He gathered his reason about him like a shield, and decided against taking the other routes. If he had gotten lost before, it could happen again. Certainly now, with his imagination running wild.

He must cross the campus.

Then it would be all right.

He began treading, timorously at first, listening with every square inch of his body.

The shaman's voice slithered into his mind. Chanting. ''. . . *you were destroying us against our will, Mr. Austin. Our world, our life. And such is your mind, and the mind of so-called 'civilized' men, that you could not see this was wrong. You have developed a culture and a social structure that pleased you, you were convinced that it was right; therefore, you could not understand the existence of any that differed. You saw us as ignorant savages—most of you did—and you were anxious to 'civilize' us. Not once did it occur to you that we, too, had our culture and our social structure;*

*that we knew right and wrong; that, perhaps, we might look upon
you as backward and uncivilized . . .''*

The sound of birds came to Austin; birds calling in high
trees, circling impossibly in the night sky.

*''. . . we have clung to our 'magic,' as you call it, and our 'su-
perstitions' for longer than you have clung to yours. Because—as
with your own—they have worked for us. Whether magic can be explained in Roman numerals or not, what is the difference, so long as
it works? Mr. Austin, there is not only one path to the Golden
City—there are many. Your people are on one path—''*

He heard the chatter of monkeys, some close, some far
away, the sound of them swinging on vines, scolding, dropping to mounds of foliage, scrambling up other trees.

*''—my people are on another. There is room in this world for both
ways. But your failure to grasp this simple fact has killed many of us
and it will kill many more of you. For we have been on our path
longer. We are closer to the Golden City . . .''*

Austin clapped his hands to his ears. But he did not stop
walking.

From the smooth stone streets, from the direction of the
physics department, came the insane trumpeting of elephants, their immense bulks crashing against brittle bark,
their huge feet crunching fallen limbs and branches . . .

The shaman's voice became the voice of Barney Chadfield
. . . He spoke again of his theory that if one could only discover the unwritten bases of black magic and apply formulae
to them, we would find that they were merely another form
of science . . . perhaps less advanced, perhaps more.

The sounds piled up, and the feelings, and the sensations.
Eyes firmly open, Austin thought of Mag and felt needled
leaves slap invisibly against his legs; he smelled the rot and
the life, the heavy, wild air of the jungle, like animal steam;
the odors of fresh blood and wet fur and decaying plants;
the short rasping breath of a million different animals—the
movement, all around him, the approaches, the retreats, the
frenzied unseen . . .

Eyes open he felt and smelled and heard all these things; and saw only the city.

A pain shot through his right arm. He tried to move it: it would not move. He thought of an old man. The old man had a doll. The old man was crushing the doll's arm, and laughing . . . He thought of reflexes and the reaction of reflexes to emotional stimuli.

He walked, ignoring the pain, not thinking about the arm at all.

". . . tell them, Mr. Austin. Make them believe. Make them believe . . . Do not kill all these people . . ."

When he had passed the Law College, he felt a pain wrench at his leg. He heard another dry-grass rustle. But not behind him: in front. Going forward.

Going toward his apartment.

Austin broke into a run, without knowing exactly why.

There was a pounding, a panting at his heels: vaguely he was aware of this. He knew only that he must get inside, quickly, to the sanity of his home. Jaws snapped, clacked. Austin stumbled on a vine, his fingers pulled at air, he leapt away and heard the sound of something landing where he had just been, something that screamed and hissed.

He ran on. At the steps, his foot pressed onto something soft. It recoiled madly. He slipped and fell again, and the feel of moist beaded skin whipped about his legs. The thunder was almost directly above. He reached out, clawed loose the thing around his leg and pulled himself forward.

There was a swarming over his hands. He held them in front of his eyes, tried to see the ants that had to be there, slapped the invisible creatures loose.

The apartment door was only a few feet away now. Austin remembered his pistol, drew it out and fired it into the night until there were no more bullets left.

He pulled himself into the lobby of the unit.

The door hissed closed.

He touched the lock, heard it spring together.

And then the noises ceased. The drums and the animals,

all the wild nightmare things—ceased to be. There was his breathing, and the pain that laced through his arm and leg.

He waited, trembling, trying to pull breath in.

Finally he rose and limped to the elevator. He did not even think about the broken machines. He knew it would work.

It did. The glass doors whirred apart at his floor, and he went out into the hall.

It was soundless.

He stood by the door, listening to his heart rattle crazily in his chest.

He opened the door.

The apartment was calm, silent. The walls glowed around the framed Mirós and Mondrians and Picassos. The furniture sat functionally on the silky white rug, black thin-legged chairs and tables . . .

Austin started to laugh, carefully checked himself. He knew he probably would not be able to stop.

He thought strongly about Tcheletchew, and of the men who would come to Mbarara in the morning. He thought of the city teeming with life. Of the daylight streaming onto the streets of people, the shops, the churches, the schools. His work. His dream . . .

He walked across the rug to the bedroom door.

It was slightly ajar.

He pushed it, went inside, closed it softly.

"Mag," he whispered. "Mag—"

There was a noise. A low, throaty rumble. Not of anger; of warning.

Richard Austin came close to the bed, adjusted his eyes to the black light.

Then he screamed.

It was the first time he had ever watched a lion feeding.

To Serve Man

Damon Knight

TELEPLAY BY ROD SERLING

AIRED MARCH 2, 1962

STARRING LLOYD BOCHNER, RICHARD KIEL, AND
SUSAN CUMMINGS

THE KANAMIT WERE NOT VERY PRETTY, IT'S TRUE.
They looked something like pigs and something like people,
and that is not an attractive combination. Seeing them for the
first time shocked you; that was their handicap. When a
thing with the countenance of a fiend comes from the stars
and offers a gift, you are disinclined to accept.

I don't know what we expected interstellar visitors to look
like—those who thought about it at all, that is. Angels, perhaps, or something too alien to be really awful. Maybe that's
why we were all so horrified and repelled when they landed
in their great ships and we saw what they really were like.

The Kanamit were short and very hairy—thick, bristly
brown-gray hair all over their abominably plump bodies.
Their noses were snoutlike and their eyes small, and they
had thick hands of three fingers each. They wore green
leather harness and green shorts, but I think the shorts were
a concession to our notions of public decency. The garments
were quite modishly cut, with slash pockets and half-belts in
the back. The Kanamit had a sense of humor, anyhow.

There were three of them at this session of the U.N., and, lord, I can't tell you how queer it looked to see them there in the middle of a solemn plenary session—three piglike creatures in green harness and shorts, sitting at the long table below the podium, surrounded by the packed arcs of delegates from every nation. They sat correctly upright, politely watching each speaker. Their flat ears drooped over the earphones. Later on, I believe, they learned every human language, but at this time they knew only French and English.

They seemed perfectly at ease—and that, along with their humor, was a thing that tended to make me like them. I was in the minority; I didn't think they were trying to put anything over.

The delegate from Argentina got up and said that his government was interested in the demonstration of a new cheap power source, which the Kanamit had made at the previous session, but that the Argentine government could not commit itself as to its future policy without a much more thorough examination.

It was what all the delegates were saying, but I had to pay particular attention to Señor Valdes, because he tended to sputter and his diction was bad. I got through the translation all right, with only one or two momentary hesitations, and then switched to the Polish-English line to hear how Grigori was doing with Janciewicz. Janciewicz was the cross Grigori had to bear, just as Valdes was mine.

Janciewicz repeated the previous remarks with a few ideological variations, and then the Secretary-General recognized the delegate from France, who introduced Dr. Denis Lévêque, the criminologist, and a great deal of complicated equipment was wheeled in.

Dr. Lévêque remarked that the question in many people's minds had been aptly expressed by the delegate from the U.S.S.R. at the preceding session, when he demanded, "What is the motive of the Kanamit? What is their purpose in offering us these unprecedented gifts, while asking nothing in return?"

The doctor then said, "At the request of several delegates and with the full consent of our guests, the Kanamit, my associates and I have made a series of tests upon the Kanamit with the equipment which you see before you. These tests will now be repeated."

A murmur ran through the chamber. There was a fusillade of flashbulbs, and one of the TV cameras moved up to focus on the instrument board of the doctor's equipment. At the same time, the huge television screen behind the podium lighted up, and we saw the blank faces of two dials, each with its pointer resting at zero, and a strip of paper tape with a stylus point resting against it.

The doctor's assistants were fastening wires to the temples of one of the Kanamit, wrapping a canvas-covered rubber tube around his forearm, and taping something to the palm of his right hand.

In the screen, we saw the paper tape begin to move while the stylus traced a slow zigzag pattern along it. One of the needles began to jump rhythmically; the other flipped halfway over and stayed there, wavering slightly.

"These are the standard instruments for testing the truth of a statement," said Dr. Lévêque. "Our first object, since the physiology of the Kanamit is unknown to us, was to determine whether or not they react to these tests as human beings do. We will now repeat one of the many experiments which were made in the endeavor to discover this."

He pointed to the first dial. "This instrument registers the subject's heartbeat. This shows the electrical conductivity of the skin in the palm of his hand, a measure of perspiration, which increases under stress. And this—" pointing to the tape-and-stylus device—"shows the pattern and intensity of the electrical waves emanating from his brain. It has been shown, with human subjects, that all these readings vary markedly depending upon whether the subject is speaking the truth."

He picked up two large pieces of cardboard, one red and one black. The red one was a square about three feet on a side; the black was a rectangle three and a half feet long. He addressed himself to the Kanama.

"Which of these is longer than the other?"

"The red," said the Kanama.

Both needles leaped wildly, and so did the line on the unrolling tape.

"I shall repeat the question," said the doctor. "Which of these is longer than the other?"

"The black," said the creature.

This time the instruments continued in their normal rhythm.

"How did you come to this planet?" asked the doctor.

"Walked," replied the Kanama.

Again the instruments responded, and there was a subdued ripple of laughter in the chamber.

"Once more," said the doctor. "How did you come to this planet?"

"In a spaceship," said the Kanama, and the instruments did not jump.

The doctor again faced the delegates. "Many such experiments were made," he said, "and my colleagues and myself are satisfied that the mechanisms are effective. Now—" he turned to the Kanama—"I shall ask our distinguished guest to reply to the question put at the last session by the delegate of the U.S.S.R.—namely, what is the motive of the Kanamit people in offering these great gifts to the people of Earth?"

The Kanama rose. Speaking this time in English, he said, "On my planet there is a saying, 'There are more riddles in a stone than in a philosopher's head.' The motives of intelligent beings, though they may at times appear obscure, are simple things compared to the complex workings of the natural universe. Therefore I hope that the people of Earth will understand, and believe, when I tell you that our mission upon your planet is simply this—to bring to you the peace and plenty which we ourselves enjoy, and which we have in the past brought to other races throughout the galaxy. When your world has no more hunger, no more war, no more needless suffering, that will be our reward.''

And the needles had not jumped once.

The delegate from the Ukraine jumped to his feet, asking to be recognized, but the time was up and the Secretary-General closed the session.

I met Grigori as we were leaving the chamber. His face was red with excitement. ''Who promoted that circus?'' he demanded.

''The tests looked genuine to me,'' I told him.

''A circus!'' he said vehemently. ''A second-rate farce! If they were genuine, Peter, why was debate stifled?''

''There'll be time for debate tomorrow, surely.''

''Tomorrow the doctor and his instruments will be back in Paris. Plenty of things can happen before tomorrow. In the name of sanity, man, how can anybody trust a thing that looks as if it ate the baby?''

I was a little annoyed. I said, ''Are you sure you're not more worried about their politics than their appearance?''

He said, ''Bah,'' and went away.

The next day reports began to come in from government laboratories all over the world where the Kanamit's power source was being tested. They were wildly enthusiastic. I don't understand such things myself, but it seemed that those little metal boxes would give more electrical power than an atomic pile, for next to nothing and nearly forever. And it was said that they were so cheap to manufacture that everybody in the world could have one of his own. In the early afternoon there were reports that seventeen countries had already begun to set up factories to turn them out.

The next day the Kanamit turned up with plans and specimens of a gadget that would increase the fertility of any arable land by 60 to 100 per cent. It speeded the formation of nitrates in the soil, or something. There was nothing in the newscasts any more but stories about the Kanamit. The day after that, they dropped their bombshell.

''You now have potentially unlimited power and increased

food supply," said one of them. He pointed with his three-fingered hand to an instrument that stood on the table before him. It was a box on a tripod, with a parabolic reflector on the front of it. "We offer you today a third gift which is at least as important as the first two."

He beckoned to the TV men to roll their cameras into closeup position. Then he picked up a large sheet of cardboard covered with drawings and English lettering. We saw it on the large screen above the podium; it was all clearly legible.

"We are informed that this broadcast is being relayed throughout your world," said the Kanama. "I wish that everyone who has equipment for taking photographs from television screens would use it now."

The Secretary-General leaned forward and asked a question sharply, but the Kanama ignored him.

"This device," he said, "generates a field in which no explosive, of whatever nature, can detonate."

There was an uncomprehending silence.

The Kanama said, "It cannot now be suppressed. If one nation has it, all must have it." When nobody seemed to understand, he explained bluntly, "There will be no more war."

That was the biggest news of the millennium, and it was perfectly true. It turned out that the explosions the Kanama was talking about included gasoline and Diesel explosions. They had simply made it impossible for anybody to mount or equip a modern army.

We could have gone back to bows and arrows, of course, but that wouldn't have satisfied the military. Besides, there wouldn't be any reason to make war. Every nation would soon have everything.

Nobody ever gave another thought to those lie-detector experiments, or asked the Kanamit what their politics were. Grigori was put out; he had nothing to prove his suspicions.

I quit my job with the U.N. a few months later, because I foresaw that it was going to die under me anyhow. U.N.

business was booming at the time, but after a year or so there was going to be nothing for it to do. Every nation on Earth was well on the way to being completely self-supporting; they weren't going to need much arbitration.

I accepted a position as translator with the Kanamit Embassy, and it was there that I ran into Grigori again. I was glad to see him, but I couldn't imagine what he was doing there.

"I thought you were on the opposition," I said. "Don't tell me you're convinced the Kanamit are all right."

He looked rather shamefaced. "They're not what they look, anyhow," he said.

It was as much of a concession as he could decently make, and I invited him down to the embassy lounge for a drink. It was an intimate kind of place, and he grew confidential over the second daiquiri.

"They fascinate me," he said. "I hate them instinctively still—that hasn't changed—but I can evaluate it. You were right, obviously; they mean us nothing but good. But do you know—" he leaned across the table—"the question of the Soviet delegate was never answered."

I am afraid I snorted.

"No, really," he said. "They told us what they wanted to do—'to bring to you the peace and plenty which we ourselves enjoy.' But they didn't say *why*."

"Why do missionaries—"

"Missionaries be damned!" he said angrily. "Missionaries have a religious motive. If these creatures have a religion, they haven't once mentioned it. What's more, they didn't send a missionary group; they sent a diplomatic delegation—a group representing the will and policy of their whole people. Now just what have the Kanamit, as a people or a nation, got to gain from our welfare?"

I said, "Cultural—"

"Cultural cabbage soup! No, it's something less obvious than that, something obscure that belongs to their psychology and not to ours. But trust me, Peter, there is no such thing as a completely disinterested altruism. In one way or another, they have something to gain."

"And that's why you're here," I said. "To try to find out what it is."

"Correct. I wanted to get on one of the ten-year exchange groups to their home planet, but I couldn't; the quota was filled a week after they made the announcement. This is the next best thing. I'm studying their language, and you know that language reflects the basic assumptions of the people who use it. I've got a fair command of the spoken lingo already. It's not hard, really, and there are hints in it. Some of the idioms are quite similar to English. I'm sure I'll get the answer eventually."

"More power," I said, and we went back to work.

I saw Grigori frequently from then on, and he kept me posted about his progress. He was highly excited about a month after that first meeting; said he'd got hold of a book of the Kanamit's and was trying to puzzle it out. They wrote in ideographs, worse than Chinese, but he was determined to fathom it if it took him years. He wanted my help.

Well, I was interested in spite of myself, for I knew it would be a long job. We spent some evenings together, working with material from Kanamit bulletin boards and so forth, and with the extremely limited English-Kanamit dictionary they issued to the staff. My conscience bothered me about the stolen book, but gradually I became absorbed by the problem. Languages are my field, after all. I couldn't help being fascinated.

We got the title worked out in a few weeks. It was *How to Serve Man*, evidently a handbook they were giving out to new Kanamit members of the embassy staff. They had new ones in, all the time now, a shipload about once a month; they were opening all kinds of research laboratories, clinics and so on. If there was anybody on Earth besides Grigori who still distrusted those people, he must have been somewhere in the middle of Tibet.

It was astonishing to see the changes that had been wrought in less than a year. There were no more standing armies, no more shortages, no unemployment. When you picked up a newspaper you didn't see H-BOMB or SATELLITE leaping out at you; the news was always good. It was a hard thing to get used to. The Kanamit were working on human biochemistry, and it was known around the embassy that they were nearly ready to announce methods of making our race taller and stronger and healthier—practically a race of supermen—and they had a potential cure for heart disease and cancer.

I didn't see Grigori for a fortnight after we finished working out the title of the book; I was on a long-overdue vacation in Canada. When I got back, I was shocked by the change in his appearance.

"What on earth is wrong, Grigori?" I asked. "You look like the very devil."

"Come down to the lounge."

I went with him, and he gulped a stiff Scotch as if he needed it.

"Come on, man, what's the matter?" I urged.

"The Kanamit have put me on the passenger list for the next exchange ship," he said. "You, too, otherwise I wouldn't be talking to you."

"Well," I said, "but—"

"They're not altruists."

I tried to reason with him. I pointed out they'd made Earth a paradise compared to what it was before. He only shook his head.

Then I said, "Well, what about those lie-detector tests?"

"A farce," he replied, without heat. "I said so at the time, you fool. They told the truth, though; as far as it went."

"And the book?" I demanded, annoyed. "What about that—*How to Serve Man*? That wasn't put there for you to read. They *mean* it. How do you explain that?"

"I've read the first paragraph of that book," he said.
"Why do you suppose I haven't slept for a week?"

I said, "Well?" and he smiled a curious, twisted smile.

"It's a cookbook," he said.

Little Girl Lost

Richard Matheson

TELEPLAY BY RICHARD MATHESON

AIRED MARCH 16, 1962

STARRING CHARLES AIDMAN AND SARAH MARSHALL

TINA'S CRYING WOKE ME UP IN A SECOND. IT WAS pitch black, middle of the night. I heard Ruth stir beside me in bed. In the front room Tina caught her breath, then started in again, louder.

"Oh, gawd," I muttered groggily.

Ruth grunted and started to push back the covers.

"I'll *get* it," I said wearily, and she slumped back on the pillow. We take turns when Tina has her nights; has a cold or a stomachache or just takes a flop out of bed.

I lifted up my legs and dropped them over the edge of the blankets. Then I squirmed myself down to the foot of the bed and slung my legs over the edge. I winced as my feet touched the icy floor boards. The apartment was arctic; it usually is these winter nights, even in California.

I padded across the cold floor, threading my way between the chest, the bureau, the bookcase in the hall and then the edge of the TV set as I moved into the livingroom. Tina sleeps there because we could only get a one-bedroom apartment. She sleeps on a couch that breaks down into a bed. And, at that moment, her crying was getting louder and she started calling for her mommy.

"All right, Tina. Daddy'll fix it all up," I told her.

She kept crying. Outside, on the balcony, I heard our collie Mack jump down from his bed on the camp chair.

I bent over the couch in the darkness. I could feel that the covers were lying flat. I backed away, squinting at the floor, but I didn't see any Tina moving around.

"Oh, my God," I chuckled to myself, in spite of irritation, "the poor kid's under the couch."

I got down on my knees and looked, still chuckling at the thought of little Tina falling out of bed and crawling under the couch.

"Tina, where are you?" I said, trying not to laugh.

Her crying got louder but I couldn't see her under the couch. It was too dark to see clearly.

"Hey, where are you, kiddo?" I asked. "Come to papa."

Like a man looking for a collar button under the bureau I felt under the couch for my daughter, who was still crying and begging for mommy, mommy.

Came the first twist of surprise. I couldn't reach her no matter how hard I stretched.

"Come on, Tina," I said, amused no longer, "stop playing games with your old man."

She cried louder. My outstretched hand jumped back as it touched the cold wall.

"Daddy!" Tina cried.

"Oh for . . . !"

I stumbled up and jolted irritably across the rug. I turned on the lamp beside the record player and turned to get her, and was stopped dead in my tracks, held there, a half-asleep mute, gaping at the couch, ice water plaiting down my back.

Then, in a leap, I was on my knees by the couch and my eyes were searching frantically, my throat getting tighter and tighter. I heard her crying under the couch, but I couldn't see her.

* * *

My stomach muscles jerked in as the truth of it struck me. I ran my hands around wildly under the bed but they didn't touch a thing. I heard her crying and, by God, she wasn't there!

"Ruth!" I yelled. "Come here."

I heard Ruth catch her breath in the bedroom and then there was a rustle of bedclothes and the sound of her feet rushing across the bedroom floor. Out of the side of my eyes I saw the light blue movement of her nightgown.

"What is it?" she gasped.

I backed to my feet, hardly able to breathe much less speak. I started to say something but the words choked up in my throat. My mouth hung open. All I could do was point a shaking finger at the couch.

"Where is she!" Ruth cried.

"I don't know!" I finally managed. "She . . ."

"*What!*"

Ruth dropped to her knees beside the couch and looked under.

"Tina!" she called.

"Mommy."

Ruth recoiled from the couch, color draining from her face. The eyes she turned to me were horrified. I suddenly heard the sound of Mack scratching wildly at the door.

"Where *is* she?" Ruth asked again, her voice hollow.

"I don't know," I said, feeling numb. I turned on the light and . . ."

"But she's *crying*," Ruth said as if she felt the same distrust of sight that I did. "I . . . Chris, *listen.*"

The sound of our daughter crying and sobbing in fright.

"Tina!" I called loudly, pointlessly, "where *are* you, angel?"

She just cried. "Mommy!" she said. "Mommy, pick me up!"

"No, no, this is crazy," Ruth said, her voice tautly held as she rose to her feet, "she's in the kitchen."

"But . . ."

I stood there dumbly as Ruth turned on the kitchen light and went in. The sound of her agonized voice made me shudder.

"Chris! *She's not in here.*"

She came running in, her eyes stark with fear. She bit her teeth into her lip.

"But where *is* . . . ?" she started to say, then stopped.

Because we both heard Tina crying and the sound of it was coming from under the couch.

But there wasn't anything under the couch.

Still Ruth couldn't accept the crazy truth. She jerked open the hall closet and looked in it. She looked behind the TV set, even behind the record player, a space of maybe two inches.

"Honey, *help* me," she begged. "We can't just leave her this way."

I didn't move.

"Honey, she's under the couch," I said.

"But she's not!"

Once more, like the crazy, impossible dream it was, me on my knees on the cold floor, feeling under the couch. I got *under* the couch, I touched every inch of floor space there. But I couldn't touch her, even though I heard her crying—*right in my ear.*

I got up, shivering from the cold and something else. Ruth stood in the middle of the livingroom rug staring at me. Her voice was weak, almost inaudible.

"Chris," she said, "Chris, what *is* it?"

I shook my head. "Honey, I don't know," I said. "I don't know what it is."

Outside, Mack began to whine as he scratched. Ruth glanced at the balcony door, her face a white twist of fear. She was shivering now in her silk gown as she looked back at the couch. I stood there absolutely helpless, my mind racing a dozen different ways, none of them toward a solution, not even toward concrete thought.

"What are we going to do?" she asked, on the verge of a scream I knew was coming.

"Baby, I . . ."

I stopped short and suddenly we were both moving for the couch.

Tina's crying was fainter.

"Oh, no," Ruth whimpered. "No. *Tina.*"

"Mommy," said Tina, further away. I could feel the chills lacing over my flesh.

"Tina, come back here!" I heard myself shouting, the father yelling at his disobedient child, who can't be seen.

"TINA!" Ruth screamed.

Then the apartment was dead silent and Ruth and I were kneeling by the couch looking at the emptiness underneath. Listening.

To the sound of our child, peacefully snoring.

"Bill, can you come right over?" I said frantically.

"What?" Bill's voice was thick and fuzzy.

"Bill, this is Chris. Tina has disappeared!"

He woke up.

"She's been kidnaped?" he asked.

"No," I said, "she's here but . . . she's not here."

He made a confused sound. I grabbed in a breath.

"Bill, for God's sake get over here!"

A pause.

"I'll be right over," he said. I knew from the way he said it he didn't know why he was coming.

I dropped the receiver and went over to where Ruth was sitting on the couch shivering and clasping her hands tightly in her lap.

"Hon, get your robe," I said. "You'll catch cold."

"Chris, I . . ." Tears running down her cheeks. "Chris, where *is* she?"

"Honey."

It was all I could say, hopelessly, weakly. I went into the bedroom and got her robe. On the way back I stooped over and twisted hard on the wall heater.

"There," I said, putting the robe over her back, "put it on."

She put her arms through the sleeves of the robe, her eyes pleading with me to do something. Knowing very well I couldn't do it, she was asking me to bring her baby back.

I got on my knees again, just to be doing something. I knew it wouldn't help any. I remained there a long time just staring at the floor under the couch. Completely in the dark.

"Chris, she's s-sleeping on the floor," Ruth said, her words faltering from colorless lips. "Won't . . . she catch cold?"

"I . . ."

That was all I could say. What could I tell her? No, she's not on the floor? How did I know? I could hear Tina breathing and snoring gently on the floor but she wasn't there to touch. She was gone but she wasn't gone. My brain twisted back and forth on itself trying to figure out that one. Try adjusting to something like that sometime. It's a fast way to breakdown.

"Honey, she's . . . she's not here," I said. "I mean . . . not on the floor."

"But . . ."

"I know, I know . . ." I raised my hands and shrugged in defeat. "I don't think she's cold, honey," I said as gently and persuasively as I could.

She started to say something too but then she stopped. There was nothing to say. It defied words.

We sat in the quiet room waiting for Bill to come. I'd called him because he's an engineering man, CalTech, top man with Lockheed over in the valley. I don't know why I thought that would help but I called him. I'd have called anyone just to have another mind to help. Parents are useless beings when they're afraid for their children.

Once, before Bill came, Ruth slipped to her knees by the couch and started slapping her hands over the floor.

"Tina, wake up!" she cried in newborn terror, "wake *up!*"

"Honey, what good is that going to do?" I asked.

She looked up at me blankly and knew. It wasn't going to do any good.

I heard Bill on the steps and reached the door before he did. He came in quietly, looking around and giving Ruth a brief smile. I took his coat. He was still in pajamas.

"What is it, kid?" he asked hurriedly.

I told him as briefly and as clearly as I could. He got down on his knees and checked for himself. He felt around underneath the couch and I saw his brow knot into lines when he heard Tina's calm and peaceful breathing.

He straightened up.

"Well?" I asked.

He shook his head. "My *God*," he muttered.

We both stared at him. Outside Mack was still scratching and whining at the door.

"Where *is* she?" Ruth asked again. "Bill, I'm about to lose my mind."

"Take it easy," he said. I moved beside her and put my arm around her. She was trembling.

"You can hear her breathing," Bill said. "It's normal breathing. She must be all right."

"But where is she?" I asked. "You can't see her, you can't even *touch* her."

"I don't know," Bill said, and was on his knees by the bed again.

"Chris, you'd better let Mack in," Ruth said, worried about that for a moment. "He'll wake all the neighbors."

"All right, I will," I said, and kept watching Bill.

"Should we call the police?" I asked. "Do you . . . ?"

"No, no, that wouldn't do any good," Bill said, "this isn't . . ." He shook his head as if he were shaking away everything he'd ever accepted. "It's not a police job," he said.

"Chris, he'll wake up all the . . ."

I turned for the door to let Mack in.

"*Wait a minute*," Bill said, and I was turned back, my heart pounding again.

Bill was half under the couch, listening hard.

"Bill, what is . . . ?" I started.

"*Shhh!*"

We were both quiet. Bill stayed there a moment longer. Then he straightened up and his face was blank.

"I can't hear her," he said.

"Oh, *no!*"

Ruth fell forward before the couch.

"Tina! Oh God, where *is* she!"

Bill was up on his feet, moving quickly around the room. I watched him, then looked back at Ruth slumped over the couch, sick with fear.

"Listen," Bill said, "do you hear anything?"

Ruth looked up. "*Hear* . . . anything?"

"Move around, move around," Bill said. "See what you hear."

Like robots Ruth and I moved around the livingroom having no idea what we were doing. Everything was quiet except for the incessant whining and scratching of Mack. I gritted my teeth and muttered a terse—"*Shut up!*"—as I passed the balcony door. For a second the vague idea crossed my mind that Mack knew about Tina. He'd always worshiped her.

Then there was Bill standing in the corner where the closet was, stretching up on his toes and listening. He noticed us watching him and gestured quickly for us to come over. We moved hurriedly across the rug and stood beside him.

"Listen," he whispered. We did.

At first there was nothing. Then Ruth gasped and none of us were letting out the noise of breath.

Up in the corner, where the ceiling met the walls, we could hear the sound of Tina sleeping.

Ruth stared up there, her face white, totally lost.

Bill just shook his head slowly. Then suddenly he held up his hand and we all froze, jolted again.

The sound was gone.

Ruth started to sob helplessly. "*Tina.*"

She started out of the corner.

"We have to find her," she said despairingly. *"Please."*

We ran around the room in unorganized circles, trying to hear Tina. Ruth's tear-streaked face was twisted into a mask of fright.

I was the one who found her this time.

Under the television set.

We all knelt there and listened. As we did we heard her murmur a little to herself and the sound of her stirring in sleep.

"Want my dolly," she muttered.

"Tina!"

I held Ruth's shaking body in my arms and tried to stop her sobbing. Without success. I couldn't keep my own throat from tightening, my heart from pounding slow and hard in my chest. My hands shook on her back, slick with sweat.

"For God's sake, *what is it?*" Ruth said, but she wasn't asking us.

Bill helped me take her to a chair by the record player. Then he stood restlessly on the rug, gnawing furiously on one knuckle, the way I'd seen him do so often when he was engrossed in a problem.

He looked up, started to say something then gave it up and turned for the door.

"I'll let the pooch in," he said. "He's making a hell of a racket."

"Don't you have any idea what might have happened to her?" I asked.

"Bill . . . ?" Ruth begged.

Bill said, "I think she's in another dimension," and he opened the door.

What happened next came so fast we couldn't do a thing to stop it.

Mack came bounding in with a yelp and headed straight for the couch.

"He *knows!*" Bill yelled, and dived for the dog.

Then happened the crazy part. One second Mack was sliding under the couch in a flurry of ears, paws and tail. Then he was gone—*just like that.* Blotted up. The three of us gaped.

Then I heard Bill say, "Yes. *Yes.*"

"Yes, *what?*" I didn't know where *I* was by then.

"The kid's in another dimension."

"What are you talking about?" I said in worried, near-angry tones. You don't hear talk like that every day.

"Sit down," he said.

"Sit down? Isn't there anything we can *do?*"

Bill looked hurriedly at Ruth. She seemed to know what he was going to say.

"I don't know if there is," was what he said.

I slumped back on the couch.

"Bill," I said. Just speaking his name.

He gestured helplessly.

"Kid," he said, "this has caught me as wide open as you. I don't even know if I'm right or not but I can't think of anything else. I think that in some way, she's gotten herself into another dimension, probably the fourth. Mack, sensing it, followed her there. But how did they get there?—I don't know. I was under that couch; so were you. Did *you* see anything?"

I looked at him and he knew the answer.

"Another . . . *dimension?*" Ruth said in a tight voice. The voice of a mother who has just been told her child is lost forever.

Bill started pacing, punching his right fist into his palm.

"Damn, damn," he muttered. "How do things like this happen?"

Then while we sat there numbly, half listening to him, half for the sound of our child, he spoke. Not to us really. To himself, to try and place the problem in the proper perspective.

"One-dimensional space a line," he threw out the words quickly. "Two-dimensional space an infinite number of lines—an infinite number of one-dimensional spaces. Three-dimensional space an infinite number of planes—an infinite

number of two-dimensional spaces. Now the basic factor
. . . the *basic* factor . . .''

He slammed his palm and looked up at the ceiling. Then
he started again, more slowly now.

''Every point in each dimension a *section* of a line in the next
higher dimension. All points in line are *sections* of the perpendicular lines that make the line a plane. All points in plane
are sections of perpendicular lines that make the plane a
solid.

''That means that in the third dimension . . .''

''Bill, for God's sake!'' Ruth burst out. ''Can't we *do* something? My *baby* is in . . . in *there*.''

Bill lost his train of thought. He shook his head.

''Ruth, I don't . . .''

I got up then and was down on the floor again, climbing
under the couch. I *had* to find it! I felt, I searched. I listened
until the silence rang. Nothing.

Then I jerked up suddenly and hit my head as Mack
barked loudly in my ear.

Bill rushed over and slid in beside me, his breath labored
and quick.

''God's sake,'' he muttered, almost furiously. ''Of all the
damn places in the world . . .''

''If the . . . the *entrance* is here,'' I muttered, ''why did we
hear her voice and breathing all over the room?''

''Well, if she moved beyond the effect of the third dimension and was entirely in the fourth—then her movement, for
us, would seem to spread over all space. Actually she'd be in
one spot in the fourth dimension but to us . . .''

He stopped.

Mack was whining. But more importantly Tina started in
again. Right by our ears.

''He brought her back!'' Bill said excitedly. ''Man, what a
mutt!''

He started twisting around, looking, touching, slapping at
empty air.

"We've got to find it!" he said. "We've got to reach in and pull them out. God knows how long this dimension pocket will last."

"What?" I heard Ruth gasp, then suddenly cry, "Tina, where are you? This is mommy."

I was about to say something about it being no use but then Tina answered.

"Mommy, mommy! Where are you, mommy?"

Then the sound of Mack growling and Tina crying angrily.

"She's trying to run around and find Ruth," Bill said. "But Mack won't let her. I don't know *how* but he seems to know where the joining place is."

"Where *are* they for God's sake!" I said in a nervous fury.

And backed right into the damn thing.

To my dying day I'll never really be able to describe what it was like. But here goes.

It was black, yes—to *me*. And yet there seemed to be a million lights. But as soon as I looked at one it disappeared and was gone. I saw them out of the sides of my eyes.

"Tina," I said, "where are you? Answer me! Please!"

And heard my voice echoing a million times, the words echoing endlessly, never ceasing but moving off as if they were alive and traveling. And when I moved my hand the motion made a whistling sound that echoed and re-echoed and moved away like a swarm of insects flowing into the night.

"Tina!"

The sound of the echoing hurt my ears.

"Chris, can you hear her?" I heard a voice. But was it a voice—or more like a thought?

Then something wet touched my hand and I jumped.

Mack.

I reached around furiously for them, every motion making whistling echoes in vibrating blackness until I felt as if I were surrounded by a multitude of birds flocking and beating insane wings around my head. The pressure pounded and heaved in my brain.

Then I felt Tina. I say I felt her but I think if she wasn't my daughter and if I didn't *know* somehow it was her, I would have thought I'd touched something else. Not a shape in the sense of third-dimension shape. Let it go at that; I don't want to go into it.

"Tina," I whispered. "Tina, baby."

"Daddy, I'm scared of dark," she said in a thin voice, and Mack whined.

Then I was scared of dark too, because a thought scared my mind.

How did I get us all out?

Then the other thought came—Chris, have you got them?

"I've got them!" I called.

And Bill grabbed my legs (which, I later learned, were still sticking out in the third dimension) and jerked me back to reality with an armful of daughter and dog and memories of something I'd prefer having no memories about.

We all came piling out under the couch and I hit my head on it and almost knocked myself out. Then I was being alternately hugged by Ruth, kissed by the dog and helped to my feet by Bill. Mack was leaping on all of us, yelping and drooling.

When I was in talking shape again I noticed that Bill had blocked off the bottom of the couch with two card tables.

"Just to be safe," he said.

I nodded weakly. Ruth came in from the bedroom.

"Where's Tina?" I asked automatically, uneasy left-overs of memory still cooking in my brain.

"She's in our bed," she said. "I don't think we'll mind for one night."

I shook my head.

"I don't think so," I said.

Then I turned to Bill.

"Look," I said. "What the hell happened?"

"Well," he said, with a wry grin, "I told you. The third dimension is just a step below the fourth. In particular, every point in our space is a section of a perpendicular line in the fourth dimension."

"So?" I said.

"So, although the lines forming the fourth dimension would be perpendicular to every point in the third dimension, they wouldn't be parallel—to *us*. But if enough of them in one area happened to be parallel in *both* dimensions—it might form a connecting corridor."

"You mean . . . ?"

"That's the crazy part," he said. "Of all the places in the world—under the couch—there's an area of points that are sections of parallel lines—parallel in both dimensions. They make a corridor into the next space."

"Or a hole," I said.

Bill looked disgusted.

"Hell of a lot of good my reasoning did," he said. "It took a *dog* to get her out."

"What about the sound?"

"You're asking me?" he said.

That's about it. Oh, naturally, Bill told his friends at CalTech, and the apartment was overrun with research physicists for a month. But they didn't find anything. They said the thing was gone. Some said worse things.

But, just the same, when we got back from my mother's house where we stayed during the scientific siege—we moved the couch across the room and stuck the television where the couch was.

So some night we may look up and hear Arthur Godfrey chuckling from another dimension. Maybe he belongs there.

Four O'Clock

Price Day

TELEPLAY BY ROD SERLING

AIRED APRIL 6, 1962

STARRING THEODORE BIKEL

THE HANDS OF THE ALARM CLOCK ON THE TABLE IN front of Mr. Crangle stood at 3:47, on a summer afternoon.

"You're wrong about that, you know," he said, not taking his eyes from the face of the clock. "You're quite wrong, Pet, as I have explained to you often enough before. The moral angle presents no difficulties at all."

The parrot, in the cage hanging above him, cocked her head and looked down with a hard, cold, reptilian eye, an ancient eye, an eye older by age upon age than the human race.

She said, "Nut."

Mr. Crangle, his eye still on the clock, took a peanut from a cracker bowl at his elbow and held it above his head, to the bars of the cage. Pet clutched it in a leathery claw. The spring-steel muscles opened the horny beak. She clinched the peanut and crushed it, the sound mingling in the furnished room with the big-city sounds coming through the open window—cars honking, feet on the sidewalk, children calling to each other, a plane overhead like a contented, industrious bee.

"It is quite true," Mr. Crangle said at 3:49, "that only someone above all personal emotions, only someone who can look at the whole thing as if from the outside, can be trusted morally to make such a decision." As the big hand reached 3:50, he felt a sense of power surge deeply through him. "Think, Pet. In ten minutes. In ten little minutes, when I say the word, all the evil people all over the world will become half their present size, so they can be known. All the uncaught murderers and the tyrants and the proud and sinful, all the bullies and the wrongdoers and the black-mailers and nicotine fiends and transgressors." His eyes blazed with omnipotence. "All of them, every one."

Pet said, "Nut."

Mr. Crangle gave her one.

"I know you don't agree fully with the half-size solution," he said, "but I do believe it to be the best one, all things considered."

He had studied over the alternatives day and night since that morning three weeks ago when, as he sat on a bench in the park, looking at the pictures in the clouds across the lake, it came to him that he had the power to do this thing, that upon him at that moment had been bestowed the gift of putting a mark on all the bad people on earth, so that they should be known.

The realization surprised him not at all. Once before, such a thing had happened. He had once held the power to stop wars. That was when the radio was telling about the big air raids on the cities. In that case the particular thing he could do was to take the stiffness out of airplane propellors, so that some morning when the crews, bundled like children against cold, went out to get in their planes, they would find the props hanging limp, like empty banana skins.

That time, he had delayed too long, waiting for just the right time and just the right plan, and they had outwitted him, unfairly. They had invented the jet, to which his power did not apply.

Then, too, there had been the thing about wheels. The

thing about wheels came to him in a coffee place as he was looking at a newspaper photograph of a bad traffic accident, three killed. The power, that was, to change all the wheels in the world from round to square, or even to triangular if he wished, so they would stub in the asphalt and stop. But he wasn't allowed to keep that power. Before he could work out a plan and a time, he had felt it taken from him.

The power over bad people had stayed. It had even grown stronger, if power like that could grow stronger. And this time he had hurried, though of course there were certain problems to be thought through.

First, who was to decide what people were evil? That wasn't too hard, really, in spite of Pet's doubts. An evil person was a person who would seem evil to a man who held within himself the knowledge of good and evil, if that man could know all the person's innermost secrets. An evil person was a person who would seem evil to an all-knowing Mr. Crangle.

Then, how to do it, the method? Mark them on the forehead, or turn them all one color, say purple? But then they would simply be able to recognize each other the more readily, and to band together in their wickedness.

When at last he hit upon the idea of a change in size, what came to him first was the thought of doubling the height and bulk of all the bad people. That would make them inefficient. They couldn't handle delicate scientific instruments or typewriters or adding machines or telephone dials. In time they would expire from bigness, like the dinosaurs in the article in the Sunday paper. But they might first run wild, with their great weight and strength, and hurt other people. Mr. Crangle wouldn't have liked that. He hated violence.

Half-size people, it was true, might be able to manipulate some of the machines. They could also be dangerous. But it would take them a long time to develop tools and weapons to their scale, and think how ridiculous they would be, meanwhile, with their clothes twice too big and their hats falling down over their ears.

At 3:54, Mr. Crangle smiled at the thought of how ridiculous they would be.

"Nut," Pet said.

He reached up and gave her one, his eyes still on the clock.

"I think," he said, "that the most interesting place to be would be at a murder trial where nobody knew whether the accused was guilty or not. And then at four o'clock, if he was guilty—"

Mr. Crangle's breath was coming faster. The clock hands stood at 3:56.

"Or watching the drunkards in a saloon," he said.

"Nut," Pet said, and he gave her one.

"Oh," he said, "there are so many places, so many places to be. But I'd rather be with you when it happens, Pet. Right here alone with you."

He sat tense in his chair. He could actually see the big hand of the clock move, in the tiniest little jerkings, leaving a hairline of white between itself and the black 3:57 dot, and moving to the 3:58 dot, narrowing the space, until it touched that dot, and then stood directly on it, and then moved past toward the 3:59 dot.

"At first," Mr. Crangle said, "the newspapers won't believe it. Even though some of it will happen right in the newspaper offices, they won't believe it. At first they won't. And then when they begin to understand that it has happened to a lot of people everybody knows are evil, then they'll see the design."

The clock said 3:59.

"A great story," Mr. Crangle said. "A great newspaper story. And nobody will know who did it, Pet, nobody but you and me."

The point of the big hand crept halfway past the 3:59 dot. Mr. Crangle's heart beat hard. His eyes were wide, his lips parted. He whispered, "Nobody will know."

The tip of the big hand touched the dot at the top of the clock face. The alarm went off. Mr. Crangle felt a great surge of strength, like water bursting a dam, and a great shock, as of a bolt of lightning. He closed his eyes.

"Now!" he said softly, and slumped exhausted.

By going to the window and looking down at the crowd in the street, he could have seen whether it had worked or not. He did not go to the window. He did not need to. He knew.

The alarm bell ran down.

Pet cocked her head and looked at him with an eye like polished stone.

"Nut," she said.

His hand, as he stretched it up, failed by a full foot and a half to reach the cage.

I Sing the Body Electric!

Ray Bradbury

TELEPLAY BY RAY BRADBURY

AIRED MAY 18, 1962

STARRING JOSEPHINE HUTCHINSON AND
VERONICA CARTWRIGHT

GRANDMA!

I remember her birth.

Wait, you say, *no* man remembers his own grandma's birth.

But, yes, *we* remember the day that she was born.

For we, her grandchildren, slapped her to life. Timothy, Agatha, and I, Tom, raised up our hands and brought them down in a huge crack! We shook together the bits and pieces, parts and samples, textures and tastes, humors and distillations that would move her compass needle north to cool us, south to warm and comfort us, east and west to travel round the endless world, glide her eyes to know us, mouth to sing us asleep by night, hands to touch us awake at dawn.

Grandma, O dear and wondrous electric dream . . .

When storm lightnings rove the sky making circuitries amidst the clouds, her name flashes on my inner lid. Sometimes still I hear her ticking, humming above our beds in the gentle dark. She passes like a clock-ghost in the long halls of memory, like a hive of intellectual bees swarming after the

Spirit of Summers Lost. Sometimes still I feel the smile I learned from her, printed on my cheek at three in the deep morn . . .

All right, all right! you cry, what was it like the day your damned and wondrous-dreadful-loving Grandma was born?

It was the week the world ended . . .

Our mother was dead.

One late afternoon a black car left Father and the three of us stranded on our own front drive staring at the grass, thinking:

That's not our grass. There are the croquet mallets, balls, hoops, yes, just as they fell and lay three days ago when Dad stumbled out on the lawn, weeping with the news. There are the roller skates that belonged to a boy, me, who will never be that young again. And yes, there the tire-swing on the old oak, but Agatha afraid to swing. It would surely break. It would fall.

And the house? Oh, God . . .

We peered through the front door, afraid of the echoes we might find confused in the halls; the sort of clamor that happens when all the furniture is taken out and there is nothing to soften the river of talk that flows in any house at all hours. And now the soft, the warm, the main piece of lovely furniture was gone forever.

The door drifted wide.

Silence came out. Somewhere a cellar door stood wide and a raw wind blew damp earth from under the house.

But, I thought, we don't *have* a cellar!

"Well," said Father.

We did not move.

Aunt Clara drove up the path in her big canary-colored limousine.

We jumped through the door. We ran to our rooms.

We heard them shout and then speak and then shout and then speak: Let the children live with me! Aunt Clara said. They'd rather kill themselves! Father said.

A door slammed. Aunt Clara was gone.

We almost danced. Then we remembered what had happened and went downstairs.

Father sat alone talking to himself or to a remnant ghost of Mother left from the days before her illness, but jarred loose now by the slamming of the door. He murmured to his hands, his empty palms:

"The children need someone. I love them but, let's face it, I must work to feed us all. You love them, Ann, but you're gone. And Clara? Impossible. She loves but smothers. And as for maids, nurses—?"

Here Father sighed and we sighed with him, remembering.

The luck we had had with maids or live-in teachers or sitters was beyond intolerable. Hardly a one who wasn't a crosscut saw grabbing against the grain. Handaxes and hurricanes best described them. Or, conversely, they were all fallen trifle, damp soufflé. We children were unseen furniture to be sat upon or dusted or sent for reupholstering come spring and fall, with a yearly cleansing at the beach.

"What we need," said Father, "is a . . ."

We all leaned to his whisper.

". . . grandmother."

"But," said Timothy, with the logic of nine years, "all our grandmothers are dead."

"Yes in one way, no in another."

What a fine mysterious thing for Dad to say.

"Here," he said at last.

He handed us a multifold, multicolored pamphlet. We had seen it in his hands, off and on, for many weeks, and very often during the last few days. Now, with one blink of our eyes, as we passed the paper from hand to hand, we knew why Aunt Clara, insulted, outraged, had stormed from the house.

Timothy was the first to read aloud from what he saw on the first page:

"I Sing the Body Electric!"

He glanced up at Father, squinting. "What the heck does that mean?"

"Read on."

Agatha and I glanced guiltily about the room, afraid Mother might suddenly come in to find us with this blasphemy, but then nodded to Timothy, who read:

" 'Fanto—' "

"Fantoccini," Father prompted.

" 'Fantoccini Ltd. *We Shadow Forth* . . . the answer to all your most grievous problems. One Model Only, upon which a thousand times a thousand variations can be added, subtracted, subdivided, indivisible, with Liberty and Justice for all.' "

"Where does it say *that?*" we all cried.

"It doesn't." Timothy smiled for the first time in days. "I just had to put that in. Wait." He read on: " 'for you who have worried over inattentive sitters, nurses who cannot be trusted with marked liquor bottles, and well-meaning Uncles and Aunts—' "

"Well-meaning, *but!*" said Agatha, and I gave an echo.

" '—we have perfected the first humanoid-genre minicircuited, rechargeable AC-DC Mark V Electrical Grandmother . . .' "

"Grandmother!?"

The paper slipped away to the floor. "Dad . . . ?"

"Don't look at me that way," said Father. "I'm half-mad with grief, and half-mad thinking of tomorrow and the day after that. Someone pick up the paper. Finish it."

"I will," I said, and did:

" 'The Toy that is more than a Toy, the Fantoccini Electrical Grandmother is built with loving precision to give the incredible precision of love to your children. The child at ease with the realities of the world and the even greater realities of the imagination, is her aim.

" 'She is computerized to tutor in twelve languages simultaneously, capable of switching tongues in a thousandth of a second without pause, and has a complete knowledge of the religious, artistic, and sociopolitical histories of the world seeded in her master hive—' "

"How great!" said Timothy. "It makes it sound as if we were to keep bees! *Educated* bees!"

"Shut up!" said Agatha.

" 'Above all,' " I read, " 'this human being, for human she seems, this embodiment in electro-intelligent facsimile of the humanities, will listen, know, tell, react and love your children insofar as such great Objects, such fantastic Toys, can be said to Love, or can be imagined to Care. This Miraculous Companion, excited to the challenge of large world and small, inner Sea or Outer Universe, will transmit by touch and tell, said Miracles to your Needy.' "

"Our Needy," murmured Agatha.

Why, we all thought, sadly, that's us, oh, yes, that's *us*.

I finished:

" 'We do not sell our Creation to able-bodied families where parents are available to raise, effect, shape, change, love their own children. Nothing can replace the parent in the home. However there are families where death or ill health or disablement undermines the welfare of the children. Orphanages seem not the answer. Nurses tend to be selfish, neglectful, or suffering from dire nervous afflictions.

" 'With the utmost humility then, and recognizing the need to rebuild, rethink, and regrow our conceptualizations from month to month, year to year, we offer the nearest thing to the Ideal Teacher-Friend-Companion–Blood Relation. A trial period can be arranged for—' "

"Stop," said Father. "Don't go on. Even *I* can't stand it."

"Why?" said Timothy. "I was just getting interested."

I folded the pamphlet up. "Do they *really* have these things?"

"Let's not talk any more about it," said Father, his hand over his eyes. "It was a mad thought—"

"Not so mad," I said, glancing at Tim. "I mean, heck, even if they tried, whatever they built, couldn't be worse than Aunt Clara, huh?"

And then we all roared. We hadn't laughed in months. And now my simple words made everyone hoot and howl and explode. I opened my mouth and yelled happily, too.

When we stopped laughing, we looked at the pamphlet and I said, "Well?"

"I—" Agatha scowled, not ready.

"We do need something, bad, right now," said Timothy.

"I have an open mind," I said, in my best pontifical style.

"There's only one thing," said Agatha. "We can try it. Sure.

"But—tell me this—when do we cut out all this talk and when does our *real* mother come home to stay?"

There was a single gasp from the family as if, with one shot, she had struck us all in the heart.

I don't think any of us stopped crying the rest of that night.

It was a clear bright day. The helicopter tossed us lightly up and over and down through the skyscrapers and let us out, almost for a trot and caper, on top of the building where the large letters could be read from the sky:

FANTOCCINI.

"What are *Fantoccini?*" said Agatha.

"It's an Italian word for shadow puppets, I think, or dream people," said Father.

"But *shadow forth*, what does that mean?"

"WE TRY TO GUESS YOUR DREAM," I said.

"Bravo," said Father. "A-Plus."

I beamed.

The helicopter flapped a lot of loud shadows over us and went away.

We sank down in an elevator as our stomachs sank up. We stepped out onto a moving carpet that streamed away on a blue river of wool toward a desk over which various signs hung:

THE CLOCK SHOP
Fantoccini Our Specialty.
Rabbits on walls, no problem.

"Rabbits on walls?"

I held up my fingers in profile as if I held them before a candle flame, and wiggled the "ears."

"Here's a rabbit, here's a wolf, here's a crocodile."

"Of course," said Agatha.

And we were at the desk. Quiet music drifted about us. Somewhere behind the walls, there was a waterfall of machinery flowing softly. As we arrived at the desk, the lighting changed to make us look warmer, happier, though we were still cold.

All about us in niches and cases, and hung from ceilings on wires and strings were puppets and marionettes, and Balinese kite-bamboo-translucent dolls which, held to the moonlight, might acrobat your most secret nightmares or dreams. In passing, the breeze set up by our bodies stirred the various hung souls on their gibbets. It was like an immense lynching on a holiday at some English crossroads four hundred years before.

You see? I know my history.

Agatha blinked about with disbelief and then some touch of awe and finally disgust.

"Well, if that's what they are, let's go."

"Tush," said Father.

"Well," she protested, "you gave me one of those dumb things with strings two years ago and the strings were in a zillion knots by dinnertime. I threw the whole thing out the window."

"Patience," said Father.

"We shall see what we can do to eliminate the strings."

The man behind the desk had spoken.

We all turned to give him our regard.

Rather like a funeral-parlor man, he had the cleverness not to smile. Children are put off by older people who smile too much. They smell a catch, right off.

Unsmiling, but not gloomy or pontifical, the man said, "Guido Fantoccini, at your service. Here's how we do it, Miss Agatha Simmons, aged eleven."

Now there was a really fine touch.

He knew that Agatha was only ten. Add a year to that, and you're halfway home. Agatha grew an inch. The man went on:

"There."

And he placed a golden key in Agatha's hand.

"To wind them up instead of strings?"

"To wind them up." The man nodded.

"Pshaw!" said Agatha.

Which was her polite form of "rabbit pellets."

"God's truth. Here is the key to your Do-it-Yourself, Select Only the Best, Electrical Grandmother. Every morning you wind her up. Every night you let her run down. You're in charge. You are guardian of the Key."

He pressed the object in her palm where she looked at it suspiciously.

I watched him. He gave me a side wink which said, well, no . . . but aren't keys fun?

I winked back before she lifted her head.

"Where does this fit?"

"You'll see when the time comes. In the middle of her stomach, perhaps, or up her left nostril or in her right ear."

That was good for a smile as the man arose.

"This way, please. Step light. Onto the moving stream. Walk on the water, please. Yes. There."

He helped to float us. We stepped from rug that was forever frozen onto rug that whispered by.

It was a most agreeable river which floated us along on a green spread of carpeting that rolled forever through halls and into wonderfully secret dim caverns where voices echoed back our own breathing or sang like Oracles to our questions.

"Listen," said the salesman, "the voices of all kinds of women. Weigh and find just the right one . . . !"

And listen we did, to all the high, low, soft, loud, in-between, half-scolding, half-affectionate voices saved over from times before we were born.

And behind us, Agatha tread backward, always fighting the river, never catching up, never with us, holding off.

"Speak," said the salesman. "Yell."

And speak and yell we did.

"Hello. You there! This is Timothy, hi!"

"What shall I say!" I shouted. "Help!"

Agatha walked backward, mouth tight.

Father took her hand. She cried out.

"Let go! No, no! I won't have my voice used! I won't!"

"Excellent." The salesman touched three dials on a small machine he held in his hand.

On the side of the small machine we saw three oscillograph patterns mix, blend, and repeat our cries.

The salesman touched another dial and we heard our voices fly off amidst the Delphic caves to hang upside down, to cluster, to beat words all about, to shriek, and the salesman itched another knob to add, perhaps, a touch of this or a pinch of that, a breath of mother's voice, all unbeknownst, or a splice of father's outrage at the morning's paper or his peaceable one-drink voice at dusk. Whatever it was the salesman did, whispers danced all about us like frantic vinegar gnats, fizzed by lightning, settling round until at last a final switch was pushed and a voice spoke free of a far electronic deep:

"Nefertiti," it said.

Timothy froze. I froze. Agatha stopped treading water.

"Nefertiti?" asked Tim.

"What does that mean?" demanded Agatha.

"I know."

The salesman nodded me to tell.

"Nefertiti," I whispered, "is Egyptian for The Beautiful One Is Here."

"The Beautiful One Is Here," repeated Timothy.

"Nefer," said Agatha, "titi."

And we all turned to stare into that soft twilight, that deep far place from which the good warm soft voice came.

And she was indeed there.

And, by her voice, she was beautiful . . .

That was it.

That was, at least, the most of it.

The voice seemed more important than all the rest.

Not that we didn't argue about weights and measures:

She should not be bony to cut us to the quick, nor so fat we might sink out of sight when she squeezed us.

Her hand pressed to ours, or brushing our brow in the middle of sick-fever nights, must not be marble-cold, dreadful, or oven-hot, oppressive, but somewhere between. The nice temperature of a baby-chick held in the hand after a long night's sleep and just plucked from beneath a contemplative hen; that, that was it.

Oh, we were great ones for detail. We fought and argued and cried, and Timothy won on the color of her eyes, for reasons to be known later.

Grandmother's hair? Agatha, with girl's ideas, though reluctantly given, she was in charge of that. We let her choose from a thousand harp strands hung in filamentary tapestries like varieties of rain we ran amongst. Agatha did not run happily, but seeing we boys would mess things in tangles, she told us to move aside.

And so the bargain shopping through the dime-store inventories and the Tiffany extensions of the Ben Franklin Electric Storm Machine and Fantoccini Pantomime Company was done.

And the always flowing river ran its tide to an end and deposited us all on a far shore in the late day . . .

It was very clever of the Fantoccini people, after that.

How?

They made us wait.

They knew we were not won over. Not completely, no, nor half completely.

Especially Agatha, who turned her face to her wall and saw sorrow there and put her hand out again and again to touch it. We found her fingernail marks on the wallpaper each morning, in strange little silhouettes, half beauty, half nightmare. Some could be erased with a breath, like ice flowers on a winter pane. Some could not be rubbed out with a washcloth, no matter how hard you tried.

And meanwhile, they made us wait.

So we fretted out June.

So we sat around July.

So we groused through August and then on August 29, ''I have this feeling,'' said Timothy, and we all went out after breakfast to sit on the lawn.

Perhaps we had smelled something on Father's conversation the previous night, or caught some special furtive glance at the sky or the freeway flapped briefly and then lost in his gaze. Or perhaps it was merely the way the wind blew the ghost curtains out over our beds, making pale messages all night.

For suddenly there we were in the middle of the grass, Timothy and I, with Agatha, pretending no curiosity, up on the porch, hidden behind the potted geraniums.

We gave her no notice. We knew that if we acknowledged her presence, she would flee, so we sat and watched the sky where nothing moved but birds and highflown jets, and watched the freeway where a thousand cars might suddenly deliver forth our Special Gift . . . but . . . nothing.

At noon we chewed grass and lay low . . .

At one o'clock, Timothy blinked his eyes.

And then, with incredible precision, it happened.

It was as if the Fantoccini people knew our surface tension.

All children are water-striders. We skate along the top skin of the pond each day, always threatening to break through, sink, vanish beyond recall, into ourselves.

Well, as if knowing our long wait must absolutely end within one minute! this *second!* no more, God, forget it!

At that instant, I repeat, the clouds above our house opened wide and let forth a helicopter like Apollo driving his chariot across mythological skies.

And the Apollo machine swam down on its own summer breeze, wafting hot winds to cool, reweaving our hair, smartening our eyebrows, applauding our pant legs against our shins, making a flag of Agatha's hair on the porch and thus settled like a vast frenzied hibiscus on our lawn, the helicopter slid wide a bottom drawer and deposited upon the grass a parcel of largish size, no sooner having laid same then the vehicle, with not so much as a god bless or farewell, sank straight up, disturbed the calm air with a mad ten thousand flourishes and then, like a skyborne dervish, tilted and fell off to be mad some other place.

Timothy and I stood riven for a long moment looking at the packing case, and then we saw the crowbar taped to the top of the raw pine lid and seized it and began to pry and creak and squeal the boards off, one by one, and as we did this I saw Agatha sneak up to watch and I thought, thank you, God, thank you that Agatha never saw a coffin, when Mother went away, no box, no cemetery, no earth, just words in a big church, no box, no box like *this* . . . !

The last pine plank fell away.

Timothy and I gasped. Agatha, between us now, gasped, too.

For inside the immense raw pine package was the most beautiful idea anyone ever dreamt and built.

Inside was the perfect gift for any child from seven to seventy-seven.

We stopped up our breaths. We let them out in cries of delight and adoration.

Inside the opened box was . . .

A mummy.

Or, first anyway, a mummy case, a sarcophagus!

"Oh, no!" Happy tears filled Timothy's eyes.

"It can't be!" said Agatha.

"It is, it is!"

"Our very own?"

"Ours!"

"It must be a mistake!"

"Sure, they'll want it back!"

"They can't *have* it!"

"Lord, Lord, is that real gold!? Real hieroglyphs! Run your fingers over them!"

"Let *me!*"

"Just like in the museums! Museums!"

We all gabbled at once. I think some tears fell from my own eyes to rain upon the case.

"Oh, they'll make the colors run!"

Agatha wiped the rain away.

And the golden mask face of the woman carved on the sarcophagus lid looked back at us with just the merest smile which hinted at our own joy, which accepted the overwhelming upsurge of a love we thought had drowned forever but now surfaced into the sun.

Not only did she have a sun-metal face stamped and beaten out of purest gold, with delicate nostrils and a mouth that was both firm and gentle, but her eyes, fixed into their sockets, were cerulean or amethystine or lapis lazuli, or all three, minted and fused together, and her body was covered over with lions and eyes and ravens, and her hands were crossed upon her carved bosom and in one gold mitten she clenched a thonged whip for obedience, and in the other a fantastic ranuncula, which makes for obedience out of love, so the whip lies unused . . .

And as our eyes ran down her hieroglyphs it came to all three of us at the same instant:

"Why, those signs!" "Yes, the hen tracks!" "The birds, the snakes!"

They didn't speak tales of the Past.

They were hieroglyphs of the Future.

This was the first queen mummy delivered forth in all time whose papyrus inkings etched out the next month, the next season, the next year, the next *lifetime!*

She did not mourn for time spent.

No. She celebrated the bright coinage yet to come, banked, waiting, ready to be drawn upon and used.

We sank to our knees to worship that possible time.

First one hand, then another, probed out to niggle, twitch, touch, itch over the signs.

"There's me, yes, look! Me, in sixth grade!" said Agatha, now in the fifth. "See the girl with my-colored hair and wearing my gingerbread suit?"

"There's me in the twelfth year of high school!" said Timothy, so very young now but building taller stilts every week and stalking around the yard.

"There's me," I said, quietly, warm, "in college. The guy wearing glasses who runs a little to fat. Sure. Heck." I snorted. "That's me."

The sarcophagus spelled winters ahead, springs to squander, autumns to spend with all the golden and rusty and copper leaves like coins, and over all, her bright sun symbol, daughter-of-Ra eternal face, forever above our horizon, forever an illumination to tilt our shadows to better ends.

"Hey!" we all said at once, having read and reread our Fortune-Told scribblings, seeing our lifelines and lovelines, inadmissible, serpentined over, around, and down. "Hey!"

And in one séance table-lifting feat, not telling each other what to do, just doing it, we pried up the bright sarcophagus lid, which had no hinges but lifted out like cup from cup, and put the lid aside.

And within the sarcophagus, of course, was the true mummy!

And she was like the image carved on the lid, but more so, more beautiful, more touching because human shaped, and shrouded all in new fresh bandages of linen, round and round, instead of old and dusty cerements.

And upon her hidden face was an identical golden mask, younger than the first, but somehow, strangely wiser than the first.

And the linens that tethered her limbs had symbols on them of three sorts, one a girl of ten, one a boy of nine, one a boy of thirteen.

A series of bandages for each of us!

We gave each other a startled glance and a sudden bark of laughter.

Nobody said the bad joke, but all thought:

She's all wrapped up in us!

And we didn't care. We loved the joke. We loved whoever had thought to make us part of the ceremony we now went through as each of us seized and began to unwind each of his or her particular serpentines of delicious stuffs!

The lawn was soon a mountain of linen.

The woman beneath the covering lay there, waiting.

"Oh, no," cried Agatha. "She's dead, too!"

She ran. I stopped her. "Idiot. She's not dead *or* alive. Where's your key?"

"Key?"

"Dummy," said Tim, "the key the man gave you to wind her up!"

Her hand had already spidered along her blouse to where the symbol of some possible new religion hung. She had strung it there, against her own skeptic's muttering, and now she held it in her sweaty palm.

"Go on," said Timothy. "Put it in!"

"But *where?*"

"Oh for God's sake! As the man said, in her right armpit or left ear. Gimme!"

And he grabbed the key and impulsively moaning with impatience and not able to find the proper insertion slot, prowled over the prone figure's head and bosom and at last, on pure instinct, perhaps for a lark, perhaps just giving up the whole damned mess, thrust the key through a final shroud of bandage at the navel.

On the instant: *spunnng!*

The Electrical Grandmother's eyes flicked wide!

Something began to hum and whir. It was as if Tim had stirred up a hive of hornets with an ornery stick.

"Oh," gasped Agatha, seeing he had taken the game away, "let *me!*"

She wrenched the key.

Grandma's nostrils *flared!* She might snort up steam, snuff out fire!

"Me!" I cried, and grabbed the key and gave it a huge . . . *twist!*

The beautiful woman's mouth popped wide.

"Me!"

"Me!"

"Me!"

Grandma suddenly sat up.

We leapt back.

We knew we had, in a way, slapped her alive.

She was born, she was *born!*

Her head swiveled all about. She gaped. She mouthed. And the first thing she said was:

Laughter.

Where one moment we had backed off, now the mad sound drew us near to peer as in a pit where crazy folk are kept with snakes to make them well.

It was a good laugh, full and rich and hearty, and it did not mock, it accepted. It said the world was a wild place, strange, unbelievable, absurd if you wished, but all in all, quite a place. She would not dream to find another. She would not ask to go back to sleep.

She was awake now. We had awakened her. With a glad shout, she would go with it all.

And go she did, out of her sarcophagus, out of her winding sheet, stepping forth, brushing off, looking around as for a mirror. She found it.

The reflections in our eyes.

She was more pleased than disconcerted with what she found there. Her laughter faded to an amused smile.

For Agatha, at the instant of birth, had leapt to hide on the porch.

The Electrical Person pretended not to notice.

She turned slowly on the green lawn near the shady street, gazing all about with new eyes, her nostrils moving as if she breathed the actual air and this the first morn of the lovely

Garden and she with no intention of spoiling the game by biting the apple . . .

Her gaze fixed upon my brother.

"You must be—?"

"Timothy. Tim," he offered.

"And you must be—?"

"Tom," I said.

How clever again of the Fantoccini Company. *They* knew. *She* knew. But they had taught her to pretend not to know. That way we could feel great, we were the teachers, telling her what she already knew! How sly, how wise.

"And isn't there another boy?" said the woman.

"Girl!" a disgusted voice cried from somewhere on the porch.

"Whose name is Alicia—?"

"Agatha!" The far voice, started in humiliation, ended in proper anger.

"Algernon, of course."

"Agatha!" Our sister popped up, popped back to hide a flushed face.

"Agatha." The woman touched the word with proper affection. "Well, Agatha, Timothy, Thomas, let me *look* at you."

"No," said I, said Tim. "Let us look at *you*. Hey . . ."

Our voices slid back in our throats.

We drew near her.

We walked in great slow circles round about, skirting the edges of her territory. And her territory extended as far as we could hear the hum of the warm summer hive. For that is exactly what she sounded like. That was her characteristic tune. She made a sound like a season all to herself, a morning early in June when the world wakes to find everything absolutely perfect, fine, delicately attuned, all in balance, nothing disproportioned. Even before you opened your eyes you knew it would be one of those days. Tell the sky what color it must be, and it was indeed. Tell the sun how to crochet its way, pick and choose among leaves to lay out carpet-ings of bright and dark on the fresh lawn, and pick and lay it did. The bees have been up earliest of all, they have already come and gone, and come and gone again to the meadow fields and returned all golden fuzz on the air, all pollen-decorated, epaulettes at the full, nectar-dripping. Don't you hear them pass? hover? dance their language? telling where all the sweet gums are, the syrups that make bears frolic and lumber in bulked ecstasies, that make boys squirm with unpronounced juices, that make girls leap out of beds to catch from the corners of their eyes their dolphin selves na-ked aflash on the warm air poised forever in one eternal glass wave.

So it seemed with our electrical friend here on the new lawn in the middle of a special day.

And she a stuff to which we were drawn, lured, spelled, doing our dance, remembering what could not be remembered, needful, aware of her attentions.

Timothy and I, Tom, that is.

Agatha remained on the porch.

But her head flowered above the rail, her eyes followed all that was done and said.

And what was said and done was Tim at last exhaling:

"Hey . . . your *eyes* . . ."

Her eyes. Her splendid eyes.

Even more splendid than the lapis lazuli on the sarcopha-gus lid and on the mask that had covered her bandaged face. These most beautiful eyes in the world looked out upon us calmly, shining.

"Your eyes," gasped Tim, "are the *exact* same color, are like—"

"Like what?"

"My favorite aggies . . ."

"What could be better than that?" she said.

And the answer was, nothing.

Her eyes slid along on the bright air to brush my ears, my nose, my chin. "And you, Master Tom?"

"Me?"

"How shall we be friends? We must, you know, if we're going to knock elbows about the house the next year . . ."

"I . . ." I said, and stopped.

"You," said Grandma, "are a dog mad to bark but with taffy in his teeth. Have you ever given a dog taffy? It's so sad and funny, both. You laugh but hate yourself for laughing. You cry and run to help, and laugh again when his first new bark comes out."

I barked a small laugh remembering a dog, a day, and some taffy.

Grandma turned, and there was my old kite strewn on the lawn. She recognized its problem.

"The string's broken. No. The ball of string's *lost*. You can't fly a kite that way. Here."

She bent. We didn't know what might happen. How could a robot grandma fly a kite for us? She raised up, the kite in her hands.

"Fly," she said, as to a bird.

And the kite flew.

That is to say, with a grand flourish, she let it up on the wind.

And she and the kite were one.

For from the tip of her index finger there sprang a thin bright strand of spider web, all half-invisible gossamer fishline which, fixed to the kite, let it soar a hundred, no, three hundred, no, a thousand feet high on the summer swoons.

Timothy shouted. Agatha, torn between coming and going, let out a cry from the porch. And I, in all my maturity of thirteen years, though I tried not to look impressed, grew taller, taller, and felt a similar cry burst out of my lungs, and burst it did. I gabbled and yelled lots of things about how I wished *I* had a finger from which, on a bobbin, I might thread the sky, the clouds, a wild kite all in one.

"If you think *that* is high," said the Electric Creature, "watch *this*!"

With a hiss, a whistle, a hum, the fishline sung out. The kite sank up another thousand feet. And again another thousand, until at last it was a speck of red confetti dancing on the very winds that took jets around the world or changed the weather in the next existence . . .

"It can't be!" I cried.

"It *is*." She calmly watched her finger unravel its massive stuffs. "I make it as I need it. Liquid inside, like a spider. Hardens when it hits the air, instant thread . . ."

And when the kite was no more than a specule, a vanishing mote on the peripheral vision of the gods, to quote from older wisemen, why then Grandma, without turning, without looking, without letting her gaze offend by touching, said:

"And, Abigail—?"

"Agatha!" was the sharp response.

O wise woman, to overcome with swift small angers.

"Agatha," said Grandma, not too tenderly, not too lightly, somewhere poised between, "and how shall *we* make do?"

She broke the thread and wrapped it about my fist three times so I was tethered to heaven by the longest, I repeat, longest kite string in the entire history of the world! Wait till I show my friends! I thought. Green! Sour apple green is the color they'll turn!

"Agatha?"

"No way!" said Agatha.

"No way," said an echo.

"There must be some—"

"We'll never be friends!" said Agatha.

"Never be friends," said the echo.

Timothy and I jerked. Where was the echo coming from? Even Agatha, surprised, showed her eyebrows above the porch rail.

Then we looked and saw.

Grandma was cupping her hands like a seashell and from within that shell the echo sounded.

"Never . . . friends . . ."

And again faintly dying, "Friends . . ."

We all bent to hear.

That is we two boys bent to hear.

"No!" cried Agatha.

And ran in the house and slammed the doors.

"Friends," said the echo from the seashell hands. "No."

And far away, on the shore of some inner sea, we heard a small door shut.

And that was the first day.

And there was a second day, of course, and a third and a fourth, with Grandma wheeling in a great circle, and we her planets turning about the central light, with Agatha slowly, slowly coming in to join, to walk if not run with us, to listen if not hear, to watch if not see, to itch if not touch.

But at least by the end of the first ten days, Agatha no longer fled, but stood in nearby doors, or sat in distant chairs under trees, or if we went out for hikes, followed ten paces behind.

And Grandma? She merely waited. She never tried to urge or force. She went about her cooking and baking apricot pies and left foods carelessly here and there about the house on mousetrap plates for wiggle-nosed girls to sniff and snitch. An hour later, the plates were empty, the buns or cakes gone and without thank-yous, there was Agatha sliding down the banister, a mustache of crumbs on her lip.

As for Tim and me, we were always being called up hills by our Electric Grandma, and reaching the top were called down the other side.

And the most peculiar and beautiful and strange and lovely thing was the way she seemed to give complete attention to all of us.

She listened, she really listened to all we said, she knew and remembered every syllable, word, sentence, punctuation, thought, and rambunctious idea. We knew that all our days were stored in her, and that any time we felt we might want to know what we said at X hour at X second on X afternoon, we just named that X and with amiable promptitude, in the form of an aria if we wished, sung with humor, she would deliver forth X incident.

Sometimes we were prompted to test her. In the midst of babbling one day with high fevers about nothing, I stopped. I fixed Grandma with my eye and demanded:

"What did I just say?"

"Oh, er—"

"Come on, spit it out!"

"I think—" she rummaged her purse. "I have it here." From the deeps of her purse she drew forth and handed me:

"Boy! A Chinese fortune cookie!"

"Fresh baked, still warm, open it."

It was almost too hot to touch. I broke the cookie shell and pressed the warm curl of paper out to read:

"—bicycle Champ of the whole West! What did I just say? Come on, spit it out!"

My jaw dropped.

"How did you *do* that?"

"We have our little secrets. The only Chinese fortune cookie that predicts the Immediate Past. Have another?"

I cracked the second shell and read:

" 'How did you *do* that?' "

I popped the messages and the piping hot shells into my mouth and chewed as we walked.

"Well?"

"You're a great cook," I said.

And, laughing, we began to run.

And that was another great thing.

She could *keep up.*

Never beat, never win a race, but pump right along in good style, which a boy doesn't mind. A girl ahead of him or beside him is too much to bear. But a girl one or two paces back is a respectful thing, and allowed.

So Grandma and I had some great runs, me in the lead, and both talking a mile a minute.

But now I must tell you the best part of Grandma.

I might not have known at all if Timothy hadn't taken

some pictures, and if I hadn't taken some also, and then compared.

When I saw the photographs developed out of our instant Brownies, I sent Agatha, against her wishes, to photograph Grandma a third time, unawares.

Then I took the three sets of pictures off alone, to keep counsel with myself. I never told Timothy and Agatha what I found. I didn't want to spoil it.

But, as I laid the pictures out in my room, here is what I thought and said:

"Grandma, in each picture, looks *different!*"

"Different?" I asked myself.

"Sure. Wait. Just a sec—"

I rearranged the photos.

"Here's one of Grandma near Agatha. And, in it, Grandma looks like . . . Agatha!

"And in this one, posed with Timothy, she looks like Timothy!

"And this last one, Holy Goll! Jogging along with me, she looks like ugly *me!*"

I sat down, stunned. The pictures fell to the floor.

I hunched over, scrabbling them, rearranging, turning upside down and sidewise. Yes. Holy Goll again, yes!

O that clever Grandmother.

O those Fantoccini people-making people.

Clever beyond clever, human beyond human, warm beyond warm, love beyond love . . .

And wordless, I rose and went downstairs and found Agatha and Grandma in the same room, doing algebra lessons in an almost peaceful communion. At least there was not outright war. Grandma was still waiting for Agatha to come round. And no one knew what day of what year that would be, or how to make it come faster. Meanwhile—

My entering the room made Grandma turn. I watched her face slowly as it recognized me. And wasn't there the merest ink-wash change of color in those eyes? Didn't the thin film of blood beneath the translucent skin, or whatever liquid they put to pulse and beat in the humanoid forms, didn't it flourish itself suddenly bright in her cheeks and mouth? I am somewhat ruddy. Didn't Grandma suffuse herself more to my color upon my arrival? And her eyes? watching Agatha-Abigail-Algernon at work, hadn't they been *her* color of blue rather than mine, which are deeper?

More important than that, in the moments as she talked with me, saying, "Good evening," and "How's your homework, my lad?" and such stuff, didn't the bones of her face shift subtly beneath the flesh to assume some fresh racial attitude?

For let's face it, our family is of three sorts. Agatha has the long horse bones of a small English girl who will grow to hunt foxes; Father's equine stare, snort, stomp, and assemblage of skeleton. The skull and teeth are pure English, or as pure as the motley isle's history allows.

Timothy is something else, a touch of Italian from Mother's side a generation back. Her family name was Mariano, so Tim has that dark thing firing him, and a small bone structure, and eyes that will one day burn ladies to the ground.

As for me, I am the Slav, and we can only figure this from my paternal grandfather's mother who came from Vienna and brought a set of cheekbones that flared, and temples from which you might dip wine, and a kind of steppeland thrust of nose which sniffed more of Tartar than of Tartan, hiding behind the family name.

So you see it became fascinating for me to watch and try to catch Grandma as she performed her changes, speaking to Agatha and melting her cheekbones to the horse, speaking to Timothy and growing as delicate as a Florentine raven pecking glibly at the air, speaking to me and fusing the hidden plastic stuffs, so I felt Catherine the Great stood there before me.

Now, how the Fantoccini people achieved this rare and subtle transformation I shall never know, nor ask, nor wish to find out. Enough that in each quiet motion, turning here, bending there, affixing her gaze, her secret segments, sections, the abutment of her nose, the sculptured chinbone, the wax-tallow plastic metal forever warmed and was forever susceptible of loving change. Hers was a mask that was all mask but only one face for one person at a time. So in crossing a room, having touched one child, on the way, beneath the skin, the wondrous shift went on, and by the time she reached the next child, why, true mother of *that* child she was! looking upon him or her out of the battlements of their own fine bones.

And when *all* three of us were present and chattering at the same time? Well, then, the changes were miraculously soft, small, and mysterious. Nothing so tremendous as to be caught and noted, save by this older boy, myself, who, watching, became elated and admiring and entranced.

I have never wished to be behind the magician's scenes. Enough that the illusion works. Enough that love is the chemical result. Enough that cheeks are rubbed to happy color, eyes sparked to illumination, arms opened to accept and softly bind and hold . . .

All of us, that is, except Agatha, who refused to the bitter last.

"Agamemnon . . ."

It had become a jovial game now. Even Agatha didn't mind, but pretended to mind. It gave her a pleasant sense of superiority over a supposedly superior machine.

"Agamemnon!" she snorted, "you *are* a d . . ."

"Dumb?" said Grandma.

"I wouldn't say that."

"Think it, then, my dear Agonistes Agatha . . . I am quite flawed, and on names my flaws are revealed. Tom there, is Tim half the time. Timothy is Tobias or Timulty as likely as not . . ."

Agatha laughed. Which made Grandma make one of her rare mistakes. She put out her hand to give my sister the merest pat. Agatha-Abigail-Alice leapt to her feet.

Agatha-Agamemnon-Alcibiades-Allegra-Alexandra-Allison withdrew swiftly to her room.

"I suspect," said Timothy, later, "because she is beginning to like Grandma."

"Tosh," said I.

"Where do you pick up words like Tosh?"

"Grandma read me some Dickens last night. 'Tosh.' 'Humbug.' 'Balderdash.' 'Blast.' 'Devil take you.' You're pretty smart for your age, Tim."

"Smart, heck. It's obvious, the more Agatha likes Grandma, the more she hates herself for liking her, the more afraid she gets of the whole mess, the more she hates Grandma in the end."

"Can one love someone so much you hate them?"

"Dumb. Of course."

"It *is* sticking your neck out, sure. I guess you hate people when they make you feel naked, I mean sort of on the spot or out in the open. That's the way to play the game, of course. I mean, you don't just love people you must LOVE them with exclamation points."

"You're pretty smart, yourself, for someone so stupid," said Tim.

"Many thanks."

And I went to watch Grandma move slowly back into her battle of wits and stratagems with what's-her-name . . .

What dinners there were at our house!

Dinners, heck; what lunches, what breakfasts!

Always something new, yet, wisely, it looked or seemed old and familiar. We were never asked, for if you ask children what they want, they do not know, and if you tell what's to be delivered, they reject delivery. All parents know this. It is a quiet war that must be won each day. And Grandma knew how to win without looking triumphant.

"Here's Mystery Breakfast Number Nine," she would say, placing it down. "Perfectly dreadful, not worth bothering with, it made me want to throw up while I was cooking it!"

Even while wondering how a robot could be sick, we could hardly wait to shovel it down.

"Here's Abominable Lunch Number Seventy-seven," she

announced. "Made from plastic food bags, parsley, and gum
from under theatre seats. Brush your teeth after or you'll
taste the poison all afternoon."

We fought each other for more.

Even Abigail-Agamemnon-Agatha drew near and circled
round the table at such times, while Father put on the ten
pounds he needed and pinkened out his cheeks.

When A. A. Agatha did not come to meals, they were left
by her door with a skull and crossbones on a small flag stuck
in a baked apple. One minute the tray was abandoned, the
next minute gone.

Other times Abigail A. Agatha would bird through during
dinner, snatch crumbs from her plate and bird off.

"Agatha!" Father would cry.

"No, wait," Grandma said, quietly. "She'll come, she'll
sit. It's a matter of time."

"What's wrong with her?" I asked.

"Yeah, for cri-yi, she's nuts," said Timothy.

"No, she's afraid," said Grandma.

"Of you?" I said, blinking.

"Not of me so much as what I might *do*," she said.

"You wouldn't do anything to hurt her."

"No, but she thinks I might. We must wait for her to find
that her fears have no foundation. If I fail, well, I will send
myself to the showers and rust quietly."

There was a titter of laughter. Agatha was hiding in the
hall.

Grandma finished serving everyone and then sat at the
other side of the table facing Father and pretended to eat. I
never found out, I never asked, I never wanted to know,
what she did with the food. She was a sorcerer. It simply
vanished.

And in the vanishing, Father made comment:

"This food. I've had it before. In a small French restaurant
over near Les Deux Magots in Paris, twenty, oh, twenty-five
years ago!" His eyes brimmed with tears, suddenly.

"How do you *do* it?" he asked, at last, putting down the

cutlery, and looking across the table at this remarkable creature, this device, this what? *woman?*

Grandma took his regard, and ours, and held them simply
in her now empty hands, as gifts, and just as gently replied:

"I am given things which I then give to you. I don't *know*
that I give, but the giving goes on. You ask what I am? Why,
a machine. But even in that answer we know, don't we, more
than a machine. I am all the people who thought of me and
planned me and built me and set me running. So I am people. I am all the things they wanted to be and perhaps could
not be, so they built a great child, a wondrous toy to represent those things."

"Strange," said Father. "When I was growing up, there
was a huge outcry at machines. Machines were bad, evil,
they might dehumanize—"

"Some machines do. It's all in the way they are built. It's
all in the way they are used. A bear trap is a simple machine
that catches and holds and tears. A rifle is a machine that
wounds and kills. Well, I am no bear trap. I am no rifle. I am a
grandmother machine, which means more than a machine."

"How can you be more than what you seem?"

"No man is as big as his own idea. It follows, then, that
any machine that embodies an idea is larger than the man
that made it. And what's so wrong with that?"

"I got lost back there about a mile," said Timothy. "Come
again?"

"Oh, dear," said Grandma. "How I do hate philosophical
discussions and excursions into esthetics. Let me put it this
way. Men throw huge shadows on the lawn, don't they?
Then, all their lives, they try to run to fit the shadows. But the
shadows are always longer. Only at noon can a man fit his
own shoes, his own best suit, for a few brief minutes. But
now we're in a new age where we can think up a Big Idea and
run it around in a machine. That makes the machine more
than a machine, doesn't it?"

"So far so good," said Tim. "I guess."

"Well, isn't a motion-picture camera and projector more

than a machine? It's a thing that dreams, isn't it? Sometimes fine happy dreams, sometimes nightmares. But to call it a machine and dismiss it is ridiculous."

"I see *that!*" said Tim, and laughed at seeing.

"You must have been invented then," said Father, "by someone who loved machines and hated people who *said* all machines were bad or evil."

"Exactly," said Grandma. "Guido Fantoccini, that was his real name, grew up among machines. And he couldn't stand the clichés any more."

"Clichés?"

"Those lies, yes, that people tell and pretend they are truths absolute. Man will never fly. That was a cliché truth for a thousand thousand years which turned out to be a lie only a few years ago. The earth is flat, you'll fall off the rim, dragons will dine on you; the great lie told as fact, and Columbus plowed it under. Well, now, how many times have you heard how inhuman machines are, in your life? How many bright fine people have you heard spouting the same tired truths which are in reality lies; all machines destroy, all machines are cold, thoughtless, awful.

"There's a seed of truth there. But only a seed. Guido Fantoccini knew that. And knowing it, like most men of his kind, made him mad. And he could have stayed mad and gone mad forever, but instead did what he had to do; he began to invent machines to give the lie to the ancient lying truth.

"He knew that most machines are amoral, neither bad nor good. But by the way you built and shaped them you in turn shaped men, women, and children to be bad or good. A car, for instance, dead brute, unthinking, an unprogrammed bulk, is the greatest destroyer of souls in history. It makes boy-men greedy for power, destruction, and more destruction. It was never *intended* to do that. But that's how it turned out."

Grandma circled the table, refilling our glasses with clear cold mineral spring water from the tappet in her left forefinger. "Meanwhile, you must use other compensating machines. Machines that throw shadows on the earth that beckon you to run out and fit that wondrous casting-forth. Machines that trim your soul in silhouette like a vast pair of beautiful shears, snipping away the rude brambles, the dire horns and hooves to leave a finer profile. And for that you need examples.''

''Examples?'' I asked.

''Other people who behave well, and you imitate them. And if you act well enough long enough all the hair drops off and you're no longer a wicked ape.''

Grandma sat again.

''So, for thousands of years, you humans have needed kings, priests, philosophers, fine examples to look up to and say, 'They are good, I wish I could be like them. They set the grand good style.' But, being human, the finest priests, the tenderest philosophers make mistakes, fall from grace, and mankind is disillusioned and adopts indifferent skepticism or, worse, motionless cynicism and the good world grinds to a halt while evil moves on with huge strides.''

''And you, why, you never make mistakes, you're perfect, you're better than anyone *ever!*''

It was a voice from the hall between kitchen and dining room where Agatha, we all knew, stood against the wall listening and now burst forth.

Grandma didn't even turn in the direction of the voice, but went on calmly addressing her remarks to the family at the table.

''Not perfect, no, for what is perfection? But this I do know: being mechanical, I cannot sin, cannot be bribed, cannot be greedy or jealous or mean or small. I do not relish power for power's sake. Speed does not pull me to madness. Sex does not run me rampant through the world. I have time and more than time to collect the information I need around and about an ideal to keep it clean and whole and intact. Name the value you wish, tell me the Ideal you want and I can see and collect and remember the good that will benefit you all. Tell me how you would like to be: kind, loving, considerate, well-balanced, humane . . . and let me run ahead on the path to explore those ways to be just that. In the darkness ahead, turn me as a lamp in all directions. I *can* guide your feet.''

''So,'' said Father, putting the napkin to his mouth, ''on the days when all of us are busy making lies—''

''I'll tell the truth.''

''On the days when we hate—''

''I'll go on giving love, which means attention, which means knowing all about you, all, all, all about you, and you knowing that I know but that most of it I will never tell to anyone, it will stay a warm secret between us, so you will never fear my complete knowledge.''

And here Grandma was busy clearing the table, circling, taking the plates, studying each face as she passed, touching Timothy's cheek, my shoulder with her free hand flowing along, her voice a quiet river of certainty bedded in our needful house and lives.

''But,'' said Father, stopping her, looking her right in the face. He gathered his breath. His face shadowed. At last he let it out. ''All this talk of love and attention and stuff. Good God, woman, you, you're not *in* there!''

He gestured to her head, her face, her eyes, the hidden sensory cells behind the eyes, the miniaturized storage vaults and minimal keeps.

''*You're* not *in* there!''

Grandmother waited one, two, three silent beats.

Then she replied: ''No. But *you* are. You and Thomas and Timothy and Agatha.

''Everything you ever say, everything you ever do, I'll keep, put away, treasure. I shall be all the things a family forgets it is, but senses, half-remembers. Better than the old family albums you used to leaf through, saying here's this winter, there's that spring, I shall recall what you forget. And though the debate may run another hundred thousand years: What is Love? perhaps we may find that love is the ability of someone to give us back to us. Maybe love is some-

one seeing and remembering, handing us back to ourselves
just a trifle better than we had dared to hope or dream . . .

"I am family memory and, one day perhaps, racial memory, too, but in the round, and at your call. I do not *know* myself. I can neither touch nor taste nor feel on any level. Yet I
exist. And my existence means the heightening of your
chance to touch and taste and feel. Isn't love in there somewhere in such an exchange? Well . . ."

She went on around the table, clearing away, sorting and
stacking, neither grossly humble nor arthritic with pride.

"What do I know?

"This, above all: the trouble with most families with many
children is someone gets lost. There isn't time, it seems, for
everyone. Well, I will give equally to all of you. I will share
out my knowledge and attention with everyone. I wish to be
a great warm pie fresh from the oven, with equal shares to be
taken by all. No one will starve. Look! someone cries, and I'll
look. Listen! someone cries, and I hear. Run with me on the
river path! someone says, and I run. And at dusk I am not
tired, nor irritable, so I do not scold out of some tired irritabil-
ity. My eye stays clear, my voice strong, my hand firm, my
attention constant."

"But," said Father, his voice fading, half convinced, but
putting up a last faint argument, "you're not *there.* As for
love—"

"If paying attention is love, I am love.

"If knowing is love, I am love.

"If helping you not to fall into error and to be good is love,
I am love.

"And again, to repeat, there are four of you. Each, in a
way never possible before in history, will get my complete attention. No matter if you all speak at once, I can channel and
hear this one and that and the other, clearly. No one will go
hungry. I will, if you please, and accept the strange word,
'love' you all."

"I *don't* accept!" said Agatha.

And even Grandma turned now to see her standing in the door.

"I won't give you permission, you can't, you mustn't!" said Agatha. "I won't let you! It's lies! You lie. No one loves me. She said she did, but she lied. She *said* but *lied!*"

"Agatha!" cried Father, standing up.

"She?" said Grandma. "Who?"

"Mother!" came the shriek. "Said: Love you! Lies! Love you! Lies! And you're like her! You lie. But you're empty, anyway, and so that's a *double* lie! I hate *her*. Now, I hate *you!*"

Agatha spun about and leapt down the hall.

The front door slammed wide.

Father was in motion, but Grandma touched his arm.

"Let me."

And she walked and then moved swiftly, gliding down the hall and then suddenly, easily, running, yes, running very fast, out the door.

It was a champion sprint by the time we all reached the lawn, the sidewalk, yelling.

Blind, Agatha made the curb, wheeling about, seeing us close, all of us yelling, Grandma way ahead, shouting, too, and Agatha off the curb and out in the street, halfway to the middle, then the middle and suddenly a car, which no one saw, erupting its brakes, its horn shrieking and Agatha flailing about to see and Grandma there with her and hurling her aside and down as the car with fantastic energy and verve selected her from our midst, struck our wonderful electric Guido Fantoccini–produced dream even while she paced upon the air and, hands up to ward off, almost in mild protest, still trying to decide what to say to this bestial machine, over and over she spun and down and away even as the car jolted to a halt and I saw Agatha safe beyond and Grandma, it seemed, still coming down or down and sliding fifty yards away to strike and ricochet and lie strewn and all of us frozen in a line suddenly in the midst of the street with one scream pulled out of all our throats at the same raw instant.

Then silence and just Agatha lying on the asphalt, intact, getting ready to sob.

And still we did not move, frozen on the sill of death, afraid to venture in any direction, afraid to go see what lay beyond the car and Agatha and so we began to wail and, I guess, pray to ourselves as Father stood amongst us: Oh, no, no, we mourned, oh no, God, no, no . . .

Agatha lifted her already grief-stricken face and it was the face of someone who has predicted dooms and lived to see and now did not want to see or live any more. As we watched, she turned her gaze to the tossed woman's body and tears fell from her eyes. She shut them and covered them and lay back down forever to weep . . .

I took a step and then another step and then five quick steps and by the time I reached my sister her head was buried deep and her sobs came up out of a place so far down in her I was afraid I could never find her again, she would never come out, no matter how I pried or pleaded or promised or threatened or just plain said. And what little we could hear from Agatha buried there in her own misery, she said over and over again, lamenting, wounded, certain of the old threat known and named and now here forever. ". . . like I said . . . told you . . . lies . . . lies . . . liars . . . all lies . . . like the other . . . other . . . just like . . . just . . . just like the other . . . other . . . other . . . !"

I was down on my knees holding onto her with both hands, trying to put her back together even though she wasn't broken any way you could see but just feel, because I knew it was no use going on to Grandma, no use at all, so I just touched Agatha and gentled her and wept while Father came up and stood over and knelt down with me and it was like a prayer meeting in the middle of the street and lucky no more cars coming, and I said, choking, "Other what, Ag, other *what?*"

Agatha exploded two words.

"Other dead!"

"You mean Mom?"

"O Mom," she wailed, shivering, lying down, cuddling up like a baby. "O Mom, dead, O Mom and now Grandma dead, she promised always, always, to love, to love, promised to be different, promised, promised and now look, look . . . I hate her, I hate Mom, I hate her, I hate *them!*"

"Of course," said a voice. "It's only natural. How foolish of me not to have known, not to have seen."

And the voice was so familiar we were all stricken.

We all jerked.

Agatha squinched her eyes, flicked them wide, blinked, and jerked half up, staring.

"How silly of me," said Grandma, standing there at the edge of our circle, our prayer, our wake.

"Grandma!" we all said.

And she stood there, taller by far than any of us in this moment of kneeling and holding and crying out. We could only stare up at her in disbelief.

"You're dead!" cried Agatha. "The car—"

"Hit me," said Grandma, quietly. "Yes. And threw me in the air and tumbled me over and for a few moments there was a severe concussion of circuitries. I might have feared a disconnection, if fear is the word. But then I sat up and gave myself a shake and the few molecules of paint, jarred loose on one printed path or another, magnetized back in position and resilient creature that I am, unbreakable thing that I am, *here* I am."

"I thought you were—" said Agatha.

"And only natural," said Grandma. "I mean, anyone else, hit like that, tossed like that. But, O my dear Agatha, not me. And now I see why you were afraid and never trusted me. You didn't know. And I had not as yet proved my singular ability to survive. How dumb of me not to have thought to show you. Just a second." Somewhere in her head, her body, her being, she fitted together some invisible tapes, some old information made new by interblending. She nodded. "Yes. There. A book of child-raising, laughed at by some few people years back when the woman who wrote the book said, as final advice to parents: 'Whatever you do, don't die. Your children will never forgive you.' "

"Forgive," some one of us whispered.

"For how can children understand when you just up and go away and never come back again with no excuse, no apologies, no sorry note, nothing."

"They can't," I said.

"So," said Grandma, kneeling down with us beside Agatha who sat up now, new tears brimming her eyes, but a different kind of tears, not tears that drowned, but tears that washed clean. "So your mother ran away to death. And after that, how *could* you trust anyone? If everyone left, vanished finally, who *was* there to trust? So when I came, half wise, half ignorant, I should have known, I did not know, why you would not accept me. For, very simply and honestly, you feared I might not stay, that I lied, that I was vulnerable, too. And two leavetakings, two deaths, were one too many in a single year. But now, do you *see*, Abigail?"

"Agatha," said Agatha, without knowing she corrected.

"Do you understand, I shall always, always be here?"

"Oh, yes," cried Agatha, and broke down into a solid weeping in which we all joined, huddled together and cars drew up and stopped to see just how many people were hurt and how many people were getting well right there.

End of story.

Well, not quite the end.

We lived happily ever after.

Or rather we lived together, Grandma, Agatha-Agamemnon-Abigail, Timothy, and I, Tom, and Father, and Grandma calling us to frolic in great fountains of Latin and Spanish and French, in great seaborne gouts of poetry like Moby Dick sprinkling the deeps with his Versailles jet somehow lost in calms and found in storms; Grandma a constant, a clock, a pendulum, a face to tell all time by at noon, or in the middle of sick nights when, raved with fever, we saw her forever by our beds, never gone, never away, always waiting, always speaking kind words, her cool hand icing our hot brows, the tappet of her uplifted forefinger unsprung to let a twine of cold mountain water touch our flannel tongues. Ten thousand dawns she cut our wildflower lawn, ten thousand nights she wandered, remembering the dust molecules that fell in the still hours before dawn, or sat whispering some lesson she felt needed teaching to our ears while we slept snug.

Until at last, one by one, it was time for us to go away to school, and when at last the youngest, Agatha, was all packed, why Grandma packed, too.

On the last day of summer that last year, we found Grandma down in the front room with various packets and suitcases, knitting, waiting, and though she had often spoken of it, now that the time came we were shocked and surprised.

"Grandma!" we all said. "What are you doing?"

"Why going off to college, in a way, just like you," she said. "Back to Guido Fantoccini's, to the Family."

"The Family?"

"Of Pinocchios, that's what he called us for a joke, at first. The Pinocchios and himself Gepetto. And then later gave us his own name: the Fantoccini. Anyway, you have been my family here. Now I go back to my even larger family there, my brothers, sisters, aunts, cousins, all robots who—"

"Who do *what?*" asked Agatha.

"It all depends," said Grandma. "Some stay, some linger. Others go to be drawn and quartered, you might say, their parts distributed to other machines who have need of repairs. They'll weigh and find me wanting or not wanting. It may be I'll be just the one they need tomorrow and off I'll go to raise another batch of children and beat another batch of fudge."

"Oh, they mustn't draw and quarter you!" cried Agatha.

"No!" I cried, with Timothy.

"My allowance," said Agatha, "I'll pay anything . . . ?"

Grandma stopped rocking and looked at the needles and

the pattern of bright yarn. "Well, I wouldn't have said, but now you ask and I'll tell. For a very *small* fee, there's a room, the room of the Family, a large dim parlor, all quiet and nicely decorated, where as many as thirty or forty of the Electric Women sit and rock and talk, each in her turn. I have not been there. I am, after all, freshly born, comparatively new. For a small fee, very small, each month and year, that's where I'll be, with all the others like me, listening to what they've learned of the world and, in my turn, telling how it was with Tom and Tim and Agatha and how fine and happy we were. And I'll tell all I learned from you."

"But . . . you taught *us!*"

"Do you *really* think that?" she said. "No, it was turn-about, roundabout, learning both ways. And it's all in here, everything you flew into tears about or laughed over, why, I have it all. And I'll tell it to the others just as they tell their boys and girls and life to me. We'll sit there, growing wiser and calmer and better every year and every year, ten, twenty, thirty years. The Family knowledge will double, quadruple, the wisdom will not be lost. And we'll be waiting there in the sitting room, should you ever need us for your own children in time of illness, or, God prevent, deprivation or death. There we'll be, growing old but not old, getting closer to the time, perhaps, someday, when we live up to our first strange joking name."

"The Pinocchios?" asked Tim.

Grandma nodded.

I knew what she meant. The day when, as in the old tale, Pinocchio had grown so worthy and so fine that the gift of life had been given him. So I saw them, in future years, the entire family of Fantoccini, the Pinocchios, trading and re-trading, murmuring and whispering their knowledge in the great parlors of philosophy, waiting for the day. The day that could never come.

Grandma must have read that thought in our eyes.

"We'll see," she said. "Let's just wait and see."

"Oh, Grandma," cried Agatha and she was weeping as

she had wept many years before. "You don't have to wait. You're alive. You've always been alive to us!"

And she caught hold of the old woman and we all caught hold for a long moment and then ran off up in the sky to far-away schools and years and her last words to us before we let the helicopter swarm us away into autumn were these:

"When you are very old and gone childish-small again, with childish ways and childish yens and, in need of feeding, make a wish for the old teacher nurse, the dumb yet wise companion, send for me. I will come back. We shall inhabit the nursery again, never fear."

"Oh, we shall never be old!" we cried. "That will never happen!"

"Never! Never!"

And we were gone.

And the years are flown.

And we are old now, Tim and Agatha and I.

Our children are grown and gone, our wives and husbands vanished from the earth and now, by Dickensian coincidence, accept it as you will or not accept, back in the old house, we three.

I lie here in the bedroom which was my childish place seventy, O seventy, believe it, seventy years ago. Beneath this wallpaper is another layer and yet another-times-three to the old wallpaper covered over when I was nine. The wallpaper is peeling. I see peeking from beneath, old elephants, familiar tigers, fine and amiable zebras, irascible crocodiles. I have sent for the paperers to carefully remove all but that last layer. The old animals will live again on the walls, revealed.

And we have sent for someone else.

The three of us have called:

Grandma! You said you'd come back when we had need. We are surprised by age, by time. We are old. We *need*.

And in three rooms of a summer house very late in time, three old children rise up, crying out in their heads: We *loved* you! We *love* you!

There! There! in the sky, we think, waking at morn. Is that the delivery machine? Does it settle to the lawn?

There! There on the grass by the front porch. Does the mummy case arrive?

Are our names inked on ribbons wrapped about the lovely form beneath the golden mask?!

And the kept gold key, forever hung on Agatha's breast, warmed and waiting? Oh God, will it, after all these years, will it wind, will it set in motion, will it, dearly, *fit?!*

The Changing of the Guard

Adapted by Anne Serling-Sutton

TELEPLAY BY ROD SERLING

AIRED JUNE 1, 1962

STARRING DONALD PLEASENCE AND
PHILIPPA BEVANS

THERE WAS NOTHING PARTICULARLY UNIQUE ABOUT the Rock Springs School for Boys, nothing to differentiate it from any other New England boys' school. Ivy clung to the brick walls, broken only where dusty, diamond-paned windows peered through. Names and thoughts of bygone times were carved deep into the wooden desks, and a musty smell seemed to cling to the long corridors, even on sunny days. The halls echoed with the same laughter, the same angers, the same disappointments one might find in any other school. No, there was nothing really distinctive about the Rock Springs School—nothing except Professor Ellis Fowler.

Professor Fowler was seventy-seven, with a great grey mop of hair and a grey beard that moved up and down as he spoke. He had a kindly, intelligent face with sparkling blue eyes that still questioned and glasses that constantly slipped down his nose, only to be fruitlessly pushed back up. He was thin and angular, resembling a rather deflated Santa Claus.

On this last day of the term his students sat before him in various postures of boredom. Professor Fowler glanced at the book in his hand, then peered toward them owlishly.

"You'll remember that we've talked of the work of Alfred Edward Housman, born—what year, Mr. Graham?"

Graham, a sixteen-year-old linebacker whose body had grown without him, blinked and suddenly came to attention. "What *year*, sir?"

There was a thin trickle of laughter. Graham shifted in his seat and fingered his varsity letter. "Ah, sometime this century. I think."

Professor Fowler smiled and nodded. "Close, Mr. Graham. Closer than usual. Sometime this century." Scratching his beard, he turned to the class. "Mr. Graham's career is laid out for him, I believe. He will be a second assistant in the information booth at Kennedy Airport."

The class sat up, anticipating a bit of fun as the professor peered at Graham over his glasses. "The date of A.E. Housman's birth, Mr. Graham—and for the benefit of the rest of the class—was 1859. His death occurred . . . what year, Mr. Butler?"

A runty little student, who had the kind of head that looked as if it would spend the rest of its life wearing a beanie, jumped to his feet. "Sir, around 1900."

Professor Fowler straightened his glasses and scratched his beard again. " 'Pon my word, young Mr. Butler, you and Mr. Graham are kindred spirits! Housman died in 1936. Now, with your and Mr. Graham's permission, this may be somewhat less moving than what a T-formation quarterback tells his team in a huddle, but I hope you'll bear with me for a moment. All of you will recall, no doubt, *A Shropshire Lad*, a little of which I will now read to you:

> "When I was one-and-twenty
> I heard a wise man say,
> 'Give crowns and pounds and guineas
> But not your heart away;' "

He continued to recite, but his eyes left the book, moved past the heads of the students, and fastened on some far-distant corner of the universe.

    '' 'Give pearls away and rubies
    But keep your fancy free.'
    But I was one-and-twenty,
    No use to talk to me.''

Slowly he lowered the book.

    ''When I was one-and-twenty
    I heard him say again,
    '' 'The heart out of the bosom
    Was never given in vain;
    'Tis paid with sighs a-plenty
    And sold for endless rue.'
    And I am two-and-twenty,
    And oh, 'tis true, 'tis true.''

Professor Fowler was suddenly aware of the boys staring at him, and closed the book. He took off his glasses and smiled from face to face. ''It is quite an odd phenomenon, really, how you react to that poem much as your fathers did. I've been reading it for fifty-one years to various classes, and not one has yet got its true meaning. Said meaning is simply—give sparingly of your youth. Embrace it for the precious thing it is. It's the most fleeting chapter in the book of your lives.'' He leaned over his desk and peered at the students. ''You will, I am sure, at some future moment of your lives, understand precisely what I'm getting at.'' Then, smiling again, he said, ''Now gentlemen, this being the last day of the semester, and this being just three days before the Christmas holidays, I thought it might behoove me to show at least a minute degree of compassion and let you out early. I might add, here, that while your final exam papers are not ready to be returned to you, you have all—amazingly enough—passed! My delight is surpassed only by my sense of shock. It is rare, young men, that in some fifty-one years of teaching, I have ever encountered such a class of dunderheads.'' His eyes twinkled. ''But nice dunderheads, and potentially fine young men who will make their marks . . . and leave their marks. God bless you all—and a merry Christmas!''

Professor Fowler made his way down the aisle, shaking an occasional hand as the students filed out, their voices rising, a spirit of the holiday season filling the halls. Locker doors slammed; books and papers were stashed away with whoops of joy. The boys were going home.

Walking through the crowded hall, Professor Fowler was about to pass the headmaster's office when the door opened and a voice called out. The headmaster was a tweedy young man still rather new to the job. He pointed an overlarge briar pipe at the professor. ''I say, Fowler, could you step in for a moment?''

''Why, of course.''

The headmaster walked over to his desk, lighting his pipe. ''Sit down, Fowler. Be comfortable.''

Professor Fowler settled himself in an overstuffed chair. Reaching into his pocket, he took out his pocket watch and peered at it.

''Am I keeping you?'' the headmaster said.

''No, no, no. There is going to be a broadcast of the *Messiah* at five o'clock, but I have plenty of time. It's a lovely thing. Very Yule-like.''

''I agree, I agree,'' said the younger man, arranging the papers on his desk. ''This won't take long.''

Fowler sat quietly, expectantly. The headmaster sucked on his pipe, made a tidy pile of the paper, and finally looked up. ''You . . .'' He cleared his throat. ''You did not respond to the letter that the Trustees sent you last week.''

The professor pushed his glasses further back on his nose. ''Letter? I'm terribly sorry. It suddenly occurs to me that I haven't opened my mail for the last few weeks. Final exams,

grading, preparation for the holiday . . . that sort of thing."
He smiled. "Anyway, I'm rather certain I know the contents
of that letter."

The headmaster looked away. "And . . . your reactions,
Professor?"

Fowler took off his glasses and went through the ritual of
checking and cleaning them. "Well, I'll naturally go along."

The headmaster beamed. "I think that's very perspica-
cious of you, Professor. Then I'll tell the Trustees that you received the communication and have agreed to it. Now, as to
your replacement—"

Fowler was no longer listening. "I told my housekeeper
not a week ago," he broke in, "that I should very likely teach
in this place until I'm a hundred years old. Two years ago I
actually taught the grandson of one of my earlier students! I
venture to say that I'll live to teach a *great*-grandson one of
these days." He smiled. "It was the Reynolds boy. You
know him. His father was Damon Reynolds, and his grandfather—a regular rascal of a boy who persisted in calling me
Weird Beard." Fowler chuckled and wiped his glasses.
"Weird Beard! He didn't know I knew that's what he was
calling me. Oh, a regular rascal of a boy! Went into the stock
market. Made himself a fortune. Came back for his twentieth
reunion, shook my hand, and said, 'Professor Fowler, please
forgive me for calling you Weird Beard.' " Fowler shook his
head and smiled.

The headmaster coughed. "Professor . . . you'll forgive
me, sir, but . . . I think you had best read the communication
that the Trustees sent."

Fowler nodded. "Oh, indeed I will. Though it's really an
odd formality, this contract signing year after year. You can
tell them for me, Headmaster, that old Fowler won't depart
the ship. Oh, no, indeed. He'll stand at the wheel through
fair weather and foul, and he'll watch the crews come aboard
and then depart . . . come aboard and then depart. And he'll
see that the ship will stay on course."

"Professor Fowler, please hear me out, sir." The headmaster rose and walked to a window, where he stared out at the snow-filled day. When he spoke again, his voice was quiet and not without pity. "The communication that the Trustees sent you was not a contract." He turned slowly from the window. "As a matter of fact, it was a notice of termination. You've been on the faculty here for over fifty years. You've passed the normal retirement age several years ago. We decided at our winter meeting that perhaps a younger man . . ." Fowler, he saw, had risen to his feet. "If you could have been at the meeting, sir, you would have been very proud of the things said about you and your work. 'A teacher of incalculable value to all of us.' But . . ." He stood with his head down, as if reluctant to look at the old man's face.

Professor Fowler's voice was almost a whisper. "Mr. Headmaster . . . am I to understand that my contract is not to be renewed? I'm discharged?"

The other began pacing the room. "Discharged? Please! Don't call it that. Retirement—*and* at half salary for the rest of your life."

Fowler said very softly, "For the rest of my life?" Suddenly he looked very old. He walked to the door and paused, his back to the headmaster. "Well, it . . . it certainly proves one thing—'pon my word it does. A man should read his mail. He most certainly should read his mail."

Outside, in the corridor, he came across two of his boys. "Merry Christmas, Professor! Have a happy holiday, sir."

Fowler studied their faces. "Mr. Halliday and Mr. Mc-Tavish . . ." His voice shook. "I wish you a safe and happy journey and a happy reunion with your families. And I trust you will not eat too much turkey . . . and too much . . . too much stuffing. I've—I've known it to happen Christmas after Christmas; you young rascals go home and eat yourselves into insensi—insensibility."

The boys looked at one another as tears ran from the old man's eyes. With trembling fingers, he touched each boy's face. "You're both fine men. Have a Merry Christmas, both of you. Have a—'' His voice broke. He turned away, hearing the boys' voices behind him. ''What's the matter with old Weird Beard? He was crying. Did you see that? He was crying.''

Fowler walked slowly down the corridor, running his hand along the wall, feeling the carved molding that had been worn smooth through the years. Pausing, he stopped and looked around, taking in the sights and sounds of this building that he had virtually lived in for half a century. Finally, pushing open the heavy oak door, he walked outside and started home, oblivious to the bitter chill. He stopped once to gaze behind him at the building he had cherished for so many years. In the twilight it was almost hidden by the falling snow.

With difficulty he climbed the steps to his house and stamped the snow off his feet, more from habit than from a conscious concern. On the hall table stood a little Christmas tree, laden with ornaments and growing more top-heavy each year. Each ornament had a special meaning because all were gifts from his ''boys.'' After the Christmas season was over, each treasure would be wrapped and, with great ceremony, stored on a high shelf. But Professor Fowler wasn't looking at the tree tonight. He was looking at the letters lying beside it. Still in his hat and coat, he fumbled through them, the door behind him still open to the winter chill.

From the dark recesses of the house, Mrs. Landers, the professor's housekeeper, materialized. After more than twenty years of living with him and caring for him, she had grown very fond of the old man, and had grown used to his absentmindedness. Closing the door, she straightened out a lock of hair that had been blown loose by a gust of wind. ''I didn't hear you come in,'' she said. ''It's certainly snowing and blowing to beat the band, isn't it?''

Fowler had finally found the letter he'd been searching for. ''I guess it is,'' he said, his thoughts elsewhere. ''I hadn't noticed.''

Mrs. Landers studied the old man's face, his stooped shoulders, and ashen color. "Is anything wrong, Professor?"

Fowler shook his head. He still held the letter. "I guess that would depend on the point of view. If you're a Trustee of this institution, anxious to inject new blood into the faculty, I'm sure you'd think there was nothing wrong at all." He paused. "But if you're an old man who has spent the better part of his life inside those halls, those classrooms, then you might be forgiven a degree of consternation." Suddenly he chuckled. "As a matter of fact, everything is *not* all right. Everything happens to be very wrong."

Mrs. Landers pointed to the letter in his hand. "What is it, Professor? What's happened?"

Fowler read aloud. " 'And since it is the policy of the school to insure our students the most up-to-date educational concepts, we think it advisable that you consider this retirement to be a mutually beneficial thing. Please understand the spirit in which this request is made and understand further that your contributions to the Rock Springs School for Boys are a matter of record, as is our appreciation.' "

"Oh, my word, Professor! That means—"

He finished her thought. "That means, Mrs. Landers—stripped of some of its sophistry, its subtlety, its backbreaking effort to break it gently—that I'm canned." He shook his head, then brightened. "Tell me, were any of my boys here?"

She looked confused. "Your boys, sir?"

"The students, Mrs. Landers, they have this wonderful tradition, on the last afternoon of the winter term, they would gather outside and sing Christmas carols."

"They haven't done that in years, Professor," she said gently. "Not since before the war, as I recall."

Fowler nodded. "Of course! I should have remembered." Removing his glasses, he started absentmindedly to clean them, then suddenly threw them on the table. "Mrs. Landers, I've become a worshipper of tradition and a fervent follower of ritual. I know it now, and I can admit it. I guess that's why this whole thing has hit me so hard." Crossing the worn oriental rug, he sat down at his desk. "I'm an antique guarding antiques. I am the curator of a museum that houses nothing but some very fragile memories."

Mrs. Landers shook her head. She was close to tears. "Professor, you're the finest man. . . . You're absolutely the finest man."

Fowler smiled. "And you, Mrs. Landers, are the most loyal woman. Now, would you do me a favor? Would you brew me up some tea? Handel's *Messiah* is on the radio in a few minutes. I'd like to listen to it."

Alone again, he sat back and carefully removed a key from his key chain. Unlocking the lower right-hand drawer of the desk, he rummaged through it and took out a revolver. He sat staring at it awhile, then placed it inside his sweater and moved to the old rocking chair.

Outside the window, the night sky was still filled with snow. Professor Fowler had finished the tea Mrs. Landers had brought him, and the empty cup sat on the table as he listened, eyes closed, to the *Messiah*. The music ended on a triumphant sweeping note just as the housekeeper entered the room. Almost on tiptoe, she walked around the chair and peered into the old man's face.

He opened his eyes. "Yes, Mrs. Landers?"

She straightened up, startled. "I thought you were asleep, Professor. Would you care for some more tea?"

He shook his head, his mind a million miles away. "Thank you, no."

"I'll have dinner ready in half an hour. Why don't you take a little nap?"

Fowler reached over and turned off the radio. "I know I'm being very difficult, but could we put off dinner this evening? I haven't much of an appetite."

"Professor, you've got to eat something. I could keep it warm for you. Perhaps after your nap . . . ?"

He studied her kindly, aging face and smiled. "Perhaps later."

She watched him as he rose from the chair and crossed the room to the bookcase, where three shelves were devoted to the Rock Springs yearbooks, the wood that supported them sagging beneath their weight. Removing one of the older books and carrying it to the desk, he opened it carefully and thumbed through the pages, studying the faces and names.

"Timothy Arnold. Never thought that one would pass. Had an incorrigible habit of chewing bubble gum and popping it. Sounded like a howitzer! 'Pon my word, it sounded like a howitzer. William Hood. Little Bill Hood . . . Smallest boy ever to play varsity football here, and had a penchant for Shelley." He turned another page, and a smile lit up his face. "Artie Beachcroft. Now there was a lad. There was a staunch lad. Full of heart, that one." He looked thoughtful. "Was he the one? Yes, yes, I recall now. His father sent me a letter. He was killed on Iwo Jima. Freckle-faced little fellow—always grinning. Never stopped grinning. Most infectious grin. He'd walk into a classroom and you had to smile."

He continued turning the pages, and at last, with a sigh, closed the book. "They come and go like ghosts. Faces, names, smiles, the funny things they did—or sad things, poignant ones. I gave them nothing at all. I realize that now. Poetry that left their minds as soon as they themselves left. Aged slogans that were already out of date when I taught them. Quotations that were so dear to me but were meaningless to them." The professor shook his head. "Mrs. Landers, I am a failure. I am an old relic that walks from class to class. Speaking by rote to unhearing ears, unwilling heads. I am an abject, dismal failure. I moved no one. I left no imprint on anyone. Now where do you suppose I got the idea that I was accomplishing anything?"

Mrs. Landers shook her head tearfully, but no words came out. Fowler smiled, understanding her silence. He walked to the door. "I will take that nap now. And I hope I haven't inconvenienced you, putting off dinner like this." He closed the door softly behind him.

Mrs. Landers slipped the yearbook back in its place on the shelf and busied herself restoring order to his desk. Lovingly she touched the pipe, the old pens, the notebooks. Some papers, she noticed, were sticking out of one of the drawers. Reaching down, she pulled the drawer open—and suddenly froze, transfixed in horror by what she saw beneath the papers: an empty holster. She picked it up, holding it at arm's length, and, after staring at it in horror, put it carefully back in the drawer. Suddenly panic-stricken, she screamed, "Professor Fowler!" and ran into the hall. The front door stood wide open. Hurriedly she picked up the telephone and dialed the headmaster.

Fowler walked slowly across the campus, his footsteps echoing in the silence, his breath coming in short, quick gasps in the cold night air. His overcoat was awry and misbuttoned, and he had forgotten his hat; he looked lost and forlorn.

Halfway across campus, he stopped in front of a large bronze statue. Wiping the snow off the base, he read the legend carved there: "Horace Mann, Educator. 1796–1859." He knelt before it in the snow. "I was just wondering if you had any self-doubts," he asked aloud, then smiled and shook his head. "I'm sure not." He brushed more snow off until he could see the quotation beneath Mann's name:

"Be ashamed to die until you have won some victory for humanity."

Fowler looked downcast. "I have won no victory," he said, "no victory at all." He felt the weight of the gun in his coat pocket. "And now I am ashamed to die."

Slowly he drew forth the revolver, snapped off the safety catch, and was about to raise it to his head when he was distracted by the sound of far-off bells pealing a melodious and strangely urgent call.

Puzzled, he peered into the distance. "Class bells? That's odd. Why would they ring now? There's no special assembly. There's nothing of that sort."

In the distance, the bells began to ring again. Slipping the gun back into his pocket, Fowler headed toward the school. The door to the main building stood curiously open. Inside, he looked into each empty classroom, then up toward the ceiling. The bells continued ringing, yet he was completely alone. He paused at the door to his classroom, then strode inside and moved up the aisle between the desks. In the middle of the room he stopped again and listened. There was a new sound now, a strange, echoing, hollow sound of talk and laughter, at once distant and very near.

At the front of the room he stopped, bewildered, amazed. Before him in each seat, a figure was gradually emerging—first no more than a ghostly transparency, then the flesh-and-blood figure of a boy, until each seat was filled. A dozen boys eyed him expectantly.

Professor Fowler unbuttoned his coat; his lips formed soundless questions. "I . . . I don't understand. Forgive me, boys, but I'm not at all sure—what I mean is, I don't recollect how—"

They smiled at him silently. At last one rose.

"Artie Beachcroft, sir. Second form. Class of 'forty-one. How have you been, Professor?"

Fowler's eyes widened. "How's that? How's that again? You say you're Artie Beachcroft?" Slowly he remembered. "Of course you are. I'd recognize you anywhere." Walking over to the boy, he reached out and gripped the boy's hand, wiping away a tear with the other. "I'm delighted to see you. I'm truly delighted to see you. I've missed you, Artie." Suddenly he paused and shook his head. "But . . . but what are you doing here? Forgive me, but you shouldn't be here. You were—"

The boy smiled. "That's right, sir. I was killed in Iwo Jima." Reaching into his pocket, he withdrew a small leather case, opened it, and displayed what was inside. "I wanted to show this to you, sir. It's the Congressional Medal of Honor. It was given to me posthumously."

"A very prideful thing, Mr. Beachcroft," said Fowler, staring into the boy's face. "A *very* prideful thing. I am indeed proud of you. You were always a fine young man. A *fine* young man." Suddenly he blinked and shook his head. "But I . . . I don't understand."

"Professor?" It was a boy from across the room. Fowler turned toward him. "I'm Bartlett—third form. Class of 'twenty-eight. I died in Roanoke, Virginia. I was doing research on x-ray treatment for cancer, and was exposed to radioactivity. I contracted leukemia."

"I remember, Bartlett," said Fowler softly. "I *do* remember. That was an incredibly brave thing you did. An incredibly brave thing."

"I kept remembering, Professor—something you'd said to me. A quote. By a poet named Walter."

Fowler nodded. "Howard Arnold Walter. I remember."

Bartlett's voice was strong as he recited:

"I would be true, for there are those who trust me;
I would be pure, for there are those who care;
I would be strong, for there is much to suffer;
I would be brave, for there is much to dare.

"I never forgot that, Professor. It was something you left me. I never forgot."

Fowler felt his lips begin to tremble. "How . . . how very decent of you, Bartlett, to say that."

From across the room, Artie Beachcroft added, "That's why I brought the medal to show you, Professor Fowler—because it's partly yours. You taught me about courage. You taught me what it meant."

"Why . . . why, how incredible," the old man said softly. His eyes scanned the room and stopped on a very small boy. "Why, it's . . . it's Weiss, isn't it? Dickie Weiss? You were the first one, Dick—"

The boy got to his feet. "The first one to die, Professor. I was at Pearl Harbor on the *Arizona*. I was an ensign."

"I remember, Dick. You saved a dozen men. You got them out of the boiler room after they were trapped—and lost your life doing it."

The boy nodded. ''You were at my elbow that day, Professor. You may not have known it, but there you were. It was a piece you had taught me by John Donne:

''Any man's death diminishes me,
because I am involved in mankind;
and therefore never send to know for
whom the bell tolls; it tolls for thee.''

Fowler's eyes were brighter in the silence that ensued. Once more the bell rung, but this time very softly. He walked up and down the aisles of boys, and they each, in turn, rose.

''I'm Thompson, sir. Second form, class of 'thirty-nine. I died on New Guinea, but you taught me about patriotism.''

''Rice, sir. Third form, class of 1917. I died of wounds at Château-Thierry. You taught me about courage.''

''Hudson, sir. Second form, class of 1922. You taught me about loyalty.''

''Whiting, sir. Fourth form, class of 'fifty-one. You taught me about honesty.''

Blinking back tears, Fowler surveyed the class and wiped his eyes. Absentmindedly he took off his glasses, peered through them, cleaned them, then put them back on.

As they watched him, the boys smiled. They remembered this ritual fondly; none of them had ever forgotten it. For a moment there was silence in the room.

At last it was Beachcroft who spoke. ''We have to go back now, Professor. But we wanted to let you know that we were grateful—that we were forever grateful, that each of us has, in turn, carried with him something that you gave him. We wanted to thank you, Professor.''

One by one the figures dimmed and disappeared. Once more, the bells began to ring.

Fowler walked slowly up the aisle, looking at the desks, touching that one, pausing by another, remembering.

* * *

Snow covered his coat by the time he arrived home. Mrs. Landers was on the telephone. She smiled with relief as he came in. "Yes, Headmaster, he's home now. He's all right. Yes, he's just fine. Thank you." She put the phone down. The two of them were beaming at one another when suddenly, from just outside, came the sound of Christmas caroling. Going to the window, Fowler saw a group of boys knee-deep in snow and heard their voices lifted in the last refrain of the song. As they finished, one boy stepped forward. "Merry Christmas, Professor! Merry Christmas to you!"

Fowler raised the window. "And a merry Christmas to you, young men, a very merry Christmas indeed! And may I add how . . . how grateful I am to all of you. I've always thought that Christmas caroling is a wonderfully special tradition. Merry Christmas, boys, and God bless you!"

The boys waved as they moved off, gradually beginning another song.

Fowler lowered the window and turned to his house-keeper. "I've had a chance to think it over, Mrs. Landers, and I think I *will* retire. I do believe that I've taught all that I can teach. And I wouldn't want the returns to diminish."

He turned once again and stared out the window. Taking off his glasses, he went through the familiar ritual of peering through them, cleaning them, and slipping them back on. From a distant tower came the sound of chimes, with the echoes of a carol beyond it.

"I do believe . . . I do believe I may have left my mark." The old man smiled. " 'Be ashamed to die . . . until you have won some victory for humanity.' Mrs. Landers, *I* didn't win them, but I helped others to win them. I believe that now. So in that way—even in a small measure—they are victories I can share."

Gazing once more out the window, he nodded. "I've had a very good life, Mrs. Landers. A rich and fruitful life. And as for this particular changing of the guard . . . I wouldn't have it any other way."

In His Image

Charles Beaumont

TELEPLAY BY CHARLES BEAUMONT

AIRED JANUARY 3, 1963

STARRING GEORGE GRIZZARD AND GAIL KOBE

"I WAITED, MISTER," THE OLD WOMAN SAID. "FOR thirty years; yes sir." She smelled of hospital corridors, pressed ferns, dust: age had devoured her. Now there was nothing left, except the eyes which flashed.

The tall young man did not smile. His hands were almost fists, but the fingers were loose.

"All my life, since I was a little girl, can you imagine? Then it came, out of a clear sky, while I was ironing. Ironing on a Sunday, God save me. It came."

"What did?" the man said, because he had to say something, he couldn't just walk away or ignore her.

"The good Lord's Own sweet breath, that's what," the old woman said. "Like an electricity shock. I was revelated. Praise God, Mister, and praise His good works."

The man looked quickly away. The station was deserted. Its floor sparkled fiercely and this gave the impression of movement, but there was no movement. And there was no sound, either, except for the miles away roar of the train, and the old woman's voice, whispering and whispering.

Please lady!

"Mister, I wonder if you'd tell me something."

The young man did not answer. *Please!*

"Do you read the book?" She cocked her head and arched and smiled.

"What book is that, ma'am?"

"Why," her eyes blinked, "the *good* book, of course."

His fingers laced together, tightly. "Yes," he told her. "All the time."

She nodded, then raised one hand. It was thin and the flesh was transparent. "You're sure you're telling the truth now? We may be a mile underground, but He hears *every word.*"

"It's the truth."

Suddenly the old woman leaned forward. Her face was sharp bones and dry flesh and tiny white hairs. "All right," she said. "All right." The smile altered. Then, almost hissing: "Leviticus; Chapter Five; Verse Two!"

Where are the people!

"Well?" She was clucking her tongue. "Well, Mister?"

The young man rose from the bench and walked to the edge of the platform. In either direction there was darkness. He stood there, watching the darkness, listening to the growing thunder of the train.

It's got to come. It's got to come soon!

The old woman's shoes rang along the cement. She looked feeble and very small. About her shoulders an orange fox lay curled, its head beneath her chin, its eyes beady with cunning.

Train!

" 'Or if a soul touch any unclean thing, whether *it be* a carcass of an unclean beast, or a carcass of unclean cattle, or the carcass of unclean creeping things, and *if* it be hidden from him; he also shall be unclean, and guilty.' "

"Go away."

"Mister," the old woman said. She reached out and touched the young man's arm. It was hard and well-muscled, as the rest of him was.

He jerked away. "Leave me alone!"

"You want His infinite love, don't you?"

"No, goddamn it, no," he shouted. "Please, lady, get away from me."

"He forgives His sheep, Mister. Maybe you're afraid it's too late but you're wrong." She moved in front of the young man. "We are all His lambs . . ."

Her words became lost in the hollow roar, growing.

Jess!

The single headlight appeared, an immense, blinding circle of sharp brilliance.

The old woman's hands were fluttering. She blinked behind thick lenses and opened and closed her cracking lips.

The first car appeared.

The young man pulled his head around. The station was still deserted. It sang piercingly, and trembled, and shook loose flaming splinters of pain.

The old woman had stopped talking.

She stood there, smiling.

The young man took a step backwards and put his hands about the old woman's shoulders.

Her eyes widened.

He waited; then, as the Express burst out of the blackness, its dark metal tons lurching and jolting along the tracks, he released his hold and pushed.

The old woman fell over the edge of the platform.

"Good-bye, Walter!"

The train scooped her up and flattened her against the headlight and held her there for half an instant like a giant moth. Then she came loose.

The young man turned around and ran up the stairs.

Outside, the streets were crowded . . .

The door was opened to the length of its chain by a girl who was mostly shadow.

Peter Nolan put his hands behind his back and smiled. "Well, ma'am," he said, "see, I'm a member of the Junior Woodchucks—"

"The what?"

"—and all I got to do is sell one more subscription to get my genuine toy dial typewriter. What do you say?"

The girl said, "No," and closed the door.

Then she opened it again. "Hi, Pete."

"Hi." He stepped inside. The apartment was thick with heat. Through the drawn shades he could see the beginnings of sunlight. "Ready?" he said.

"And willing," the girl said. "Are you disappointed?"

"Just a little surprised." He put his hand on the back of the girl's neck and pulled gently. He kissed her.

"Pete! I've told you, there are lines I just don't cross."

"I was going to wait till after we got married, but then I figured what the hell." He touched her nose.

She wriggled out of his arms. "How come so late?"

"What am I, three minutes off schedule?"

"That's close. You miss by only half an hour."

He walked over to the couch, lay down, and groaned theatrically. "I keep telling you to get rid of that sun dial!"

"Okay, so you overslept," the girl said. "God knows leaving at six o'clock wasn't *my* idea."

He lit a cigarette. "I did not oversleep. I left the hotel at four-thirty A.M., got on a subway, got off the subway, and came directly here. Therefore—"

"Therefore, you're nuts. It's now five past six."

He sat upright, pulled back his coatsleeves, glared at a small Benrus.

"Don't worry about it, dear," she said, patting his knee. "I'm just glad I found out now."

She sniffed. "Oh-oh."

"Oh-oh what?"

"I think I smell the maid burning." She rushed across the room and into the kitchen. "You said you wanted to bring some food along, didn't you?"

"Sure."

"So I roasted us a chicken. We can have sandwiches."

He rose and walked into the kitchen. "You," he said, "are only the wildest."

She did not turn around.

He leaned against the refrigerator. "I know what you mean," he said. "It's too good."

"No." Jess did busy things with the chicken. "It's just that I'm happy—understand? And that's enough to give any girl the creeps this day and age."

He watched her work and was quiet for a while. Then he said, "Maybe you ought to change your mind."

She tried to press her hand against his mouth.

"I mean it. Do you really know what the hell you're doing?"

"Of course I do. I—a twenty-eight-year-old spinster, of sound mind and body—am going to run away to a town I never even heard of for the purpose of marrying a guy I've known exactly seven days. Is there anything odd about that?"

"I'm serious, Jess. Shouldn't you know a little more about me, or something?"

"Like what? I know that your name is Peter Nolan. I know that you live in Coeurville, New York, in a big white house surrounded by rose bushes and trees. I know that you do scientific research on a bomb—"

"Not a bomb," he smiled. "A computer. Electronics. See, you're romanticizing me already."

"Don't interrupt. You are visiting New York City for the pure morbid pleasure of it, currently rooming at the Chesterfield Inn. You make five hundred dollars a month, but have saved nothing—which tells me a good deal more about you than I care to know. But—let me finish! Apart from the libertine side of your personality, you are moderately intelligent—and immoderately handsome—kind to small dogs and old chestnut vendors but cool towards the rest of humanity. You prefer Basie to Bach, Grandma Moses to Van Gogh, and haven't made up your mind about this Faulkner critter. Above all, you're lonely and in desperate need of a woman five feet nine inches tall with black hair answering to the name of Jessica." She exhaled. "Now, is there anything important that I've missed? Not counting the multitudes of dark women out of your past, of course."

He picked up the wicker basket. "Okay," he said. "You got me dead to rights."

"In that case, let us away—before you start asking questions about *me*."

He kissed her very hard and held her.

"You'll like Coeurville, Jess," he said. "I know you will."

"I'd *better*, if I expect you to make an honest woman out of me! That town is rough competition."

"It's a good town."

She took the basket and waited for him to gather up the suitcases. "Homesick already," she murmured, "after not even two weeks away."

"You'll see," he said. "It's quite a place."

She nodded and looked around the apartment. Then she closed the door and locked it.

"Come on," she said, "let's go make it legal."

Fire!

A bright leaf on the rotted curtain first and then two leaves and three, and then the curtain falling and the leaves turned into blazing yellow ivy, reaching up the wall, across the floor, over all the tables and chairs, growing—

"*Walter!*"

—a forest of flame, hungry . . . and the man with the bandage quiet, still and quiet, waiting to be eaten . . .

Peter Nolan opened his eyes, quickly. The dream lingered a moment, and vanished.

"Has nightmares," Jess said, "screams, twitches, talks gibberish. *This* you didn't tell me."

The dream was gone. He tried to remember it, but it was gone. "Must have been the pastrami," he said, yawning, vaguely aware of the heat inside his skull. "Pastrami doesn't care much for me."

"I'd say it hates your guts." She whistled. "And who, may I inquire, is Walter?"

"Who is who?"

"You kept yelling Walter."

"Well," he said, "this is a poor time to be telling you, I suppose, but . . . he happens to be my brother."

"What?"

"Yes. We keep him in the cellar. I don't like to think about it."

"Pete."

"I don't know any Walter."

"Really?"

"Not that I can remember, anyway. Maybe he's the Father-Symbol . . . or would that be the Mother-Symbol?"

"Probably," Jess said, "it's the Sex-Symbol. Walter is your repressed libido, and he's champing at the bit."

The highway sloped gently and curved past an immense field of wild growth. Beyond the field there were farmhouses and straggles of horses and wild shade trees, small and bright in the clean air. The thunder of rockets rumbled distantly.

Peter Nolan stretched and yawned again. "Want me to take over?"

"If you want to," Jess stopped the car and they switched seat positions.

"Which reminds me," she said, "just how far is this rustic paradise?"

"Well . . ." He studied the countryside. "I *ought* to know, but I generally come through at night . . ."

"Pretty country, anyway," she said.

"The prettiest." He squinted, leaned close to the windshield. "I know where we are now. See that scatter creek?"

"Yup."

"Used to play there when I was a kid. Every time I ran away from home, this is as far as I got. Water's ice cold."

"Good old Scatter Creek!"

He nudged her. "Don't be so damn big-city. I intend to ac-

quaint you with every square inch of Coeurville, and you're
going to love it.''

"Aye, aye," she said, sleepily.

"Over there's Lonely Yew Lane. Great place for sparking
with the girlies.''

"How would you know?"

"Among sparking circles," he said, "I was referred to as
The Electrode.''

She made feline movements against him. "I'll just bet
you're the best known figure in town.''

"Only one of the best," he admitted. Then, "Lean your
head on my shoulder—we've got an hour anyway.''

She closed her eyes. In a tired, contented voice she whispered, "Pete Nolan, you have the sharpest, boniest, damndest shoulders in all the world.''

He slipped his arm around her, and they drove in silence
for a while. Things, he thought, are very good. Things are
about as good as they can be. If they were any better, I would
go berserk.

He thought of how he and Jess had met, only a week before. It had been late at night, and he had been walking . . .
where? Somewhere. And he was in the middle of the street,
when the light changed to red. Then something happened
—he couldn't figure out what, or why. Shock, maybe. Anyway, suddenly he was lying on his back, with the bumper of
a car less than three feet from his head. This car. And Jess,
standing there, whitefaced and trembling. *'Are you hurt, Mister?' 'You never laid a wheel on me.' 'In that case, I don't mind telling you, buddy, you have reduced me to a nervous wreck.' 'How
about a drink?' 'A drink would be fine.'* . . .

The field gave way to lawns and small houses and fresh-
fruit stands.

Peter Nolan eased off the accelerator. They passed a sign
which read: *You are entering Coeurville, N. Y.—Pop. 3,550.*

Then the houses multiplied and soon there were stores
and motels.

"Mah plantation," he boomed. "Fur as th' eye kin see!"

It was a very small town, and very narrow, pressed by grassy knolls and shaded by giant poplars which burst from the sidewalks. The streets were white and clean. Above the streets banners announcing a fair drifted calmly in the breeze, all reds and greens. There were a lot of women, but also a number of old men.

Peter Nolan smoothed the powerful turbines down and dropped rapidly from 114 miles-per-hour to a calm 40. He sighed. "There's the New Brunswick," he gestured. "Got an ice cream parlor and a magazine shop. You can get cigarettes there, too, if you can prove you're over twenty-one—Mr. van Brooks is very strict about that."

"I shouldn't have too much trouble."

"Over there's the Foodbag grocery where we trade. Depot's over to the right, you can't see it now. And—"

He narrowed his eyes.

He looked at a large red office building on the corner.

"Come on, don't stop now."

He shook his head, almost imperceptibly. "—library's down Elm Street, there—"

A red office building in Coeurville?

As he tried to place it, a clothing store glided slowly past the car window. Helmer's Men's Wear. Wide glass front, yellow plastic shade, perfectly ordinary and not in the least peculiar—except, he couldn't recall any Helmer's Men's Wear.

It was brand new to him.

Brother, you're an observant one, all right. Too much work . . . Town could burn down, you wouldn't know it.

Burn down . . .

"Pete, do me a favor."

"Sure."

"Let's get a quick one before meeting the gang, huh? Just one quick one."

"No can do," he said. "Have to go into Temple for liquor. That's four miles away."

"I thought I saw a bar back there on the main drag."

"Not in Coeurville you didn't." He frowned, felt a tenseness spring into life inside him. "How about coffee?"

"Okay."

He nosed the car onto a shoulder and cut the engine. *Burn . . .*

"Hey."

They walked past a dry goods store and a motion picture theatre and a drugstore.

And entered a small hotel lobby.

"Pete, what's biting you?"

He dropped the frown. "Nothing. The nervous bridegroom is all."

"Maybe we ought to get married right away," Jess said. She looked around the deserted lobby. It was dark and musty. "You want to get coffee here?" she said, dubiously.

"Down the street," someone said. Jess turned and faced an amiable old man in a blue suit. He was standing behind a desk. "Four stores down. Kelsey's Cafe."

Peter Nolan walked over to the man. "This is the Imperial, isn't it?" he asked, and thought, Of course this is the Imperial. What a stupid question.

"Sure is, Mister."

Sure is, Mister. Who is this old bird anyway?

"You close up your coffee shop?"

"Nope. Never had a coffee shop. Just the hotel."

The tenseness increased. "That's certainly very interesting," he told the man, remembering the five hundred or more times he'd eaten lunch here.

He snorted and walked across the lobby. It looked the same. Even the dust looked the same. He returned to the desk. "Is this a gag?"

The old man took a step backwards. "Beg pardon?"

Jess laughed. "Come on," she said, "they're probably using it for an orgy, stag only."

"But—"

Outside in the sunlight, Peter Nolan looked at the building carefully.

"It was here," he said, pointing to the brick wall. "At least, I think it was. Or else—did he say Kelsey's Cafe?"

"That's what he said."

"I never heard in my entire life of a Kelsey's Cafe." He turned his head, peered up and down the street. It was the same, and yet, somehow, it wasn't the same.

"You sure we're in the right town, Petesey?" Jess said. "I know how absent-minded you scientific men are."

"Of course I'm sure."

"Well, don't snap at me . . ."

"Look, Jess—let's go on home, get something there. I think maybe I'm a little upset. All right?"

"Sure."

They went back to the car.

"Is it far?"

"Just a few blocks." He felt the tenseness growing. As the houses passed, it grew. He thought about the red building, the bar Jess said she'd seen, and now this ridiculous business with the coffee shop . . . Just a mix-up, of course, that and his natural nervousness.

No. Something was wrong. He knew it, he could feel the wrongness all around him.

"That's it, isn't it?" Jess said. She was looking at a large square white house.

"Yeah." The familiarity of the house restored his spirits. The feeling drained away. "Your future home, Miss Lang." He stopped the car.

"It's beautiful, Pete. Really."

He got out of the car.

"Think I better go in first," he said. "The shock would be too great for Aunt Mildred."

"I thought you'd written her."

"I did, but I forgot to—" He took the letter from his inside coat pocket, and grinned.

"God, and you worry about forgetting coffee shops!"

He walked across the porch and tried the door.

It was locked.

He removed a key from his pocket and inserted it. It didn't work.

The feeling came back, sickeningly. He twisted the key first one way and then the other, and examined the chain to see that he'd not made a mistake.

The door opened.

"What is it?" A fat man with a fat red face stood glaring.

Peter Nolan glanced at the house numbers: 515. He glared back at the man. "Who are you?"

The fat man closed one eye. An old friend of Mildred's, probably—Mildred had so many screwy friends. Or a plumber, maybe. "Look, my name's Nolan. I live here. I own the house."

The fat man scratched his chin. He said nothing.

"Where's Mildred?"

"Who?"

"Mildred Nolan! Say, what the hell are you doing here, anyway?"

"It's none of your business," the fat man told him, "but I happen to live here. I've lived here for nine years, bought the place from Gerald Butler, got the deed to prove it. There ain't nobody named Mildred here and I never saw you before in my life." He started to close the door. "You got the wrong house."

"Look, fella, you're headed for a lot of trouble. I mean it. Now open up, and—"

The fat man slammed the door hurriedly.

Peter Nolan walked back to the car. He turned and stared.

"What's up?" Jess asked.

He looked at the house. At the curtains he'd never seen, and the *fresh* white paint, and the green doormat . . . He thought about the key that didn't fit the lock.

"Pete."

Goddamn it, what was happening? This was his house, all right, there wasn't any doubt of that. No doubt at all. None.

He looked at Jess, opened his mouth, closed it, and walked quickly across the street.

He went up the steps of a brown shake bungalow, and rapped on the door.

"Mrs. Cook! Hey, Jennie!"

A young girl appeared at the open window. "Who'd you want?" she said.

"Mrs. Cook. I've got to talk with her."

The girl leaned on her elbows. "Mrs. Cook died," she said. "Didn't you know?"

"What . . . did you say?"

"Three years ago. You aren't her cousin from Chicago, are you?"

"No," he said, dazedly. "No, I'm not. Sorry." He walked slowly back across the street and got into the car.

Jess was frowning, searching his face. "What is it, Pete?" she said. "Don't you think you better clue me in?"

"I don't—" He ran a hand through his hair. "The kid over there claims Mrs. Cook has been dead for three years."

"So what?"

"I had lunch with Mrs. Cook just before I left for New York . . . a week and a half ago."

For a long time now he had driven in silence, gazing directly ahead at the road, his hands tight about the steering wheel. The tachometer needle was hovering around the danger mark.

Jess sat close to the door. The smile that usually played about her face was gone. She looked different, just as everything looked different, and she no longer had the sixteen or seventeen year old's look.

For Peter Nolan the tension was now like a steel rail bent almost to the breaking point. It would snap at any moment, he felt sure. Because there was no suspecting now, only knowing, knowing absolutely. They'd driven from his house—*that* house, he wasn't sure whose it was any longer—to the city hall. Fred Dickey would clear things up, make the proper explanations, good old Fred. Except good old Fred hadn't recognized him. Neither had Bert Zangwill over at the sheriff's office—Bert, who used to tell them stories, who was a hero to him! And the others, the friends he had known all his life—all dead, or gone away, or unable to remember him . . .

But not completely unable. That was the strangest thing of all. The way they would stare and seem about to greet him and then shake their heads . . .

He felt like screaming now, as he remembered how Jess' face had changed in the past two hours, how her eyes had changed, how she looked at him, the suspicion and the wonder only too obvious.

God, maybe I am nuts, he thought, maybe I really am. Then, No, dammit! This is Coeurville and this is my home and I know every foot of it. That tree over there, the strawberry patch we're passing, everything. I do!

Jess was rubbing the back of her neck. ''Pete—''

''Yes?''

''You said something a little while ago, back in town . . . You said it was as though Coeurville had aged twenty years. Didn't you?''

''That's right. Twenty years—in a week and a half.''

''Maybe not,'' she said.

''What do you mean?''

''I'm not really sure, but—this is going to sound corny. I just mean, what if it's true? What if twenty years actually have gone by?''

''Rip van Winkle?''

She shrugged. ''Well, why not? At least it's a possibility.''

''No,'' he said. ''I thought of it, but it doesn't hold up. For a lot of reasons. One, it would make me at least forty-five—unless I left at age ten. Which couldn't very well be, because I went to high school and college here. And that,'' he sighed, nervously, ''brings us to the real beaut. There are no records of my having attended Coeurville High. Remember?''

She nodded.

"And the university I work for, dear old Coeurville U., it doesn't even exist. It never existed." He thought of the feeling in his chest when they'd driven out onto that unbroken field of grass which had been a campus, had been, he knew, had to have been. "And what about Mildred?"

Jess shivered slightly.

"Mildred was the head of the Garden Club," he continued. "She got around town like a visiting Congressman, all the time. Everybody knew her. And now there isn't a single trace of evidence to show that Mildred Nolan ever lived in Coeurville, New York."

"Okay, so it won't work. It was an idea."

The berry patches became fields once more, golden brown and dark, almost black, green. Peter Nolan turned down a small gravel road and decelerated sharply and drove the road that wound through the fields.

He hit the brake at a curve and slid to a stop.

"Wait here," he said.

He got out of the car and walked through the rusted wire gate of the cemetery. It was a small place, and very old. The gravestones were ornate carvings of fat children with wings or great scrolls or filagreed crosses, all grimed with age.

He walked across the raised humps of neglected lawn, toward the east end of the cemetery. Beyond the fence was rich grass, dairy cows grazing in utter silence, and a dark stream crossed by a trestle.

Peter Nolan approached two marble tombstones, and remembered with every step the sadness he had felt when he had stood exactly here, in the foul rain, and watched them lower his mother's casket, down close to the father he had never known.

The memory was alive and strong. It was the one thing he was sure of, now.

He knelt and stared at the twin epitaphs on the tombstones.

And felt the steel bar of tenseness inside him snap and explode into a million white-hot fragments.

The epitaphs read:

MARY F. CUMMINGS
1883 – 1931
and
WALTER B. CUMMINGS, SR.
1879 – 1909

The sky was a deep red stain now. Jess pushed hard on the pedal, keeping it at a steady 140. Her lips were dry.

"We'll be home in a little while," she said, softly, "and then it'll be okay. Go on, pass out again. Rest."

The speed lane merged with the narrow highway and the traffic thinned and disappeared. Barns and farmhouses flashed past the window in a darkening blur.

Peter Nolan sat very still. He clutched his knees.

The pain that was not precisely that vanished and returned and grew and diminished. He fought it with all of his strength. But it would not stay away. Nothing he did would make it stay away.

Memories skirted close, and he kept reaching for them.

Fire. A man with bandages. A house.

He reached and sometimes came very near, and always missed. No. It would take something more than reaching. But what? And for what?

The car pulled into a service station and he shut his eyes against the sudden brilliance.

What was she trying to do, anyway, blind him?

And who the hell did she think she was to order him around?

He looked at Jess. She smiled.

Then he remembered that she had used the word *doctor*. Why? To cure him, or—to get rid of him, quietly?

Of course. One of her doctor friends would slip him a

needle and that would be that. Never mind the reason. Women have their own reasons.

He waited until the sky had turned almost completely black, then he said, "Jess, would you please stop the car?"

She pulled over onto the dirt. "You going to be sick?"

"Yeah," he said. "I'll be back in a minute. I don't feel so good."

He went outside, leaped the shallow ditch, and walked into the dense foliage.

His shoe scraped. He bent down and patted the ground and closed his fingers about a large jagged stone.

Good. We'll see about doctors now.

"Jess!" he called. "Could you give me a hand?"

A pause. Then the sound of the metal door opening and slamming and the sound of movement in the brush.

Jess walked over to him and touched his arm.

"Is it better?" she asked.

"Yes."

Her eyes moved to his hand.

He raised the stone, stood there with it raised, staring; then he turned and threw the stone into the foliage in back of him.

"What is it, Pete?"

"Stubbed my damn toe." He moved toward Jess and pulled her close. "Stubbed my toe on the rock." The pain was leaving. It had torn across his mind like a sheet of flame, until there had been only a dancing blackness. Now it was leaving.

Jess put her fingers against his face, gently. "Come on back to the car," she said.

He took his hands from her.

"Come on, Pete."

"All right. You go on—I'll be there in a minute."

She looked at him helplessly, then she walked back. When she was gone, when he heard the door again, Peter Nolan closed his eyes. He waited for the pain to return, but it did not return. He tried to hang on to the memories that had been flying quickly through his brain, but they were elusive. Something about an old woman, something about a train, they were, and fire, and—

He realized, suddenly, why he had picked up the stone.

He had meant to kill Jess.

Why?

He bunched his fingers into fists and drove them, hard, into a tree, again, and again.

Then he stopped. The moon slid out of a clump of blackness, and spilled light over the land—cool, soft, clear light.

Peter Nolan looked at his hands. He turned them over and looked at them.

They were white and dry.

The tree bark had torn away small strips and pieces of flesh, but there was no blood.

He carefully pulled a flap of skin down three inches below the wrist, and focused his eyes.

Beneath the flap of skin, where veins ought to have been, and cartilage, and bone, were hundreds of tiny flexible rods, jointed and gleaming, and infinitesimal springs, turning, and bright yellow coils of wire.

He looked at his wrist watch for a long time. Then he wrapped a handkerchief around the torn section, and went back to the car.

Jess was waiting. "Better now?" she asked in the same genuine, unfrightened tone she had used before.

"Better," he said. Everything was returning now. Like relays clicking into place. Everything.

He threw his head back. "Drive to your apartment," he said, expressionlessly. "Let me off when I tell you to, then drive to your apartment and wait for me."

Jess said nothing. She started the car.

Soon they were in the outskirts of the city.

He walked up the circular driveway and stood for a moment, looking at the house. It was fat and sprawling and ugly: a little of 1860 and a little of 1960, brick and wood, gabled windows, false pilasters. Its color was gray. Where once had been white paint was now only this grayness. The age-bulged slats were pocked and cancered, held by crumbling nails.

He walked to the machine-carved door.

The knocker put out deep sound.

He waited, knocked again.

The door opened.

"Hello, Walter."

The tall man with the bandaged face sighed. "Pete," he said, extending his hand. "I've been waiting for you."

Peter Nolan walked with the tall man into a large room.

There were hundreds of books in this room, all shabby and worn, a few heavy pieces of furniture, mostly ancient, fancy letter openers, dark lace curtains.

"Sit down," the tall man said. "Over there." He walked over to a small cupboard and poured whiskey into a glass. "You've been to Coeurville, haven't you?"

"Yes. Tell me about it, Walter."

"But you know already. How else could you have come here?"

"I asked you to talk. Please."

The tall man paused, then shrugged. "All right." He reached up and tore loose from his forehead the upper strips of adhesive tape.

The bandages fell.

Peter Nolan stared at an exact duplicate of himself. Except for the stitched scar running from just below the left eye to the mouth, the face was a mirrored reflection.

"As you can see, you nearly blinded me with those scissors."

"From the beginning, Walter."

"But this *is* the beginning," the tall man said. Then, "All right. Your name is Peter Nolan—you know that."

"Yes."

"And you know that you were born eight days ago. I made the delivery: Doctor W. B. Cummings, Jr., Ph.D. I'm your mother. I'm also your father—and every single one of your ancestors, too, unless we count the first adding machine."

"You're drunk."

"Aye. Drunk as an owl. Drunk as a lord. Care to join me? It's quite possible, and I guarantee no hangover—"

"All I want is for you to stow the colorful dialogue and tell me things."

The tall man tilted his glass. "You've been to Coeurville, so you've learned that Peter Nolan never lived there. You also know that you've been behaving—oddly—of late. And from the handkerchief around your hand, I should judge you know about that, too. With this information what can *I* tell you?"

"Who am I?" The heat was beginning again.

"You're nobody," the tall man said. "You're nobody at all."

"Stop it, Walter."

"Who is this watch I'm wearing? Ask me that. Who is the refrigerator in the kitchen? Don't you understand?" The man's eyes glinted briefly. "You're a machine, Pete."

Memories took solider form. They came into focus.

But not entirely. Pieces were missing.

"Go on."

The tall man pulled his dressing gown closer about his unshaven throat. He seemed to talk to himself alone.

"You were born a long time ago, actually," he said. "Inside my head. All kids have dreams, don't they? You were mine. The others thought about ice cream mountains and success with the F.B.I. and going to Mars, and swapped their dreams, and finally forgot them. I didn't. I thought about one thing and longed for one thing, always; just one: a *perfect* artificial man. Not just a robot, but a duplicate of a human being." He laughed. "It was harmless—and not even terribly imaginative for a child. I became an adult—only, I didn't forget my dream."

Peter Nolan picked up one of the letter openers. It was sturdy and sharp.

"All right," the tall man said, "I made you. Is that straight enough? It took a lot of years and a lot of money, and more failures than I like to think about. But I was patient. I studied, I read, I experimented. I'd already built a man—also Peter Nolan: I like the name: no reason—but he was nothing. A crude job. So I started all over again from scratch, duplicating from every manner of material the physical elements of the human body. People helped me, but they didn't know what it was for. Some of them solved problems I could never have solved. But—don't you see? I wanted to give my man a brain that worked like a brain; and emotions; and intelligence." He refilled the glass, took another swallow. "All that—I dreamed. Of course, intelligence was the most difficult. You have no idea how difficult. My man had to have memories, he had to have reasoning power—abstract reasoning power —a past, a personality—millions of intricate facets multiplied by millions to make up *intelligence*. Inventing these things from whole cloth would have taken forever. So I worked and found the answer. I would use myself. On certain cells I made certain impressions. My own memories went into the cells. Some of my talent. Some of my knowledge. Bits and pieces, of myself. It took a long time . . . a very long time."

They were silent for a time. Peter Nolan gripped the letter opener and struggled against the heat.

"You were perfect, I felt," the tall man went on. "But I had to be sure. Ten years ago you would have been impossible: since the discoveries in plastics, however, you were merely improbable. My plastic felt like flesh to *me*, and I had cushioned the mechanical parts so that they felt exactly like human bones when touched, but—it would be the final test: to let you mingle with crowds, and observe closely their reactions. I blocked out—or tried to—all memory of me and your actual construction. You were Peter Nolan, research scientist, in New York on a sabbatical . . ."

"You lived in Coeurville?" The question leapt out.

"Of course. For your past, I gave you my memories of the

town. Some of them were probably quite inaccurate and incomplete—I left Coeurville many years ago. Going there must have been an experience . . .''

"It was." Peter Nolan closed his eyes. "What about the University?"

"Fictitious. I had to give you a job."

"And Aunt Mildred?"

"A conceit. All the old women I've known in one. I worked out your relationship with her very carefully—not at all necessary, I suppose. The female conquests, by the way, are also—I regret to report—imaginary." He shook a cigarette loose from a pack. "That's about all," he said. "You can fill in the rest. Up to last week, anyway."

"What about last week."

The tall man shook his head. "I wish I knew," he said. "Something went wrong, something mechanical . . . I couldn't tell. You attacked me with a pair of scissors and I couldn't stop you. As you know, I've been unable to find you since."

"What's wrong with me?"

"I'm not sure. But—look, Pete. You're me. Everything you know or feel or think reflects some portion of myself, Walter Cummings. If you wished to kill—I've read the papers, I know about it; the conductor caught a glimpse of you—it could only mean that there is some part of me that wished to kill. *My* own death-wish, inverted. Everyone has it. I mean, we're all potential suicides or murderers or rapists or thieves. We all have the seeds of paranoia, schizophrenia, or worse, lying inside us, somewhere—from the moment we're born to the moment we die. But—and here's the thing—if we're normal, we're protected. We're protected by our inhibitions. These instincts are never given a chance to get out of hand. We may *want* to kill the loudmouthed woman downstairs, or we may *want* to commit suicide at times—but usually we don't."

"So?"

"So, Pete, it would appear that my own 'seeds' are more

developed than I'd realized. In you, they are. In giving you parts of myself, I also gave you—although unintentionally—my latent psychoses. Big ones. Big enough to break through . . .''

There was a long silence.

"To put it even clearer," the tall man said, "you're insane."

Peter Nolan rose from the couch and walked over to the window. The night pressed, moved, tugged at the branches of dead trees.

"Can I be—fixed?"

The tall man shrugged.

The heat dripped faster, melting into pain. Whirlings and bright dots and pain. "Can I?"

"I don't know."

"Why don't you know?"

"Because . . . much as I hated to admit it, luck had a great deal to do with your success." The man stared at the letter opener in Peter Nolan's hand. "Skill alone wasn't enough. There were so many failures before, they should have made it clear—but they didn't. I was obsessed."

"What are you saying?"

"That you were an accident. I was a blind man with a machine gun, Pete. I kept shooting and reloading and shooting and finally I hit the target; but it was off-center. I don't know that I could even come close again."

Peter Nolan fought the pain, grasped at the picture of an old woman falling toward dark tracks.

The tall man smiled, wanly. "But that's the story of my life, right down the line. A long series of failures. I told myself that I wanted to make an artificial man, but I think my real aim was simply to build another Walter Cummings. Only, without the shyness, without the frustration—a reverse Jekyll and Hyde. All I wished I was. The 'real' me . . ."

Peter Nolan turned. "I came here to kill you," he said.

The tall man nodded.

"I was going to kill you and set fire to the house."

"I know: I felt like doing it myself. It's what I'd do if I were in your shoes."

"There's a girl, Walter."

The tall man raised his eyebrows; then he lit another cigarette, slowly, off the old one.

"Does she know?" he said.

"No. I took her with me to Coeurville; we were going to get married there; and she thinks I'm probably nuts—but she doesn't know. She's in love with me."

"Pretty?"

"And intelligent. And lonely—something you ought to be able to understand. She's got a fine life all mapped out, for her and me, together."

"That's—too bad," the tall man said. He pressed his fingertips into his temples. "I'm truly sorry, Pete."

"Her name is Jessica Lang. She has old-fashioned ideas about virtue: that's why she never found out, I imagine." Peter Nolan gripped the edge of the chair. "That would have been a nice scene."

"No," the tall man said. "You're perfect. It would have gone all right—that is, if she's a virgin. It would seem strange, but then, it always does. Or so I've heard."

The pain jabbed in and out, fire-tipped needles, jabbing.

The tall man rose from the couch-arm on which he had been seated. "Well," he said, "what are we going to do?"

"You can't fix me for sure?"

"No."

"You can't stop me from killing. You can't make me grow old, either—I'll always be like this. I'm insane and I'll stay insane, until something goes out—then I'll die. Is that it?"

"I'm sorry, Pete. I wanted you to be all the things I wasn't; that's the truth. If I'd known—"

Peter Nolan put his hands out. "She'd learn about it, some day," he said.

"Yes. She would."

"She'd find out, or I'd kill her—I almost did, tonight. I might kill Jess."

"You might."

The two figures were very quiet for a time. The wind beat against the loose window panes, and against the shutters of the house.

They were quiet, listening.

Then Peter Nolan said: "Do you want to make it right, Walter?"

The tall man clenched his fists. "I would give anything to do that."

"Are you telling the truth?"

"Yes."

"Then listen to me carefully. You're going to build another Peter Nolan—"

"What?"

"That's right. You're going to build another me, and it's going to be right, this time, and you're going to do it tonight. This Peter Nolan is going to marry Jess; and he's going to be happy, for the first time in his life."

The tall man stared.

Understanding came into his eyes, slowly.

"It's something you can do—*now*—isn't it?"

"I think so."

"Then let's get to work, before I jam this letter opener into your chest."

"Pete—"

"Come on."

Together, they walked into the hall and down the long flight of stairs to the laboratory below.

Hours later one of them returned to the study.

The door was opened to the length of its chain by a girl who was mostly shadow.

The tall man put his hands behind his back and smiled. "Well, ma'am," he said, "see, I'm a member of the Junior Woodchucks—"

"Pete, get in here this minute. I've been worried sick."

The tall man walked into the apartment. He paused for a moment, then he took the girl into his arms and kissed her. She pulled away. "And now, before I go crazy," she said, "will you please tell me what this is all about?"

The tall man smiled. "I'll tell you what it's all about," he promised. "But let's not talk here."

"I want to know if you're all right," Jess said, looking at him. "What's that scar on your face?"

"I'm all right," the tall man said. "Come on, a drink. Get your coat."

Jess went to the closet and pulled out a jacket and slipped it on.

They went out of the apartment.

A cold gray moon spread light across the streets.

"Pete, something is wrong. I know it is."

"No," the tall man said. "Other way around. Something is right, for a change." He held her arm and looked at her and then she saw his smile and stopped talking.

They went into a bar.

At a table, after they ordered, he lit a cigarette for her. Then he lit one for himself. He held the flame of the lighter before his face for a long moment, and he heard her exclaim as he ran his index finger through the flame. Hot pain seared through him. He pulled his finger away, snapped off the lighter and grinned at her.

"What did you burn your finger for, Pete? You did it deliberately . . ."

He laughed. "Couldn't help it. Had to prove something to myself."

"What?"

He shrugged, still smiling. "Had to make sure I was really flesh and blood and not some part of a plastic nightmare . . ."

"I don't understand, Pete."

"Not necessary, honey. Not at all. Everything's ok. The past is gone and for the first time in my life I'm looking forward to the future. In a way I guess we're seeing each other for the first time. What I see is nice.''

The waiter brought their drinks. He raised his, wiggled his burnt finger for her to do likewise, and proffered a toast.

Outside the bar an old man in a dirty white raincoat walked up and down, carrying newspapers.

''Subway killer still at large!'' the old man shouted.

His voice was a whisper in the wind.

Mute

Richard Matheson

Teleplay by Richard Matheson

Aired January 31, 1963

Starring Ann Jillian, Frank Overton, and
Barbara Baxley

THE MAN IN THE DARK RAINCOAT ARRIVED IN GERman Corners at two-thirty that Friday afternoon. He walked
across the bus station to a counter behind which a plump,
grey-haired woman was polishing glasses.

"Please," he said. "Where might I find authority?"

The woman peered through rimless glasses at him. She
saw a man in his late thirties, a tall, good-looking man.

"Authority?" she asked.

"Yes—how do you say it? The constable? The—?"

"Sheriff?"

"Ah." The man smiled. "Of course. The sheriff. Where
might I find him?"

After being directed, he walked out of the building into the
overcast day. The threat of rain had been constant since he'd
woken up that morning as the bus was pulling over the
mountains into Casca Valley. The man drew up his collar,
then slid both hands into the pockets of his raincoat and
started briskly down Main Street.

Really, he felt tremendously guilty for not having come

sooner; but there was so much to do, so many problems to overcome with his own two children. Even knowing that something was wrong with Holger and Fanny, he'd been unable to get away from Germany until now—almost a year since they'd last heard from the Nielsens. It was a shame that Holger had chosen such an out-of-the-way place for his corner of the four-sided experiment.

Professor Werner walked more quickly, anxious to find out what had happened to the Nielsens and their son. Their progress with the boy had been phenomenal—really an inspiration to them all. Although Werner felt, deep within himself, that something terrible had happened, he hoped they were all alive and well. Yet, if they were, how to account for the long silence?

Werner shook his head worriedly. Could it have been the town? Elkenberg had been compelled to move several times in order to avoid the endless prying—sometimes innocent, more often malicious—into *his* work. Something similar might have happened to Nielsen. The workings of the small-town composite mind could, sometimes, be a terrible thing.

The sheriff's office was in the middle of the next block. Werner strode more quickly along the narrow sidewalk, then pushed open the door and entered the large, warmly heated room.

"Yes?" the sheriff asked, looking up from his desk.

"I have come to inquire about a family," Werner said. "The name of Nielsen."

Sheriff Harry Wheeler looked blankly at the tall man.

Cora was pressing Paul's trousers when the call came. Setting the iron on its stand, she walked across the kitchen and lifted the receiver from the wall telephone.

"Yes?" she said.

"Cora, it's me."

Her face tightened. "Is something wrong, Harry?"

He was silent.

"Harry?"

"The one from Germany is here."

Cora stood motionless, staring at the calendar on the wall, the numbers blurred before her eyes.

"Cora, did you hear me?"

She swallowed dryly. "Yes."

"I-I have to bring him out to the house," he said.

She closed her eyes.

"I know," she murmured, and hung up.

Turning, she walked slowly to the window. It's going to rain, she thought. Nature was setting the scene well.

Abruptly, her eyes shut, her fingers drew in tautly, the nails digging at her palms.

"No." It was almost a gasp. *"No."*

After a few moments she opened her tear-glistening eyes and looked out fixedly at the road. She stood there numbly, thinking of the day the boy had come to her.

If the house hadn't burned in the middle of the night there might have been a chance. It was twenty-one miles from German Corners but the state highway ran fifteen of them and the last six—the six miles of dirt road that led north into the wood-sloped hills—might have been navigated had there been more time.

As it happened, the house was a night-lashing sheet of flame before Bernhard Klaus saw it.

Klaus and his family lived some five miles away on Sky-touch Hill. He had gotten out of bed around one-thirty to get a drink of water. The window of the bathroom faced north and that was why, entering, Klaus saw the tiny flaring blaze out in the darkness.

"Gott'n'immel!" he slung startled words together and was out of the room before he'd finished. He thumped heavily down the carpeted steps, then, feeling at the wall for guidance, hurried for the livingroom.

"Fire at Nielsen house!" he gasped after agitated cranking had roused the night operator from her nap.

The hour, the remoteness, and one more thing doomed

the house. German Corners had no official fire brigade. The security of its brick and timbered dwellings depended on voluntary effort. In the town itself this posed no serious problem. It was different with those houses in the outlying areas.

By the time Sheriff Harry Wheeler had gathered five men and driven them to the fire in the ancient truck, the house was lost. While four of the six men pumped futile streams of water into the leaping, crackling inferno, Sheriff Wheeler and his deputy, Max Ederman, circuited the house.

There was no way in. They stood in back, raised arms warding off the singeing buffet of heat, grimacing at the blaze.

"They're done for!" Ederman yelled above the windswept roar.

Sheriff Wheeler looked sick. "The *boy*," he said, but Ederman didn't hear.

Only a waterfall could have doused the burning of the old house. All the six men could do was prevent ignition of the woods that fringed the clearing. Their silent figures prowled the edges of the glowing aura, stamping out sparks, hosing out the occasional flare of bushes and tree foliage.

They found the boy just as the eastern hill peaks were being edged with grey morning.

Sheriff Wheeler was trying to get close enough to see into one of the side windows when he heard a shout. Turning, he ran toward the thick woods that sloped downward a few dozen yards behind the house. Before he'd reached the underbrush, Tom Poulter emerged from them, his thin frame staggering beneath the weight of Paal Nielsen.

"Where'd you find him?" Wheeler asked, grabbing the boy's legs to ease weight from the other man's back.

"Down the hill," Poulter gasped. "Lyin' on the ground."

"Is he burned?"

"Don't look it. His pajamas ain't touched."

"Give him here," the sheriff said. He shifted Paal into his own strong arms and found two large, green-pupiled eyes staring blankly at him.

"You're awake," he said, surprised.

The boy kept staring at him without making a sound.

"You all right, son?" Wheeler asked. It might have been a statue he held, Paal's body was so inert, his expression so dumbly static.

"Let's get a blanket on him," the sheriff muttered aside, and started for the truck. As he walked he noticed how the boy stared at the burning house now, a look of masklike rigidity on his face.

"*Shock*," murmured Poulter, and the sheriff nodded grimly.

They tried to put him down on the cab seat, a blanket over him, but he kept sitting up, never speaking. The coffee Wheeler tried to give him dribbled from his lips and across his chin. The two men stood beside the truck while Paal stared through the windshield at the burning house.

"Bad off," said Poulter. "Can't talk, cry nor nothin'."

"He isn't burned," Wheeler said, perplexed. "How'd he get out of the house without getting burned?"

"Maybe his folks got out too," said Poulter.

"Where are they then?"

The older man shook his head. "Dunno, Harry."

"Well, I better take him home to Cora," the sheriff said. "Can't leave him sitting out here."

"Think I'd better go with you," Poulter said. "I have t'get the mail sorted for delivery."

"All right."

Wheeler told the other four men he'd bring back food and replacements in an hour or so. Then Poulter and he climbed into the cab beside Paal and he jabbed his boot toe on the starter. The engine coughed spasmodically, groaned over, then caught. The sheriff raced it until it was warm, then eased it into gear. The truck rolled off slowly down the dirt road that led to the highway.

Until the burning house was no longer visible, Paal stared out the back window, face still immobile. Then, slowly, he turned, the blanket slipping off his thin shoulders. Tom Poulter put it back over him.

"Warm enough?" he asked.

The silent boy looked at Poulter as if he'd never heard a human voice in his life.

As soon as she heard the truck turn off the road, Cora Wheeler's quick right hand moved along the stove-front switches. Before her husband's bootfalls sounded on the back porch steps, the bacon lay neatly in strips across the frying pan, white moons of pancake batter were browning on the griddle, and the already brewed coffee was heating.

"*Harry.*"

There was a sound of pitying distress in her voice as she saw the boy in his arms. She hurried across the kitchen.

"Let's get him to bed," Wheeler said. "I think maybe he's in shock."

The slender woman moved up the stairs on hurried feet, threw open the door of what had been David's room, and moved to the bed. When Wheeler passed through the doorway she had the covers peeled back and was plugging in an electric blanket.

"Is he hurt?" she asked.

"No." He put Paal down on the bed.

"Poor darling," she murmured, tucking in the bedclothes around the boy's frail body. "Poor little darling." She stroked back the soft blonde hair from his forehead and smiled down at him.

"There now, go to sleep, dear. It's all right. Go to sleep."

Wheeler stood behind her and saw the seven-year-old boy staring up at Cora with that same dazed, lifeless expression. It hadn't changed once since Tom Poulter had brought him out of the woods.

The sheriff turned and went down to the kitchen. There he phoned for replacements, then turned the pancakes and bacon, and poured himself a cup of coffee. He was drinking it when Cora came down the back stairs and returned to the stove.

"Are his parents—?" she began.

"I don't know," Wheeler said, shaking his head. "We couldn't get near the house."

"But the boy—?"

"Tom Poulter found him outside."

"Outside."

"We don't know how he got out," he said. "All we know's he was there."

His wife grew silent. She slid pancakes on a dish and put the dish in front of him. She put her hand on his shoulder.

"You look tired," she said. "Can you go to bed?"

"Later," he said.

She nodded, then, patting his shoulder, turned away. "The bacon will be done directly," she said.

He grunted. Then, as he poured maple syrup over the stack of cakes, he said, "I expect they are dead, Cora. It's an awful fire; still going when I left. Nothing we could do about it."

"That poor boy," she said.

She stood by the stove watching her husband eat wearily.

"I tried to get him to talk," she said, shaking her head, "but he never said a word."

"Never said a word to us either," he told her. "Just stared."

He looked at the table, chewing thoughtfully.

"Like he didn't even know how to talk," he said.

A little after ten that morning the waterfall came—a waterfall of rain—and the burning house sputtered and hissed into charred, smoke-fogged ruins.

Red-eyed and exhausted, Sheriff Wheeler sat motionless in the truck cab until the deluge had slackened. Then, with a chest-deep groan, he pushed open the door and slid to the ground. There, he raised the collar of his slicker and pulled down the wide-brimmed Stetson more tightly on his skull. He walked around to the back of the covered truck.

"Come on," he said, his voice hoarsely dry. He trudged through the clinging mud toward the house.

The front door still stood. Wheeler and the other men bypassed it and clambered over the collapsed livingroom wall. The sheriff felt thin waves of heat from the still-glowing timbers, and the throat-clogging reek of wet, smoldering rugs and upholstery turned his edgy stomach.

He stepped across some half-burned books on the floor and the roasted bindings crackled beneath his tread. He kept moving, into the hall, breathing through gritted teeth, rain spattering off his shoulders and back. I hope they got out, he thought. I hope to God they got out.

They hadn't. They were still in their bed, no longer human, blackened to a hideous, joint-twisted crisp. Sheriff Wheeler's face was taut and pale as he looked down at them.

One of the men prodded a wet twig at something on the mattress.

"Pipe," Wheeler heard him say above the drum of rain. "Must have fell asleep smokin'."

"Get some blankets," Wheeler told them. "Put them in the back of the truck."

Two of the men turned away without a word and Wheeler heard them clump away over the rubble.

He was unable to take his eyes off Professor Holger Nielsen and his wife, Fanny, scorched into grotesque mockeries of the handsome couple he remembered—the tall, big-framed Holger, calmly imperious; the slender, auburn-haired Fanny, her face a soft, rose-cheeked—

Abruptly, the sheriff turned and stumbled from the room, almost tripping over a fallen beam.

The boy—what would happen to the boy now? That day was the first time Paal had ever left this house in his life. His parents were the fulcrum of his world; Wheeler knew that much. No wonder there had been that look of shocked incomprehension on Paal's face.

Yet how did he know his mother and father were dead?

As the sheriff crossed the livingroom, he saw one of the men looking at a partially charred book.

"Look at this," the man said, holding it out.

Wheeler glanced at it, his eyes catching the title: *The Unknown Mind.*

He turned away tensely. "Put it down!" he snapped, quitting the house with long, anxious strides. The memory of how the Nielsens looked went with him; and something else. A question.

How did Paal get out of the house?

Paal woke up.

For a long moment he stared up at the formless shadows that danced and fluttered across the ceiling. It was raining out. The wind was rustling tree boughs outside the window, causing shadow movements in this strange room. Paal lay motionless in the warm center of the bed, air crisp in his lungs, cold against his pale cheeks.

Where were they? Paal closed his eyes and tried to sense their presence. They weren't in the house. Where then? Where were his mother and father?

Hands of my mother. Paal washed his mind clean of all but the trigger symbol. They rested on the ebony velvet of his concentration—pale, lovely hands, soft to touch and be touched by, the mechanism that could raise his mind to the needed level of clarity.

In his own home it would be unnecessary. His own home was filled with the sense of them. Each object touched by them possessed a power to bring their minds close. The very air seemed charged with their consciousness, filled with a constancy of attention.

Not here. He needed to lift himself above the alien drag of here.

Therefore, I am convinced that each child is born with this instinctive ability. Words given to him by his father appearing again like dew-jeweled spider web across the fingers of his mother's hands. He stripped it off. The hands were free again, stroking slowly at the darkness of his mental focus. His eyes were shut; a tracery of lines and ridges scarred his brow, his tightened jaw was bloodless. The level of awareness, like waters, rose.

His senses rose along, unbidden.

Sound revealed its woven maze—the rushing, thudding, drumming, dripping rain; the tangled knit of winds through air and tree and gabled eave; the crackling settle of the house; each whispering transience of process.

Sense of smell expanded to a cloud of brain-filling odors—wood and wool, damp brick and dust and sweet starched linens. Beneath his tensing fingers weave became apparent—coolness and warmth, the weight of covers, the delicate, skin-scarring press of rumpled sheet. In his mouth the taste of cold air, old house. Of sight, only the hands.

Silence; lack of response. He'd never had to wait so long for answers before. Usually, they flooded on him easily. His mother's hands grew clearer. They pulsed with life. Unknown, he climbed beyond. *This bottom level sets the stage for more important phenomena.* Words of his father. He'd never gone above that bottom level until now.

Up, up. Like cool hands drawing him to rarified heights. Tendrils of acute consciousness rose toward the peak, searching desperately for a holding place. The hands began breaking into clouds. The clouds dispersed.

It seemed he floated toward the blackened tangle of his home, rain a glistening lace before his eyes. He saw the front door standing, waiting for his hand. The house drew closer. It was engulfed in licking mists. Closer, closer—

Paal, no.

His body shuddered on the bed. Ice frosted his brain. The house fled suddenly, bearing with itself a horrid image of two black figures lying on—

Paal jolted up, staring and rigid. Awareness maelstromed into its hiding place. One thing alone remained. He knew that they were gone. He knew that they had guided him, sleeping, from the house.

Even as they burned.

* * *

That night they knew he couldn't speak.

There was no reason for it, they thought. His tongue was there, his throat looked healthy. Wheeler looked into his opened mouth and saw that. But Paal did not speak.

"So *that's* what it was," the sheriff said, shaking his head gravely. It was near eleven. Paal was asleep again.

"What's that, Harry?" asked Cora, brushing her dark blonde hair in front of the dressing table mirror.

"Those times when Miss Frank and I tried to get the Nielsens to start the boy in school." He hung his pants across the chair back. "The answer was always no. Now I see why."

She glanced up at his reflection. "There must be something wrong with him, Harry," she said.

"Well, we can have Doc Steiger look at him but I don't think so."

"But they were college people," she argued. "There was no earthly reason why they shouldn't teach him how to talk. Unless there was some reason he *couldn't*."

Wheeler shook his head again.

"They were strange people, Cora," he said. "Hardly spoke a word themselves. As if they were too good for talking—or something." He grunted disgustedly. "No wonder they didn't want that boy to school."

He sank down on the bed with a groan and shucked off boots and calf-high stockings. "What a day," he muttered.

"You didn't find anything at the house?"

"Nothing. No identification papers at all. The house is burned to a cinder. Nothing but a pile of books and they don't lead us anywhere."

"Isn't there any way?"

"The Nielsens never had a charge account in town. And they weren't even citizens, so the professor wasn't registered for the draft."

"Oh." Cora looked a moment at her face reflected in the oval mirror. Then her gaze lowered to the photograph on the dressing table—David as he was when he was nine. The Nielsen boy looked a great deal like David, she thought. Same height and build. Maybe David's hair had been a trifle darker but—

"What's to be done with him?" she asked.

"Couldn't say, Cora," he answered. "We have to wait till the end of the month, I guess. Tom Poulter says the Nielsens got three letters the end of every month. Come from Europe, he said. We'll just have to wait for them, then write back to the addresses on them. May be the boy has relations over there."

"Europe," she said, almost to herself. "That far away."

Her husband grunted, then pulled the covers back and sank down heavily on the mattress.

"Tired," he muttered.

He stared at the ceiling. "Come to bed," he said.

"In a little while."

She sat there brushing distractedly at her hair until the sound of his snoring broke the silence. Then, quietly, she rose and moved across the hall.

There was a river of moonlight across the bed. It flowed over Paal's small, motionless hands. Cora stood in the shadows a long time looking at the hands. For a moment she thought it was David in his bed again.

It was the sound.

Like endless club strokes across his vivid mind, it pulsed and throbbed into him in an endless, garbled din. He sensed it was communication of a sort but it hurt his ears and chained awareness and locked incoming thoughts behind dense, impassable walls.

Sometimes, in an infrequent moment of silence he would sense a fissure in the walls and, for that fleeting moment, catch hold of fragments—like an animal snatching scraps of food before the trap jaws clash together.

But then the sound would start again, rising and falling in rhythmless beat, jarring and grating, rubbing at the live, glis-

tening surface of comprehension until it was dry and aching
and confused.

"Paal," she said.

A week had passed; another week would pass before the
letters came.

"Paal, didn't they ever talk to you? Paal?"

Fists striking at delicate acuteness. Hands squeezing sensitivity from the vibrant ganglia of his mind.

"Paal, don't you know your name? Paal? *Paal.*"

There was nothing physically wrong with him. Doctor
Steiger had made sure of it. There was no reason for him not
to talk.

"We'll teach you, Paal. It's all right, darling. We'll teach
you." Like knife strokes across the weave of consciousness.
"Paal. Paal."

Paal. It was himself; he sensed that much. But it was different in the ears, a dead, depressive sound standing alone and
drab, without the host of linked associations that existed in
his mind. In thought, his name was more than letters. It was
him, every facet of his person and its meaning to himself, his
mother and his father, to his life. When they had summoned
him or thought his name it had been more than just the small
hard core which sound made of it. It had been everything in-
terwoven in a flash of knowing, unhampered by sound.

"Paal, don't you understand? It's your name. Paal Nielsen. Don't you understand?"

Drumming, pounding at raw sensitivity. Paal. The sound
kicking at him. *Paal. Paal.* Trying to dislodge his grip and
fling him into the maw of sound.

"Paal. *Try,* Paal. Say it after me. Pa-al. *Pa-al.*"

Twisting away, he would run from her in panic and she
would follow him to where he cowered by the bed of her son.

Then, for long moments, there would be peace. She would
hold him in her arms and, as if she understood, would not
speak. There would be stillness and no pounding clash of
sound against his mind. She would stroke his hair and kiss
away sobless tears. He would lie against the warmth of her,

his mind, like a timid animal, emerging from its hiding place again—to sense a flow of understanding from this woman. Feeling that needed no sound.

Love—wordless, unencumbered, and beautiful.

Sheriff Wheeler was just leaving the house that morning when the phone rang. He stood in the front hallway, waiting until Cora picked it up.

"Harry!" he heard her call. "Are you gone yet?"

He came back into the kitchen and took the receiver from her. "Wheeler," he said into it.

"Tom Poulter, Harry," the postmaster said. "Them letters is in."

"Be right there." Wheeler said, and hung up.

"The letters?" his wife asked.

Wheeler nodded.

"*Oh*," she murmured so that he barely heard her.

When Wheeler entered the post office twenty minutes later, Poulter slid the three letters across the counter. The sheriff picked them up.

"Switzerland," he read the postmarks, "Sweden, Germany."

"That's the lot," Poulter said. "Like always. On the thirtieth of the month."

"Can't open them, I suppose," Wheeler said.

"Y'know I'd say yes if I could, Harry," Poulter answered. "But law's law. You know that. I got t'send them back unopened. That's the law."

"All right." Wheeler took out his pen and copied down the return addresses in his pad. He pushed the letters back. "Thanks."

When he got home at four that afternoon, Cora was in the front room with Paal. There was a look of confused emotion on Paal's face—a desire to please coupled with a frightened need to flee the disconcertion of sound. He sat beside her on the couch looking as if he were about to cry.

"Oh, *Paal*," she said as Wheeler entered. She put her arms

around the trembling boy. "There's nothing to be afraid of, darling."

She saw her husband.

"What did they *do* to him?" she asked, unhappily.

He shook his head. "Don't know," he said. "He should have been put in school though."

"We can't very well put him in school when he's like *this*," she said.

"We can't put him anywhere till we see what's what," Wheeler said. "I'll write to those people tonight."

In the silence, Paal felt a sudden burst of emotion in the woman and he looked up quickly at her stricken face.

Pain. He felt it pour from her like blood from a mortal wound.

And while they ate supper in an almost silence, Paal kept sensing tragic sadness in the woman. It seemed he heard sobbing in a distant place. As the silence continued he began to get momentary flashes of remembrance in her pain-opened mind. He saw the face of another boy. Only it swirled and faded and there was *his* face in her thoughts. The two faces, like contesting wraiths, lay and overlay upon each other as if fighting for the dominance of her mind.

All fleeing, locked abruptly behind black doors as she said, "You have to write to them, I suppose."

"You know I do, Cora," Wheeler said.

Silence. Pain again. And when she tucked him into bed, he looked at her with such soft, apparent pity on his face that she turned quickly from the bed and he could feel the waves of sorrow break across his mind until her footsteps could no longer be heard. And, even then, like the faint fluttering of bird wings in the night, he felt her pitiable despair moving in the house.

"What are you writing?" she asked.

Wheeler looked over from his desk as midnight chimed its seventh stroke in the hall. Cora came walking across the room and set the tray down at his elbow. The steamy fra-

grance of freshly brewed coffee filled his nostrils as he
reached for the pot.

"Just telling them the situation," he said. "About the fire,
the Nielsens dying. Asking them if they're related to the boy
or know any of his relations over there."

"And what if his relations don't do any better than his parents?"

"Now, Cora," he said, pouring cream, "I thought we'd already discussed that. It's not our business."

She pressed pale lips together.

"A frightened child *is* my business," she said angrily.
"Maybe you—"

She broke off as he looked up at her patiently, no argument in his expression.

"*Well*," she said, turning from him, "it's true."

"It's not our business, Cora." He didn't see the tremor of
her lips.

"So he'll just go on not talking. I suppose! Being afraid of
shadows!"

She whirled. "It's *criminal!*" she cried, love and anger
bursting from her in a twisted mixture.

"It's got to be done, Cora." He said it quietly. "It's our
duty."

"*Duty.*" She echoed it with an empty lifelessness in her
voice.

She didn't sleep. The liquid flutter of Harry's snoring in
her ears, she lay staring at the jump of shadows on the ceiling, a scene enacted in her mind.

A summer's afternoon; the back doorbell ringing. Men
standing on the porch, John Carpenter among them, a blanket-
covered stillness weighing down his arms, a blank look on
his face. In the silence, a drip of water on the sunbaked
boards—slowly, unsteadily, like the beats of a dying heart.
He was swimming in the lake, Miz Wheeler and—

She shuddered on the bed as she had shuddered then—
numbly, mutely. The hands beside her were a crumpled

whiteness, twisted by remembered anguish. All those years waiting, waiting for a child to bring life into her house again.

At breakfast she was hollow-eyed and drawn. She moved about the kitchen with a willful tread, sliding eggs and pancakes on her husband's plate, pouring coffee, never speaking once.

Then he had kissed her goodbye and she was standing at the livingroom window watching him trudge down the path to the car. Long after he'd gone, staring at the three envelopes he'd stuck into the side clip of the mailbox.

When Paal came downstairs he smiled at her. She kissed his cheek, then stood behind him, wordless and watching, while he drank his orange juice. The way he sat, the way he held his glass; it was so like—

While Paal ate his cereal she went out to the mailbox and got the three letters, replacing them with three of her own— just in case her husband ever asked the mailman if he'd picked up three letters at their house that morning.

While Paal was eating his eggs, she went down into the cellar and threw the letters into the furnace. The one to Switzerland burned, then the ones to Germany and Sweden. She stirred them with a poker until the pieces broke and disappeared like black confetti in the flames.

Weeks passed; and, with every day, the service of his mind grew weaker.

"Paal, dear, don't you understand?" The patient, loving voice of the woman he needed but feared. "Won't you say it once for me? Just for me? *Paal?*"

He knew there was only love in her, but sound would destroy him. It would chain his thoughts—like putting shackles on the wind.

"Would you like to go to school, Paal? Would you? *School?*" Her face a mask of worried devotion.

"Try to talk, Paal. Just *try.*"

He fought it off with mounting fear. Silence would bring him scraps of meaning from her mind. Then sound returned and grossed each meaning with unwieldy flesh. Meanings joined with sounds. The links formed quickly, frighteningly. He struggled against them. Sounds could cover fragile, darting symbols with a hideous, restraining dough, dough that would be baked in ovens of articulation, then chopped into the stunted lengths of words.

Afraid of the woman, yet wanting to be near the warmth of her, protected by her arms. Like a pendulum he swung from dread to need and back to dread again.

And still the sounds kept shearing at his mind.

"We can't wait any longer to hear from them," Harry said. "He'll have to go to school, that's all."

"No," she said.

He put down his newspaper and looked across the living-room at her. She kept her eyes on the movements of her knitting needles.

"What do you mean, no?" he asked, irritably. "Every time I mention school you say no. Why *shouldn't* he go to school?"

The needles stopped and were lowered to her lap. Cora stared at them.

"I don't know," she said. "It's just that—" A sigh emptied from her. "I don't know," she said.

"He'll start on Monday," Harry said.

"But he's frightened," she said.

"Sure he's frightened. You'd be frightened too if you couldn't talk and everybody around you was talking. He needs education, that's all."

"But he's not *ignorant*, Harry. I—I swear he understands me sometimes. *Without* talking."

"*How?*"

"I don't know. But—well, the Nielsens weren't stupid people. They wouldn't just *refuse* to teach him."

"Well, whatever they taught him," Harry said, picking up his paper, "it sure doesn't show."

When they asked Miss Edna Frank over that afternoon to meet the boy she was determined to be impartial.

That Paal Nielsen had been reared in miserable fashion was beyond dispute but the maiden teacher had decided not to allow the knowledge to affect her attitude. The boy needed understanding. The cruel mistreatment of his parents had to be undone and Miss Frank had elected herself to the office.

Striding with a resolute quickness down German Corners' main artery, she recalled that scene in the Nielsen house when she and Sheriff Wheeler had tried to persuade them to enter Paal in school.

And such a smugness in their faces, thought Miss Frank, remembering. Such a polite disdain. *We do not wish our boy in school,* she heard Professor Nielsen's words again. Just like that, Miss Frank recalled. Arrogant as you please. *We do not wish—* Disgusting attitude.

Well, at least the boy was out of it now. That fire was probably the blessing of his life, she thought.

"We wrote to them four, five weeks ago," the sheriff explained, "and we haven't gotten an answer yet. We can't just let the boy go on the way he is. He needs schooling."

"He most certainly does," agreed Miss Frank, her pale features drawn into their usual sum of unyielding dogmatism. There was a wisp of mustache on her upper lip, her chin came almost to a point. On Halloween the children of German Corners watched the sky above her house.

"He's very shy," Cora said, sensing that harshness in the middle-aged teacher. "He'll be terribly frightened. He'll need a lot of understanding."

"He shall receive it," Miss Frank declared. "But let's see the boy."

Cora led Paal down the steps speaking to him softly. "Don't be afraid, darling. There's nothing to be afraid of."

Paal entered the room and looked into the eyes of Miss Edna Frank.

Only Cora felt the stiffening of his body—as though, instead of the gaunt virgin, he had looked into the petrifying gaze of the Medusa. Miss Frank and the sheriff did not catch the flare of iris in his bright, green eyes, the minute twitching at one corner of his mouth. None of them could sense the leap of panic in his mind.

Miss Frank sat smiling, holding out her hand.

"Come here, child," she said and, for a moment, the gates slammed shut and hid away the shimmering writhe.

"Come on, darling," Cora said, "Miss Frank is here to help you." She led him forward, feeling beneath her fingers the shuddering of terror in him.

Silence again. And, in the moment of it, Paal felt as though he were walking into a century-sealed tomb. Dead winds gushed out upon him, creatures of frustration slithered on his heart, strange flying jealousies and hates rushed by—all obscured by clouds of twisted memory. It was the purgatory that his father had pictured to him once in telling him of myth and legend. This was no legend though.

Her touch was cool and dry. Dark wrenching terrors ran down her veins and poured into him. Inaudibly, the fragment of a scream tightened his throat. Their eyes met again and Paal saw that, for a second, the woman seemed to know that he was looking at her brain.

Then she spoke and he was free again, limp and staring.

"I think we'll get along just fine," she said.

Maelstrom!

He lurched back on his heels and fell against the sheriff's wife.

All the way across the grounds, it had been growing, growing—as if he were a geiger counter moving toward some fantastic pulsing strata of atomic force. Closer, yet closer, the delicate controls within him stirring, glowing, trembling, reacting with increasing violence to the nearness of power. Even though his sensitivity had been weakened by over three months of sound he felt this now, strongly. As though he walked into a center of vitality.

It was *the young*.

Then the door opened, the voices stopped, and all of it rushed through him like a vast, electric current—all wild and unharnessed. He clung to her, fingers rigid in her skirt, eyes widened, quick breaths falling from his parted lips. His gaze moved shakily across the rows of staring children faces and waves of distorted energies kept bounding out from them in a snarled, uncontrolled network.

Miss Frank scraped back her chair, stepped down from her six-inch eminence and started down the aisle toward them.

"Good morning," she said, crisply. "We're just about to start our classes for the day."

"I—do hope everything will be all right," Cora said. She glanced down. Paal was looking at the class through a welling haze of tears. "Oh, *Paal.*" She leaned over and ran her fingers through his blonde hair, a worried look on her face. "Paal, don't be afraid, dear," she whispered.

He looked at her blankly.

"Darling, there's nothing to be—"

"Now just you leave him here," Miss Frank broke in, putting her hand on Paal's shoulder. She ignored the shudder that rippled through him. "He'll be right at home in no time, Mrs. Wheeler. But you've got to leave him by himself."

"Oh, but—" Cora started.

"No, believe me, it's the only way," Miss Frank insisted. "As long as you stay he'll be upset. Believe me. I've seen such things before."

At first he wouldn't let go of Cora but clung to her as the one familiar thing in this whirlpool of frightening newness. It was only when Miss Frank's hard, thin hands held him back that Cora backed off slowly, anxiously, closing the door and cutting off from Paal the sight of her soft pity.

He stood there trembling, incapable of uttering a single word to ask for help. Confused, his mind sent out tenuous shoots of communication but in the undisciplined tangle they were broken off and lost. He drew back quickly and tried, in vain, to cut himself off. All he could manage to do was let the torrent of needling thoughts continue unopposed until they had become a numbing, meaningless surge.

"Now, Paal," he heard Miss Frank's voice and looked up

gingerly at her. The hand drew him from the door. *"Come along."*

He didn't understand the words but the brittle sound of them was clear enough, the flow of irrational animosity from her was unmistakable. He stumbled along at her side, threading a thin path of consciousness through the living undergrowth of young, untrained minds; the strange admixture of them with their retention of born sensitivity overlaid with the dulling coat of formal inculcation.

She brought him to the front of the room and stood him there, his chest laboring for breath as if the feelings around him were hands pushing and constraining on his body.

"This is Paal Nielsen, class," Miss Frank announced, and sound drew a momentary blade across the stunted weave of thoughts. "We're going to have to be very patient with him. You see, his mother and father never taught him how to talk."

She looked down at him as a prosecuting lawyer might gaze upon exhibit A.

"He can't understand a word of English," she said.

Silence a moment, writhing. Miss Frank tightened her grip on his shoulder.

"Well, we'll help him learn, won't we, class?"

Faint mutterings arose from them; one thin, piping, *"Yes, Miss Frank."*

"Now, Paal," she said. He didn't turn. She shook his shoulder. *"Paal,"* she said.

He looked at her.

"Can you say your name?" she asked. "Paal? Paal Nielsen? Go ahead. Say your name."

Her fingers drew in like talons.

"Say it. Paal. *Pa-al.*"

He sobbed. Miss Frank released her hand.

"You'll learn," she said calmly.

It was not encouragement.

He sat in the middle of it like hooked bait in a current that

swirled with devouring mouths, mouths from which endlessly came mind-deadening sounds.

"This is a boat. A boat sails on the water. The men who
live on the boat are called sailors."

And, in the primer, the words about the boat printed under a picture of one.

Paal remembered a picture his father had shown him once.
It had been a picture of a boat too; but his father had not spoken futile words about the boat. His father had created about
the picture every sight and sound heir to it. Great blue rising
swells of tide. Grey-green mountain waves, their white tops
lashing. Storm winds whistling through the rigging of a
bucking, surging, shuddering vessel. The quiet majesty of an
ocean sunset, joining, with a scarlet seal, sea and sky.

"This is a farm. Men grow food on the farm. The men who
grow food are called farmers."

Words. Empty, with no power to convey the moist, warm
feel of earth. The sound of grain fields rustling in the wind
like golden seas. The sight of sun setting on a red barn wall.
The smell of soft lea winds carrying, from afar, the delicate
clank of cowbells.

"This is a forest. A forest is made of trees."

No sense of presence in those black, dogmatic symbols
whether sounded or looked upon. No sound of winds rushing like eternal rivers through the high green canopies. No
smell of pine and birch, oak and maple and hemlock. No feel
of treading on the century-thick carpet of leafy forest floors.

Words. Blunt, sawed-off lengths of hemmed-in meaning;
incapable of evocation, of expansion. Black figures on white.
This is a cat. This is a dog. Cat, dog. This is a man. This is a
woman. Man, woman. Car. Horse. Tree. Desk. Children.
Each word a trap, stalking his mind. A snare set to enclose
fluid and unbounded comprehension.

Every day she stood him on the platform.

"Paal," she would say, pointing at him, "Paal. Say it.
Paal."

He couldn't. He stared at her, too intelligent not to make the connection, too much afraid to seek further.

"Paal." A bony finger prodding at his chest. "Paal. Paal. *Paal.*"

He fought it. He had to fight it. He blanked his gaze and saw nothing of the room around him, concentrating only on his mother's hands. He knew it was a battle. Like a jelling of sickness, he had felt each new encroachment on his sensitivity.

"You're not listening, Paal Nielsen!" Miss Frank would accuse, shaking him. "You're a stubborn, ungrateful boy. Don't you want to be like *other* children?"

Staring eyes; and her thin, never-to-be-kissed lips stirring, pressing in.

"Sit down," she'd say. He didn't move. She'd move him off the platform with rigid fingers.

"Sit *down*," she'd say as if talking to a mulish puppy.

Every day.

She was awake in an instant; in another instant, on her feet and hurrying across the darkness of the room. Behind her, Harry slept with laboring breaths. She shut away the sound and let her hand slip off the door knob as she started across the hall.

"*Darling.*"

He was standing by the window looking out. As she spoke, he whirled and, in the faint illumination of the night light, she could see the terror written on his face.

"Darling, come to bed." She led him there and tucked him in, then sat beside him, holding his thin, cold hands.

"What is it, dear?"

He looked at her with wide, pained eyes.

"*Oh—*" She bent over and pressed her warm cheek to his. "What are you afraid of?"

In the dark silence it seemed as if a vision of the schoolroom and Miss Frank standing in it crossed her mind.

"Is it the school?" she asked, thinking it only an idea which had occurred to her.

The answer was in his face.

"But school is nothing to be afraid of, darling," she said. "You—"

She saw tears welling in his eyes, and abruptly she drew him up and held him tightly against herself. *Don't be afraid,* she thought. *Darling, please don't be afraid. I'm here and I love you just as much as they did. I love you even more—*

Paal drew back. He stared at her as if he didn't understand.

As the car pulled up in back of the house, Werner saw a woman turn away from the kitchen window.

"If we'd only heard from you," said Wheeler, "but there was never a word. You can't blame us for adopting the boy. We did what we thought was best."

Werner nodded with short, distracted movements of his head.

"I understand," he said quietly. "We received no letters however."

They sat in the car in silence, Werner staring through the windshield, Wheeler looking at his hands.

Holger and Fanny *dead,* Werner was thinking. A horrible discovery to make. The boy exposed to the cruel blunderings of people who did not understand. That was, in a way, even more horrible.

Wheeler was thinking of those letters and of Cora. He should have written again. Still, those letters should have reached Europe. Was it possible they were all missent?

"Well," he said, finally, "you'll—want to see the boy."

"Yes," said Werner.

The two men pushed open the car doors and got out. They walked across the back yard and up the wooden porch steps. Have you taught him how to speak?—Werner almost said but couldn't bring himself to ask. The concept of a boy like Paal exposed to the blunt, deadening forces of usual speech was something he felt uncomfortable thinking about.

"I'll get my wife," said Wheeler. "The livingroom's in there."

After the sheriff had gone up the back stairs, Werner walked slowly through the hall and into the front room. There he took off his raincoat and hat and dropped them over the back of a wooden chair. Upstairs he could hear the faint sound of voices—a man and woman. The woman sounded upset.

When he heard footsteps, he turned from the window.

The sheriff's wife entered beside her husband. She was smiling politely, but Werner knew she wasn't happy to see him there.

"Please sit down," she said.

He waited until she was in a chair, then settled down on the couch.

"What is it you want?" asked Mrs. Wheeler.

"Did your husband tell you—?"

"He told me who you were," she interrupted, "but not why you want to see Paul."

"*Paul?*" asked Werner, surprised.

"We—" Her hands sought out each other nervously. "—we changed it to Paul. It—seemed more appropriate. For a Wheeler, I mean."

"I see." Werner nodded politely.

Silence.

"Well," Werner said then, "you wish to know why I am here to see—the boy. I will explain as briefly as possible.

"Ten years ago, in Heidelburg, four married couples—the Elkenbergs, the Kalders, the Nielsens, and my wife and I—decided to try an experiment on our children—some not yet born. An experiment of the mind.

"We had accepted, you see, the proposition that ancient man, deprived of the dubious benefit of language, had been telepathic."

Cora started in her chair.

"Further," Werner went on, not noticing, "that the basic organic source of this ability is still functioning though no longer made use of—a sort of ethereal tonsil, a higher appendix—not used but neither useless.

"So we began our work, each searching for physiological facts while, at the same time, developing the ability in our children. Monthly correspondence was exchanged, a systematic methodology of training was arrived at slowly. Eventually, we planned to establish a colony with the grown children, a colony to be gradually consolidated until these abilities would become second nature to its members.

"Paal is one of these children."

Wheeler looked almost dazed.

"This is a *fact?*" he asked.

"A fact," said Werner.

Cora sat numbly in her chair staring at the tall German. She was thinking about the way Paal seemed to understand her without words. Thinking of his fear of the school and Miss Frank. Thinking of how many times she had woken up and gone to him even though he didn't make a sound.

"What?" she asked, looking up as Werner spoke.

"I say—may I see the boy now?"

"He's in school," she said. "He'll be home in—"

She stopped as a look of almost revulsion crossed Werner's face.

"School?" he asked.

"Paal Nielsen, stand."

The young boy slid from his seat and stood beside the desk. Miss Frank gestured to him once and, more like an old man than a boy, he trudged up to the platform and stood beside her as he always did.

"Straighten up," Miss Frank demanded. "Shoulders back."

The shoulders moved, the back grew flat.

"What's your name?" asked Miss Frank.

The boy pressed his lips together slightly. His swallowing made a dry, rattling noise.

"What is your name?"

He made no reply.

The virgin teacher looked at him and, in the moment that she did, through her mind ran memories of her childhood. Of her gaunt, mania-driven mother keeping her for hours at a time in the darkened front parlor, sitting at the great round table, her fingers arched over the smoothly worn ouija board—making her try to communicate with her dead father.

Memories of those terrible years were still with her—always with her. Her minor sensitivity being abused and twisted into knots until she hated every single thing about perception. Perception was an evil, full of suffering and anguish.

The boy must be freed of it.

"Class," she said, "I want you all to think of Paal's name." (This was his name no matter what Mrs. Wheeler chose to call him.) "Just think of it. Don't say it. Just think: Paal, Paal, Paal. When I count three. Do you understand?"

They stared at her, some nodding. *"Yes,* Miss Frank," piped up her only faithful.

"All right," she said. "One—two—*three."*

It flung into his mind like the blast of a hurricane, pounding and tearing at his hold on wordless sensitivity. He trembled on the platform, his mouth fallen ajar.

The blast grew stronger, all the power of the young directed into a single, irresistible force. Paal, *Paal, PAAL!!* it screamed into the tissues of his brain.

Until, at the very peak of it, when he thought his head would explode, it was all cut away by the voice of Miss Frank scalpeling into his mind.

"Say it! Paal!"

"Here he comes," said Cora. She turned from the window. "Before he gets here, I want to apologize for my rudeness."

''Not at all,'' said Werner, distractedly. ''I understand perfectly. Naturally, you would think that I had come to take the
boy away. As I have said, however, I have no legal powers
over him—being no relation. I simply want to see him as the
child of my two colleagues—whose shocking death I have
only now learned of.''

He saw the woman's throat move and picked out the leap
of guilty panic in her mind. She had destroyed the letters her
husband wrote. Werner knew it instantly but said nothing.
He sensed that the husband also knew it; she would have
enough trouble as it was.

They heard Paal's footsteps on the bottom step of the front
porch.

''I *will* take him out of school,'' Cora said.

''Perhaps not,'' said Werner, looking toward the door. In
spite of everything he felt his heartbeat quicken, felt the fingers of his left hand twitch in his lap. Without a word, he sent
out the message. It was a greeting the four couples had decided on; a sort of password.

Telepathy, he thought, *is the communication of impressions of
any kind from one mind to another independently of the recognized
channels of sense.*

Werner sent it twice before the front door opened.

Paal stood there, motionless.

Werner saw recognition in his eyes, but in the boy's mind
was only confused uncertainty. The misted vision of Werner's face crossed it. In his mind, all the people had existed—
Werner, Elkenberg, Kalder, all their children. But now it was
locked up and hard to capture. The face disappeared.

''Paul, this is Mister Werner,'' Cora said.

Werner did not speak. He sent the message out again—
with such force that Paal could not possibly miss it. He saw a
look of uncomprehending dismay creep across the boy's features, as if Paal suspected that something was happening yet
could not imagine what.

The boy's face grew more confused. Cora's eyes moved
concernedly from him to Werner and back again. Why didn't

Werner speak? She started to say something, then remembered what the German had said.

"Say, what—?" Wheeler began until Cora waved her hand and stopped him.

Paal, think!—Werner thought desperately—*Where is your mind?*

Suddenly, there was a great, wracking sob in the boy's throat and chest. Werner shuddered.

"My name is Paal," the boy said.

The voice made Werner's flesh crawl. It was unfinished, like a puppet voice, thin, wavering, and brittle.

"My name is Paal."

He couldn't stop saying it. It was if he were whipping himself on, knowing what had happened and trying to suffer as much as possible with the knowledge.

"My name is Paal. My name is Paal." An endless, frightening babble; in it, a panic-stricken boy seeking out an unknown power which had been torn from him.

"My name is Paal." Even held tightly in Cora's arms, he said it. "My name is Paal." Angrily, pitiably, endlessly. *"My name is Paal. My name is Paal."*

Werner closed his eyes.

Lost.

Wheeler offered to take him back to the bus station, but Werner told him he'd rather walk. He said goodbye to the sheriff and asked him to relay his regrets to Mrs. Wheeler, who had taken the sobbing boy up to his room.

Now, in the beginning fall of a fine, mistlike rain, Werner walked away from the house, from Paal.

It was not something easily judged, he was thinking. There was no right and wrong of it. Definitely, it was not a case of evil versus good. Mrs. Wheeler, the sheriff, the boy's teacher, the people of German Corners—they had, probably, all meant well. Understandably, they had been outraged at the idea of a seven-year-old boy's not having been taught to speak by his parents. Their actions were, in light of that, justifiable and good.

It was simply that, so often, evil could come of misguided good.

No, it was better left as it was. To take Paal back to Europe—back to the others—would be a mistake. He could if he wanted to; all the couples had exchanged papers giving each other the right to take over rearing of the children should anything happen to the parents. But it would only confuse Paal further. He had been a trained sensitive, not a born one. Although, by the principle they all worked on, all children were born with the atavistic ability to telepath, it was so easy to lose, so difficult to recapture.

Werner shook his head. It was a pity. The boy was without his parents, without his talent, even without his name.

He had lost everything.

Well, perhaps, not everything.

As he walked, Werner sent his mind back to the house to discover them standing at the window of Paal's room, watching sunset cast its fiery light on German Corners. Paal was clinging to the sheriff's wife, his cheek pressed to her side. The final terror of losing his awareness had not faded but there was something else counterbalancing it. Something Cora Wheeler sensed yet did not fully realize.

Paal's parents had not loved him. Werner knew this. Caught up in the fascination of their work, they had not had the time to love him as a child. Kind, yes, affectionate, always; still, they had regarded Paal as their experiment in flesh.

Which was why Cora Wheeler's love was, in part, as strange a thing to Paal as all the crushing horrors of speech. It would not remain so. For, in that moment when the last of his gift had fled, leaving his mind a naked rawness, she had been there with her love, to soothe away the pain. And always would be there.

"Did you find who you were looking for?" the grey-haired

woman at the counter asked Werner as she served him coffee.

"Yes. Thank you," he said.

"Where was he?" asked the woman.

Werner smiled.

"At home," he said.

Death Ship

Richard Matheson

TELEPLAY BY RICHARD MATHESON

AIRED FEBRUARY 7, 1963

STARRING JACK KLUGMAN AND ROSS MARTIN

MASON SAW IT FIRST.

He was sitting in front of the lateral viewer taking notes as the ship cruised over the new planet. His pen moved quickly over the graph-spaced chart he held before him. In a little while they'd land and take specimens. Mineral, vegetable, animal—if there were any. Put them in the storage lockers and take them back to Earth. There the technicians would evaluate, appraise, judge. And, if everything was acceptable, stamp the big, black INHABITABLE on their brief and open another planet for colonization from overcrowded Earth.

Mason was jotting down items about general topography when the glitter caught his eye.

"I saw something," he said.

He flicked the viewer to reverse lensing position.

"Saw what?" Ross asked from the control board.

"Didn't you see a flash?"

Ross looked into his own screen.

"We went over a lake, you know," he said.

"No, it wasn't that," Mason said. "This was in that clearing beside the lake."

332

"I'll look," said Ross, "but it probably was the lake."

His fingers typed out a command on the board and the big ship wheeled around in a smooth arc and headed back.

"Keep your eyes open now," Ross said. "Make sure. We haven't got any time to waste."

"Yes sir."

Mason kept his unblinking gaze on the viewer, watching the earth below move past like a slowly rolled tapestry of woods and fields and rivers. He was thinking, in spite of himself, that maybe the moment had arrived at last. The moment in which Earthmen would come upon life beyond Earth, a race evolved from other cells and other muds. It was an exciting thought. 1997 might be the year. And he and Ross and Carter might now be riding a new *Santa Maria* of discovery, a silvery, bulleted galleon of space.

"There!" he said. "There it is!"

He looked over at Ross. The captain was gazing into his viewer plate. His face bore the expression Mason knew well. A look of smug analysis, of impending decision.

"What do you think it is?" Mason asked, playing the strings of vanity in his captain.

"Might be a ship, might not be," pronounced Ross.

Well, for God's sake, let's go down and see, Mason wanted to say, but knew he couldn't. It would have to be Ross's decision. Otherwise they might not even stop.

"I guess it's nothing," he prodded.

He watched Ross impatiently, watched the stubby fingers flick buttons for the viewer. "We might stop," Ross said. "We have to take samples anyway. Only thing I'm afraid of is . . ."

He shook his head. Land, man! The words bubbled up in Mason's throat. For God's sake, let's go down!

Ross evaluated. His thickish lips pressed together appraisingly. Mason held his breath.

Then Ross's head bobbed once in that curt movement which indicated consummated decision. Mason breathed again. He watched the captain spin, push and twist dials.

Felt the ship begin its tilt to upright position. Felt the cabin shuddering slightly as the gyroscope kept it on an even keel. The sky did a ninety-degree turn, clouds appeared through the thick ports. Then the ship was pointed at the planet's sun and Ross switched off the cruising engines. The ship hesitated, suspended a split second, then began dropping toward the earth.

"Hey, we settin' down already?"

Mickey Carter looked at them questioningly from the port door that led to the storage lockers. He was rubbing greasy hands over his green jumper legs.

"We saw something down there," Mason said.

"No kiddin'," Mickey said, coming over to Mason's viewer. "Let's see."

Mason flicked on the rear lens. The two of them watched the planet billowing up at them.

"I don't know whether you can . . . oh, yes, there it is," Mason said. He looked over at Ross.

"Two degrees east," he said.

Ross twisted a dial and the ship then changed its downward movement slightly.

"What do you think it is?" Mickey asked.

"Hey!"

Mickey looked into the viewer with even greater interest. His wide eyes examined the shiny speck enlarging on the screen.

"Could be a ship," he said. "Could be."

Then he stood there silently, behind Mason, watching the earth rushing up.

"Reactors," said Mason.

Ross jabbed efficiently at the button and the ship's engines spouted out their flaming gases. Speed decreased. The rocket eased down on its roaring fire jets. Ross guided.

"What do *you* think it is?" Mickey asked Mason.

"I don't know," Mason answered. "But if it's a ship," he added, half wishfully thinking, "I don't see how it could possibly be from Earth. We've got this run all to ourselves."

"Maybe they got off course," Mickey dampened without knowing.

Mason shrugged. "I doubt it," he said.

"What if it is a ship?" Mickey said. "And it's not ours?"

Mason looked at him and Carter licked his lips.

"Man," he said, "that'd be somethin'."

"Air spring," Ross ordered.

Mason threw the switch that set the air spring into operation. The unit which made possible a landing without them having to stretch out on thick-cushioned couches. They could stand on deck and hardly feel the impact. It was an innovation on the newer government ships.

The ship hit on its rear braces.

There was a sensation of jarring, a sense of slight bouncing. Then the ship was still, its pointed nose straight up, glittering brilliantly in the bright sunlight.

"I want us to stay together," Ross was saying. "No one takes any risks. That's an order."

He got up from his seat and pointed at the wall switch that let atmosphere into the small chamber in the corner of the cabin.

"Three to one we need our helmets," Mickey said to Mason.

"You're on," Mason said, setting into play their standing bet about the air or lack of it in every new planet they found. Mickey always bet on the need for apparatus. Mason for unaided lung use. So far, they'd come out about even.

Mason threw the switch, and there was a muffled sound of hissing in the chamber. Mickey got the helmet from his locker and dropped it over his head. Then he went through the double doors. Mason listened to him clamping the doors behind him. He kept wanting to switch on the side viewers and see if he could locate what they'd spotted. But he didn't. He let himself enjoy the delicate nibbling of suspense.

Through the intercom they heard Mickey's voice.

"Removing helmet," he said.

Silence. They waited. Finally, a sound of disgust.

"I lose again," Mickey said.

The others followed him out.

"God, did they hit!"

Mickey's face had an expression of dismayed shock on it. The three of them stood there on the greenish-blue grass and looked.

It *was* a ship. Or what was left of a ship for, apparently, it had struck the earth at terrible velocity, nose first. The main structure had driven itself about fifteen feet into the hard ground. Jagged pieces of superstructure had been ripped off by the crash and were lying strewn over the field. The heavy engines had been torn loose and nearly crushed the cabin. Everything was deathly silent, and the wreckage was so complete they could hardly make out what type of ship it was. It was as if some enormous child had lost fancy with the toy model and had dashed it to earth, stamped on it, banged on it insanely with a rock.

Mason shuddered. It had been a long time since he'd seen a rocket crash. He'd almost forgotten the everpresent menace of lost control, of whistling fall through space, of violent impact. Most talk had been about being lost in an orbit. This reminded him of the other threat in his calling. His throat moved unconsciously as he watched.

Ross was scuffing at a chunk of metal at his feet.

"Can't tell much," he said. "But I'd say it's our own."

Mason was about to speak, then changed his mind.

"From what I can see of that engine up there, I'd say it was ours," Mickey said.

"Rocket structure might be standard," Mason heard himself say, "everywhere."

"Not a chance," Ross said. "Things don't work out like that. It's ours all right. Some poor devils from Earth. Well, at least their death was quick."

"Was it?" Mason asked the air, visualizing the crew in their cabin, rooted with fear as their ship spun toward earth, maybe straight down like a fired cannon shell, maybe end-over-end like a crazy, fluttering top, the gyroscope trying in vain to keep the cabin always level.

The screaming, the shouted commands, the exhortations to a heaven they had never seen before, to a God who might be in another universe. And then the planet rushing up and blasting its hard face against their ship, crushing them, ripping the breath from their lungs. He shuddered again, thinking of it.

"Let's take a look," Mickey said.

"Not sure we'd better," Ross said. "We say it's ours. It might not be."

"Jeez, you don't think anything is still alive in there, do you?" Mickey asked the captain.

"Can't say," Ross said.

But they all knew he could see that mangled hulk before him as well as they. Nothing could have survived that.

The look. The pursed lips. As they circled the ship. The head movement, unseen by them.

"Let's try that opening there," Ross ordered. "And stay together. We still have work to do. Only doing this so we can let the base know which ship this is." He had already decided it was an Earth ship.

They walked up to a spot in the ship's side where the skin had been laid open along the welded seam. A long, thick plate was bent over as easily as a man might bend paper.

"Don't like this," Ross said. "But I suppose . . ."

He gestured with his head and Mickey pulled himself up to the opening. He tested each handhold gingerly, then slid on his work gloves as he found some sharp edge. He told the other two and they reached into their jumper pockets. Then Mickey took a long step into the dark maw of the ship.

"Hold on, now!" Ross called up. "Wait until I get there."

He pulled himself up, his heavy boot toes scraping up the rocket skin. He went into the hole too. Mason followed.

It was dark inside the ship. Mason closed his eyes for a moment to adjust to the change. When he opened them, he saw two bright beams searching up through the twisted tangle of beams and plates. He pulled out his own flash and flicked it on.

"God, is this thing wrecked," Mickey said, awed by the sight of metal and machinery in violent death. His voice echoed slightly through the shell. Then, when the sound ended, an utter stillness descended on them. They stood in the murky light and Mason could smell the acrid fumes of broken engines.

"Watch the smell, now," Ross said to Mickey who was reaching up for support. "We don't want to get ourselves gassed."

"I will," Mickey said. He was climbing up, using one hand to pull his thick, powerful body up along the twisted ladder. He played the beam straight up.

"Cabin is all out of shape," he said, shaking his head.

Ross followed him up. Mason was last, his flash moving around endlessly over the snapped joints, the wild jigsaw of destruction that had once been a powerful new ship. He kept hissing in disbelief to himself as his beam came across one violent distortion of metal after another.

"Door's sealed," Mickey said, standing on a pretzel-twisted catwalk, bracing himself against the inside rocket wall. He grabbed the handle again and tried to pull it open.

"Give me your light," Ross said. He directed both beams at the door and Mickey tried to drag it open. His face grew red as he struggled. He puffed.

"No," he said, shaking his head. "It's stuck."

Mason came up beside them. "Maybe the cabin is still pressurized," he said softly. He didn't like the echoing of his own voice.

"Doubt it," Ross said, trying to think. "More than likely the jamb is twisted." He gestured with his head again. "Help Carter."

Mason grabbed one handle and Mickey the other. Then they braced their feet against the wall and pulled with all their strength. The door held fast. They shifted their grip, pulled harder.

"Hey, it slipped!" Mickey said. "I think we got it."

They resumed footing on the tangled catwalk and pulled the door open. The frame was twisted, the door held in one corner. They could only open it enough to wedge themselves in sideways.

The cabin was dark as Mason edged in first. He played his light beam toward the pilot's seat. It was empty. He heard Mickey squeeze in as he moved the light to the navigator's seat.

There was no navigator's seat. The bulkhead had been stove in there, the viewer, the table and the chair all crushed beneath the bent plates. There was a clicking in Mason's throat as he thought of himself sitting at a table like that, in a chair like that, before a bulkhead like that.

Ross was in now. The three beams of light searched. They all had to stand, legs spraddled, because the deck slanted.

And the way it slanted made Mason think of something. Of shifting weights, of *things* sliding down. . . .

Into the corner where he suddenly played his shaking beam.

And felt his heart jolt, felt the skin on him crawling, felt his unblinking eyes staring at the sight. Then felt his boots thud him down the incline as if he were driven.

"Here," he said, his voice hoarse with shock.

He stood before the bodies. His foot had bumped into one of them as he held himself from going down any further, as he shifted his weight on the incline.

Now he heard Mickey's footsteps, his voice. A whisper. A bated, horrified whisper.

"Mother of God."

Nothing from Ross. Nothing from any of them then but stares and shuddering breaths.

Because the twisted bodies on the floor were theirs, all three of them. And all three . . . dead.

Mason didn't know how long they stood there, wordlessly, looking down at the still, crumpled figures on the deck.

How does a man react when he is standing over his own corpse? The question plied unconsciously at his mind. What does a man say? What are his first words to be? A poser, he seemed to sense, a loaded question.

But it was happening. Here he stood—and there he lay dead at his own feet. He felt his hands grow numb and he rocked unsteadily on the tilted deck.

"God."

Mickey again. He had his flash pointed down at his own face. His mouth twitched as he looked. All three of them had their flash beams directed at their own faces, and the bright ribbons of light connected their dual bodies.

Finally Ross took a shaking breath of the stale cabin air.

"Carter," he said, "find the auxiliary light switch, see if it works." His voice was husky and tightly restrained.

"Sir?"

"The light switch—the light switch!" Ross snapped.

Mason and the captain stood there, motionless, as Mickey shuffled up the deck. They heard his boots kick metallic debris over the deck surface. Mason closed his eyes, but was unable to take his foot away from where it pressed against the body that was his. He felt bound.

"I don't understand," he said to himself.

"Hang on," Ross said.

Mason couldn't tell whether it was said to encourage him or the captain himself.

Then they heard the emergency generator begin its initial whining spin. The light flickered, went out. The generator coughed and began humming and the lights flashed on brightly.

They looked down now. Mickey slipped down the slight deck hill and stood beside them. He stared down at his own body. Its head was crushed in. Mickey drew back, his mouth a box of unbelieving terror.

"I don't get it," he said. "I don't get it. What *is* this?"

"Carter," Ross said.

"That's *me!*" Mickey said. "God, it's *me!*"

"Hold on!" Ross ordered.

"The three of us," Mason said quietly, "and we're all dead."

There seemed nothing to be said. It was a speechless nightmare. The tilted cabin all bashed in and tangled. The three corpses all doubled over and tumbled into one corner, arms and legs flopped over each other. All they could do was stare.

Then Ross said, "Go get a tarp. Both of you."

Mason turned. Quickly. Glad to fill his mind with simple command. Glad to crowd out tense horror with activity. He took long steps up the deck. Mickey backed up, unable to take his unblinking gaze off the heavy-set corpse with the green jumper and the caved-in, bloody head.

Mason dragged a heavy, folded tarp from the storage locker and carried it back into the cabin, legs and arms moving in robotlike sequence. He tried to numb his brain, not think at all until the first shock had dwindled.

Mickey and he opened up the heavy canvas sheet with wooden motions. They tossed it out and the thick, shiny material fluttered down over the bodies. It settled, outlining the heads, the torsos, the one arm that stood up stiffly like a spear, bent over wrist and hand like a grisly pennant.

Mason turned away with a shudder. He stumbled up to the pilot's seat and slumped down. He stared at his outstretched legs, the heavy boots. He reached out and grabbed his leg and pinched it, feeling almost relief at the flaring pain.

"Come away," he heard Ross saying to Mickey, "I said, *come away!*"

He looked down and saw Ross half dragging Mickey up from a crouching position over the bodies. He held Mickey's arm and led him up the incline.

"We're dead," Mickey said hollowly. "That's us on the deck. We're *dead.*"

Ross pushed Mickey up to the cracked port and made him look out.

"There," he said. "There's our ship over there. Just as we

left it. This ship isn't ours. And those bodies. They . . . can't be ours.''

He finished weakly. To a man of his sturdy opinionation, the words sounded flimsy and extravagant. His throat moved, his lower lip pushed out in defiance of this enigma. Ross didn't like enigmas. He stood for decision and action. He wanted action now.

"You saw yourself down there," Mason said to him. "Are you going to say it isn't you?''

"That's exactly what I'm saying," Ross bristled. "This may seem crazy, but there's an explanation for it. There's an explanation for everything.''

His face twitched as he punched his bulky arm.

"This is me," he claimed. "I'm solid." He glared at them as if daring opposition. "I'm alive," he said.

They stared blankly at him.

"I don't get it," Mickey said weakly. He shook his head and his lips drew back over his teeth.

Mason sat limply in the pilot's seat. He almost hoped that Ross's dogmatism would pull them through this. That his staunch bias against the inexplicable would save the day. He wanted for it to save the day. He tried to think for himself, but it was so much easier to let the captain decide.

"We're all dead," Mickey said.

"Don't be a fool!" Ross exclaimed. "Feel yourself!"

Mason wondered how long it would go on. Actually, he began to expect a sudden awakening, him jolting to a sitting position on his bunk to see the two of them at their tasks as usual, the crazy dream over and done with.

But the dream went on. He leaned back in the seat and it was a solid seat. From where he sat he could run his fingers over solid dials and buttons and switches. All real. It was no dream. Pinching wasn't even necessary.

"Maybe it's a vision," he tried, vainly attempting thought, as an animal mired tries hesitant steps to solid earth.

"That's enough," Ross said.

Then his eyes narrowed. He looked at them sharply. His

face mirrored decision. Mason almost felt anticipation. He tried to figure out what Ross was working on. Vision? No, it couldn't be that. Ross would hold no truck with visions. He noticed Mickey staring open-mouthed at Ross. Mickey wanted the consoling of simple explanation too.

"Time warp," said Ross.

They still stared at him.

"What?" Mason asked.

"Listen," Ross punched out his theory. More than his theory, for Ross never bothered with that link in the chain of calculation. His certainty.

"Space bends," Ross said. "Time and space form a continuum. Right?"

No answer. He didn't need one.

"Remember they told us once in training of the possibility of circumnavigating time. They told us we could leave Earth at a certain time. And when we came back we'd be back a year earlier than we'd calculated. Or a year later.

"Those were just theories to the teachers. Well, I say it's happened to us. It's logical, it could happen. We could have passed right through a time warp. We're in another galaxy, maybe different space lines, maybe different time lines."

He paused for effect.

"I say we're in the future," he said.

Mason looked at him.

"How does that help us?" he asked. "If you're right."

"We're not dead!" Ross seemed surprised that they didn't get it.

"If it's in the future," Mason said quietly, "then we're going to die."

Ross gaped at him. He hadn't thought of that. Hadn't thought that his idea made things even worse. Because there was only one thing worse than dying. And that was knowing you were going to die. And where. And how.

Mickey shook his head. His hands fumbled at his sides. He raised one to his lips and chewed nervously on a blackened nail.

"No," he said weakly, "I don't get it."

Ross stood looking at Mason with jaded eyes. He bit his lips, feeling nervous with the unknown crowding him in, holding off the comfort of solid, rational thinking. He pushed, he shoved it away. He persevered.

"Listen," he said, "we're agreed that those bodies aren't ours."

No answer.

"Use your heads!" Ross commanded. "Feel yourself!"

Mason ran numbed fingers over his jumper, his helmet, the pen in his pocket. He clasped solid hands of flesh and bone. He looked at the veins in his arms. He pressed an anxious finger to his pulse. It's true, he thought. And the thought drove lines of strength back into him. Despite all, despite Ross's desperate advocacy, he was alive. Flesh and blood were his evidence.

His mind swung open then. His brow furrowed in thought as he straightened up. He saw a look almost of relief on the face of a weakening Ross.

"All right then," he said, "we're in the future."

Mickey stood tensely by the port. "Where does that leave us?" he asked.

The words threw Mason back. It was true, where did it leave them?

"How do we know how distant a future?" he said, adding weight to the depression of Mickey's words. "How do we know it isn't in the next twenty minutes?"

Ross tightened. He punched his palm with a resounding smack.

"How do we know?" he said strongly. "We don't go up, we can't crash. That's how we know."

Mason looked at him.

"Maybe if we went up," he said, "we might bypass our death altogether and leave it in this space-time system. We could get back to the space-time system of our own galaxy and . . ."

His words trailed off. His brain became absorbed with twisting thought.

Ross frowned. He stirred restlessly, licked his lips. What had been simple was now something else again. He resented the uninvited intrusion of complexity.

"We're alive now," he said, getting it set in his mind, consolidating assurance with reasonable words, "and there's only one way we can stay alive."

He looked at them, decision reached. "We have to stay here," he said.

They just looked at him. He wished that one of them, at least, would agree with him, show some sign of definition in their minds.

"But . . . what about our orders?" Mason said vaguely.

"Our orders don't tell us to kill ourselves!" Ross said. "No, it's the only answer. If we never go up again, we never crash. We . . . we avoid it, we prevent it!"

His head jarred once in a curt nod. To Ross, the thing was settled.

Mason shook his head.

"I don't know," he said. "I don't . . ."

"I do," Ross stated. "Now let's get out of here. This ship is getting on our nerves."

Mason stood up as the captain gestured toward the door. Mickey started to move, then hesitated. He looked down at the bodies.

"Shouldn't we . . . ?" he started to inquire.

"What, what?" Ross asked, impatient to leave.

Mickey stared at the bodies. He felt caught up in a great, bewildering insanity.

"Shouldn't we . . . bury ourselves?" he said.

Ross swallowed. He would hear no more. He herded them out of the cabin. Then, as they started down through the wreckage, he looked in at the door. He looked at the tarpaulin with the jumbled mound of bodies beneath it. He pressed his lips together until they were white.

"I'm alive," he muttered angrily.

Then he turned out the cabin light with tight, vengeful fingers and left.

They all sat in the cabin of their own ship. Ross had ordered food brought out from the lockers, but he was the only one eating. He ate with a belligerent rotation of his jaw as though he would grind away all mystery with his teeth.

Mickey stared at the food.

"How long do we have to stay?" he asked, as if he didn't clearly realize that they were to remain permanently.

Mason took it up. He leaned forward in his seat and looked at Ross.

"How long will our food last?" he said.

"There's edible food outside, I've no doubt," Ross said, chewing.

"How will we know which is edible and which is poisonous?"

"We'll watch the animals," Ross persisted.

"They're a different type of life," Mason said. "What they can eat might be poisonous to us. Besides, we don't even know if there are any animals here."

The words made his lips raise in a brief, bitter smile. And he'd actually been hoping to contact another people. It was practically humorous.

Ross bristled. "We'll . . . cross each river as we come to it," he blurted out as if he hoped to smother all complaint with this ancient homily.

Mason shook his head. "I don't know," he said.

Ross stood up.

"Listen," he said. "It's easy to ask questions. We've all made a decision to stay here. Now let's do some concrete thinking about it. Don't tell me what we can't do. I know that as well as you. Tell me what we can do."

Then he turned on his heel and stalked over to the control board. He stood there glaring at blank-faced gauges and dials. He sat down and began scribbling rapidly in his log as if something of great note had just occurred to him. Later Mason looked at what Ross had written and saw that it was a long paragraph which explained in faulty but unyielding logic why they were all alive.

Mickey got up and sat down on his bunk. He pressed his large hands against his temples. He looked very much like a little boy who had eaten too many green apples against his mother's injunction and who feared retribution on both counts. Mason knew what Mickey was thinking. Of that still body with the skull forced in. The image of himself brutally killed in collision. He, Mason, was thinking of the same thing. And, behavior to the contrary, Ross probably was too.

Mason stood by the port looking out at the silent hulk across the meadow. Darkness was falling. The last rays of the planet's sun glinted off the skin of the crashed rocket ship. Mason turned away. He looked at the outside temperature gauge. Already it was seven degrees and it was still light. Mason moved the thermostat needle with his right forefinger.

Heat being used up, he thought. The energy of our grounded ship being used up faster and faster. The ship drinking its own blood with no possibility of transfusion. Only operation would recharge the ship's energy system. And they were without motion, trapped and stationary.

"How long can we last?" he asked Ross again, refusing to keep silence in the face of the question. "We can't live in this ship indefinitely. The food will run out in a couple of months. And a long time before that the charging system will go. The heat will stop. We'll freeze to death."

"How do we know the outside temperature will freeze us?" Ross asked, falsely patient.

"It's only sundown," Mason said, "and already it's . . . minus thirteen degrees."

Ross looked at him sullenly. Then he pushed up from his chair and began pacing.

"If we go up," he said, "we risk . . . *duplicating* that ship over there."

"But would we?" Mason wondered. "We can only die

once. It seems we already have. In this galaxy. Maybe a person can die once in every galaxy. Maybe that's afterlife. Maybe . . ."

"Are you through?" asked Ross coldly.

Mickey looked up.

"Let's go," he said. "I don't want to hang around here."

He looked at Ross.

Ross said, "Let's not stick out our necks before we know what we're doing. Let's think this out."

"I have a wife!" Mickey said angrily. "Just because you're not married—"

"Shut up!" Ross thundered.

Mickey threw himself on the bunk and turned to face the cold bulkhead. Breath shuddered through his heavy frame. He didn't say anything. His fingers opened and closed on the blanket, twisting it, pulling it out from under his body.

Ross paced the deck, abstractedly punching at his palm with a hard fist. His teeth clicked together, his head shook as one argument after another fell before his bullheaded determination. He stopped, looked at Mason, then started pacing again. Once he turned on the outside spotlight and looked to make sure it was not imagination.

The light illumined the broken ship. It glowed strangely, like a huge, broken tombstone. Ross snapped off the spotlight with a soundless snarl. He turned to face them. His broad chest rose and fell heavily as he breathed.

"All right," he said. "It's *your* lives too. I can't decide for all of us. We'll hand vote on it. That thing out there may be something entirely different from what we think. If you two think it's worth the risk of our lives to go up, we'll . . . go up."

He shrugged. "Vote," he said. "I say we stay here."

"I say we go," Mason said.

They looked at Mickey.

"Carter," said Ross, "what's your vote?"

Mickey looked over his shoulder with bleak eyes.

"Vote," Ross said.

"Up," Mickey said. "Take us up. I'd rather die than stay here."

Ross's throat moved. Then he took a deep breath and squared his shoulders.

"All right," he said quietly. "We'll go up."

"God have mercy on us," Mickey muttered as Ross went quickly to the control board.

The captain hesitated a moment. Then he threw switches. The great ship began shuddering as gases ignited and began to pour like channeled lightning from the rear vents. The sound was almost soothing to Mason. He didn't care any more; he was willing, like Mickey, to take a chance. It had only been a few hours. It had seemed like a year. Minutes had dragged, each one weighted with oppressive recollections. Of the bodies they'd seen, of the shattered rocket— even more of the Earth they would never see, of parents and wives and sweethearts and children. Lost to their sight forever. No, it was far better to try to get back. Sitting and waiting was always the hardest thing for a man to do. He was no longer conditioned for it.

Mason sat down at his board. He waited tensely. He heard Mickey jump up and move over to the engine control board.

"I'm going to take us up easy," Ross said to them. "There's no reason why we should . . . have any trouble."

He paused. They snapped their heads over and looked at him with muscle-tight impatience.

"Are you both ready?" Ross asked.

"*Take us up*," Mickey said.

Ross jammed his lips together and shoved over the switch that read: *Vertical Rise.*

They felt the ship tremble, hesitate. Then it moved off the ground, headed up with increasing velocity. Mason flicked on the rear viewer. He watched the dark earth recede, tried not to look at the white patch in the corner of the screen, the patch that shone metallically under the moonlight.

"Five hundred," he read. "Seven-fifty . . . one thousand . . . fifteen hundred. . . ."

He kept waiting. For explosion. For an engine to give out. For their rise to stop.

They kept moving up.

"Three thousand," Mason said, his voice beginning to betray the rising sense of elation he felt. The planet was getting farther and farther away. The other ship was only a memory now. He looked across at Mickey. Mickey was staring, openmouthed, as if he were about ready to shout out *"Hurry!"* but was afraid to tempt the fates.

"Six thousand . . . *seven thousand!"* Mason's voice was jubilant. "We're *out* of it!"

Mickey's face broke into a great, relieved grin. He ran a hand over his brow and flicked great drops of sweat on the deck.

"God," he said, gasping, "my God."

Mason moved over to Ross's seat. He clapped the captain on the shoulder.

"We made it," he said. "Nice flying."

Ross looked irritated.

"We shouldn't have left," he said. "It was nothing all the time. Now we have to start looking for another planet." He shook his head. "It wasn't a good idea to leave," he said.

Mason stared at him. He turned away shaking his head, thinking . . . you can't win.

"If I ever see another glitter," he thought aloud, "I'll keep my big mouth shut. To hell with alien races anyway."

Silence. He went back to his seat and picked up his graph chart. He let out a long shaking breath. Let Ross complain, he thought, I can take anything now. Things are normal again. He began to figure casually what might have occurred down there on that planet.

Then he happened to glance at Ross.

Ross was thinking. His lips pressed together. He said something to himself. Mason found the captain looking at him.

"Mason," he said.

"What?"

"Alien race, you said."

Mason felt a chill flood through his body. He saw the big head nod once in decision. Unknown decision. His hands started to shake. A crazy idea came. No, Ross wouldn't do that, not just to assuage vanity. Would he?

"I don't . . ." he started. Out of the corner of his eye he saw Mickey watching the captain too.

"*Listen*," Ross said. "I'll tell you what happened down there. I'll *show* you what happened!"

They stared at him in paralyzing horror as he threw the ship around and headed back.

"What are you doing!" Mickey cried.

"Listen," Ross said. "Didn't you understand me? Don't you see how we've been tricked?"

They looked at him without comprehension. Mickey took a step toward him.

"Alien race," Ross said. "That's the short of it. That time-space idea is all wet. But I'll tell you what idea isn't all wet. So we leave the place. What's our first instinct as far as reporting it? Saying it's uninhabitable? We'd do more than that. We wouldn't report it at all."

"Ross, you're not taking us back!" Mason said, standing up suddenly as the full terror of returning struck him.

"You bet I am!" Ross said, fiercely elated.

"You're crazy!" Mickey shouted at him, his body twitching, his hands clenched at his sides menacingly.

"Listen to me!" Ross roared at them. "Who would be benefited by us not reporting the existence of that planet?"

They didn't answer. Mickey moved closer.

"Fools!" he said. "Isn't it obvious? There *is* life down there. But life that isn't strong enough to kill us or chase us away with force. So what can they do? They don't want us there. So what can they do?"

He asked them like a teacher who cannot get the right answers from the dolts in his class.

Mickey looked suspicious. But he was curious now, too,

and a little timorous as he had always been with his captain, except in moments of greatest physical danger. Ross had always led them, and it was hard to rebel against it even when it seemed he was trying to kill them all. His eyes moved to the viewer screen where the planet began to loom beneath them like a huge dark ball.

"We're alive," Ross said, "and I say there never *was* a ship down there. We saw it, sure. We *touched* it. But you can see anything if you believe it's there! All your senses can tell you there's something when there's nothing. All you have to do is *believe* it!"

"What are you getting at?" Mason asked hurriedly, too frightened to realize. His eyes fled to the altitude gauge. Seventeen thousand . . . sixteen thousand . . . fifteen . . .

"Telepathy," Ross said, triumphantly decisive. "I say those men, or whatever they are, saw us coming. And they didn't want us there. So they read our minds and saw the death fear, and they decided that the best way to scare us away was to show us our ship crashed and ourselves dead in it. And it worked . . . until now."

"So it worked!" Mason exploded. "Are you going to take a chance on killing us just to prove your damn theory?"

"It's *more* than a theory!" Ross stormed, as the ship fell, then Ross added with the distorted argument of injured vanity, "My orders say to pick up specimens from every planet. I've always followed orders before and, by God, I still will!"

"You saw how cold it was!" Mason said. "No one can live there anyway! Use your head, Ross!"

"Damn it, *I'm* captain of this ship!" Ross yelled, "and I give the orders!"

"Not when our lives are in your hands!" Mickey started for the captain.

"Get back!" Ross ordered.

That was when one of the ship's engines stopped and the ship yawed wildly.

"You fool!" Mickey exploded, thrown off balance. "You *did* it, you *did* it!"

Outside the black night hurtled past.

The ship wobbled violently. *Prediction true* was the only phrase Mason could think of. His own vision of the screaming, the numbing horror, the exhortations to a deaf heaven—all coming true. That hulk would be this ship in a matter of minutes. Those three bodies would be . . .

"Oh . . . *damn!*" He screamed it at the top of his lungs, furious at the enraging stubbornness of Ross in taking them back, of causing the future to be as they saw—all because of insane pride.

"No, they're not going to fool us!" Ross shouted, still holding fast to his last idea like a dying bulldog holding its enemy fast in its teeth.

He threw switches and tried to turn the ship. But it wouldn't turn. It kept plunging down like a fluttering leaf. The gyroscope couldn't keep up with the abrupt variations in cabin equilibrium and the three of them found themselves being thrown off balance on the tilting deck.

"Auxiliary engines!" Ross yelled.

"It's no use!" Mickey cried.

"*Damn it!*" Ross clawed his way up the angled deck, then crashed heavily against the engine board as the cabin inclined the other way. He threw switches over with shaking fingers.

Suddenly Mason saw an even spout of flame through the rear viewer again. The ship stopped shuddering and headed straight down. The cabin righted itself.

Ross threw himself into his chair and shot out furious hands to turn the ship about. From the floor Mickey looked at him with a blank, white face. Mason looked at him, too, afraid to speak.

"Now shut up!" Ross said disgustedly, not even looking at them, talking like a disgruntled father to his sons. "When we get down there you're going to see that it's true. That ship'll be gone. And we're going to go looking for those bastards who put the idea in our minds!"

They both stared at their captain humbly as the ship

headed down backwards. They watched Ross's hands move efficiently over the controls. Mason felt a sense of confidence in his captain. He stood on the deck quietly, waiting for the landing without fear. Mickey got up from the floor and stood beside him, waiting.

The ship hit the ground. It stopped. They had landed again. They were still the same. And . . .

"Turn on the spotlight," Ross told them.

Mason threw the switch. They all crowded to the port. Mason wondered for a second how Ross could possibly have landed in the same spot. He hadn't even appeared to be following the calculations made on the last landing.

They looked out.

Mickey stopped breathing. And Ross's mouth fell open.

The wreckage was still there.

They had landed in the same place and they had found the wrecked ship still there. Mason turned away from the port and stumbled over the deck. He felt lost, a victim of some terrible universal prank, a man accursed.

"You said . . ." Mickey said to the captain.

Ross just looked out of the port with unbelieving eyes.

"Now we'll go up again," Mickey said, grinding his teeth. "And we'll *really* crash this time. And we'll be killed. Just like those . . . those . . ."

Ross didn't speak. He stared out of the port at the refutation of his last clinging hope. He felt hollow, void of all faith in belief in sensible things.

Then Mason spoke.

"We're not going to crash—" he said somberly—"ever."

"What?"

Mickey was looking at him. Ross turned and looked too.

"Why don't we stop kidding ourselves?" Mason said. "We all know what it is, don't we?"

He was thinking of what Ross had said just a moment before. About the senses giving evidence of what was believed. Even if there was nothing there at all . . .

Then, in a split second, with the knowledge, he saw Ross

and he saw Carter. As they *were*. And he took a short shuddering breath, a last breath until illusion would bring breath and flesh again.

"Progress," he said bitterly, and his voice was an aching whisper in the phantom ship. "The Flying Dutchman takes to the universe."

The Devil, You Say?

Charles Beaumont

TELEPLAY BY CHARLES BEAUMONT

AIRED FEBRUARY 28, 1963, AS "PRINTER'S DEVIL"

STARRING BURGESS MEREDITH, ROBERT STERLING,
AND PATRICIA CROWLEY

IT WAS TWO O'CLOCK IN THE MORNING WHEN I DE-
cided that my attendance at a meeting of The International
Newspapermen's Society for the Prevention of Thirst was a
matter of moral necessity. This noble Brotherhood, steeped
in tradition and by now as immortal as the institution of the
public press, has always been a haven, a refuge and an inspiration to weary souls in the newspaper profession. Its gather-
ings at Ada's Bar & Grill—Open 24 Hours A Day have made
more than a few dismiss their woes for a while.

I had just covered a terrifically drab story which depended
nine tenths upon the typewriter for its effect, and both brain
and throat had grown quite dry in consequence. The extra
block and a half over to Ada's was a completely natural de-
tour.

As usual at this time of day, the only customers were
newspapermen.

Joe Barnes of the *Herald* was there, also Marv Kepner and
Frank Monteverdi of the *Express*. Warren Jackson, the *Globe*'s
drama critic, sat musing over a cigar, and Mack Sargent, who

got paid for being the *News'* sports man, seemed to be fascinated by improvising multiple beer rings on the table cloth.

The only one I was surprised to see was Dick Lewis, a featured columnist for the *Express* who'd lately hit the syndicates. He usually didn't drop in to Ada's more than two or three times a month, and then he never added much to the conversation.

Not that he wasn't likable. As a matter of fact, Dick always put a certain color into the get-togethers, by reason of being such a clam. It gave him a secretive or "Mystery-Man" appearance, and that's always stimulating to gab-fests which occasionally verge towards the monotonous.

He sat in one of the corner booths, looking as though he didn't give a damn about anything. A little different this time, a little lower at the mouth. Having looked into mirrors many times myself, I'd come to recognize the old half-closed eyelids that didn't result from mere tiredness. Dick sat there considering his half-empty stein and stifling only a small percentage of burps. Clearly he had been there some time and had considered a great many such half-empty steins.

I drew up a chair, tossed off an all-inclusive nod of greeting and listened for a few seconds to Frank's story of how he had scooped everybody in the city on the *Lusitania* disaster, only to get knocked senseless by an automobile ten seconds before he could get to a phone. The story died in the midsection, and we all sat for a half hour or so quaffing cool ones, hiccoughing and apologizing.

One of the wonderful things about beer is that a little bit, sipped with the proper speed, can give one the courage to do and say things one would ordinarily not have the courage to even dream of doing and saying. I had absorbed, *presto*, sufficient of the miracle drug by the time the clock got to three A.M., to do something I guess I'd wanted to do in the back of my mind for a long time. My voice was loud and clear and charged with insinuation. Everybody looked up.

"Dammit, Lewis," I said, pointing directly at him, "in order to be a member in good standing of this Society, you've just got to say something interesting. A guy simply doesn't look as inscrutable as you do without having something on his mind. You've listened to our stories. Now how about one of your own?"

"Yeah," joined Monteverdi, "Ed's right. You might call it your dues."

Jackson looked pleased and put in: "See here, Lewis, you're a newsman, aren't you? Surely you have *one* halfway diverting story."

"If it's personal," I said, "so much the better. I mean, after all, we're a Brotherhood here."

And that started it. Pretty soon we were all glaring at poor Dick, looking resentful and defiant.

He then surprised us. He threw down the last of his drink, ordered three more, stared us each in the face one by one and said:

"Okay. All right. You're all just drunk enough to listen without calling for the boys in white, though you'll still think I'm the damndest liar in the state. All right, I admit it. I do have something on my mind. Something you won't believe worth beans. And let me tell you something else. I'm quitting this screwball racket, so I don't care what you think."

He drained another stein-full.

"I'm going to tell you why as of tomorrow I start looking for some nice quiet job in a boiler factory. Or maybe as a missionary."

And this is the story Dick Lewis told that night. He was either mighty drunk or crazy as a coot, because you could tell he believed every word he said.

I'm not so sure about any of it, myself. All I know for certain is that he actually did quit the game just as he said he would, and since that night I haven't even heard his name.

When my father died he left me a hundred and twenty-two dollars, his collection of plastic-coated insects and complete ownership of the *Danville Daily Courier*. He'd owned and edited the *Courier* for fifty-five years and although it never

made any money for him, he loved it with all his heart. I
sometimes used to think that it was the most precious thing
in life to him. For whenever there wasn't any news—which
was all the time—he'd pour out his inner thoughts, his history, his whole soul into the columns. It was a lot more than
just a small town newspaper to Dad: it was his life.

I cut my first teeth on the old hand press and spent most of
my time in the office and back room. Pop used to say to me,
"You weren't born, lad, you appeared one day out of a bottle
of printer's ink." Corny, but I must have believed him, because I grew up loving it all.

What we lived on those days was a mystery to me. Not
enough issues of the *Courier* were sold even to pay for the paper stock. Nobody bought it because there was never anything to read of any interest—aside from Dad's personal
column, which was understandably limited in its appeal. For
similar reasons, no one ever advertised. He couldn't afford
any of the press services or syndicates, and Danville wasn't
homebody enough a town to give much of a darn how Mrs.
Piddle's milk cows were coming along.

I don't even know how he managed to pay the few hands
around the place. But Dad didn't seem to worry, so I never
gave the low circulation figures a great deal of thought.

That is, I didn't until it was my turn to take over.

After the first month I began to think about it a lot. I remember sitting in the office alone one night, wondering just
how the hell Dad ever did it. And I don't mind saying, I
cussed his hide for not ever telling me. He was a queer old
duck and maybe this was meant as a test or something.

If so, I had flunked out on the first round.

I sat there staring dumbly at the expense account and wondering, in a half-stupid way, how such a pretty color as red
ever got mixed up with so black a thing as being broke.

I wondered what earthly good a newspaper was to
Danville. It was a town unusual only because of its concentrated monotony: nothing ever happened. Which is news
just once, not once a day. Everybody was happy, nobody

was starving; everlasting duties were tended to with a complete lack of reluctance. If every place in the world had been like Danville, old Heraclitus wouldn't have been given a second thought. It hadn't had so much as a drunken brawl since 1800.

So I figured it all out that night. I'd take the sheets of paper in front of me and pitch them into the waste basket. Within an hour I'd call up everyone who worked with me, including the delivery boys, and tell them that the *Danville Daily Courier* had seen its day. Those people with subscriptions, I thought, would have to try to find me. I had about ten dollars left and owed twenty times that in rent and credit.

I suppose you just don't decide to close up business and actually close it up—right down to firing all the help—in an hour's time. But that's what I was going to do. I didn't take anything into consideration except the fact that I had to go somewhere and get a job quick, or I'd end up being the first person in Danville's history to die of starvation. So I figured to lock up the office, go home and get my things together and leave the next afternoon for some nearby city.

I knew that if I didn't act that fast, if I stayed and tried to sell the office and the house, I'd never get out of Danville. You don't carry out flash decisions if you wait around to weigh their consequences. You've got to act. So that's what I started to do.

But I didn't get far. About the time I had it all nicely resolved and justified, I was scared out of my shoes by a polite sort of cough, right next to me. It was after midnight and subconsciously I realized that this was neither the time nor the place for polite coughs—at least ones I didn't make. Especially since I hadn't heard anyone come in.

An old boy who must have been crowding ninety stood in front of the desk, staring at me. And I stared right back. He was dressed in the sporty style of the eighteen nineties, with whiskers all over his face and a little black derby which canted jauntily over his left eye.

''Mr. Lewis?'' he said, hopping on the side of the desk and

taking off his white gloves, finger by finger. ''Mr. Richard Lewis?''

''Yes, that's right'' is what I said.

''The son of Elmer Lewis?''

I nodded, and I'll bet my mouth was wide open. He took out a big cigar and lit it.

''If I may be so rude,'' I finally managed to get out, ''who the hell are you and how did you get in here?''

His eyes twinkled and immediately I was sorry for having been so abrupt. I don't know why, but I added, ''After all, y'know, it's pretty late.''

The old geezer just sat there smiling and puffing smoke into the air.

''Did you want to see me about something, Mr.—''

''Call me Jones, my boy, call me Jones. Yes, as a matter of fact, I do have some business with you. Y'see, I knew your father quite well once upon a time—might say he and I were very close friends. Business partners too, you might say. Yes. Business partners. Tell me, Richard, did you ever know your father to be unhappy?''

It was an odd conversation, but Mr. Jones was far too friendly and ingratiating to get anything but courtesy out of me. I answered him honestly.

''No, Dad was always about the happiest person I've ever seen. Except when Mother died, of course.''

Jones shifted and waved his cane in the air.

'Of course, of course. But aside from that. Did he have any grievances about life, any particular concern over the fact that his newspaper was never very, shall we say, successful? In a word, Richard, was your father content to the day he died?''

''Yes, I'd say he was. At least I never heard him complain. Dad never wanted anything but a chance to putter around the office, write his column and collect bugs.''

At this he whacked the desk and grinned until all I could see was teeth.

''Ah, that's very good, m'boy, very good. Times haven't been like they were in the old days. I'd begun to wonder if I was as good as I made out to be. Why, do you know that Elmer was my first customer since that time Dan'l Webster made such a fool of me! Oh, that was rich. You've got to hand it to those New Hampshire lawyers, you've just got to hand it to them.''

He sat chuckling and puffing out smoke, and, looking squarely at the situation, I began to get a very uncomfortable sensation along the back of my spine.

''Your dad wasn't any slouch, though, let me tell you, Dick. That part of the deal is over. He got what he wanted out of his life on Earth and now he's—what's that wonderful little expression somebody started a few centuries ago?—oh yes, he's paying the fiddler. But things were almost as bad then as they are now, I mean as far as signed, paid-up contracts go. Oh, I tell you, you humans are getting altogether too shrewd for your own good. What with wars and crime and politicians and the like, I scarcely have anything to do these days. No fun in merely shoveling 'em in.''

A long, gassy sigh.

''Yes sir, Elmer was on to me all right. He played his cards mighty clever. Included you, Dick m'boy. So all I have to do is make you happy and, well then, the deal's closed.''

By this time I felt pretty much like jumping out the window, but shot nerves or not, I was able to say:

''Look, Grandpa, I don't know what in hell you're talking about. I'm in no mood for this sort of thing and don't particularly care to be. If you were a friend of Pop's I'm glad to see you and all that, but if you came here for hospitality I'm afraid you're out of luck. I'm leaving town tomorrow. If you'd like, I'll walk you to a nice clean hotel.''

''Ah,'' he said, pushing me back into my chair with his cane, ''you don't understand. Lad, I've not had much practice lately and may be a trifle on the rusty side, but you must give me my dues. Let me see—if I remember correctly, the monthly cash stipend was not included and therefore was not passed on to you.''

''Look—''

"The hundred and fifty a month your father got, I mean. I see you know nothing of it. Cautious one, Elmer. Take it easy, son, take it easy. Your troubles are over."

This was too much. I got up and almost shouted at him.

"I've got enough troubles already, without a loony old bird like you busting in on me. Do we take you to a hotel, or do you start traveling?"

He just sat there and laughed like a jackass, poking me with his cane and flicking cigar ashes all over the floor.

"Dick m'boy, it's a pity you don't want out of life what your father did. In a way, that would have simplified things. As it is, I'm going to have to get out the old bag of tricks and go to work. Answer one more question and you may go your way."

I said, "All right, make it snappy, Pop. I'm getting tired of this game."

"Am I right in assuming that your principal unhappiness lies in the fact that your newspaper is not selling as you would like it to, and that this is due to the categorical fact that nothing newsworthy ever takes place in this town?"

"Yeah, that's right on the button. Now—"

"Very well, Dick. That's what I wanted to know. I advise you to go home now and get a good night's sleep."

"Exactly what I plan to do. It's been charming, Mr. Jones. I don't mind saying I think you're a nosy galoot with squirrels in the head. Anyway, do you want to go to a hotel?"

He jumped down off the desk and started to walk with me towards the front door.

"No thank you, Richard lad; I have much work to do. I tell you, stop worrying. Things are going to be rosy for you and, if you watch your step, *you'll* have no fiddler to pay. And now, good night."

Jones then dug me in the ribs with his cane and strode off, whistling "There'll Be a Hot Time in the Old Town Tonight."

He was headed straight for the Litthe Creek bridge, which gradually opened off into flap pastures and a few farm houses. Nothing lay beyond that except the graveyard.

I supposed he didn't know where he was going, but I was too confused and tired to care much. When I looked again there wasn't hide nor hair of Mr. Jones.

He was promptly forgotten. Almost, anyway. When you're broke and owe everybody in town, you're able to forget just about anything. Except, of course, that you're broke and owe everybody in town.

I locked up the office and started for home. The fire and fury were gone: I couldn't get up the gall to phone everyone and do all the things I'd planned to do.

So, miserable as a wet dog, I trudged a few blocks to the house, smoked a half dozen cigarettes and went to bed, hoping I'd have the guts to get on the train the next day.

I woke up early feeling like a fish left out in the sun too long. It was six o'clock and, like always at this time, I wished that I had a wife or a mistress to get me a big breakfast. Instead I hobbled downstairs and knew exactly what Mother Hubbard felt like. I fixed a lousy cup of coffee and sat down to a glorious dish of corn flakes. I knew that train was mighty far away and that in a little while I'd go to the office, reach in the filler box and help set up another stinking issue of the *Daily Courier*. Then would come the creditors and the long line of bushwa. Even the corn flakes tasted rancid.

Then I heard a distinct thud against the front door. It struck me as being odd, because there had never before been any thuds at that particular front door, which made precisely that sound.

I opened it, looked around and finally at my feet. There, folded magnificently and encircled with a piece of string, was a newspaper.

Since the *Courier* was the only paper Danville had ever known, and since I never read the thing anyway, it all looked very peculiar. Besides, none of my delivery boys ever folded in such a neat, professional manner.

There wasn't anybody in sight, but I noticed, before I picked it up, that there was a paper on the doorstep of every house and store around. Then people started coming out and noticing the bundles, so I gathered it up and went back inside. Maybe I scratched my head. I know I felt like it.

There was a little card attached to the string. It read:

COMPLIMENTARY ISSUE

If You Desire To Begin Or Rebegin Your Subscription, Send Checks Or Cash To The Office Of The Danville Daily Courier. Rates Are Listed Conveniently Within.

That was a laugh, but I didn't. Something was screwy somewhere. In the first place, there weren't supposed to be any morning deliveries. I, Ernie Meyer and Fred Scarborough (my staff) started the edition around eight o'clock, and it didn't get delivered until six that night. Also, since no one was in the office after I left and nothing whatsoever had been done on the next day's issue—let alone the fancy printing on that card, which could have been done only on a large press—well, I got an awfully queer feeling in the pit of my stomach.

When I opened up the paper I about yelled out loud. It looked like the biggest, most expensive highfalutin' city paper ever put together. The legend still read *Danville Daily Courier*, but I'd have felt better if it had said the *Tribune*.

Immediately upon reading the double-inch headlines, I sat down and started to sweat. There, in black, bold letters were the words:

MAYOR'S WIFE GIVES BIRTH
TO BABY HIPPOPOTAMUS

And underneath:

At three A.M. this morning, Mayor and Mrs. Fletcher Lindquist were very much startled to find themselves the parents of a healthy, 15 pound baby hippo. Most surprising is the fact that nowhere in the lineage of either the Mayor or his wife is there record of a hippopotamus strain. Mrs. Lindquist's great-grandfather, reports show, was a raving lunatic from the age of twenty-three to the time of his death, fifty years later, but it is biologically unsound to assume that such ancestral proclivities would necessarily introduce into later generations so unusual a result.

Therefore, Danville's enterprising, precedent-setting Mayor Lindquist may be said to have proved his first campaign promise, to wit, "I will make many changes!"

Continued on page 15

I don't have to recount what I did or thought at all this. I merely sat there and numbly turned to page fifteen.

Displaying his usual cool and well-studied philosophy, the Mayor announced that, in view of the fact that the Lindquists' expected baby was to have been called either Edgar Bernhardt or Louisa Ann, and inasmuch as the hippopotamus was male in sex, the name Edgar Bernhardt would be employed as planned.

When queried, the Mayor said simply, "I do not propose that our son be victim to unjudicious slander and stigmatic probings. Edgar will lead a healthy, normal life." He added brusquely: "I have great plans for the boy!"

Both Mrs. Lindquist and the attending physician, Dr. Forrest Peterson, refrained from comment, although Dr. Peterson was observed in a corner from time to time, mumbling and striking his forehead.

I turned back to the front page, feeling not at all well. There, 3 inches by 5 inches, was a photograph of Mrs. Fletcher Lindquist, holding in her arms (honest to God!) a pint-sized hippopotamus.

I flipped feverishly to the second sheet, and saw:

FARMER BURL ILLING COMPLAINS
OF MYSTERIOUS APPEARANCE
OF DRAGONS IN BACK YARD.

And then I threw the damn paper as far as I could and began pinching myself. It only hurt; I didn't wake up. I closed
my eyes and looked again, but there it was, right where I'd
heaved it.

I suppose I should have, but I didn't for a moment get the
idea I was nuts. A real live newspaper had been delivered at
my door. I owned the only newspaper in town and called it
the *Danville Daily Courier*. This paper was also called the
Danville Daily Courier. I hadn't put together an issue since the
day before. This one was dated today. The only worthwhile
news *my* paper had ever turned out was a weather report.
This one had stuff that would cause the Associated Press to
drop its teeth.

Somebody, I concluded, was nuts.

And then I slowly remembered Mr. Jones. That screwy Mr.
Jones, that loony old bird-brain.

He'd broken into the office after I'd left and somehow put
together this fantastic issue. Where he got the photograph I
didn't know, but that didn't bother me. It was the only answer. Sure—who else would have done such a thing?
Thought he'd help me by making up a lot of tall tales and
peddling them to everyone in town.

I got sore as hell. So this was how he was going to "help"
me! If he'd been there at the moment I would have broken
every bone in his scrawny old body. My God, I thought,
how'll I get out of this? What would I say when the Mayor
and Illing and Lord knows how many others got wind of it?

Dark thoughts of me, connected to a long rail, coated from
head to toe with a lot of tar and a lot of feathers, floated
clearly before my eyes. Or me at the stake, with hungry
flames lapping up . . . Who could blame them? *Some* big time
magazine or tabloid would get a copy—they'd never miss a
story like this. And then Danville would be the laughing

stock of the nation, maybe the world. At the very best, I'd be sued blue.

I took one last look at that paper on the floor and lit out for the office. I was going to tear that old jerk limb from limb—I was going to make some *real* news.

Halfway there the figure of Fred Scarborough rushed by me a mile a minute. He didn't even turn around. I started to call, but then Ernie Meyer came vaulting down the street. I tried to dodge, but the next thing I knew Ernie and I were sitting on top of each other. In his eyes was an insane look of fear and confusion.

"Ernie," I said, "what the devil's the matter with you? Has this town gone crazy or have I?"

"Don't know about that, Mr. Lewis," he panted, "but I'm headin' for the hills."

He got up and started to take off again. I grabbed him and shook him till his teeth rattled.

"What *is* the matter with you? Where's everybody running? Is there a fire?"

"Look, Mr. Lewis, I worked for your dad. It was a quiet life and I got paid regular. Elmer was a little odd, but that didn't bother me none, because I got paid regular, see. But things is happening at the office now that I don't have to put up with. 'cause, Mr. Lewis, I don't get paid at all. And when an old man dressed like my grandfather starts a lot of brand new presses running all by himself and, on top of that, chases me and Fred out with a pitchfork, well, Mr. Lewis, I'm quittin'. I resign. Goodbye, Mr. Lewis. Things like this just ain't ever happened in Danville before."

Ernie departed in a hurry, and I got madder at Mr. Jones.

When I opened the door to the office, I wished I was either in bed or had a drink. All the old hand-setters and presses were gone. Instead there was a huge, funny looking machine, popping and smoking and depositing freshly folded newspapers into a big bin. Mr. Jones, with his derby still on his head, sat at my desk pounding furiously at the typewriter and chuckling like a lunatic. He ripped a sheet out and started to insert another, when he saw me.

"Ah, Dick m'boy! How are you this morning? I must say, you don't look very well. Sit down, won't you. I'll be finished in a second."

Back he went to his writing. All I could do was sit down and open and close my mouth.

"Well," he said, taking the sheets and poking them through a little slot in the machine. "Well, there's tomorrow's edition, all—how does it go?—all put to bed. They'll go wild over that. Just think, Reverend Piltzer's daughter was found tonight with a smoking pistol in her hand, still standing over the body of her—"

I woke up.

"Jones!"

"Of course, it's not front page stuff. Makes nice filler for page eight, though."

"Jones!"

"Yes, m'boy?"

"I'm going to kill you. So help me, I'm going to murder you right now! Do you realize what you've done? Oh Lord, don't you know that half the people in Danville are going to shoot me, burn me, sue me and ride me out on a rail? Don't you—but they won't. No sir, I'll tell them everything. And you're going to stick right here to back me up. Of all the—"

"Why, what's the matter, Dick? Aren't you happy? Look at all the news your paper is getting."

"Hap—Happy? You completely ruin me and ask if I'm happy! Go bar the door, Jones; they'll be here any second."

He looked hurt and scratched the end of his nose with his cane.

"I don't quite understand, Richard. *Who* will be here? Out of town reporters?"

I nodded weakly, too sick to talk.

"Oh no, they won't arrive until tomorrow. You see, they're just getting this morning's issue. Why are you so distraught? Ah, I know what will cheer you up. Take a look at the mail box.''

I don't know why, but that's what I did. I knew the mail wasn't supposed to arrive until later, and vaguely I wanted to ask what had happened to all the old equipment. But I just went over and looked at the mail box, like Mr. Jones had suggested. I opened the first letter. Three dollars dropped out. Letter number two, another three bucks. Automatically I opened letter after letter, until the floor was covered with currency. Then I imagine I looked up piteously at Mr. J.

''Subscriptions, m'boy, subscriptions. I hurried the delivery a bit, so you'd be pleased. But that's just a start. Wait'll tomorrow, Dick. This office will be knee-deep in money!''

At this point I finally did begin to think I was crazy.

''What is all this about, Jones? *Please* tell me, or call the little white wagon. Am I going soggy in the brain?''

''Come, come! Not a bit of it! I've merely fulfilled my promise. Last night you told me that you were unhappy because the *Courier* wasn't selling. Now, as you can see, it *is* selling. And not only to Danville. No sir, the whole world will want subscriptions to your paper, Richard, before I'm through.''

''But you don't understand, Jones. You just can't make up a lot of news and expect to get by with it. It's been tried a hundred different times. People are going to catch on. And you and me, we're going to be jailed sure as the devil. Do you see now what you've done?''

He looked at me quizzically and burst out laughing.

''Why, Dick, you *don't* understand yet, do you! Come now, surely you're not such a dunce. Tell me, exactly what do you think?''

''Merely that an old man stepped into my life last night and that my life has been a nightmare ever since.''

''But beyond that. Who am I and why am I here?''

''Oh, I don't know, Mr. Jones. You're probably just a friend of Dad's and thought you could help me out by this crazy scheme. I can't even get angry with you anymore.

Things were going to hell without you—maybe I can get a job on the prison newspaper.''

''Just a queer old friend of Elmer's, eh? And you think I did no more than 'make up' those headlines. You don't wonder about this press—'' he waved his cane toward the large machine which had supplanted the roll-your-own— ''or how the papers got delivered or why they look so professional? Is that press your imagination?''

I looked over at the machine. It was like nothing I'd ever seen before. Certainly it was not an ordinary press. But it was real enough. Actual papers were popping out of it at the rate of two or three a second. And then I thought of that photograph.

''My God, Jones, do you mean to tell me that you're—''

''Precisely, my lad, precisely. A bit rusty, as I said, but with many a unique kick left.''

He kicked his heels together and smiled broadly.

''Now, you can be of no help here whatever. So, since you look a bit peaked around the face, it is my suggestion that you go home and rest for a few days.''

''That news . . . those things in the paper, you mean they were—''

''Absolutely factual. Everything that is printed in the *Danville Daily Courier*,'' he said gaily, ''is the, er, the gospel truth. Go home, Dick: I'll attend to the reporters and editors and the like. When you're feeling better, come back and we'll work together. Perhaps you'll have a few ideas.''

He put another sheet in the typewriter, rested his bushy chin on the head of the cane for a moment, twinkled his eyes and then began typing like mad.

I staggered out of the office and headed straight for Barney's Grill. All it had was beer, but that would have to do. I had to get drunk: I knew that.

When I got to Barney's, the place was crowded. I ordered a beer and then almost dropped it when the waiter said to me:

''You certainly were right on the ball, Mr. Lewis, you and your paper. Who'd a'ever thought the Mayor's wife would have a hippopotamus? Yes sir, right on the ball. I sent in my subscription an hour ago!''

Then Mrs. Olaf Jaspers, a quiet old lady who always had her coffee and doughnut at Barney's before going to work at the hospital, said:

''Oh, it was certainly a sight to see. Miz Lindquist is just as proud. Fancy, a hippopotamus!''

I quickly gulped the beer.

''You mean you actually saw it, Mrs. Jaspers?''

''Oh my yes,'' she answered. ''I was there all the time. We can't any of us figure it out, but it was the cutest thing you ever did see. Who was that old fellow that took the picture, Richard? A new man?''

Everyone began talking to me then, and my head swam around and around.

''Mighty quick of you, Lewis! You've got *my* subscription for two years!''

''Poor Burl never did catch those pesky dragons. Ate up every one of his turnips, too.''

''You're a real editor, Mr. Lewis. We'll all going to take the *Courier* from now on. Imagine; all these funny things happen and you're right there to get all the news!''

I bought a case of beer, excused myself, went home and got blind drunk.

It was nice to wake up the next morning, because, even though my head split I felt sure this was every bit a dream. The hope sank fast when I saw all the beer bottles lying on the floor. With an empty feeling down below, I crawled to the front door and opened it.

No dream.

The paper lay there, folded beautifully. I saw people running down the streets, lickity split, toward Main Street.

Thinking was an impossibility. I made for the boy's room, changed clothes, fixed some breakfast and only then had the courage to unfold the issue. The headlines cried: EXTRA!! Underneath, almost as large:

S. S. QUEEN MARY DISCOVERED
ON MAIN STREET

An unusual discovery today made Danville, U.S.A., a center of world-wide attention. The renowned steam ship, the S.S. *Queen Mary*, thought previously to be headed for Italy enroute from Southampton, appeared suddenly in the middle of Main Street in Danville, between Geary and Orchard Ave.

Imbedded deep in the cement so that it remains upright, the monstrous vessel is proving a dangerous traffic hazard, causing many motorists to go an entire mile out of their way.

Citizens of Danville view the phenomenon with jaundiced eyes, generally considering it a great nuisance.

Empty whiskey bottles were found strewn about the various decks, and all of the crew and passengers remain under the influence of heavy intoxication.

In the words of the Captain, J. E. Cromerlin:

"I din' have a thing to do with it. It wash that damned navigator, all his fault."

Officials of the steam ship line are coming from London and New York to investigate the situation.

Continued on page 20

That's what it said, and, so help me, there was another photograph, big and clear as life.

I ran outside, and headed for Main Street. But the minute I turned the corner, I saw it.

There, exactly as the paper had said, was the *Queen Mary*, as quiescent and natural as though she'd been in dock. People were gathered all around the giant ship, jabbering and yelling.

In a dazed sort of way, I got interested and joined them.

Lydia Murphy, a school teacher, was describing the nautical terms to her class, a gang of kids who seemed happy to get out of school.

Arley Taylor, a fellow who used to play checkers with Dad, walked over to me.

"Now, ain't that something, Dick! I ask ya, ain't that something!"

"That, Arley," I agreed, "is something."

I saw Mr. Jones standing on the corner, swinging his cane and puffing his cigar. I galloped over to him.

"Look, Jones, I believe you. Okay, you're the devil. But you just can't do this. First a hippopotamus, now the world's biggest ocean liner in the middle of the street— You're driving me nuts!"

"Why, hello Dick. Say, you ought to see those subscriptions now! I'd say we have five thousand dollars' worth. They're beginning to come in from the cities now. Just you wait, boy, you'll have a newspaper that'll beat 'em all!"

Arguing didn't faze him. I saw then and there that Mr. Jones wouldn't be stopped. So I cussed a few times and started off. Only I was stopped short by an expensive looking blonde, with horn-rimmed glasses and a notebook.

"Mr. Richard Lewis, editor of the *Danville Courier*?" she said.

"That's me."

"My name is Elissa Traskers. I represent the *New York Mirror*. May we go somewhere to talk?"

I mumbled, "Okay," and took one more look at the ship.

Far up on the deck I could see a guy in a uniform chasing what couldn't have been anything else but a young lady without much clothes on.

When two big rats jumped out of the lowest port hole and scampered down the street, I turned around sharply and almost dragged the blonde the entire way to my house.

Once inside, I closed the door and locked it. My nerves were on the way out.

"Mr. Lewis, why did you do that?" asked the blonde.

"Because I like to lock doors, I *love* to lock doors. They fascinate me."

"I see. Now then, Mr. Lewis, we'd like a full account, in your own words, of all these strange happenings."

She crossed a tan leg and that didn't help much to calm me down.

"Miss Traskers," I said, "I'll tell you just once, and then I want you to go away. I'm not a well man.

"My father, Elmer Lewis, was a drifter and a floater all his life, until he met the devil. Then he decided what would really make him happy. So he asked the devil to set him up in a small town with a small town newspaper. He asked for a monthly cash stipend. He got all this, so for fifty years he sat around happy as a fool, editing a paper which didn't sell and collecting lousy little bugs—"

The blonde baby looked worried, because I must have sounded somewhat unnatural. But maybe the business with the boat had convinced her that unusual things do, occasionally, happen.

"Mr. Lewis," she said sweetly, "before you go on, may I offer you a drink?"

And she produced from her purse a small, silver flask. It had scotch in it. With the elan of the damned, I got a couple of glasses and divided the contents of the flask into each.

"Thanks."

"Quite all right. Now, enough kidding, Mr. Lewis. I must turn in a report to my paper."

"I'm *not* kidding, honey. For fifty-five years my dad did this, and my mother stuck right by him. The only thing out of the ordinary they ever had was me."

The scotch tasted wonderful. I began to like Miss Traskers a lot.

"All this cost Pop his soul, but he was philosophic and I guess that didn't matter much to him. Anyway, he tricked the devil into including me into the bargain. So after he died and left the paper to me, and I started to go broke, Mr. Jones appeared and decided to help me out."

"To help you out?"

"Yeah. All this news is his work. Before he's done he'll send the whole world off its rocker, just so I can get subscriptions."

She'd stopped taking it down a long time ago.

"I'd think you were a damned liar, Mr. Lewis—"

"Call me Dick."

"—if I hadn't seen the *Queen Mary* sitting out there. Frankly, Mr. Lew— Dick, if you're telling the truth, something's got to be done."

"You're darn right it does, Elissa. But *what*? The old boy is having too much fun now to be stopped. He told me himself that he hasn't had anything to do like this for centuries."

"Besides," she said, "how did I get here so quickly? The ship was discovered only this morning, yet I can't remember—"

"Oh, don't worry about it, kid. From now on *anything* is likely to happen."

Something did. I went over and kissed her, for no apparent reason except that she was a pretty girl and I was feeling rotten. She didn't seem to mind.

Right on cue, the doorbell rang.

"Who is it?" I shouted.

"We're from the Associated Press. We want to see Mr. Richard Lewis," came a couple of voices. I could hear more footsteps coming up the front porch.

"I'm sorry," I called, "he's just come down with Yellow Fever. He can't see anybody."

But it wasn't any use. More and more steps and voices, and I could see the door being pushed inward. I grabbed Elissa's hand and we ran out the back way, ran all the way to the office.

Strangely, there weren't many people around. We walked in, and there, of course, was Mr. Jones at the typewriter. He looked up, saw Elissa and winked at me.

"Listen to this, boy. BANK PRESIDENT'S WIFE CLAIMS DIVORCE—EXPLAINS CAUGHT HUSBAND TRIFLING

WITH THREE MERMAIDS IN BATHTUB. 'course, it's rather long, but I think we can squeeze it in. Well, well, who have you there?''

I couldn't think of anything else, so I introduced Elissa.

"Ah, from the *Mirror*! I got you down here this morning, didn't I?''

Elissa looked at me and I could tell she didn't think I had been trying to fool her.

"Have you turned in your report yet, Miss?''

She shook her head.

"Well, do so immediately! Why do you think I took the trouble of sending you in the first place? Never mind, I'll attend to it. Oh, we're terribly busy here. But a shapely lass like you shouldn't have to work for a living, now should she, Dick?''

And with this, Jones nudged Elissa with his cane, in a spot which caused me to say:

"Now see here, Jones—this is going too far! Do that again and I'll punch you in the snoot.''

"I must say, Richard, you're just like your father. Don't lose a minute, do you!''

I reached out to grab him, but the second afterwards he was over on the other side of the room.

"Tut tut, m'boy, not a very nice way to treat your benefactor! Look at that basket there.''

I looked and so did Elissa. She looked long and hard. The room was full of money and checks, and Mr. Jones danced over with a mischievous glint in his eyes.

"Bet a couple could take just what's there and live comfortably for a year on it. That is, if they were sure there would be more to come.''

He sidled over to Elissa and nudged her again, and I started swinging.

Before I landed on my face, a thought came to me. It was a desperate, long-odds, crazy thought, but it seemed the answer to everything.

"Tell you what, Jones,'' I said, picking myself up off the

floor and placing Elissa behind me. "This is a little silly after all. I think you're right. I think I've acted in a very ungrateful fashion and I want to apologize. The *Courier* is really selling now, and it appears that it'll make me a lot of money. All thanks to you. I'm really sorry."

He put the chair down and seemed pleased.

"Now then, that's more like it, Dick. And, er, I apologize, young lady. I was only being devilish."

Elissa was a sophisticated girl: she didn't open her mouth.

"I can see that you're busy, Mr. Jones, so if you don't mind, Elissa and I will take a little walk."

I gave him a broad wicked wink, which delighted him.

"That's *fine,* m'boy. I want to get this evening's edition ready. Now let's see, where was I . . ."

By this time it was getting dark. Without saying a word, I pushed Elissa into the alley behind the shop. You could hear the press chugging away inside, so I began to talk fast.

"I like you," I said, "and maybe after all this is over, we can get together somewhere. But right now the important thing is to stop that bird."

She looked beautiful there in the shadows, but I couldn't take the time to tell her so. Vaguely I sensed that I'd somehow fallen in love with this girl whom I'd met that same day. She looked in all ways cooperative.

I did manage to ask: "You got a boyfriend?"

Again she shook that pretty blonde head, so I got right back to the business at hand.

"Jones *has* to be stopped. What he's done so far is fantastic, all right, but comparatively harmless. However, we've got to remember that he's the devil after all, and for sure he's up to something. Things won't stay harmless, you can count on that. Already he's forgotten about the original idea. Look at him in there, having the time of his life. This was all he needed to cut loose. Dad made the mistake of leaving the *idea* of my happiness up to Mr. Jones' imagination."

"All right, Dick, but what do we do?"

"Did you notice that he read aloud what's *going* to happen tonight, Elissa?"

"You mean about the mermaids in the bathtub?"

"Yes. Don't you get it? That hasn't happened yet. He thinks up these crazy ideas, types 'em out, gets 'em all printed and *then* they take place. He goes over, takes a few pictures and in some way gets the papers delivered a few minutes later, complete with the news. Don't ask me why he doesn't just snap his fingers—maybe he enjoys it this way more."

"I suppose that's, uh, sensible. What do you want me to do, Dick?"

"It's asking a lot, I suppose, but we can't let him wreck the whole world. Elissa, do you think you could divert the devil for about a half hour?"

Looking at her, I knew she could.

"I get it now. Okay, if you think it'll work. First, do me a favor?"

"Anything."

"Kiss me again, would you?"

I complied, and let me tell you, there was nothing crazy about that kiss. I was honestly grateful to Mr. Jones for *one* thing at least.

Elissa opened the front door of the office, threw back her hair and crooked a finger at the devil.

"Oh Mr. Jones!"

From the alley I could see him stop typing abruptly. More than abruptly. So would I.

"Why, my dear! Back from your walk so soon? Where is Richard?"

"I don't know—he just walked off and didn't say anything. Now I'm all alone."

The devil's eyes looked like tiny red hot coals, and he bit clean through his cigar.

"Well," he said. "Well, well, *well!*"

"You wouldn't like to take me out for a few drinks, would you, Mr. Jones?"

The way she moved her hips would have made me bite through my cigar, if I'd had a cigar. She was doing beautifully.

"Well, I had rather planned to—no, it can wait. Certainly, Miss Traskers, I'd be pleased, more than pleased, oh, *very* pleased to accompany you somewhere for a spot. Richard has probably gone home to talk to other reporters."

With this he hopped over the desk and took Elissa's arm.

"Oh, my dear girl, it has been so long, so very long. Voluntarily, I mean."

She smiled at the old goat and in a few moments they were headed straight for Barney's Grill. I almost chased them when I heard him say, "And afterwards, perhaps we could take a stroll through the woods, eh?"

As soon as they were out of sight, I ran into the office, took his material out of the typewriter and inserted a new sheet.

I thought for a few moments, and then hurriedly typed:

DEVIL RETURNS HOME

The devil, known also as Mr. Jones, cut short his latest visit to Earth because of altercations in Gehenna. Mr. Elmer Lewis, for some years a resident of the lower regions, successfully made his escape and entry into heaven, where he joined his wife, Elizabeth. The devil can do nothing to alter this, but has decided to institute a more rigorous discipline among his subjects still remaining.

And then, on another sheet I wrote:

OFFICE OF DANVILLE DAILY COURIER DISAPPEARS

The citizens of Danville were somewhat relieved this morning as they noticed the disappearance of the office of the town's only newspaper, the *Courier*. All the news reported in the pages of this tabloid since April 11, furthermore, was found to be totally false and misrepresentational, except the information printed in this edition. Those who paid for subscriptions have all received their money in full.

Richard Lewis, the editor, is rumored to be in New York, working for one of the large metropolitan newspapers.

The community of Danville continues a normal, happy existence, despite the lack of a news organ.

I walked over to the machine, which still ejected papers, and quickly inserted the two sheets into the slot, exactly as I'd observed Jones do.

At which point the universe blew up in my face. The entire office did a jig and then settled gently but firmly, on top of my head.

When things unfuzzed and I could begin to see straight, I found myself sitting at a typewriter in a very large and very strange office.

A fellow in shirt-sleeves and tortoise-shells ambled over and thumped me on the back.

"Great work, Dick," he said. "Great job on that city hall fire. C'mon, break down, ye set it yourself?"

Of course, as was becoming a habit, I stared dumbly.

"Always the dead-pan—wotta joker! So now you're in the syndicates. Some guys are just plain old lucky, I guess. Do *I* ever happen to be around when things like that bust out? Huh!"

He walked away, and by degrees, very carefully, I learned that I'd just scooped everybody on a big fire that had broken out in the city hall.

I was working for the *Mirror*, making $75.00 per week. I'd been with them only a few days, but everyone seemed very chummy.

It had worked. I'd outsmarted the devil! I'd gotten rid of him and the paper and everything. And then I remembered.

I remembered Elissa. So, come quitting time, I asked the first guy I saw:

"Where does Miss Elissa Traskers work, you know?"

The fellow's eyes lit up and he looked melancholy.

"You mean The Blonde Bomber? Whatta gal, whatta gal! Those legs, those—"

"Yeah—where does she work?"

"Second floor. Flunks for Davidson, that lucky—"

I got down to the second floor quick. There she was, as pretty as I remembered her. I walked up and said:

"Hello, honey. It worked!"

"I beg your pardon?"

She didn't have to say any more. I realized with a cold, heartless feeling what it was I'd forgotten. I'd forgotten Elissa. Didn't even mention her on either of those sheets, didn't even mention her!

"Don't you remember, honey? You were doing me a favor, coaxing the devil to buy you a few drinks . . ."

It was there in her eyes. She could have been staring at an escaped orangoutang.

"Excuse me," she said, picked up her coat and trotted out of the office. And out of my life.

I tried to get in touch with her any number of times after that, but she didn't know me each time. Finally I saw it was no good. I used to sit by the window and watch her leave the building with some guy or another, sit there and wish I'd just left things like they were while Mr. Jones was having fun.

It wasn't very peaceful, but so what. I ask you, so what?

Dick sat in his corner, looking serious as a lawyer. We'd all stopped laughing quite a while back, and he was actually so convincing that I piped up:

"Okay, what happened then? That why you want to quit newspaper work—because of her?"

He snickered out the side of his mouth and lit another cigarette.

"Yeah, that's why. Because of her. But that isn't all. You guys remember what happened to the Governor's wife last week?"

We remembered. Governor Parker's spouse had gone berserk and run down Fifth Avenue without a stitch on.

"You know who covered that story, who was right there again?"

It had been Lewis. That story was what had entrenched him solidly with the biggest syndicate in the country.

"All right. Can any of you add two and two?"

We were all silent.

"What are you talking about?" Jackson asked.

Dick threw down a beer and laughed out loud, though he didn't seem particularly amused.

"I wasn't so smart. I didn't stop the devil; I just stalled him awhile. He's back, y'understand, he's back! And this time he's going to get mad. That's why I'm quitting the newspapers. I don't know what I'll do, but whatever it is Mr. Jones is going to do his damndest to make me successful."

I was about to start the laughter, when I saw something that cut it off sharp.

I saw a very old gentleman, with derby, spats and cane, leaning against the bar and winking at me.

It didn't take me long to get home.

Blind Alley

Malcolm Jameson

TELEPLAY BY ROD SERLING

AIRED APRIL 11, 1963, AS "OF LATE I THINK
OF CLIFFORDSVILLE"

STARRING ALBERT SALMI, JULIE NEWMAR, AND
JOHN ANDERSON

NOTHING WAS FURTHER FROM MR. FEATHERSMITH'S
mind than dealings with streamlined, mid-twentieth-century
witches or dickerings with the Devil. But something *had* to be
done. The world was fast going to the bowwows, and he suffered from an overwhelming nostalgia for the days of his
youth. His thoughts constantly turned to Cliffordsville and
the good old days when men were men and God was in His
heaven and all was right with the world. He hated modern
women, the blatancy of the radio, That Man in the White
House, the war . . .

Mr. Feathersmith did not feel well. His customary grouch
—which was a byword throughout all the many properties of
Pyramidal Enterprises, Inc.—had hit an all-time high. The
weather was rotten, the room too hot, business awful, and
everybody around him a dope. He loathed all mention of the
cold war, which in his estimation had been bungled from the
start. He writhed and cursed whenever he thought of priori-
ties, quotas and taxes; he frothed at the mouth at every new

government regulation. His plants were working night and day on colossal contracts that under any reasonable regime would double his wealth every six months, but what could he expect but a few paltry millions?

He jabbed savagely at a button on his desk, and before even the swiftest-footed of messengers could have responded, he was irritably rattling the hook of his telephone.

"Well?" he snarled, as a tired, harassed voice answered. "Where's Paulson? Wake him up! I want him."

Paulson popped into the room with an inquiring, "Yes, sir?" Mr. Paulson was his private secretary and to his mind stupid, clumsy and unambitious. But he was a male. For Mr. Feathersmith could not abide the type of woman that cluttered up offices in these decadent days. Everything about them was distasteful—their bold, assured manner, their calm assumption of efficiency, their persistent invasion of fields sacred to the stronger and wiser sex. He abhorred their short skirts, their painted faces and their varnished nails, the hussies! And the nonchalance with which they would throw a job in an employer's face if he undertook to drive them was nothing short of maddening. Hence Mr. Paulson.

"I'm roasting," growled Mr. Feathersmith. "This place is an oven."

"Yes, sir," said the meek Paulson, and went to the window where an expensive air-conditioning unit stood. It regulated the air, heating it in winter, cooling it in summer. It was cold and blustery out and snow was in the air; Mr. Feathersmith should have been grateful. But he was not. It was a modern gadget, and though a touch of the hand was all that was needed to regulate it, he would have nothing to do with it. All Paulson did was move a knob one notch.

"What about the Phoenix Development Shares?" barked the testy old man. "Hasn't Ulrich unloaded those yet? He's had time enough."

"The S. E. C. hasn't approved them yet," said Paulson, apologetically. He might have added, but thought best not to, that Mr. Farquhar over there had said the prospectus stank and that the whole proposition looked like a bid for a long-term lease on a choice cell in a Federal penitentiary.

"*Aw-r-rk,*" went Mr. Feathersmith, "a lot of Communists, that's what they are. What are we coming to? Send Clive in."

"Mr. Clive is in court, sir. And so is Mr. Blakeslee. It's about the reorganization plan for the Duluth, Moline & Southern—the bondholders' protective committee . . ."

"*Aw-r-rk,*" choked Mr. Feathersmith. Yes, those accursed bondholders—always yelping and starting things. "Get out. I want to think."

His thoughts were bitter ones. Never in all his long and busy life had things been as tough as now. When he had been simply Jack Feathersmith, the promoter, it had been possible to make a fortune overnight. You could lose at the same rate, too, but still a man had a chance. There were no starry-eyed reformers always meddling with him. Then he had become the more dignified "entrepreneur," but the pickings were still good. After that he had styled himself "investment banker" and had done well, though a certain district attorney raised some nasty questions about it and forced some refunds and adjustments. But that had been in the 30's when times were hard for everybody. Now, with a war on and everything, a man of ability and brains ought to mop up. But would they let him? *Aw-r-rk!*

Suddenly he realized he was panting and heaving and felt very, very weak. He must be dying. But that couldn't be right. No man of any age kept better fit. Yet his heart was pounding and he had to gasp for every breath. His trembling hand fumbled for the button twice before he found it. Then, as Paulson came back, he managed a faint, "Get a doctor—I must be sick."

For the next little while things were vague. A couple of the hated females from the outer office were fluttering and cooing about the room, and one offered him a glass of water which he spurned. Then he was aware of a pleasant-faced young chap bending over him listening to his chest through a stethoscope. He discovered also that one of those tight, blood-pressure contraptions was wrapped around his arm. He felt the prick of a needle. Then he was lifted to a sitting position and given a couple of pills.

"A little stroke, eh?" beamed the young doctor, cheerily. "Well, you'll be all right in a few minutes. The ephedrine did the trick."

Mr. Feathersmith ground his teeth. If there was anything in this topsy-turvy modern age he liked less than anything else it was the kind of doctors they had. A little stroke, eh? The young whippersnapper! A fresh kid, no more. Now take old Dr. Simpson, back at Cliffordsville. There was a doctor for you—a sober, grave man who wore a beard and a proper Prince Albert coat. There was no folderol about him—new-fangled balderdash about basal metabolism, X-rays, electrocardiograms, blood counts and all that rot. He simply looked at a patient's tongue, asked him about his bowels, and then wrote a prescription. And he charged accordingly.

"Do you have these spells often?" asked the young doctor. He was so damn cheerful about it, it hurt.

"Never," blared Mr. Feathersmith. "Never was sick a day in my life. Three of you fellows pawed me over for three days, but couldn't find a thing wrong. Consolidated Mutual wrote me a million straight life on the strength of that and tried their damnedest to sell me another million. That's how good I am."

"Pretty good," agreed the doctor with a laugh. "When was that?"

"Oh, lately—fifteen years ago, about."

"Back in '28, huh? That was when even life insurance companies didn't mind taking a chance now and then. You were still in your fifties then, I take it?"

"I'm fit as a fiddle yet," asserted the old man doggedly. He wanted to pay this upstart off and be rid of him.

"Maybe," agreed the doctor, commencing to put his gear away, "but you didn't look it a little while ago. If I hadn't got here when I did . . ."

"Look here, young man," defied Mr. Feathersmith, "you can't scare me."

"I'm not trying to," said the young man, easily. "If a heart block can't scare you, nothing can. Just the same, you've got to make arrangements. Either with a doctor or an undertaker. Take your choice. My car's downstairs if you think I'll do."

"*Aw-r-rk*," sputtered Mr. Feathersmith, but when he tried to get up he realized how terribly weak he was. He let them escort him to the elevator, supporting him on either side, and a moment later was being snugged down on the back seat of the doctor's automobile.

The drive uptown from Wall Street was as unpleasant as usual. More so, for Mr. Feathersmith had been secretly dreading the inevitable day when he would fall into doctors' hands, and now that it had happened, he looked out on the passing scene in search of diversion. The earlier snow had turned to rain, but there were myriads of men and lots of equipment clearing up the accumulation of muck and ice. He gazed at them sourly—*scrape, scrape, scrape*—noise, clamor and dirt, all symptomatic of the modern city. He yearned for Cliffordsville where it rarely snowed, and when it did it lay for weeks in unsullied whiteness on the ground. He listened to the gentle swishing of the whirling tires on the smooth, wet pavement, disgusted at the monotony of it. One street was like another, one city like another—smooth, endless concrete walled in by brick and plate glass and dreary rows of light poles. No one but a fool would live in a modern city. Or a modern town, for that matter, since they were but unabashed tiny imitations of their swollen sisters. He sighed. The good old days were gone beyond recapture.

It was that sigh and that forlorn thought that turned his mind to Forfin. Forfin was a shady fellow he knew and once or twice had employed. He was a broker of a sort, for the lack of better designation. He hung out in a dive near Chatham Square and was altogether a disreputable person, yet he could accomplish strange things. Such as dig up information known only to the dead, or produce prophecies that could actually be relied on. The beauty of dealing with him was that so long as the fee was adequate—and it had to be that—he delivered the goods and asked no questions. His only explanation of his peculiar powers was that he had contacts—gifted astrologers and numerologists, unprincipled demonologists and their ilk. He was only a go-between, he insisted, and invariably required a signed waiver before undertaking any assignment. Mr. Feathersmith recalled now that once, when he had complained of a twinge of rheumatism, Forfin had hinted darkly at being able to produce some of the water of the Fountain of Youth. At a price, of course. And when the price was mentioned, Mr. Feathersmith had haughtily ordered him out of the office.

The doctor's office was the chamber of horrors he had feared. There were many rooms and cubbyholes filled with shiny adjustable enameled torture chairs and glassy cabinets in which rows of cruel instruments were laid. There were fever machines and other expensive-looking apparatus, and a laboratory full of mysterious tubes and jars. White-smocked nurses and assistants flitted noiselessly about like helpful ghosts. They stripped him and weighed him and jabbed needles in him and took his blood. They fed him messy concoctions and searched his innards with a fluoroscope; they sat him in a chair and snapped electrodes on his wrists and ankle to record the pounding of his heart on a film. And after other thumpings, listenings and measurings, they left him weary and quivering to dress himself alone.

Naked as he was, and fresh from the critical probing of the doctor and his gang, he was unhappily conscious of how harshly age had dealt with him after all. He was pink and lumpy now where he had once been firm and tanned. His spindly shanks seemed hardly adequate for the excess load he now carried about his middle. Until now he had valued the prestige and power that goes with post-maturity, but now, for the first time in his life, he found himself hankering after youth again. Yes, youth would be desirable on any terms. It was a thoughtful Mr. Feathersmith who finished dressing that afternoon.

The doctor was waiting for him in his study, as infernally cheerful as ever. He motioned the old man to a chair.

"You are a man of the world," he began, "so I guess you can take it. There is nothing to be alarmed over—immediately. But you've got to take care of yourself. If you do, there are probably a good many years left in you yet. You've got a cardiac condition that has to be watched, some gastric impairments, your kidneys are pretty well shot, there are signs of senile arthritis, and some glandular failure and vitamin deficiency. Otherwise, you are in good shape."

"Go on." Now Mr. Feathersmith knew he would have to get in touch with Forfin.

"You've got to cut out all work, avoid irritation and excitement, and see me at least weekly. No more tobacco, no liquor, no spicy or greasy foods, no late hours. I'm giving you a diet and some prescriptions as to pills and tablets you will need . . ."

The doctor talked on, laying down the law in precise detail. His patient listened dumbly, resolving steadfastly that he would do nothing of the sort. Not so long as he had a broker on the string who could contact magicians.

That night Mr. Feathersmith tried to locate Forfin, but Forfin could not be found. The days rolled by and the financier felt better. He was his old testy self again and promptly disregarded all his doctor's orders. Then he had his second heart attack, and that one nearly took him off. After that he ate the vile diet, swallowed his vitamin and gland-extract pills, and duly went to have his heart examined. He began liquidating his many business interests. Sooner or later his scouts would locate Forfin. After that he would need cash, and lots of it. Youth, he realized now, was worth whatever it could be bought for.

The day he met with his lawyers and the buyers' lawyers

to complete the sale of Pyramidal Enterprises, Inc., Mr. Blakeslee leaned over and whispered that Forfin was back in town. He would be up to see Mr. Feathersmith that night. A gleam came into the old man's eye and he nodded. He was ready. By tomorrow all his net worth would be contained in cash and negotiable securities. It was slightly over thirty-two million dollars altogether, an ample bribe for the most squeamish demonologist and enough left over for the satisfaction of whatever dark powers his incantations might raise. He was confident money would do the trick. It always had, for him, and was not the love of it said to be the root of all evil?

Mr. Feathersmith was elated. Under ordinary circumstances he would have conducted a transaction of the magnitude of selling Pyramidal with the maximum of quibbling and last-minute haggling. But today he signed all papers with alacrity. He even let Polaris Petroleum & Pipeline go without a qualm, though the main Polaris producing field was only a few miles south of his beloved Cliffordsville. He often shuddered to think of what an oil development would do to a fine old town like that, but it made him money and, anyhow, he had not been back to the place since he left it years ago to go and make his fortune.

After the lawyers had collected their papers and gone, he took one last look around. In his office, as in his apartment, there was no trace of garish chromium and red leather. It was richly finished in quiet walnut paneling with a single fine landscape on one wall. A bookcase, a big desk, two chairs and a Persian rug completed the furnishings. The only ultramodern feature was the stock ticker and the news teletype. Mr. Feathersmith liked his news neat and hot off the griddle. He couldn't abide the radio version, for it was adorned and embellished with the opinions and interpretations of various commentators and self-styled experts.

It was early when he got home. By chance it was raining again, and as he stepped from his limousine under the marquee canopy that hung out over the sidewalk, the doorman rushed forward with an umbrella lest a stray drop wet his financial highness. Mr. Feathersmith brushed by the man angrily—he did not relish sycophantism, he thought. Flunkies, pah! He went up in the elevator and out into the softly lit corridor that led to his apartment. Inside he found his houseboy, Felipe, listening raptly to a swing version of a classic, playing it on his combination FM radio and Victrola.

"Shut that damn thing off!" roared Mr. Feathersmith. Symphonic music he liked, when he was in the mood for it, but nothing less.

Then he proceeded to undress and have his bath. It was the one bit of ritual in his day that he really enjoyed. His bathroom was a marvel of beauty and craftsmanship—in green and gold tile with a sunken tub. There was a needle bath, too, a glass-enclosed shower, and a sweat chamber. He reveled for a long time in the steamy water. Then, remembering that Forfin might come at any time, he hurried out.

His dinner was ready. Mr. Feathersmith glowered at the table as he sat down. It was a good table to look at, but that was not the way he felt about it. The cloth was cream-colored damask and the service exquisitely tooled sterling; in the center sat a vase of roses with sprays of ferns. But the crystal pitcher beside his plate held certified milk, a poor substitute for the vintage Pommard he was accustomed to. Near it lay a little saucer containing the abominable pills—six of them, two red, two brown, one black, and one white.

He ate his blue points. After that came broiled pompano, for the doctor said he could not get too much fish. Then there was fresh asparagus and creamed new potatoes. He topped it off with fresh strawberries and cream. No coffee, no liqueur.

He swallowed the stuff mechanically, thinking all the while of Chub's place, back in Cliffordsville. There a man could get an honest-to-goodness beefsteak, two inches thick and reeking with fat, fresh cut from a steer killed that very day in Chub's back yard. He thought, too, of Pablo, the tamale man. His stand was on the corner by the Opera House, and he kept his sizzling product in a huge lard can wrapped in an old red tablecloth. The can sat on a small charcoal stove so as to keep warm, and the whole was in a basket. Pablo dished out the greasy, shuck-wrapped morsels onto scraps of torn newspaper and one sat down on the curb and ate them with his fingers. They may have been made of fragments of dog—as some of his detractors alleged—but they were good. Ten cents a dozen, they were. Mr. Feathersmith sighed another mournful sigh. He would give ten thousand dollars for a dozen of them right now—and the ability to eat them.

Feathersmith waited impatiently for Forfin to come. He called the operator and instructed her to block all calls except that announcing his expected guest. Damn that phone, anyway. All that any Tom, Dick or Harry who wanted to intrude had to do was dial a number. The old man had an unlisted phone, but people who knew where he lived called through the house switchboard notwithstanding.

At length the shifty little broker came. Mr. Feathersmith lost no time in approaches or sparring. Forfin was a practical man like himself. You could get down to cases with him without blush or apology.

"I want," Mr. Feathersmith said, baldly, "to turn the hand of the clock back forty years. I want to go to the town of Cliffordsville, where I was born and raised, and find it just as I left it. I propose to start life all over again. Can you contact the right people for the job?"

"*Phew!*" commented Mr. Forfin, mopping his head. "That's a big order. It scares me. That'll involve Old Nick himself . . ."

He looked uneasily about, as if the utterance of the name was a sort of inverted blasphemy.

"Why not?" snapped the financier, bristling. "I always deal with principals. They can act. Skip the hirelings, demons, or whatever they are."

"I know," said Forfin, shaking his head disapprovingly, "but he's a slick bargainer. Oh, he keeps his pacts—to the dot. But he'll slip a fast one over just the same. It's his habit. He gets a kick out of it—outsmarting people. And it'll cost. Cost like hell."

"I'll be the judge of the cost," said the old man, stiffly, thinking of the scant term of suffering, circumscribed years that was the best hope the doctor had held out to him, "and as to bargaining, I'm not a pure sucker. How do you think I got where I am?"

"O. K.," said Forfin, with a shrug. "It's your funeral. But it'll take some doing. When do we start?"

"Now."

"He sees mortals only by appointment, and I can't make 'em. I'll arrange for you to meet Madame Hecate. You'll have to build yourself up with her. After that you're on your own. You'd better have plenty of ready dough. You'll need it."

"I've got it," said Mr. Feathersmith shortly. "And yours?"

"Forget it. I get my cut from *them*."

That night sleep was slow in coming. He reviewed his decision and did not regret it. He had chosen the figure of forty deliberately. Forty from seventy left thirty—in his estimation the ideal age. If he were much younger, he would be pushed around by his seniors; if he were much older, he wouldn't gain so much by the jump back. But at thirty he would be in the prime of physical condition, old enough to be thought of as mature by the youngsters, and young enough to command the envy of the oldsters. And, as he remembered it, the raw frontier days were past, the effete modernism yet to come.

He slept. He dreamed. He dreamed of old Cliffordsville, with its tree-lined streets and sturdy houses sitting way back, each in its own yard and behind its own picket fence. He remembered the soft clay streets and how good the dust felt between the toes when he ran barefoot in the summertime. Memories of good things to eat came to him—the old spring house and watermelons hung in bags in the well, chickens running the yard, and eggs an hour old. There was Sarah, the cow, and old Aunt Anna, the cook. And then there were the wideopen business opportunities of those days. A man could start a bank or float a stock company and there were no snooping inspectors to tell him what he could and couldn't do. There were no blaring radios, or rumbling, stinking trucks or raucous auto horns. People stayed healthy because they led the good life. Mr. Feathersmith rolled over in bed and smiled. It wouldn't be long now!

The next afternoon Forfin called him. Madame Hecate would see him at five; and he gave a Fifth Avenue address. That was all.

Mr. Feathersmith was really surprised when he entered the building. He had thought a witch would hang out in some dubious district where there were grime and cobwebs. But this was one of the swankiest buildings in a swanky street. It was filled with high-grade jewelers and diamond merchants, for the most part. He wondered if he had heard the address wrong.

At first he was sure he had, for when he came to examine the directory board he could find no Hecate under the H's or any witches under the W's. He stepped over to the elevator starter and asked him whether there was a tenant by that name.

"If she's on the board, there is," said that worthy, looking Mr. Feathersmith up and down in a disconcerting fashion. He went meekly back to the board. He rubbed his eyes. There was her name—in both places. "Madame Hecate, Consultant Witch, Suite 1313."

He went back to the elevators, then noticed that the telltale arcs over the doors were numbered—10, 11, 12, 14, 15, and so on. There was no thirteenth floor. He was about to turn to the starter again when he noticed a small car down at the end of the hall. Over its door was the label, "Express to 13th Floor." He walked down to it and stepped inside. An insolent little guy in a red monkey jacket lounged against the starting lever. He leered up at Mr. Feathersmith and said, "Are you *sure* you want to go up, pop?"

Mr. Feathersmith gave him the icy stare he had used so often to quell previous impertinences, and then stood rigidly looking out the door. The little hellion slid the door to with a shrug and started the cab.

When it stopped he got off in a small foyer that led to but a single door. The sign on the door said merely, "Enter," so Mr. Feathersmith turned the knob and went in. The room looked like any other midtown reception room. There was a desk presided over by a lanky, sour woman of uncertain age, whose only noteworthy feature was her extreme pallor and haggard eyes. The walls were done in a flat blue-green pastel color that somehow hinted at iridescence, and were relieved at the top by a frieze of interlaced pentagons of gold and black. A single etching hung on the wall, depicting a conventionalized witch astride a broomstick silhouetted against a full moon, accompanied by a flock of bats. A pair of chairs and a sofa completed the furnishings. On the sofa a huge black cat slept on a red velvet pillow.

"Madame Hecate is expecting you," said the cadaverous receptionist in a harsh, metallic voice. "Please be seated."

"Ah, a zombie," thought Mr. Feathersmith, trying to get into the mood of his environment. Then as a gesture of good will, though he had no love for any animal, he bent over and stroked the cat. It lifted its head with magnificent deliberation, regarded him venomously for a moment through baleful green eyes; then, with the most studied contempt, spat. After that it promptly tucked its head back in its bosom as if that disposed of the matter for all eternity.

"Lucifer doesn't like people," remarked the zombie, powdering her already snowy face. Just then a buzzer sounded faintly, three times.

"The credit man is ready for you," said the ghostly receptionist. "You'll have to pass him first. This way, please."

For some reason that did not astonish Mr. Feathersmith as much as some other features of the place. After all, he was a businessman, and even in dealing with the myrmidons of Hell, business was business. He followed her through the inner door and down a side passage to a little office. The fellow who received him was an affable, thin young man, with brooding, dark-brown eyes, and an errant black lock that kept falling down and getting in his eyes.

"A statement of your net worth, please," asked the young man, indicating a chair. He turned and waved a hand about the room. It was lined with fat books, shelf after shelf of them, and there were filing cases stuffed with loose papers and photographs. "I should warn you in advance that we have already made an independent audit and know the answer. It is a formality, as it were. Thought you ought to know."

Mr. Feathersmith gazed upon the books with wonderment. Then his blood ran chill and he felt the gooseflesh rise on him and a queer bristly feeling among the short hairs on the back of his neck. The books were all about *him!* There were two rows of thick volumes neatly titled in gold leaf, such as "J. Feathersmith—Private Life—Volume IX." There was one whole side of the room lined with other books, in sets. One set was labeled "Business Transactions," another "Subconscious Thoughts and Dreams," and then other volumes on various related aspects of their subject. One that shocked him immensely bore the horrid title of "Indirect Murders, Et Cetera." For an instant he did not grasp its import, until he recalled the aftermath of the crash of Trans-Mississippi Debentures. It was a company he had bought into only to find it mostly water. He had done the only thing to do and get out with a profit—he blew the water up into vapor, then pulled the plug. A number of suicides resulted. He supposed the book was about that and similar fiascoes.

He turned to face the credit man and was further dismayed to see that gentleman scrutinizing a copy of the contract of sale of the Pyramidal company. So he knew the terms exactly! Worse, on the blotter in plain sight was a photostat copy of a will that he had made out that very morning. It was an attempt on Mr. Feathersmith's part to hedge. He had left all his money to the Simonist Brotherhood for the propagation of religion, thinking to use it as a bargaining point with whatever demon showed up to negotiate with him. Mr. Feathersmith scratched his neck—a gesture of annoyance at being forestalled that he had not used for years. It was all the more irritating that the credit man was purring softly and smiling to himself.

"Well?" said the credit man.

Mr. Feathersmith had lost the first round and knew it. He had come in to arrange a deal and to dictate, more or less, his own terms. Now he was at a distinct disadvantage. There was only one thing to do if he wanted to go on; that was to come clean. He reached into his pocket and pulled out a slip of paper. There was one scribbled line on it. "Net worth— $32,673,251.03, plus personal effects."

"As of noon, today," added Mr. Feathersmith, handing the paper across the desk.

The credit man glanced at it, then shoved it into a drawer with the comment that it appeared to be substantially correct. Then he announced that that was all. He could see Madame Hecate now.

Madame Hecate turned out to be the greatest surprise so far. Mr. Feathersmith had become rather dubious as to his ability to previse these strange people he was dealing with, but he was quite sure the witch would be a hideous creature with an outjutting chin meeting a down-hanging beak and with the proverbial hairy warts for facial embellishments. She was not like that at all. Madame Hecate was as cute a little trick as could be found in all the city. She was a vivacious, tiny brunette with sparkling eyes and a gay, carefree manner, and was dressed in a print housedress covered by a tan smock.

"You're a lucky man, Mr. Feathersmith," she gurgled, wiping her hands on a linen towel and tossing it into a handy container. "The audience with His Nibs is arranged for about an hour from now. Ordinarily he only comes at midnight, but lately he has had to spend so much time on Earth he works on a catch-as-catch-can basis. At the moment he is in

Germany—it is midnight there now, you know—giving advice to one of his most trusted mortal aides. No doubt you could guess the name, but for reasons you will appreciate, our clientele is regarded as confidential. But he'll be along shortly."

"Splendid," said Mr. Feathersmith. For a long time it had been a saying of his that he wouldn't wait an hour for an appointment with the Devil himself. But circumstances had altered. He was glad that he had *only* an hour to wait.

"Now," said the witch, shooting him a coy, sidelong glance, "let's get the preliminaries over with. A contract will have to be drawn up, of course, and that takes time. Give me the main facts as to what you want, and I'll send them along to the Chief Fiend in the Bureau of Covenants. By the time His Nibs gets here, the scribes will have everything ready."

She produced a pad and a pencil and waited, smiling sweetly at him.

"Well, uh," he said, a trifle embarrassed because he did not feel like telling her *quite* all that was in his mind—she seemed such an innocent to be in the witch business. "I had an idea it would be nice to go back to the town of my boyhood to spend the rest of my life . . ."

"Yes?" she said eagerly. "And then . . ."

"Well," he finished lamely, "I guess that's about all. Just put me back in Cliffordsville as of forty years ago—that's all I want."

"How unique!" she exclaimed, delightedly. "You know, most men want power and wealth and success in love and all that sort of thing. I'm sure His Nibs will grant this request instantly."

Mr Feathersmith grunted. He was thinking that he had already acquired all those things from an uninformed, untrained start in that same Cliffordsville just forty years ago. Knowing what he did now about men and affairs and the subsequent history of the world, what he would accomplish on the second lap would astonish the world. But the thought suggested an addendum.

"It should be understood," he appended, "that I am to retain my present—uh—wisdom, unimpaired, and complete memory."

"A trifle, Mr. Feathersmith," she bubbled. "A trifle, I assure you."

He noticed that she had noted the specifications on separate sheets of paper, and since he indicated that was all, she advanced to a nearby brazier that stood on a tripod and lit them with a burning candle she borrowed from a sconce. The papers sizzled smartly into greenish flame, curled and disappeared without leaving any ash.

"They are there now," she said. "Would you like to see our plant while you wait?"

"With pleasure," he said, with great dignity. Indeed, he was most curious about the layout, for the room they were in was a tiny cubicle containing only a high desk and a stool and the brazier. He had expected more demoniac paraphernalia.

She led the way out and he found the place was far more extensive than he thought. It must cover the entire floor of the building. There was a long hall, and off it many doors.

"This is the Alchemical Department," she said, turning into the first one. "I was working in here when you came. That is why my hands were so gummy. Dragon fat is vile stuff, don't you think?"

She flashed those glowing black eyes on him and a dazzling smile.

"I can well imagine," he replied.

He glanced into the room. At first sight it had all the appearance of a modern chemical laboratory, though many of the vessels were queerly shaped. The queerest of all were the alchemists, of whom about a dozen sat about on high stools. They were men of incalculable age, bearded and wearing heavy-rimmed octagonal-lensed eyeglasses. All wore black smocks spattered with silvery crescents, sunbursts, stars, and such symbols. All were intent on their work. The bottles on the tables bore fantastic labels, such as "asp venom," "dried cameleopard blood," and "powdered unicorn horn."

"The man at the alembic," explained the witch, sweetly, "is compounding a modified love philter. You'd be surprised how many star salesmen depend on it. It makes them virtually irresistible. We let them have it on a commission basis."

She pointed out some other things, such as the two men adjusting the rheostat on an electric athanor, all of which struck Mr. Feathersmith as being extremely incongruous. Then they passed on.

The next room was the Voodoo Department, where a black sculptress was hard at work fashioning wax dolls from profile and front-view photographs of her client's most hated enemies. An assistant was studying a number of the finished products and occasionally thrusting pins into certain vital parts. There were other unpleasant things to be seen there and Mr. Feathersmith shuddered and suggested they pass on.

"If it affects you that way," said the witch, with her most beguiling smile, "maybe we had better skip the next."

The next section was devoted to Demonology and Mr. Feathersmith was willing to pass it by, having heard something of the practices of that sect. Moreover, the hideous moans and suppressed shrieks that leaked through the wall were sufficient to make him lose any residual interest in the orgies. But it was not to be. A door was flung open and an old hag tottered out, holding triumphantly aloft a vial of glowing violet vapor.

"Look," she cackled with hellish glee, "I caught it! The anguish of a dying hen! He! He!"

Mr. Feathersmith suffered a twinge of nausea and a bit of fright, but the witch paused long enough to coo a few words of praise.

She popped her head into the door beyond where a senile practitioner could be seen sitting in a black robe and dunce's cap spangled with stars and the signs of the zodiac. He was in the midst of a weird planetarium.

"This is the phoniest racket in the shop," she murmured, "but the customers love it. The old guy is a shrewd guesser.

That's why he gets by. Of course, his horoscopes and all these props are just so much hogwash—custom, you know."

Mr. Feathersmith flicked a glance at the astrologer, then followed her into the next room. A class of neophytes appeared to be undergoing instruction in the art of Vampirism. A demon with a pointer was holding forth before a set of wall charts depicting the human circulatory system and emphasizing the importance of knowing just how to reach the carotid artery and jugular vein. The section just beyond was similar. It housed the Department of Lycanthropy and a tough-looking middle-aged witch was lecturing on the habits of predatory animals. As Mr. Feathersmith and his guide looked in, she was just concluding some remarks on the value of prior injections of aqua regia as a resistant to possible silver bullets.

He never knew what other departments were in the place, for the witch happened to glance up at one of the curious clocks that adorned the walls. She said it kept Infernal time. At any rate, His Nibs was due shortly. They must hurry to the Apparition Chamber.

That awesome place was in a class by itself. Murals showing the torments of Hell covered the long walls. At one end was a throne, at the other a full-length portrait of His Nibs himself, surrounded by numerous photographs. The portrait was the conventional one of the vermilion anthropoid modified by barbed tail, cloven hoofs, horns, and a wonderfully sardonic leer. The rest of the pictures were of ordinary people—some vaguely familiar to Mr. Feathersmith.

"His Vileness always appears to mortals as one of their own kind," explained the witch, seeing Mr. Feathersmith's interest in the gallery. "It works out better that way."

Two imps were bustling about, arranging candles and bowls of incense about a golden pentagon embedded in the black composition floor. There were other cabalistic designs worked into the floor by means of metallic strips set edgewise, but apparently they were for lesser demons or jinn. The one receiving attention at the moment was immediately before the throne. The witch produced a pair of ear plugs and inserted them into Mr. Feathersmith's ears. Then she blind-folded him, patted him soothingly and told him to take it easy—it was always a little startling the first time.

It was. He heard the spewing of some type of fireworks, and the monotone of the witch's chant. Then there was a splitting peal of thunder, a blaze of light, and a suffocating sulphurous atmosphere. In a moment that cleared and he found his bandage whisked off. Sitting comfortably on the throne before him was a chubby little man wearing a gray pin-striped business suit and smoking a cigar. He had large blue eyes, several chins, and a jovial, back-slapping expression. He might have been a Rotarian and proprietor of a moderate-sized business anywhere.

"Good morning," he said affably. "I understand you want transportation to Cliffordsville of four decades ago. My Executive Committee has approved it, and here it is . . ."

Satan snapped his fingers. There was a dull *plop* and an ex-plosion of some sort overhead. Then a document fluttered downward. The witch caught it deftly and handed it to His Nibs, who glanced at it and presented it to Mr. Feathersmith.

Whether the paper was parchment or fine-grained asbes-tos/mat, that gentleman could not say. But it was covered with leaping, dazzling letters of fire that were exceedingly hard to read, especially in the many paragraphs of fine print that made up the bulk of the document. Its heading was:

COMPACT *between His Infernal Highness Satan, known hereinafter as The Party of the First Part, and one J. Feather-smith, a loyal and deserving servant, known as The Party of the Second Part. To wit:*

The perusal of such a contract would have been child's play for the experienced Mr. Feathersmith, had it not been for the elusive nature of the dancing letters, since only the part directly under his eye was legible. The rest was lost in the fiery interplay of squirming script and had the peculiar property of seeming to give a different meaning at every reading. Considered as a legal document, thought Mr. Feathersmith out of the depths of his experience, it was a honey. It seemed to mean what it purported to mean, yet . . .

At any rate, there was a clause there that plainly stated, even after repeated readings, that The Party of the Second Part would be duly set down at the required destination, furnished with necessary expense money and a modest stake, and thereafter left on his own.

"The compensation?" queried Mr. Feathersmith, having failed to see mention of it. "You'll want my soul, I presume."

"Dear me, no," responded Satan cheerily, with a friendly pat on the knee. "We've owned that outright for many, many years. Money's all we need. You see, if anything happened to you as you are, the government would get about three quarters of it and the lawyers the rest. We hate to see that three quarters squandered in subversive work—such as improved housing and all that rot. So, if you'll kindly give us your check . . ."

"How much?" Mr. Feathersmith wanted to know, reaching for his checkbook.

"Thirty-three million," said Satan calmly.

"That's outrageous!" shouted the client. "I haven't that much . . ."

"There was to be 1 per cent off for cash, Your Vileness," reminded the witch sweetly.

Mr. Feathersmith glared at both of them. He had been neatly trimmed—right down to chicken feed. His first impulse was to terminate the interview then and there. But he remembered that, given youth and opportunity, he could make any number of fortunes. He also had in mind the dismal future forecast for him by the doctor. No. The transaction had to be gone through with. He meekly signed checks for his full balance, and an order on his brokers for the delivery of all other valuables.

There was one more thing to do—sign the pact.

"Roll up your left sleeve," said the witch. He noticed she held a needle-tipped syringe in one hand and a pad damp- ened with alcohol in the other. She rubbed him with the cotton, then jabbed him with the needle. When she had with- drawn a few cubic centimeters of blood, she yanked the needle out, unscrewed it and replaced it by a fountain-pen point.

"Our practitioners did awfully sloppy work in the old days," she laughed, as she handed him the gruesomely charged pen and the pact. "You have no idea how many were lost prematurely through infection."

"Uh-huh," said Mr. Feathersmith, rolling down his sleeve and getting ready to sign. He might as well go through with it—the sooner the better.

"Your transportation," she added, handing him a folding railroad ticket with a weird assortment of long-defunct or merged railroads on it, queer dates and destinations. But he saw that it ended where and when he wanted to go.

"Grand Central Station, Track 48, 10:34 tonight."

"Better give him some cash," suggested Satan, hauling out a roll of bills and handing them to her. Mr. Feathersmith looked at them with fast-rising anxiety; the sight of them shook him to the foundations. For they were large, blanket- like sheets of paper, none smaller than a fifty, and many with yellow backs. Satan also handed over a coin purse, in which were some gold pieces and six or eight big silver dollars. Mr. Feathersmith had completely forgotten that they used such money in the old days—pennies and dollar bills were un- known in the West, and fives and tens in paper so rare as to be refused by shopkeepers. How much else had he forgot- ten? It rattled him so that he did not notice when Satan disap- peared, and he allowed himself to be ushered out in a mumbling daze by the little witch.

By train time, though, he had cheered up. There was just the little journey halfway across the continent to be negoti- ated and the matter of the forty years. No doubt that would occur during the night as a miracle of sorts. He let the redcap carry his luggage aboard the streamlined flier and snugged himself down in his compartment. He had not had to bother with having clothes of the period made to order, for the witch had intimated that those details would be taken care of automatically.

His next job was to compose the story he was going to tell to explain his return to Cliffordsville. Besides other excellent reasons, he had chosen the particular time for his rejuvenation so as not to run foul of himself in his earlier personality or any of his family. It had been just at the close of the Spanish War that both parents had died of yellow fever, leaving him an orphan and in possession of the old homestead and the parental bank account. He had lost little time in selling the former and withdrawing the latter. After that he had shaken the dust of Cliffordsville from his feet for what he thought was to be all time. By 1902 there was no member of the Feathersmith family residing in the county. His return, therefore, would be regarded merely as an ordinary return. He would give some acceptable explanations, then take up where he had left off. Sooner or later he would pull out again—probably to Detroit to get in on the ground floor with Henry Ford, and he thought it would be a good idea, too, to grab himself some U. S. Steel, General Motors and other comers-to-be. He licked his lips in anticipation of the killing he would make in the subsequent World War I years when he could ride Bethlehem all the way to the top, pyramiding as he went, without a tremor of fear. He also thought with some elation of how much fun it would be to get reaquainted with Daisy Norton, the girl he might have married if he had but stayed in Cliffordsville. She was cold to him then, but that was because her father was a rich aristocrat and looked down upon the struggling Feathersmiths. But this time he would marry her and the Norton acres under which the oil field lay. After that . . .

He had undressed automatically and climbed into his berth. He let his feverish anticipations run on, getting dozier all the time. He suddenly recalled that he really should have seen the doctor before leaving, but dismissed it with a happy smile. By the time he had hit his upper twenties he was done with whooping cough, measles and mumps. It had been all these years since, before he required the services of a doctor again. He made a mental note that when he next reached sixty he would take a few precautions. And with that happy thought he dropped off into sound sleep.

The Limited slid on through the night, silently and jarless. Thanks to its air conditioning, good springs, well-turned wheels, smooth traction, rock-ballasted roadbed and heavy rails, it went like the wind. For hundreds of miles the green lights of block signals flickered by, but now and again another train would thunder by on an eastbound track. Mr. Feathersmith gave no thought to those things as he pillowed deeper into the soft blankets, or worried about the howling blizzard raging outside. The Limited would get there on time and with the minimum of fuss. That particular Limited went fast and far that night—mysteriously it must have covered in excess of a thousand miles and got well off its usual route. For when Mr. Feathersmith did wake, along toward dawn, things were uncannily different.

To begin with, the train was lurching and rocking violently from side to side, and there was a persistent slapping of a flat wheel underneath. The blizzard had abated somewhat, but the car was cold. He lifted the curtain a bit and looked out on a snow-streaked, hilly landscape that strongly suggested Arkansas. Then the train stopped suddenly in the middle of a field and men came running alongside with lanterns. A hotbox, he heard one call, which struck him as odd, for he had not heard of hotboxes for a long time.

After about an hour, and after prolonged whistling, the train slowly gathered way again. By that time Mr. Feathersmith noticed that his berth had changed during the night. It was an old-fashioned fore-and-aft berth with an upper pressing down upon it. He discovered he was wearing a flannel nightgown, too—another item of his past he had failed to remember, it had been so long since he had changed to silk pajamas. But by then the porter was going through the car rousing all the passengers.

"Gooch Junction in half a' hour, folks," he was saying. "Gotta get up now—dey drop the sleeper dere."

Mr. Feathersmith groaned and got up. Yes, yes, of course. Through sleepers were the exception, not the rule, forty years ago. He found his underwear—red flannel union suit it was—and his shirt, a stiff-bosomed affair with detachable cuffs and a complicated arrangement of cuff holders. His shoes were Congress gaiters with elastic in the sides, and his suit of black broadcloth beginning to turn green. He got on the lower half of it and bethought himself of his morning shave. He fished under the berth for his bag and found it—a rusty old Gladstone, duly converted as promised. But there was no razor in it of any type he dared use. There was a set of straight razors and strops and a mug for soap, but he would not trust himself to operate with them. The train was much too rough for that.

But he had to wash, so he climbed out of the berth, bumping others, and found the lavatory. It was packed with half-dressed men in the process of shaving. The basins were miserable affairs of marble and supplied by creaky pumps that delivered a tablespoonful of water at a time. The car was finished in garish quartered oak, mahogany, mother-of-pearl and bright woods fitted into the most atrocious inlays Mr. Feathersmith could have imagined. The taste in decoration, he realized, had made long steps since 1902.

His companions were "drummers"—heavy, well-fed men, all. One was in dry goods; one in coffee, tea and spices; another in whiskey; and two of the rest in patent medicines. Their conversation touched on Bryan and Free Silver, and one denounced Theodore Roosevelt's imperialism—said it was all wrong for us to annex distant properties like the Sandwich Islands and the Philippines. One man thought Aguinaldo was a hero, another that Funston was the greatest general of all time. But what worried them most was whether they would get to Gooch Junction at all, and if so, how much late.

"We're only an hour behind now," said the whiskey drummer, "but the brakeman told me there's a bad wreck up ahead and it may take 'em all day to clear it . . ."

"Many killed?"

"Naw. Just a freight—engine crew and brakeman and about a dozen tramps. That's all."

"Shucks. They won't hold us up for that. They'll just pile the stuff up and burn it."

It was ten when they reached the Junction, which consisted of only a signal tower, a crossing, and several sidings. There was no diner on, but the news butcher had a supply of candy, paper-thin ham sandwiches on stale bread, and soda pop. If one did not care for those or peanuts, he didn't eat. Dropping the sleeper took a long time and much backing and filling, during which the locomotive ran off the rails and had to be jockeyed back on. Mr. Feathersmith was getting pretty disgusted by the time he reached the day coach and found he had to share a seat with a raw farm boy in overalls and a sloppy old felt hat. The boy had an aroma that Mr. Feathersmith had not smelled for a long, long time. And then he noticed that the aroma prevailed in other quarters, and it came to him all of a sudden that the day was Thursday and considerably removed from last Saturday and presumptive baths.

It was about that time that Mr. Feathersmith became aware that he himself had been unchanged except for wardrobe and accessories. He had expected to wake up youthful. But he did not let it worry him unduly, as he imagined the Devil would come through when he had gone all the way back. He tried to get a paper from the butcher, but all there were were day-old St. Louis papers and the news was chiefly local. He looked for the financial section and only found a quarter of a column where a dozen railroad bonds were listed. The editor seemed to ignore the Orient and Europe altogether, and there was very little about Congress. After that he settled down and tried to get used to the temperature. At one end of the car there was a pot-bellied cast-iron stove, kept roaring by volunteer stokers, but despite its ruddy color and the tropic heat in the two seats adjacent, the rest of the car was bitter cold.

The train dragged on all day, stopping often on bleak sidings and waiting for oncoming trains to pass. He noticed on the blackboards of the stations they passed that they were now five hours late and getting later. But no one seemed to worry. It was the expected. Mr. Feathersmith discovered he had a great turnip of a gold watch in the pocket of his waistcoat—a gorgeously flowered satin affair, incidentally—and the watch was anchored across his front by a chain heavy enough to grace the bows of a young battleship. He consulted it often, but it was no help. They arrived at Florence, where they should have been before noon, just as the sun was setting. Everybody piled out of the train to take advantage of the twenty-minute stop to eat at the Dining House there.

The food was abundant—fried ham, fried steaks, cold turkey, roast venison and fried chicken and slabs of fried salt pork. But it was all too heavy and greasy for his worn stomach. The fact that the vegetables consisted of four kinds of boiled beans plus cabbage reminded him that he did not have his vitamin tablets with him. He asked for asparagus, but people only looked amused. That was stuff for the rich and it came in little cans. No, no asparagus. Fish? At breakfast they might have salt mackerel. They *could* open a can of salmon. Would that do? He looked at the enormous, floury biscuits, the heavy pitchers of honey and sorghum molasses and a bowl of grits, and decided he would have just a glass of milk. The butter he never even considered, as it was a pale, anemic salvy substance. They brought him an immense tumbler of buttermilk and he had to make the best of that.

By the time they were back in the cars, the brakeman was going down the aisle, lighting the Pintsch lamps overhead with a lamplighter. The gas had a frightful odor, but no one seemed to mind. It was "up-to-date," not the smelly kerosene they used on some lines.

The night wore on, and in due time the familiar landscape of old Cliffordsville showed up outside the window. Another item he discovered he had forgotten was that Cliffordsville had been there before the railroad was run through. On account of curves and grades, the company had by-passed the town by a couple of miles, so that the station—or depot—stood that distance away. It would have been as good a way as any to approach the town of his childhood, except that on this day the snow had turned to drizzling rain. The delightful clay roads were all right in dry weather, but a mass of bottomless, sticky, rutted mud on a day like this. Mr. Feathersmith walked out onto the open platform of the car and down its steps. He viewed the sodden station and its waterlogged open platform with misgiving. There was but one rig that had come to meet the train. It was the Planter's Hotel bus—a rickety affair with facing fore-and-aft seats approached from the rear by three steps and grab-irons, à la Black Maria. The driver had his storm curtains up, but they were only fastened by little brass gimmicks at the corners and flapped abominably. There were four stout horses drawing the vehicle, but they were spattered with mud up to the belly and the wheels were encrusted with foot-thick adhesions of clay.

"Stranger here?" asked the driver, as he gathered up his reins and urged the animals to break the bus out of the quagmire it had sunk down in.

"I've been here before," said Mr. Feathersmith, wondering savagely why—back in those good old days—somebody had not had enough gumption to grade and gravel-surface this road. "Does Mr. Toler still run the hotel?"

"Yep. Swell hotel he's got, too. They put in a elevator last year."

That was a help, thought Mr. Feathersmith. As he remembered the place it had twenty-foot ceilings and was three stories high. With *his* heart, at least for the first day here, he was just as happy at not having to climb those weary, steep stairs. And, now that he thought of it, the Planter's Hotel *was* a darn good hotel for its day and time. People said there was nothing like it closer than Dallas.

The drive in took the best part of two hours. The wind tore at the curtains and gusts of rain blew in. Three times they bogged down completely and the driver had to get out and put his shoulder to a wheel as the four horses lay belly-flat against the oozy mud and strained as if their hearts and backs would break. But eventually they drew up before the hotel, passing through streets that were but slightly more passable than the road. Mr. Feathersmith was shocked at the utter absence of concrete or stone sidewalks. Many blocks boasted no sidewalks at all; the others were plank affairs.

A couple of Negro boys lounged before the hotel and upon the arrival of the bus got into a tussle as to which should carry the Gladstone bag. The tussle was a draw, with the result that they both carried it inside, hanging it between them.

The hotel was a shattering disappointment from the outset. Mr. Feathersmith's youthful memories proved very false indeed. The lobby's ceiling was thirty feet high, not twenty, and supported by two rows of cast-iron fluted columns topped with crudely done Corinthian caps. The bases and caps had been gilded once, but they were tarnished now, and the fly-specked marble painting of the shafts was anything but convincing. The floor was alternate diamond squares of marble—black with blue, and spotted with white enameled cast-iron cuspidors of great capacity, whose vicinity attested the poor marksmanship of Cliffordsville's chewers of the filthy weed. The marble-topped desk was decorated by a monstrous ledger, an inkpot and pens, and presided over by a supercilious young man with slicked-down hair neatly parted in the middle and a curly, thick brown mustache.

"A three-dollar room, of course, sir?" queried the clerk, giving the register a twirl and offering the pen.

"Of course," snapped Mr. Feathersmith, "the best. And with bath."

"With bath, sir?" deprecated the young man, as if taking it

as a joke. "Why, there is a bath on every floor. Just arrange with the bellboy."

The old financier grunted. He was forgetting things again. He glanced over his shoulder toward the rear of the lobby where a red-hot stove was closely surrounded by a crowd of drummers. It seemed to be the only spot of warmth in the place, but he was intent on his bath. So he accepted the huge key and tag and followed the boy to the elevator. That proved to be a loosely woven, open-cage affair in an open shaft and operated by a cable that ran vertically through it. The boy slammed the outer door—there was no inner—and grasped the cable with both hands and pulled. There was a throaty rumble down below and the car began gradually to ascend. Inch by inch it rose, quivering, at about half the speed of a modern New York escalator. Mr. Feathersmith fumed and fidgeted, but there was no help for it. The elevators of forty years ago were like that. It was just too bad his room was 303.

It was big enough, twenty by twenty by twenty. A perfect cube, containing two gigantic windows which only a Sandow could manage. The huge double bed with heavy mahogany head and foot pieces was lost in it. Several rocking chairs stood about, and a rag rug was on the floor. But the *pièce de résistance* of the room was the marble-topped washstand. On it rested a porcelain bowl and pitcher and beside it a slop jar. Mr. Feathersmith knew without looking what the cabinet beneath it contained. He walked over to it and looked into the pitcher. The water had a crust of ice on top of it. The room had not a particle of heat!

"I want a bath. Right away," he said to the bellboy. "Hot."

"Yassir," said the boy, scratching his head, "but I ain't know ef the chambermaid's got around to cleaning hit yit. They ain't many as want bath till tomorrow. I kin go look and see, though."

"I've got some laundry, too. I want it back tomorrow."

"Oh, mister—you-all must be from New Yawk. They ain't

no such thing here. They's a steam laundry, but they only take up Mondays and gita it back on Sat'day. My ma kin do it fer you, but that'll have to be Monday, too. She irons awful nice. They's mighty little she ever burns—and steal!—why, white folks, you could trust her with anything you got. Now'n then she loses a hand'chuf er some little thing like that, but steal—nossir."

"Skip it," snorted Mr. Feathersmith, "and see about that bath." He was relearning his lost youth fast. There had been times when metropolitan flunkyism had annoyed him, but he would give something for some of it now. He pulled out a dime and gave it to the boy, who promptly shuffled out for a conference with the maid over the unheard-of demand of a bath on Friday afternoon.

One look at the bathroom was enough. It was twenty feet high, too, but only eight feet long by three wide, so that it looked like the bottom of a dark well. A single carbon filament lamp dangled from a pair of black insulated wires, led across the ceiling, and gave a dim orange light—as did the similar one in the bedroom. The bathtub was a tin affair, round-bottomed and standing on four cast-iron legs. It was dirty, and fed by a half-inch pipe that dribbled a pencil-thin stream of water. In about two hours, Mr. Feathersmith estimated, his bath would be drawn and ready—provided, of course, that the maid should remove in the meantime the mass of buckets, pans, brooms, mops and scrub rags that she stored in the place. One glance at the speckled, chocked other piece of plumbing in the place made him resolve he would use the gadget underneath his own washstand.

"I kin bring hot water—a pitcher ur so," suggested the colored boy, "ef you want it."

"Never mind," said Mr. Feathersmith. He remembered now that a barber shop was just around the corner and they had bathtubs as well. It would be easier to go there, since he needed a shave, anyway, and pay an extra quarter and get it over with.

He slept in his new bed that night and found it warm despite the frigidness of the room, for the blankets of the time were honest wool and thick. But it was the only crumb of comfort he could draw from his new surroundings.

The next morning. Mr. Feathersmith's troubles truly began. He got up, broke the crust of ice in his pitcher, and gaspingly washed his face and hands. He waited tediously for the slow-motion elevator to come up and take him down to breakfast. That meal was inedible, too, owing to its heaviness. He marveled that people could eat so much so early in the morning. He managed some oatmeal and buttered toast, but passed up all the rest. He was afraid that grapefruit was unheard of; as to the other fruits, there were apples. Transportation and storage had evidently not solved the out-of-season fruit and vegetable problem.

It also worried him that Satan had done nothing so far about his rejuvenation. He got up with the same gnarled, veiny hands, florid face, and bald head. He wished he had insisted on a legible copy of the contract at the time, instead of waiting for the promised confirmation copy. But all that was water over the dam. He was here, so, pending other developments, he must see about establishing his daily comforts and laying the foundation for his fortune.

There were several things he wanted: to acquire the old Feathersmith homestead; to marry Daisy Norton; to bring in the Cliffordsville oil field—wasn't there already Spindletop, Batson and Sour Lake making millions?—then go back to New York, where, after all, there was a civilization of a sort, however primitive.

He took them in order. Representing himself as a granduncle of his original self, he inquired at the local real-estate man's office. Yes, the Feathersmith place was for sale—cheap. The former cook, Anna, was living near it and available for hire. It did not take Mr. Feathersmith long to get to the local livery stable and hire a two-horse rig to take him out there.

The sight of the place was a shock to him. The road out was

muddy in stretches, and rocky and bumpy in others. At last they came to a sagging plank gate in a barbed-wire fence and the driver dragged it open. The great trees Mr. Feathersmith had looked back on with fond memory proved to be post oaks and cedars. There was not a majestic elm or pecan tree in the lot. The house was even more of a disappointment. Instead of the vast mansion he remembered, it was a rambling, run-down building whose porches sagged and where the brown remnant of last summer's honeysuckle still clung to a tangle of cotton strings used for climbers. They should have a neat pergola built for them, he thought, and entered.

The interior was worse. One room downstairs had a fireplace. Upstairs there was a single sheet-iron wood stove. What furniture that was left was incredibly tawdry; there was no telephone and no lights except kerosene wick lamps. The house lacked closets or a bath, and the back yard was adorned with a crazy Chic Sale of the most uninviting pattern. A deserted hog-pen and a dilapidated stable completed the assets. Mr. Feathersmith decided he wouldn't live there again on any terms.

But a wave of sentimentality drove him to visit Anna, the former cook. She, at least, would not have depreciated like the house had done in a paltry two years. He learned she lived in a shack close by, so he went. He introduced himself as an elder of the Feathersmith family, and wanted to know if she would cook and wash for him.

"I doan want no truck with any kind of Feathersmith," she asserted. "They're po' white trash—all of 'em. The ole man and the missus wan't so bad, but that young skunk of a Jack sold out before they was hardly cold and snuck outa town twixt sundown and daylight an' we ain't never seed ur heard tell of him since. Jus' let me alone—that's all I ask."

With that she slammed the cabin door in his face.

So! thought Mr. Feathersmith. Well, he guessed he didn't want her, either. He went back to town and straight to the bank. Having discovered he had three thousand dollars in big bills and gold, a sizable fortune for Cliffordsville of the period, since the First National Bank was capitalized for only ten, he went boldly in to see Mr. Norton. He meant to suggest that they jointly exploit the Norton plantation for the oil that was under it. But on the very moment he was entering the portals of the bank he suddenly remembered that the Cliffordsville field was a very recent one, circa 1937, and therefore deep. Whereas Spindletop had been discovered by boring shallow wells—a thousand feet and mostly less—later-day wells had depths of something over a mile. In 1902 the suggestion of drilling to six thousand feet and more would have been simply fantastic. There was neither the equipment nor the men to undertake it. Mr. Feathersmith gulped the idea down and decided instead to make a deposit and content himself with polite inquiries about the family.

Mr. Norton was much impressed with the other's get-up and the cash deposit of three thousand dollars. That much currency was not to be blinked at in the days before the Federal Reserve Board Act. When money stringencies came—and they did often—it was actual cash that counted, not that ephemeral thing known as credit. He listened to Mr. Feathersmith's polite remarks and observed that he would consider it an honor to permit his wife and daughter to receive the new depositor at their home. Personally fingering the beloved bank notes, Mr. Norton ushered out his new customer with utmost suavity.

The call was arranged, and Mr. Feathersmith put in his appearance at exactly 4:30 p.m. of the second day following. Ransacking his mind for memories of customs of the times, he bethought himself to take along a piece of sheet music, a pound of mixed candies, and a bouquet of flowers.

The visit was a flop. Befitting his new status as an important depositor, he took a rubber-tired city hack to the door, and then, to avoid the charge of sinful extravagance, he dismissed the fellow, telling him to come back at five. After that, bearing his gifts, he maneuvered the slippery pathway of pop bottles planted neck down, bordered by bricks and desiccated rosebushes. He mounted the steps and punched the doorbell. After that there was a long silence, but he knew that there was tittering inside and that several persons pulled the curtains softly and surveyed him surreptitiously. At length the door opened cautiously and an old black mammy dressed in silk to match let him in and led him into the parlor.

It was a macabre room, smelling of mold. She seated him in a horsehair-covered straight chair, then went about the business of opening the inside folding blinds. After that she flitted from the room. After a long wait Mrs. Norton came in, stately and dignified, and introduced herself. Whereupon she plumped herself down on another chair and stared at him. A few minutes later the giggling Daisy came in and was duly introduced. She also bowed stiffly, without offering a hand, and sat down. Then came the grandmother. After that they just sat—the man at one end of the room, and the three sedate women in a row at the other, their knees and ankles tightly compressed together and their hands folded in their laps. Mr. Feathersmith got up and tried to manage a courtly bow while he made his presentations, thinking they were awfully stuffy.

He thought so particularly, because he had formerly had Daisy out on a buggy ride and knew what an expert kisser she could be when the moon was right. But things were different. He introduced various possible topics of conversation, such as the weather, the latest French styles, and so forth. But they promptly—and with the utmost finality—disposed of each with a polite, agreeing "Yes, sir." It was maddening. And then he saw that Daisy Norton was an empty-headed little doll who could only giggle, kiss, as required, and say, "Yes, sir." She had no conception of economics, politics, world affairs . . .

"*Aw-r-rk!*" thought Mr. Feathersmith. The thought took him back to those hellcats of modern women—like Miss Tomlinson, in charge of his Wall Street office force—the very type he wanted to get away from, but who was alert and alive.

He listened dully while Daisy played a "Valse Brilliante" on the black square piano, and saw the embroideries her fond mother displayed. After that he ate the little cakes and coffee they brought. Then left. That was Daisy Norton. Another balloon pricked.

On the trip back to the hotel he was upset by seeing a number of yellow flags hung out on houses. It puzzled him at first, until he remembered that that was the signal for smallpox within. It was another thing he had forgotten about the good old days. They had smallpox, yellow fever, diphtheria, scarlet fever, and other assorted diseases that raged without check except constitutional immunity. There was the matter of typhoid, too, which depended on water and milk-supply surveillance. And it came to him that so long as Satan chose to keep him aged, he must live chiefly on milk. Cliffordsville, he well remembered, annually had its wave of typhoid, what with its using unfiltered creek water and the barbarian habit of digging wells in the vicinity of cesspools. Mr. Feathersmith was troubled. Didn't he have enough physical complaints as it was?

He was reminded even more forcibly of that shortly afterward when he came to, sitting up on the floor of a barroom with someone forcing whiskey into his mouth.

"You fainted, mister, but you'll be all right now."

"Get me a doctor," roared Mr. Feathersmith. "Its ephedrine I want, not whiskey!"

The doctor didn't come. There was only the one, and he was out miles in the country administering to a case of "cramp colic"—a mysterious disease later to achieve the more fashionable notoriety of "acute appendicitis." The patient died, unhappily, but that did not bring the doctor back to town any quicker.

The next morning Mr. Feathersmith made a last desperate effort to come back. There was a bicycle mechanic in town who had recently established a garage in order to take care of Mr. Norton's lumbering Ford and Dr. Simpson's buggylike

Holtzmann. Those crude automobiles thought it a triumph to make ten miles without a tow, had to be cranked by hand, and were lighted at night by kerosene carriage lamps or acetylene bicycle lamps.

"Why not devise a self-starter," suggested Mr. Feathersmith, recalling that millions had been made out of them, "a gadget you press with the foot, you know, that will crank the engine with an electric motor?"

"Why not wings?" asked the surly mechanic. He did not realize that both were practical, or that Mr. Feathersmith had seen better days. The trouble with Mr. Feathersmith was that he had always been a promoter and a financier, with little or no knowledge of the mechanical end of the game.

"It works," he insisted solemnly, "a storage battery, a motor, and a gilhookey to crank the motor. Think it over. It would make us rich."

"So would perpetual motion," answered the garage man. And that was that.

Dr. Simpson, when contact was made, was even a poorer consolation.

"Ephedrine? Vitamins? Thyroxin? You're talking gibberish—I don't know what you mean. Naturally, a man of your age is likely to get short of breath at times—even faint. But shucks, Mr. Feathersmith, don't let that bother you. I've known men to live to a hundred that didn't stack up as well as you. Take it easy, rest plenty with a nap every afternoon, and you'll be all right. We're only young once, you know."

When Mr. Feathersmith found that the good doctor had nothing to offer better than a patented "tonic" and poultices for his rheumatism, he thereafter let him strictly alone. The situation as to vitamins and glandular extracts was worse than hopeless—the dieticians had not got around yet to finding out about calories, let alone those. Mr. Feathersmith worried more and more over Satan's inexplicable delay in bestowing youth befitting the age, for Forfin had insisted the Old Boy would fulfill his promise if the price was paid. But until that was done, the old financier could only wait and employ his time as profitably as he could.

He kept ransacking his brains for things he could invent, but every avenue proved to be a blind alley. He mentioned the possibility of flying to the circle that sat about the lobby stove, but they scornfully laughed it down. It was an obvious impossibility, except for the dirigible gas bags Santos-Dumont was playing with in France. He tried to organize a company to manufacture aluminum, but unfortunately no one had heard of the stuff except one fellow who had been off to school and seen a lump of it in the chemical laboratory. It was almost as expensive as gold, and what good was it?

Mr. Feathersmith realized then that if he were in possession of a 1942 automobile no one could duplicate it, for the many alloys were unknown and the foundry and machine-shop practice necessary were undeveloped. There was nothing to paint it with but carriage paint—slow-drying and sticky. There were no fuels or lubricants to serve it, or any roads fit to run it on.

He played with other ideas, but they all came croppers. He dared not even mention radio—it smacked too much of magic—or lunacy. And he most certainly did not want to be locked up as a madman in an insane asylum of the era. If standard medicine was just beginning to crawl, psychiatry was simply nonexistent. So he kept quiet about his speculations.

Since life had become so hard and he was cut off from any normal intercourse with his fellow townsmen, he yearned for good music. But, alas, that likewise was not to be had outside one or two metropolitan orchestras. He went once to church and heard a homegrown, self-taught soprano caterwaul in a quavering voice. After that he stayed away. He caught himself wishing for a good radio program—and he had altered considerably his standards of what was good.

A week rolled by. During it he had another stroke that was almost his last. The New York doctor had warned him that if he did not obey all the rules as to diet and other palliatives, he might expect to be taken off at any time. Mr. Feathersmith knew that his days were numbered—and the number was far fewer than it would have been if he had remained in the modern age he had thought so unbearable. But still there was the hope that the Devil would yet do the right thing by him.

That hope was finally and utterly blasted the next day. Mr. Feathersmith was in the grip of another devastating fit of weakness and knew that shortly he would be unable to breathe and would therefore fall into a faint and die. But just before his last bit of strength and speck of consciousness faded, there was a faint plop overhead and an envelope fluttered down and into his lap. He looked at it, and though the stamp and cancellation were blurred and illegible, he saw the return address in the corner was ''Bureau of Complaints and Adjustments, Gehenna.'' His trembling fingers tore the missive open. A copy of his contract fell into his lap.

He scanned it hurriedly. As before, it seemed flawless. Then he discovered a tiny memorandum clipped to its last page. He read it and knew his heart would stand no more. It was from the cute little witch of Fifth Avenue.

DEAREST SNOOKY-WOOKY:

His Nibs complains you keep on bellyaching. That's not fair. You said you wanted to be where you are, and there you are. You wanted your memory unimpaired. Can we help it if your memory is lousy? And not once, old dear, did you cheep about also having your youth restored. So that lets us out. Be seeing you in Hell, old thing.

Cheerio!

He stared at it with fast-dimming eyes.

''The little witch—the bad, badgering little . . .'' and then an all-engulfing blackness saved him from his mumbling alliteration.

Song for a Lady

Charles Beaumont

TELEPLAY BY CHARLES BEAUMONT

AIRED MAY 9, 1963, AS "PASSAGE ON THE *LADY ANNE*"

STARRING LEE PHILIPS, JOYCE VAN PATTEN,
WILFRID HYDE-WHITE, AND CECIL KELLAWAY

THE TRAVEL AGENT HAD WARNED US. IT WAS AN old ship, very old, very tired. And slow. "In fact," said Mr. Spierto, who had been everywhere and knew all about travel, "there's nothing slower afloat. Thirteen days to Le Havre, fourteen to Southampton. Provided there are favorable winds, of course! No; I doubt that we'll spend our honeymoon on her. Besides, this will be her last crossing. They're going to scrap the old relic in a month." And I think that's the reason we picked the *Lady Anne* for our first trip abroad. There was something appealing about taking part in a ship's last voyage, something, Eileen said, poignant and special.

Or maybe it was simply the agent's smirk. He might have been able to talk us out of it otherwise, but he had to smirk— the veteran of Katmandu and the innocent untraveled Iowans—and that got us mad. Anyway, we made two first class reservations, got married and caught a plane for New York.

What we saw at the dock surprised us. Spierto's horrified

descriptions of the ship had led us to expect something between a kayak and The Flying Dutchman, whereas at first glance the *Lady Anne* seemed to be a perfectly ordinary ocean liner. Not that either of us had ever actually *seen* an ocean liner, except in films; but we'd decided what one should look like, and this looked like one. A tall giant of a vessel, it was, with a bright orange hull and two regal smokestacks; and a feeling of lightness, of grace, almost, despite the twenty thousand tons.

Then we got a little closer. And the *Lady Anne* turned into one of those well-dressed women who look so fine a block away and then disintegrate as you approach them. The orange on the hull was bright, but it wasn't paint. It was rust. Rust, like fungus, infecting every inch, trailing down from every port hole. Eating through the iron.

We gazed at the old wreck for a moment, then resolutely made our way past some elderly people on the dock and, at the gangplank, stopped. There was nothing to say, so Eileen said: "It's beautiful."

I was about to respond when a voice snapped: "No!" An aged man with thin but fierce red hair was standing behind us, bags in hand. "Not 'it,' " he said, angrily. "*She*. This ship is a lady."

"Oh, I'm sorry." My wife nodded respectfully. "Well, then, *she's* beautiful."

"Indeed she is!" The man continued to glare, not malevolently, not furiously, but with great suspicion. He started up the plank, then paused. "You're seeing someone off?"

I told him no.

"Visitors, then."

"No," I said. "Passengers."

The old man's eyes widened. "How's that?" he said, exactly as if I'd just admitted that we were Russian spies. "You're what?"

"Passengers," I said again.

"Oh, no," he said, "no, no, I hardly think so. I hardly

think that. This, you see, is the *Lady Anne*. There's been a mistake."

"Jack, please!" A small square woman with thick glasses shook her head reproachfully.

"Be still," the old man snapped at her. His voice was becoming reedy with excitement. "If you'll consult your tickets, young fellow, I think you'll find that a serious error has occurred here. I repeat, this is the *Lady Anne*—"

"—and I repeat," I said, not too patiently, "that we're passengers." However, he didn't move, so I fished the tickets out of my pocket and shoved them at him.

He stared at the papers for a long time; then, sighing, handed them back. "Private party," he muttered; "excursion, might say. Planned so long. Outsiders! I . . ." And without another word, he turned and marched stiffly up the gangplank. The small square woman followed him, giving us a thin, curious smile.

"Well!" Eileen grinned, after the slightest hesitation. "I guess that means 'Welcome Aboard' in British."

"Forget it." I took her hand and we went directly to the cabin. It was small, just as the friendly travel agent had prophesied: two bunks, an upper and a lower, a sink, a crown-shaped *pot du chambre*. But it wasn't stark. Incredible fat cupids stared blindly from the ceiling, the door was encrusted with flaked gold paint, and there was a chipped chandelier. Grotesque, but cheerful, somehow. Of course, it would have been cheerful at half the size—with a few rats thrown in—because we'd gotten ourselves into this mess against everyone's advice and, one way or another, we were determined to prove that our instincts had been right.

"Nice," said Eileen, reaching up and patting a cupid's belly.

I kissed her and felt, then, that things wouldn't be too bad. It would take more than a grumpy old Englishman and a crazy stateroom to spoil our trip. A lot more.

Unfortunately, a lot more was fast in coming.

When we took a stroll out on deck, we noticed a surprisingly large number of elderly people standing at the rail; but, we were excited, and somehow this didn't register. We waved at the strangers on the dock, watched the passengers still coming aboard, and began to feel the magic. Then I saw the old redheaded gentleman tottering toward us, still glaring and blinking. In a way he looked like the late C. Aubrey Smith, only older and thinner. Just as straight, though, and just as bushy in the eyebrows.

"See here," he said, pointing at me with his cane, "you aren't really serious about this, are you?"

"About what?" I asked.

"Traveling on the *Lady Anne*. That is, hate to sound cliqueish and all that, but—"

"We're serious," Eileen said, curtly.

"Dear me." The old man clucked his tongue. "Americans, too. British ship, y'know. Sort of reunion and—" He motioned toward another man in tweeds. "Burgess! Over here!" The man, if anything older than our friend, caned his way across the wooden planks. "Burgess, these are the ones I mean. They've tickets!"

"No, no, no," said the man with the cane. "Whole thing obviously a ghastly blunder. Calm yourself, McKenzie: we've time yet. Now then." He gave us a crafty, crooked smile. "No doubt you young people aren't aware that this is rather a, how shall I put it, private, sort of, cruise; d'ye see? Very tight. Dear me, yes. Unquestionably a slip-up on the part of—"

"Look," I said, "I'm getting tired of this routine. There hasn't been any slip-up or anything else. This is our ship and by God we're sailing to Europe on it. Her."

"That," said Burgess, "is bad news indeed."

I started to walk away, but the old man's fingers gripped my arm. "Please," he said. "I expect this may seem odd to you, quite odd, but we're actually trying to be of help."

"Exactly so," said the redheaded man, McKenzie. "There are," he whispered darkly, "things you don't know about this ship."

"For example," Burgess cut in, "she is over sixty-five years old. No ventilation, y'know; no modern conveniences whatever on her. And she takes forever to cross."

"And dangerous," said the redheaded man. "Dear me, yes."

The two old fellows pulled us along the deck, gesturing with their canes.

"Look at those deck chairs, just look at 'em. Absolute antiques. Falling to pieces. Wouldn't trust the best of 'em to hold a baby."

"And the blankets, as you see, are rags. Quite threadbare."

"And look at that staircase. Shameful! Shouldn't be at all surprised to see it collapse at any moment."

"Oh, we can tell you, the *Lady Anne* is nothing but an ancient rust bucket."

"So you see, of course, how impractical the whole idea is."

They looked at us.

Eileen smiled her sweetest smile. "As a matter of fact," she said, "I think this is the most darling little boat I've ever seen. Don't you agree, Alan?"

"Definitely," I said.

The old men stared in disbelief; then Burgess said: "You'll get bored."

"We never get bored," Eileen said.

McKenzie said, "You'll get sick, then!"

"Never."

"Wait!" Burgess was frowning. "We're wasting time. Look here, why you are both so damned determined to travel on an outdated ship when there are dozens of fine modern vessels available, I shan't pretend to understand. Perhaps it is typical American stubbornness. Flying in the face of convention, that sort of thing. Eh? Admirable! However, we must insist that you overcome this determination."

Eileen opened her mouth, then shut it when she saw the roll of money clutched in the old man's fist.

"I am prepared," he said, in a firm voice, "to pay you double the amount you spent for your tickets, provided you will abandon your plan."

There was a short silence.

"Well?"

I glanced at Eileen. "Not a chance," I said.

"Triple the amount?"

"No."

"Very well. I am forced to extremes. If you will leave the *Lady Anne* now, I will give you the equivalent of five thousand American dollars."

"Which," McKenzie said, "I will meet."

"Making it ten thousand dollars."

Eileen seemed almost on the edge of tears. "Not for a million," she said. "Now let me tell you gentlemen something. Ever since we picked this ship, people have been doing their best to discourage us. I don't know why and I don't care. If you're so afraid the brash Americans are going to upset your British tea—"

"My good lady, we—"

"—you can forget it. We won't go near you. But we paid for our tickets and that gives us every bit as much right to the *Lady Anne* as you have! Now just go away and leave us alone!"

The conversation ended. We walked back to the bow and waited, in silence, until the line had been cast off and the tugs had begun to pull us out to sea; then, still not mentioning the episode, we wandered around to the other side of the ship. I know now that there were elderly people there, too, and only elderly people, but again, we were too sore—and the adventure was too new—to notice this.

It wasn't, in fact, until the fire drill, with the corridor packed, that it first began to sink in. There weren't any young people to be seen. No students. No children. Only old men and women, most of them walking, but several on canes and on crutches, a few in wheelchairs. And, judging from the number of tweed suits, pipes, mustaches, and woollen dresses, mostly all British.

I was thinking about the two weeks to Southampton and the ten thousand dollars, when Eileen said, "Look."

I looked. And ran into hundreds of unblinking eyes, turned directly on us. Staring as though we were a new species.

"Don't worry," I whispered, without much assurance, "we'll find somebody our age on board. It stands to reason."

And it did stand to reason. But although we looked everywhere, everywhere it was the same: old men, old women. British. Silent. Staring.

Finally we got tired of the search and walked into the ship's single public room. It was called The Imperial Lounge: a big hall with hundreds of chairs and tables, a tiny dance floor, a podium for musicians, and a bar. All done in the rococo style you'd expect to find on the *Titanic*: purples and greens, faded to gray, and chipped gold. People sat in the chairs, neither reading nor playing cards nor talking. Just sitting, with hands folded. We tiptoed across a frayed rug to the bar and asked the grandfather in charge for two double-Scotches; then we ordered two more.

"Housie-Housie tonight," Eileen said, gesturing toward a blackboard. "That's British bingo. But I suppose we won't be invited."

"Nuts to 'em," I said. We looked at each other, then out over the white-thatched balding sea of heads—some drooping in afternoon sleep already—and back at each other; and I'm proud to say that neither of us wept.

After the drinks we exited The Imperial Lounge, softly, and queued up for lunch. The restaurant was Empire style, the silks smelling of age and dust, the tapestries blurred. We ordered something called Bubble and Squeak because it sounded jolly, but it wasn't. And neither were the diners surrounding us. Particularly those who sat alone. They all had an air of melancholy, and they stared at us throughout the meal, some surreptitiously, some openly.

Finally we gave up trying to eat and fled back to the Imperial Lounge, because where else was there to go?

The sea of heads was calm. Except for one. It was red, and when we entered it nodded and bounced up.

Mr. Friendly's eyes were snapping. "I beg your pardon," he said. "Hate to bother you. But my wife, Mrs. McKenzie, over there—she, uh, points out that I've been rude. Quite rude. And I expect I ought to apologize."

"Do you?" I asked.

"Oh, yes! But there is something more important. Really good news, in fact." It was strange to see the old boy smiling so happily; the frown seemed to have been a fixture. "Mr. Burgess and I talked the whole thing over," he said, "and we've decided that you won't have to leave the ship after all."

"Say," I said, a trifle bitterly, "that *is* good news. We were afraid we'd have to swim back and it's had us sick with worry."

"Really?" Mr. McKenzie cocked his head to one side. "Sorry about that, my boy. But we were quite concerned, all of us, as I daresay you gathered. Y'see, it simply hadn't occurred to us that an *outsider* would ever want to go on the *Lady*. I mean, she's primarily a freighter, as it were; and the last time she took on a new passenger was, according to Captain Protheroe, the summer of '48. So you can understand— but never mind that, never mind that. It's all settled now."

"*What's* all settled?" asked my wife.

"Why, everything," said the old man, expressively. "But come, you really must join Mrs. McKenzie and me for a bit of tea. That's one thing that hasn't changed on the *Lady*. She still has the finest tea of any ship afloat. Eh, my dear?"

The small square woman nodded.

We exchanged introductions as if we were meeting for the first time. The man named Burgess extended his hand and shook mine with real warmth, which was quite a shock. His wife, a quiet, pale woman, smiled. She stared at her cup for a moment, then said, "Ian, I expect the Ransomes are wondering a bit about your and Mr. McKenzie's behavior this morning.''

"Eh?" Burgess coughed. "Oh, yes. But it's all right now, Cynthia; I told you that."

"Still—"

"Perhaps I can help," said Mrs. McKenzie, who had not yet spoken. Her voice was a lovely soft thing, yet, oddly, commanding. She looked at Eileen. "But first you must tell us why you chose the *Lady Anne.*"

Eileen told them.

Mrs. Mckenzie's smile changed her face, it washed away the years and she became almost beautiful. "My dear," she said, "you were quite right. The *Lady* is special. More special, I should say, than either you or your husband might imagine. You see, this is the ship Jack and I sailed on when we were married—which would be fifty-six years ago."

"Fifty-five," said the redheaded man. He took a drink of tea and set the cup down gently. "She was a splendid thing then, though. The ship, I mean!"

"Jack, really."

Eileen looked at McKenzie and said, in an even voice: "I thought you told us that it was an old rust bucket."

"Not 'it.' *She.*" Burgess blushed. "Should both have been struck down by lightning," he said. "Greatest lie ever uttered. Mrs. Ransome, mark this: the *Lady Anne* was and is now the finest ship that ever crossed the sea. Queen of the fleet, she was."

"And quite unusual," put in McKenzie. "Only one of her kind, I believe. Y'see, she specialized in honeymooners. That was her freight then: young people in love; aye. That's what makes your presence so—what shall I say—ironic? Eh? No, that isn't it. Not ironic. Sally, what is the damned word I'm looking for?"

"Sweet," said his wife, smiling.

"No, no. Anyway, that was it. A regular floating wedding suite, y'might say. Young married couples, that's all you'd ever see on her. Full of juice and the moon in their eyes. Dear me. It was funny, though. All those children trying to act grown-up and worldly, trying to act married and used to it, d'you see, and every one of 'em as nervous as a mouse. Remember, Burgess?''

''I do. Of course, now, that only lasted for a few days, McKenzie. The *Lady Anne* gave 'em time to know each other.'' The old man laughed. ''She was a wise ship. She understood such things.''

Mrs. McKenzie lowered her eyes, but not, I thought, out of embarrassment. ''At any rate,'' she said, ''although it was, needless to say, unofficial, that did seem to be the policy of the owners, then. *Everything* was arranged for young people. For anyone else, I imagine the ship must have been a bit on the absurd side. Love has its own particular point of view, you know: it sees everything larger than life. Nothing is too ornate for it, or too fancy, or too dramatic. If it is a good love, it demands the theatrical—and then transfigures it. It turns the grotesque into the lovely, as a child does . . .'' The old woman raised her eyes. ''Where a shipping line ever found that particular vision, I shall never know. But they made the *Lady Anne* into an enchanted gondola and took that moment of happiness and—pure—sweet pain that all lovers have and made the moment live for two really unspeakably pleasant weeks . . .''

The redheaded McKenzie cleared his throat loudly. ''Quite so,'' he said, glancing at his wife, who smiled secretly. ''Quite so. I expect they get the drift, my dear. No need to go sticky.''

''But,'' said his wife, ''I feel sticky.''

''Eh? Oh.'' He patted her hand. ''Of course. Still—''

Burgess removed his pipe. ''The point is,'' he said, ''that we spent a good many fine hours aboard this old scow. The sort of hours one doesn't forget. When we heard that they were going to . . . retire . . . the *Lady*, well, it seemed right, somehow, that we should join her on her last two-way sailing. And that, I think, accounts for the number of old parties aboard. Most of 'em here for the same reason, actually.

Boshier-Jones and his wife over there, sound asleep: the bald chap. Engineer in his day, and a good one. The Whiteaways, just past the column. They were on our first sailing. Innes Champion, the writer: quite a droll fellow most of the time, though you wouldn't guess it now. A widower, y'know. Wife passed on in '29. They had their honeymoon on the *Lady*—a better one, if possible, than ours: propeller fell off— that would be in 1906—and they were four days in repairing it, so he says. Terrible liar, though. Don't know that chap in the wheelchair; do you, McKenzie?''

"Brabham. Nice enough, but getting on, if you know what I mean. Tends to tremble and totter. Still, a decent sort.''

"Alone?''

"I fear so.''

Mrs. McKenzie took a sip of cold tea and said: "I hope you understand a bit more of our attitude, Mrs. Ransome. And I do hope you will forgive us for staring at you and your husband occasionally. It's quite impolite, but I think we are not actually seeing *you* so much as we are seeing ourselves, as we were fifty years ago. Isn't that foolish?''

Eileen tried to say something, but it didn't work. She shook her head.

"One other thing," Mrs. McKenzie said. "You *are* in love with each other, aren't you?''

"Yes," I said. "Very much.''

"Splendid, I told Jack that when I first saw you this morning. But, of course, that wasn't the point. I'd forgotten the plan.''

"Sally!" McKenzie frowned. "Do watch it.''

The old woman put a hand to her mouth, and we sat there quietly. Then Burgess said, "I think it's time for the men to adjourn for a cigar. With your permission?''

We walked to the bar and Burgess introduced me around. "Van Vlyman, this is Ransome. He's American but he's all right. Nothing to worry about." "Sanders, shake hands with young Ransome. He and his wife are on their honeymoon, y'know. Picked the *Lady Anne!* No, no, I tell you: it's all been straightened out.'' ''Fairman, here now, wake up; this is—''

The warmth of these men suddenly filled me, and after a while it seemed as though, magically, I wasn't thirty-two at all, but seventy-two, with all the wisdom of those years.

The man called Sanders insisted upon buying a round and raised his glass. ''To the finest, loveliest, happiest ship that ever was!'' he said, and we drank, solemnly.

''Pity,'' someone said.

''No!'' The portly ex-colonel, Van Vlyman, crashed his fist down upon the polished mahogany. ''Not a 'pity'! A *crime*. An evil, black-hearted crime, perpetrated by stupid little men with bow ties.''

''Easy, Van Vlyman. Nothing to get heated over now.''

''Nothing, indeed!'' roared the old soldier. ''Easy, indeed! God Almighty, are all of you so ancient, so feeble that you can't see the truth? Don't you know why they want to scrap the *Lady*?''

Sanders shrugged. ''Outlived her usefulness,'' he said.

''Usefulness? Usefulness to whom, sir? Nonsense! D'you hear? She's the best ship on the sea.'' Van Vlyman scowled darkly. ''A little slow, perhaps—but, I put it to you, Sanders, by whose standards? Yours? Mine? Thirteen, fourteen days for a crossing is fast enough for anyone in his right mind. Only people aren't in their right minds any more, that's the trouble. That's the core of it right there. People, I say, have forgotten how to relax. They've forgotten how to appreciate genuine luxury. Speed: that's all that counts nowadays. Get it over with! Why? Why are they in such a hurry?'' He glared at me. ''What's the damned rush?''

Burgess looked sad. ''Van Vlyman, aren't you being a bit—''

''To the contrary. I am merely making an observation upon the state of the world today. Also, I am attempting to point out the true reason for this shameful decision.''

''Which is?''

"A plot, *doubt*less of Communist origin," declared the colonel.

"Oh, really, Van Vlyman—"

"Haven't you eyes? Are you all that senile? The *Lady Anne* was condemned because she represents a way of life. A better way of life, by God, sir, than anything they're brewing up today; and they can't stand that. She's not just a ship, I tell you; she's the old way. She's grace and manners and tradition. Don't you see? She's the Empire!"

The old man's eyes were flashing.

"Nothing," he said, in a lower voice, "is sacred any more. The beasts are at the gate, and we're all too old to fight them. Like the *Lady* herself, too old and too tired. So we stand about in stone fury like pathetic statues with our medals gone to rust and our swords broken while the vandals turn our castles into sideshows, put advertisements for soap along our roads, and—wait! the time is soon!—reach up their hairy hands and pull the Queen down from her throne. Scrap the *Lady*! No. But how are we to stop them from scrapping England?"

The old man stood quite still for several minutes, then he turned and walked away; and McKenzie said, beneath his breath: "Poor chap. He'd planned this with his wife, and then she had to go and die on him."

Burgess nodded. "Well, we'll have some cards tonight and he'll feel better."

We drank another; then Eileen and I had dinner with the McKenzies and retired to our cabin.

Mrs. McKenzie had been right. Love does have its own particular vision: the plaster cupids and golden door didn't seem grotesque at all; in fact, very late at night, with the moon striping the calm black ocean, it seemed to me that there could hardly be a nicer room.

The next twelve days were like a lazy, endless dream. We had trouble, at first, adjusting to it. When you've lived most of your life in a city, you forget that leisure can be a creative thing. You forget that there is nothing sinful in relaxation.

But the *Lady Anne* was good to us. She gave us time, plenty of time. And on the fourth day I stopped fidgeting and began to enjoy the pleasures of getting to know the woman I'd married. Eileen and I talked together and made love together and walked the ancient deck together, hoping that it would never end, secure in the knowledge that it would . . . but not for a while.

We forgot, too, that the other passengers were in their seventies and eighties. It wasn't important, any longer. They were married couples, as we were, and in a very real way, they were on their honeymoons, too. Twice we surprised McKenzie and his wife on the promenade deck well after midnight, and the Burgesses hardly ever stopped holding hands. The women and men who were alone looked melancholy, but somehow not sad. Even the old colonel, Van Vlyman, had stopped being angry. We'd see him every now and then seated on the deck, his eyes looking out over the Atlantic, dreaming.

Then, treacherously, as if it had sneaked up on us, the twelfth day came, and the smell of land was in the air. Far in the distance we could see the gray spine of Cherbourg, and we wondered what had happened to the hours.

McKenzie stopped us in The Imperial Lounge. His face wore a slightly odd expression. "Well," he said, "it's almost over. I expect you're glad."

"No," I told him. "Not really."

That pleased him. "The *Lady*'s done her job for you, then?"

"She has," said Eileen, a different, softer, more feminine Eileen than I'd known two weeks before.

"Well, then; you'll be coming to the dance tonight?"

"Wouldn't miss it."

"Capital! Uh . . . one thing. Have you packed your luggage?"

"No. I mean, we don't dock till tomorrow night, so—"

"Quite. Still, it would do no harm to pack them anyhow," said McKenzie. "See you at the dance!"

Like so many of the others, the things he said frequently sounded peculiar and meant nothing. We went outside and stood at the rail and watched the old sailors—who were all part of the original crew—scrubbing down the ship. They seemed to be working especially hard, removing every trace of dirt, scraping the rails with stiff wire brushes, getting things neat.

At eight we went back to the cabin and changed into our evening dress; and at nine-thirty joined the others in The Imperial Lounge.

The incredible little band was playing antique waltzes and fox trots, and the floor was filled with dancing couples. After a few drinks, we became one of the couples. I danced with Eileen for a while, then with almost every other woman aboard. Everyone seemed to be happy again. Eileen was trying to rumba with Colonel Van Vlyman, who kept sputtering that he didn't know how, and Mrs. McKenzie taught me a step she'd learned in 1896. We drank some more and danced more and laughed, and then the clock struck midnight and the band stood up and played Auld Lang Syne and the people held hands and were quiet.

McKenzie and Burgess walked up then, and Burgess said: "Mr. Ransome, Mrs. Ransome: we'd like you to meet our captain, Captain Protheroe. He's been here as long as the *Lady* has; isn't that right, sir?"

An unbelievably old man in a neat blue uniform nodded his head. His hair was thin and white, his eyes were clear.

"A most unusual man, the captain," said Burgess. "He understands things. Like the rest of us, actually—except that his wife is a ship. Still, I doubt I love my Cynthia more than he loves the *Lady Anne*."

The captain smiled and looked directly at us. "You've had a pleasant voyage?" he asked, in a good strong voice.

"Yes, sir," I said. "We're grateful to have been part of it."

"Indeed? Well, that's very nice."

There was a pause, and I suddenly became aware of a curious fact. The vibration of the engines, deep below us, had stopped. The ship itself had stopped.

Captain Protheroe's smile broadened. "Very nice, indeed," he said. "As Mr. McKenzie pointed out to me earlier, your presence aboard has been rather symbolic, if I may use the word. Us ending, you beginning; that sort of thing, eh?" He rose from the chair. "Now then. I'm afraid that I must say good bye to you. We've radioed your position and you oughtn't to be inconvenienced for more than a few hours."

"Beg pardon?" I said.

Burgess coughed. "They don't know," he said. "Thought it would be better that way."

"Eh? Oh, yes, how stupid of me. Of course." Captain Protheroe turned his clear eyes back to us. "You won't mind obliging us," he said, "by gathering up your things?"

"Gathering up our things?" I parroted, stupidly. "Why?"

"Because," he said, "we are going to put you off the ship."

Eileen grabbed my arm, but neither of us could think of a thing to say. I was vaguely conscious of the stillness of the boat, of the people in the room, staring at us.

"I'm very much afraid that I shall have to ask you to hurry," said the captain, "for it is getting rather late. The rescue vessel is already on its way, you see. You, uh, *do* understand?"

"No," I said, slowly, "we don't. And we're certainly not going anywhere until we do."

Captain Protheroe drew up to his full height and glanced sharply at McKenzie. "Really," he said, "I should've thought you'd have anticipated this."

McKenzie shrugged. "Didn't want to worry them."

"Indeed. And now we're in a mess, for, of course, we've no time at all for lengthy explanations."

"In that case," said Burgess, "Let's skip them." His eyes were twinkling. "I rather think they'll understand eventually."

The captain nodded. He said, "Excuse me," walked out of

the room, returned a moment later with a pistol. Then, aiming the pistol at me: "Sorry, but I must insist you do as we say. McKenzie, take this thing and see to it that the Ransomes are ready within ten minutes."

McKenzie nodded, brandished the gun. "Come along," he said. "And don't take it too hard, my boy."

He prodded us down to the cabin and kept waving the pistol until we'd packed our bags. He seemed hugely delighted with his new role.

"Now, gather up the life jackets and follow me."

We returned to the boat station, where almost everyone on the ship had gathered.

"Lower away!" cried the captain, and a useless-looking white lifeboat was cranked over the side.

"Now then, if you will please climb down the ladder . . ."

"For God's sake," I said. "This—"

"The *ladder*, Mr. Ransome. And do be careful!"

We clambered down into the lifeboat, which was rocking gently, and watched them raise the rope.

We could see the McKenzies, the Burgesses, Van Vlyman, Sanders and Captain Protheroe standing by the rail, waving. They had never looked so pleasant, so happy.

"Don't worry," one of them called, "you'll be picked up in no time at all. Plenty of water and food there; and a light. You're sure you have all your luggage?"

I heard the ship's engines start up again, and I yelled some idiotic things; but then the *Lady Anne* began to pull away from us. The old people at the rail, standing very close to one another, waved and smiled and called: "Good bye! Good bye!"

"Come back!" I screamed, feeling, somehow, that none of this was actually happening. "Damn it, come back here!" Then Eileen touched my shoulder, and we sat there listening to the fading voices and watching the immense black hull drift away into the night.

It became suddenly very quiet, very still. Only the sound of water slapping against the lifeboat.

We waited. Eileen's eyes were wide; she was staring into the darkness, her hand locked tightly in mine.

"Shhh," she said.

We sat there for another few minutes, quietly, rocking; then there was a sound, soft at first, hollow, but growing.

"Alan!"

The explosion thundered loose in a swift rushing fury, and the water began to churn beneath us.

Then, as suddenly, it was quiet again.

In the distance I could see the ship burning. I could feel the heat of it. Only the stern was afire, though: all the rest of it seemed untouched—and I was certain, oddly certain that no one had been harmed by the blast.

Eileen and I held each other and watched as, slowly, as, gracefully and purposefully, the *Lady Anne* listed on her side. For an eternity she lay poised, then the dark mass of her slipped with incredible speed down beneath the waves, sliding, sinking into the water as quickly and smoothly as a giant needle into velvet.

It could not have taken more than fifteen minutes. Then the sea was as calm and as empty as it ever was before there were such things as ships and men.

We waited for another hour in the lifeboat, and I asked Eileen if she felt cold but she said no. There was a wind across the ocean, but my wife said that she had never felt so warm before.

Steel

Richard Matheson

TELEPLAY BY RICHARD MATHESON

AIRED OCTOBER 4, 1963

STARRING LEE MARVIN

THE TWO MEN CAME OUT OF THE STATION ROLLING a covered object. They rolled it along the platform until they reached the middle of the train, then grunted as they lifted it up the steps, the sweat running down their bodies. One of its wheels fell off and bounced down the metal steps and a man coming up behind them picked it up and handed it to the man who was wearing a rumpled brown suit.

''Thanks,'' said the man in the brown suit and he put the wheel in his side coat pocket.

Inside the car, the men pushed the covered object down the aisle. With one of its wheels off, it was lopsided and the man in the brown suit—his name was Kelly—had to keep his shoulder braced against it to keep it from toppling over. He breathed heavily and licked away tiny balls of sweat that kept forming over his upper lip.

When they reached the middle of the car, the man in the wrinkled blue suit pushed forward one of the seat backs so there were four seats, two facing two. Then the two men pushed the covered object between the seats and Kelly reached through a slit in the covering and felt around until he found the right button.

The covered object sat down heavily on a seat by the window.

"Oh, God, listen to'm squeak," said Kelly.

The other man, Pole, shrugged and sat down with a sigh. "What d'ya expect?" he asked.

Kelly was pulling off his suit coat. He dropped it down on the opposite seat and sat down beside the covered object.

"Well, we'll get 'im some o' that stuff soon's we're paid off," he said worriedly.

"If we can find some," said Pole, who was almost as thin as one. He sat slumped back against the hot seat watching Kelly mop at his sweaty cheeks.

"Why shouldn't we?" asked Kelly, pushing the damp handkerchief down under his shirt collar.

"Because they don't make it no more," Pole said with the false patience of a man who has had to say the same thing too many times.

"Well, that's crazy," said Kelly. He pulled off his hat and patted at the bald spot in the center of his rust-colored hair. "There's still plenty B-twos in the business."

"Not many," said Pole, bracing one foot upon the covered object.

"*Don't,*" said Kelly.

Pole let his foot drop heavily and a curse fell slowly from his lips. Kelly ran the handkerchief around the lining of his hat. He started to put the hat on again, then changed his mind and dropped it on top of his coat.

"God, but it's hot," he said.

"It'll get hotter," said Pole.

Across the aisle a man put his suitcase up on the rack, took off his suit coat, and sat down, puffing. Kelly looked at him, then turned back.

"Ya think it'll be hotter in Maynard, huh?" he asked.

Pole nodded. Kelly swallowed dryly.

"Wish we could have another o' them beers," he said.

Pole stared out the window at the heat waves rising from the concrete platform.

"I had three beers," said Kelly, "and I'm just as thirsty as I was when I started."

"Yeah," said Pole.

"Might as well've not had a beer since Philly," said Kelly.

Pole said, "Yeah."

Kelly sat there staring at Pole a moment. Pole had dark hair and white skin and his hands were the hands of a man who should be bigger than Pole was. But the hands were as clever as they were big. Pole's one o' the best, Kelly thought, one o' the best.

"Ya think he'll be all right?" he asked.

Pole grunted and smiled for an instant without being amused.

"If he don't get hit," he said.

"No, no, I mean it," said Kelly.

Pole's dark, lifeless eyes left the station and shifted over to Kelly.

"So do I," he said.

"Come *on*," Kelly said.

"Steel," said Pole, "ya know just as well as me. He's shot t'hell."

"That ain't true," said Kelly, shifting uncomfortably. "All he needs is a little work. A little overhaul 'n' he'll be good as new."

"Yeah, a little three-four-grand overhaul," Pole said, "with parts they don't make no more." He looked out the window again.

"Oh . . . it ain't as bad as that," said Kelly. "Hell, the way you talk you'd think he was ready for scrap."

"Ain't he?" Pole asked.

"No," said Kelly angrily, "he *ain't*."

Pole shrugged and his long white fingers rose and fell in his lap.

"Just 'cause he's a little old," said Kelly.

"Old." Pole grunted. *"Ancient."*

"Oh . . ." Kelly took a deep breath of the hot air in the car and blew it out through his broad nose. He looked at the covered object like a father who was angry with his son's faults but angrier with those who mentioned the faults of his son.

"Plenty o' fight left in him," he said.

Pole watched the people walking on the platform. He watched a porter pushing a wagon full of piled suitcases.

"Well . . . is he okay?" Kelly asked finally as if he hated to ask.

Pole looked over at him.

"I dunno, Steel," he said. "He needs work. Ya know that. The trigger spring in his left arm's been rewired so many damn times it's almost shot. He's got no protection on that side. The left side of his face's all beat in, the eye lens is cracked. The leg cables is worn, they're pulled slack, the tension's gone to hell. Even his gyro's off."

Pole looked out at the platform again with a disgusted hiss.

"Not to mention the oil paste he ain't got in 'im," he said.

"We'll get 'im some," Kelly said.

"Yeah, *after* the fight, *after* the fight!" Pole snapped. "What about *before* the fight? He'll be creakin' around that ring like a goddam—*steam shovel.* It'll be a miracle if he does two rounds. They'll prob'ly ride us outta town on a rail."

Kelly swallowed. "I don't think it's that bad," he said.

"The *hell* it ain't," said Pole. "It's worse. Wait'll that crowd gets a load of 'Battling Maxo' from Philadelphia. They'll blow a nut. We'll be lucky if we get our five hundred bucks."

"Well, the contract's signed," said Kelly firmly. "They can't back out now. I got a copy right in the old pocket." He leaned over and patted at his coat.

"That contract's for Battling Maxo," said Pole. "Not for this—steam shovel here."

"Maxo's gonna do all right," said Kelly as if he was trying hard to believe it. "He's not as bad off as you say."

"Against a B-*seven?*" Pole asked.

"It's just a *starter* B-*seven*," said Kelly. "It ain't got the kinks out yet."

Pole turned away.

"Battling Maxo," he said. "One-round Maxo. The battling steam shovel."

"Aw, shut the hell up!" Kelly snapped suddenly, getting redder.

"You're always knockin' 'im down. Well, he's been doin' OK for twelve years now and he'll keep on doin' OK. So he needs some oil paste. And he needs a little work. *So what?* With five hundred bucks we can get him all the paste he needs. And a new trigger spring for his arm and—and new leg cables! And everything. Chris*sake.*"

He fell back against the seat, chest shuddering with breath, and rubbed at his cheeks with his wet handkerchief. He looked aside at Maxo. Abruptly, he reached over a hand and patted Maxo's covered knee clumsily and the steel clanked hollowly under his touch.

"You're doin' all right," said Kelly to his fighter.

The train was moving across a sun-baked prairie. All the windows were open but the wind that blew in was like blasts from an oven.

Kelly sat reading his paper, his shirt sticking wetly to his broad chest. Pole had taken his coat off too and was staring morosely out the window at the grass-tufted prairie that went as far as he could see. Maxo sat under his covering, his heavy steel frame rocking a little with the motion of the train.

Kelly put down his paper.

"Not even a word," he said.

"What d'ya expect?" Pole asked. "They don't cover Maynard."

"Maxo ain't just some clunk from Maynard," said Kelly. "He was big time. Ya'd think they'd"—he shrugged—"remember him."

"Why? For a coupla prelims in the Garden three years ago?" Pole asked.

"It wasn't no three years, buddy," said Kelly definitely.

"It was in 1977," said Pole, "and now it's 1980. That's three years where I come from."

"It was late '77," said Kelly. "Right before Christmas. Don't ya remember? Just before—Marge and me . . ."

Kelly didn't finish. He stared down at the paper as if Marge's picture were on it—the way she looked the day she left him.

"What's the difference?" Pole asked. "They don't remember *them*, for Chrissake. With a coupla thousand o' the damn things floatin' around? How could they remember 'em? About the only ones who get space are the champeens and the new models."

Pole looked at Maxo. "I hear Mawling's puttin' out a B-nine this year," he said.

Kelly refocused his eyes. "Yeah?" he said uninterestedly.

"Hyper-triggers in both arms—*and* legs. All steeled aluminum. Triple gyro. Triple-twisted wiring. God, they'll be beautiful."

Kelly put down the paper.

"Think they'd remember him," he muttered. "It wasn't so long ago."

His face relaxed in a smile of recollection.

"Boy, will I ever forget that night?" he said. "No one gives us a tumble? It was all Dimsy the Rock, Dimsy the Rock. *Three* t'one for Dimsy the Rock. Dimsy the Rock—fourth-rankin' light heavy. On his way t'the top."

He chuckled deep in his chest. "And did we ever put him away," he said. "*Oooh.*" He grunted with savage pleasure. "I can see that left cross now. *Bang!* Right in the chops. And old Dimsy the Rock hittin' the canvas like a—like a *rock,* yeah, *just* like a rock!"

He laughed happily. "Boy, what a night, what a night," he said. "Will I ever forget that night?"

Pole looked at Kelly with a somber face. Then he turned away and stared at the dusty sun-baked plain again.

"I wonder," he muttered.

Kelly saw the man across the aisle looking again at the covered Maxo. He caught the man's eye and smiled, then gestured with his head toward Maxo.

"That's my fighter," he said loudly.

The man smiled politely, cupping a hand behind one ear.

"My fighter," said Kelly. "Battling Maxo. Ever hear of 'im?"

The man stared at Kelly a moment before shaking his head.

Kelly smiled. "Yeah, he was almost light-heavyweight champ once," he told the man. The man nodded politely.

On an impulse, Kelly got up and stepped across the aisle. He reversed the seat back in front of the man and sat down facing him.

"Pretty damn hot," he said.

The man smiled. "Yes. Yes it is," he said.

"No new trains out here yet, huh?"

"No," said the man. "Not yet."

"Got all the new ones back in Philly," said Kelly. "That's where"—he gestured with his head—"my friend 'n' I come from. And Maxo."

Kelly stuck out his hand.

"The name's Kelly," he said. "Tim Kelly."

The man looked surprised. His grip was loose.

When he drew back his hand he rubbed it unobtrusively on his pants leg.

"I used t'be called 'Steel' Kelly," said Kelly. "Used t'be in the business m'self. Before the war, o' course. I was a light heavy."

"Oh?"

"Yeah. That's right. Called me 'Steel' cause I never got knocked down once. Not *once*. I was even number nine in the ranks once. Yeah."

"I see." The man waited patiently.

"My—fighter," said Kelly, gesturing toward Maxo with his head again. "He's a light heavy too. We're fightin' in Maynard t'night. You goin' that far?"

"Uh-no," said the man. "No, I'm—getting off at Hayes."

"Oh." Kelly nodded. "Too bad. Gonna be a good scrap."
He let out a heavy breath. "Yeah, he was—fourth in the
ranks once. He'll be *back* too. He—uh—knocked down Dimsy
the Rock in late '77. Maybe ya read about that."

"I don't believe . . ."

"Oh. Uh-huh." Kelly nodded. "Well . . . it was in all the
East Coast papers. You know. New York, Boston, Philly.
Yeah it—got a hell of a spread. Biggest upset o' the year."

He scratched at his bald spot.

"He's a B-two, y'know, but—that means he's the second
model Mawling put out," he explained, seeing the look on
the man's face. "That was back in—let's see—'67, I think it
was. Yeah, '67."

He made a smacking sound with his lips. "Yeah, that was
a good model," he said. "The best. Maxo's still goin' strong."
He shrugged depreciatingly. "I don't go for these new
ones," he said. "You know. The ones made o' steeled aluminum with all the doo-dads."

The man stared at Kelly blankly.

"Too . . . flashy—flimsy. Nothin' . . ." Kelly bunched his
big fist in front of his chest and made a face. "Nothin' *solid*,"
he said. "No. Mawling don't make 'em like Maxo no more."

"I see," said the man.

Kelly smiled.

"Yeah," he said. "Used t'be in the game m'self. When
there was enough men, o' course. Before the bans." He
shook his head, then smiled quickly. "Well," he said, "we'll
take this B-seven. Don't even know what his name is," he
said, laughing.

His face sobered for an instant and he swallowed.

"We'll take 'im," he said.

Later on, when the man had gotten off the train, Kelly
went back to his seat. He put his feet up on the opposite seat
and, laying back his head, he covered his face with the newspaper.

"Get a little shut-eye," he said.

Pole grunted.

Kelly sat slouched back, staring at the newspaper next to his eyes. He felt Maxo bumping against his side a little. He listened to the squeaking of Maxo's joints. "Be all right," he muttered to himself.

"What?" Pole asked.

Kelly swallowed. "I didn't say anything," he said.

When they got off the train at six o'clock that evening they pushed Maxo around the station and onto the sidewalk. Across the street from them a man sitting in his taxi called them.

"We got no taxi money," said Pole.

"We can't just push 'im through the streets," Kelly said. "Besides, we don't even know where Kruger Stadium is."

"What are we supposed to eat with then?"

"We'll be loaded after the fight," said Kelly. "I'll buy you a steak three inches thick."

Sighing, Pole helped Kelly push the heavy Maxo across the street that was still so hot they could feel it through their shoes. Kelly started sweating right away and licking at his upper lip.

"God, how d'they live out here?" he asked.

When they were putting Maxo inside the cab the base wheel came out again and Pole, with a snarl, kicked it away.

"What're ya *doin'*?" Kelly asked.

"Oh . . . sh—" Pole got into the taxi and slumped back against the warm leather of the seat while Kelly hurried over the soft tar pavement and picked up the wheel.

"Chris*sake*," Kelly muttered as he got in the cab. "What's the—"

"Where to, chief?" the driver asked.

"Kruger Stadium," Kelly said.

"You're there." The cab driver pushed in the rotor button and the car glided away from the curb.

"What the hell's wrong with you?" Kelly asked Pole in a low voice. "We wait more'n half a damn year t'get us a bout and you been nothin' but bellyaches from the start."

"Some bout," said Pole. "Maynard, Kansas—the prize-fightin' center o' the nation."

"It's a start, ain't it?" Kelly said. "It'll keep us in coffee 'n' cakes a while, won't it? It'll put Maxo back in shape. And if we take it, it could lead to—"

Pole glanced over disgustedly.

"I don't *get* you," Kelly said quietly. "He's our fighter. What're ya writin' 'im off for? Don't ya want 'im t'win?"

"I'm a class-A mechanic, Steel," Pole said in his falsely patient voice. "I'm not a daydreamin' kid. We got a piece o' dead iron here, not a B-seven. It's simple mechanics, Steel, that's all. Maxo'll be lucky if he comes out o' that ring with his head still on."

Kelly turned away angrily.

"It's a *starter* B-seven," he muttered. "Full o' kinks. *Full* of 'em."

"Sure, sure," said Pole.

They sat silently a while looking out the window, Maxo between them, the broad steel shoulders bumping against theirs. Kelly stared at the building, his hands clenching and unclenching in his lap as if he was getting ready to go fifteen rounds.

"Have you seen this Maynard Flash?" Pole asked the driver.

"The Flash? You bet. Man, there's a fighter on his way. Won seven straight. He'll be up there soon, ya can bet ya life. Matter o' fact he's fightin' t'night too. With some B-two heap from back East, I hear."

The driver snickered. "Flash'll slaughter 'im," he said.

Kelly stared at the back of the driver's head, the skin tight across his cheekbones.

"Yeah?" he said flatly.

"Man, he'll—"

The driver broke off suddenly and looked back. "Hey, you ain't—" he started, then turned front again. "Hey, I didn't know, mister," he said. "I was only ribbin'."

"Skip it," Pole said. "You're right."

Kelly's head snapped around and he glared at the sallow-faced Pole.

"*Shut-up,*" he said in a low voice.

He fell back against the seat and stared out the window, his face hard.

"I'm gonna get 'im some oil paste," he said after they'd ridden a block.

"Swell," said Pole. "We'll eat the tools."

"Go to hell," said Kelly.

The cab pulled up in front of the brick-fronted stadium and they lifted Maxo out onto the sidewalk. While Pole tilted him, Kelly squatted down and slid the base wheel back into its slot. Then Kelly paid the driver the exact fare and they started pushing Maxo toward the alley.

"Look," said Kelly, nodding toward the poster board in front of the stadium. The third fight listed was

MAYNARD FLASH
(B-7, L.H.)
VS.
BATTLING MAXO
(B-2, L.H.)

"Big deal," said Pole.

Kelly's smile disappeared. He started to say something, then pressed his lips together. He shook his head irritably and big drops of his sweat fell to the sidewalk.

Maxo creaked as they pushed him down the alley and carried him up the steps to the door. The base wheel fell out again and bounced down the cement steps. Neither one of them said anything.

It was hotter inside. The air didn't move.

"Get the wheel," Kelly said and started down the narrow hallway, leaving Pole with Maxo. Pole leaned Maxo against the wall and turned for the door.

Kelly came to a half-glassed office door and knocked.

"Yeah," said a voice inside. Kelly went in, taking off his hat.

The fat bald man looked up from his desk. His skull glistened with sweat.

"I'm Battling Maxo's owner," said Kelly, smiling. He extended his big hand but the man ignored it.

"Was wonderin' if you'd make it," said the man whose name was Mr. Waddow. "Your fighter in decent shape?"

"The best," said Kelly cheerfully. "The best. My mechanic—he's class-A—just took 'im apart and put 'im together again before we left Philly."

The man looked unconvinced.

"He's in good shape," said Kelly.

"You're lucky t'get a bout with a B-two," said Mr. Waddow. "We ain't used nothin' less than B-fours for more than two years now. The fighter we was after got stuck in a car wreck and got ruined."

Kelly nodded. "We'll, ya got nothin' t'worry about," he said. "My fighter's in top shape. He's the one knocked down Dimsy the Rock in Madison Square year or so ago."

"I want a good fight," said the fat man.

"You'll get a good fight," Kelly said, feeling a tight pain in his stomach muscles. "Maxo's in good shape. You'll see. He's in top shape."

"I just want a good fight."

Kelly stared at the fat man a moment. Then he said, "You got a ready room we can use? The mechanic 'n' me'd like t'get something t'eat."

"Third door down the hall on the right side," said Mr. Waddow. "Your bout's at eight thirty."

Kelly nodded. "OK."

"Be there," said Mr. Waddow, turning back to his work.

"Uh . . . what about—?" Kelly started.

"You get ya money after ya deliver a fight," Mr. Waddow cut him off.

Kelly's smile faltered.

"OK," he said. "See ya then."

When Mr. Waddow didn't answer, he turned for the door.

"Don't slam the door," Mr. Waddow said. Kelly didn't.

"Come on," he said to Pole when he was in the hall again. They pushed Maxo down to the ready room and put him inside it.

"What about checkin' 'im over?" Kelly said.

"What about my *gut?*" snapped Pole. "I ain't eaten in six hours."

Kelly blew out a heavy breath. "All right, let's go then," he said.

They put Maxo in a corner of the room.

"We should be able t'lock him in," Kelly said.

"Why? Ya think somebody's gonna *steal* 'im?"

"He's valuable," said Kelly.

"Sure, he's a priceless antique," said Pole.

Kelly closed the door three times before the latch caught. He turned away from it, shaking his head worriedly. As they started down the hall he looked at his wrist and saw for the fiftieth time the white band where his pawned watch had been.

"What time is it?" he asked.

"Six twenty-five," said Pole.

"We'll have t'make it fast," Kelly said. "I want ya t'check 'im over good before the fight."

"What for?" asked Pole.

"Did ya *hear* me?" Kelly said angrily.

"Sure, sure," Pole said.

"He's gonna take that son-of-a-bitch B-seven," Kelly said, barely opening his lips.

"Sure he is," said Pole. "With his teeth."

"Some town," Kelly said disgustedly as they came back in the side door of the stadium.

"I told ya they wouldn't have any oil paste here," Pole said. "Why should they? B-twos are dead. Maxo's probably the only one in a thousand miles."

Kelly walked quickly down the hall, opened the door of the

ready room and went in. He crossed over to Maxo and pulled off the covering.

"Get to it," he said. "There ain't much time."

Blowing out a slow, tired breath, Pole took off his wrinkled blue coat and tossed it over the bench standing against the wall. He dragged a small table over to where Maxo was, then rolled up his sleeves. Kelly took off his hat and coat and watched while Pole worked loose the nut that held the tool cavity door shut. He stood with his big hands on his hips while Pole drew out the tools one by one and laid them down on the table.

"Rust," Pole muttered. He rubbed a finger around the inside of the cavity and held it up, copper-colored rust flaking off the tip.

"Come on," Kelly said irritably. He sat down on the bench and watched as Pole pried off the sectional plates on Maxo's chest. His eyes ran up over Maxo's leonine head. If I didn't see them coils, he thought once more, I'd swear he was real. Only the mechanics in a B-fighter could tell it wasn't real men in there. Sometimes people were actually fooled and sent in letters complaining that real men were being used. Even from ringside the flesh tones looked human. Mawling had a special patent on that.

Kelly's face relaxed as he smiled fondly at Maxo.

"Good boy," he murmured. Pole didn't hear. Kelly watched the sure-handed mechanic probe with his electric pick, examining connections and potency centers.

"Is he all right?" he asked, without thinking.

"Sure, he's great," Pole said. He plucked out a tiny steel-caged tube. "If this doesn't blow out," he said.

"Why should it?"

"It's sub-par," Pole said jadedly. "I told ya that after the last fight *eight months* ago."

Kelly swallowed. "We'll get 'im a new one after this bout," he said.

"Seventy-five bucks," muttered Pole as if he were watching the money fly away on green wings.

"It'll hold," Kelly said, more to himself than to Pole.

Pole shrugged. He put back the tube and pressed in the row of buttons on the main autonomic board. Maxo stirred.

"Take it easy on the left arm," said Kelly. "Save it."

"If it don't work here, it won't work out there," said Pole.

He jabbed at a button and Maxo's left arm began moving with little, circling motions. Pole pushed over the safety-block switch that would keep Maxo from counterpunching and stepped back. He threw a right at Maxo's chin and the robot's arm jumped up with a hitching motion to cover his face. Maxo's left eye flickered like a ruby catching the sun.

"If that eye cell goes . . ." Pole said.

"It *won't*," said Kelly tensely. He watched Pole throw another punch at the left side of Maxo's head. He saw the tiny ripple of the flexo-covered cheek, then the arm jerked up again. It squeaked.

"That's enough," he said. "It works. Try the rest of 'im."

"He's gonna get more than two punches throwed at his head," Pole said.

"*His arm's all right*," Kelly said. "Try something else, I said."

Pole reached inside Maxo and activated the leg-cable centers. Maxo began shifting around. He lifted his left leg and shook off the base wheel automatically. Then he was standing lightly on black-shoed feet, feeling at the floor like a cured cripple testing for stance.

Pole reached forward and jabbed in the FULL button, then jumped back as Maxo's eye beams centered on him and the robot moved forward, broad shoulders rocking slowly, arms up defensively.

"Damn," Pole muttered, "they'll hear 'im squeakin' in the back row."

Kelly grimaced, teeth set. He watched Pole throw another right and Maxo's arm lurch up raggedly. His throat moved with a convulsive swallow and he seemed to have trouble breathing the close air in the little room.

Pole shifted around the floor quickly, side to side. Maxo

followed lumberingly, changing direction with visibly jerking motions.

"Oh, he's *beautiful,*" Pole said, stopping. "Just beautiful." Maxo came up, arms still raised, and Pole jabbed in under them, pushing the OFF button. Maxo stopped.

"Look, we'll have t'put 'im on *de*fense, Steel," Pole said. "That's all there is to it. He'll get chopped t'pieces if we have 'im movin' in."

Kelly cleared his throat. "No," he said.

"Oh for—will ya use ya *head?*" snapped Pole. "He's a B-two, f'Chrissake. He's gonna get slaughtered anyway. Let's save the pieces."

"They want 'im on the *off*ense," said Kelly. "It's in the contract."

Pole turned away with a hiss.

"What's the use?" he muttered.

"Test 'im some more."

"What for? He's as good as he'll ever be."

"Will ya do what I say!" Kelly shouted, all the tension exploding out of him.

Pole turned back and jabbed in a button. Maxo's left arm shot out. There was a snapping noise inside it and it fell against Maxo's side with a dead clank.

Kelly started up, his face stricken. "My God what did ya *do!*" he cried. He ran over to where Pole was pushing the button again. Maxo's arm didn't move.

"I *told* ya not t'fool with that arm!" Kelly yelled. "What the hell's the *matter* with ya!" His voice cracked in the middle of the sentence.

Pole didn't answer. He picked up his pry and began working off the left shoulder plate.

"So help me God, if you broke that arm . . ." Kelly warned in a low, snaking voice.

"If *I* broke it!" Pole snapped. "Listen, you dumb mick! This heap has been runnin' on borrowed time for three years now! Don't talk t'me about breakages!"

Kelly clenched his teeth, his eyes small and deadly.

"Open it up," he said.

"Son-of-a—" Pole muttered as he got the plate off. "You find another goddam mechanic that coulda kep' this steam shovel together any better these last years. You just *find* one."

Kelly didn't answer. He stood rigidly, watching while Pole put down the curved plate and looked inside.

When Pole touched it, the trigger spring broke in half and part of it jumped across the room.

Pole started to say something, then stopped. He looked at the ashen-faced Kelly without moving.

Kelly's eyes moved to Pole.

"Fix it," he said hoarsely.

Pole swallowed. "Steel, I—"

"*Fix* it!"

"I can't! That spring's been fixin' t'break for—"

"You broke it! Now *fix* it!" Kelly clamped rigid fingers on Pole's arm. Pole jerked back.

"Let go of me!" he said.

"What's the matter with you!" Kelly cried. "Are you crazy? He's got t'be fixed. He's *got* t'be!"

"Steel, he needs a new spring."

"Well, *get* it!"

"They don't *have* 'em here, Steel," Pole said. "I *told* ya. And if they *did* have 'em, we ain't got the sixteen fifty t'get one."

"Oh— Oh, God," said Kelly. His hand fell away and he stumbled to the other side of the room. He sank down on the bench and stared without blinking at the tall, motionless Maxo.

He sat there a long time, just staring, while Pole stood watching him, the pry still in his hand. He saw Kelly's broad chest rise and fall with spasmodic movements. Kelly's face was a blank.

"If he don't watch 'em," muttered Kelly finally.

"What?"

Kelly looked up, his mouth set in a straight, hard line. "If he don't watch, it'll work," he said.

"What're ya talkin' about?"

Kelly stood up and started unbuttoning his shirt.

"What're ya—"

Pole stopped dead, his mouth falling open. "Are you *crazy?*" he asked.

Kelly kept unbuttoning his shirt. He pulled it off and tossed it on the bench.

"Steel, you're out o' your mind!" Pole said. "You can't do that!"

Kelly didn't say anything.

"But you'll—Steel, you're *crazy!*"

"We deliver a fight or we don't get paid," Kelly said.

"But—you'll get *killed!*"

Kelly pulled off his undershirt. His chest was beefy, there was red hair swirling around it. "Have to shave this off," he said.

"Steel, *come on,*" Pole said. "You—"

His eyes widened as Kelly sat down on the bench and started unlacing his shoes.

"They'll never let ya," Pole said. "You can't make 'em think you're a—" He stopped and took a jerky step forward. "Steel, fuh Chrissake!"

Kelly looked up at Pole with dead eyes.

"You'll help me," he said.

"But they—"

"Nobody knows what Maxo looks like," Kelly said. "And only Waddow saw me. If he don't watch the bouts we'll be all right."

"But—"

"They won't know," Kelly said. "The B's bleed and bruise too."

"Steel, come on," Pole said shakily. He took a deep breath and calmed himself. He sat down hurriedly beside the broad-shouldered Irishman.

"Look," he said. "I got a sister back East—in Maryland. If I wire 'er, she'll send us the dough t'get back."

Kelly got up and unbuckled his belt.

"Steel, I know a guy in Philly with a B-five wants t'sell cheap," Pole said desperately. "We could scurry up the cash and— Steel, fuh Chrissake, you'll get *killed!* It's a B-seven! Don't ya understand? A B-*seven!* You'll be mangled!"

Kelly was working the dark trunks over Maxo's hips.

"I won't let ya do it, Steel," Pole said, "I'll go to—"

He broke off with a sucked-in gasp as Kelly whirled and moved over quickly to haul him to his feet. Kelly's grip was like the jaws of a trap and there was nothing left of him in his eyes.

"You'll help me," Kelly said in a low, trembling voice. "You'll help me, or I'll beat ya brains out on the wall."

"You'll get killed," Pole murmured.

"Then I will," said Kelly.

Mr. Waddow came out of his office as Pole was walking the covered Kelly toward the ring.

"Come on, come on," Mr. Waddow said. "They're waitin' on ya."

Pole nodded jerkily and guided Kelly down the hall.

"Where's the owner?" Mr. Waddow called after them.

Pole swallowed quickly. "In the audience," he said.

Mr. Waddow grunted and, as they walked on, Pole heard the door to the office close. Breath emptied from him.

"I should've told 'im," he muttered.

"I'd o' killed ya," Kelly said, his voice muffled under the covering.

Crowd sounds leaked back into the hall now as they turned a corner. Under the canvas covering, Kelly felt a drop of sweat trickle down his temple.

"Listen," he said, "you'll have t'towel me off between rounds."

"Between what rounds?" Pole asked tensely. "You won't even last one."

"Shut up."

"You think you're just up against some tough fighter?" Pole asked. "You're up against a machine! Don't ya—"

"I said shut up."

"Oh . . . you dumb—" Pole swallowed. "If I towel ya off, they'll know," he said.

"They ain't seen a B-two in years," Kelly broke in. "If anyone asks, tell 'em it's an oil leak."

"Sure," said Pole disgustedly. He bit his lips. "Steel, ya'll never get away with it."

The last part of his sentence was drowned out as, suddenly, they were among the crowd, walking down the sloping aisle toward the ring. Kelly held his knees locked and walked a little stiffly. He drew in a long, deep breath and let it out slowly.

The heat burdened in around him like a hanging weight. It was like walking along the sloping floor of an ocean of heat and sound. He heard voices drifting past him as he moved.

"Ya'll take 'im home in a box!"

"Well, if it ain't *Rattlin'* Maxo!"

And the inevitable, "*Scrap iron!*"

Kelly swallowed dryly, feeling a tight, drawing sensation in his loins. Thirsty, he thought. The momentary vision of the bar across from the Kansas City train station crossed his mind. The dim-lit booth, the cool fan breeze on the back of his neck, the icy, sweat-beaded bottle chilling his palm. He swallowed again. He hadn't allowed himself one drink in the last hour. The less he drank the less he'd sweat, he knew.

"Watch it."

He felt Pole's hand slide in through the opening in the back of the covering, felt the mechanic's hand grab his arm and check him.

"Ring steps," Pole said out of a corner of his mouth.

Kelly edged his right foot forward until the shoe tip touched the riser of the bottom step. Then he lifted his foot to the step and started up.

At the top, Pole's fingers tightened around his arm again.

"Ropes," Pole said, guardedly.

It was hard getting through the ropes with the covering on. Kelly almost fell and hoots and catcalls came at him like spears out of the din. Kelly felt the canvas give slightly under his feet and then Pole pushed the stool against the back of his legs and he sat down a little too jerkily.

"Hey, get that derrick out o' here!" shouted a man in the second row. Laughter and hoots.

Then Pole drew off the covering and put it down on the ring apron.

Kelly sat there staring at the Maynard Flash.

The B-seven was motionless, its gloved hands hanging across its legs. There was imitation blonde hair, crew cut, growing out of its skull pores. Its face was that of an impassive Adonis. The simulation of muscle curve on its body and limbs was almost perfect. For a moment Kelly almost thought that years had been peeled away and he was in the business again, facing a young contender. He swallowed carefully. Pole crouched beside him, pretending to fiddle with an arm plate.

"Steel, *don't*," he muttered again.

Kelly didn't answer. He kept staring at the Maynard Flash, thinking of the array of instant-reaction centers inside the smooth arch of chest. The drawing sensation reached his stomach. It was like a cold hand pulling in at strands of muscle and ligament.

A red-faced man in a white suit climbed into the ring and reached up for the microphone which was swinging down to him.

"Ladies and gentlemen," he announced, "the opening bout of the evening. A ten-round light-heavyweight bout. From Philadelphia, the B-two, *Battling Maxo.*"

The crowd booed and hissed. They threw up paper airplanes and shouted, *"Scrap iron!"*

"His opponent, our own B-seven, the *Maynard Flash!*"

Cheers and wild clapping. The Flash's mechanic touched a button under the left armpit and the B-seven jumped up and held his arms over his head in the victory gesture. The crowd laughed happily.

"God," Pole muttered, "I never saw that. Must be a new gimmick."

Kelly blinked to relieve his eyes.

"Three more bouts to follow," said the red-faced man and then the microphone drew up and he left the ring. There was no referee. B-fighters never clinched—their machinery rejected it—and there was no knockdown count. A felled B-fighter stayed down. The new B-nine, it was claimed by the Mawling publicity staff, would be able to get up, which would make for livelier and longer bouts.

Pole pretended to check over Kelly.

"Steel, it's your last chance," he begged.

"*Get out,*" said Kelly without moving his lips.

Pole looked at Kelly's immobile eyes a moment, then sucked in a ragged breath and straightened up.

"Stay *away* from him," he warned as he started through the ropes.

Across the ring, the Flash was standing in its corner, hitting its gloves together as if it were a real young fighter anxious to get the fight started. Kelly stood up and Pole drew the stool away. Kelly stood watching the B-seven, seeing how its eye centers were zeroing in on him. There was a cold sinking in his stomach.

The bell rang.

The B-seven moved out smoothly from its corner with a mechanical glide, its arms raised in the traditional way, gloved hands wavering in tiny circles in front of it. It moved quickly toward Kelly, who edged out of his corner automatically, his mind feeling, abruptly, frozen. He felt his own hands rise as if someone else had lifted them and his legs were like dead wood under him. He kept his gaze on the bright, unmoving eyes of the Maynard Flash.

They came together. The B-seven's left flicked out and Kelly blocked it, feeling the rock-hard fist of the Flash even through his glove. The fist moved out again. Kelly drew back his head and felt a warm breeze across his mouth. His own left shot out and banged against the Flash's nose. It was like hitting a doorknob. Pain flared in Kelly's arm and his jaw muscles went hard as he struggled to keep his face blank.

The B-seven feinted with a left and Kelly knocked it aside. He couldn't stop the right that blurred in after it and grazed his left temple. He jerked his head away and the B-seven threw a left that hit him over the ear. Kelly lurched back, throwing out a left that the B-seven brushed aside. Kelly caught his footing and hit the Flash's jaw solidly with a right uppercut. He felt a jolt of pain run up his arm. The Flash's head didn't budge. He shot out a left that hit Kelly on the right shoulder.

Kelly backpedaled instinctively. Then he heard someone yell, "Get 'im a bicycle!" and he remembered what Mr. Waddow had said. He moved in again.

A left caught him under the heart and he felt the impact shudder through his frame. Pain stabbed at his heart. He threw a spasmodic left which banged against the B-seven's nose again. There was only pain. Kelly stepped back and staggered as a hard right caught him high on the chest. He started to move back. The B-seven hit him on the chest again. Kelly lost his balance and stepped back quickly to catch equilibrium. The crowd booed. The B-seven moved in without making a single mechanical sound.

Kelly regained his balance and stopped. He threw a right that missed. The momentum of his blow threw him off center and the Flash's left drove hard against his upper right arm. The arm went numb. Even as Kelly was sucking in a teeth-clenched gasp the B-seven shot in a hard right under his guard that slammed into Kelly's spongy stomach. Kelly felt the breath go out of him. His right slapped ineffectively across the Flash's right cheek. The Flash's eyes glinted.

As the B-seven moved in again, Kelly sidestepped and, for a moment, the radial eye centers lost him. Kelly moved out of range dizzily, pulling air in through his nostrils.

"Get that heap out o' there!" a man yelled.

Breath shook in Kelly's throat. He swallowed quickly and started forward just as the Flash picked him up again. He stepped in close, hoping to outtime electrical impulse, and threw a hard right at the Flash's body.

The B-seven's left shot up and Kelly's blow was deflected by the iron wrist. Kelly's left was thrown off too and then the Flash's left shot in and drove the breath out of Kelly again. Kelly's left barely hit the Flash's rock-hard chest. He staggered back, the B-seven following. He kept jabbing but the B-seven kept deflecting the blows and counterjabbing with almost the same piston-like motion. Kelly's head kept snapping back. He fell back more and saw the right coming straight at him. He couldn't stop it.

The blow drove in like a steel battering ram. Spears of pain shot behind Kelly's eyes and through his head. A black cloud seemed to flood across the ring. His muffled cry was drowned out by the screaming crowd as he toppled back, his nose and mouth trickling bright blood that looked as good as the dye they used in the B-fighters.

The rope checked his fall, pressing in rough and hard against his back. He swayed there, right arm hanging, limp, left arm raised defensively. He blinked his eyes instinctively, trying to focus them. I'm a robot, he thought, a robot.

The Flash stepped in and drove a violent right into Kelly's chest, a left to his stomach. Kelly doubled over, gagging. A right slammed off his skull like a hammer blow, driving him back against the ropes again. The crowd screamed.

Kelly saw the blurred outline of the Maynard Flash. He felt another blow smash into his chest like a club. With a sob he threw a wild left that the B-seven brushed off. Another sharp blow landed on Kelly's shoulder. He lifted his right and managed to deflect the worst of a left thrown at his jaw. Another right concaved his stomach. He doubled over. A hammering right drove him back on the ropes. He felt hot, salty blood in his mouth and the roar of the crowd seemed to swallow him. Stay up!—he screamed at himself. Stay up, goddam you! The ring wavered before him like dark water.

With a desperate surge of energy, he threw a right as hard as he could at the tall, beautiful figure in front of him. Something cracked in his wrist and hand and a wave of searing pain shot up his arm. His throat-locked cry went unheard. His arm fell, his left went down, and the crowd shrieked and howled for the Flash to finish it.

There were only inches between them now. The B-seven rained in blows that didn't miss. Kelly lurched and staggered under the impact of them. His head snapped from side to side. Blood ran across his face in scarlet ribbons. His arm hung like a dead branch at his side. He kept getting slammed back against the ropes, bouncing forward and getting slammed back again. He couldn't see anymore. He could only hear the screaming of the crowd and the endless swishing and thudding of the B-seven's gloves. Stay up, he thought. I have to stay up. He drew in his head and hunched his shoulders to protect himself.

He was like that seven seconds before the bell when a clubbing right on the side of his head sent him crashing to the canvas.

He lay there gasping for breath. Suddenly, he started to get up, then, equally as suddenly, realized that he couldn't. He fell forward again and lay on his stomach on the warm canvas, his head throbbing with pain. He could hear the booing and hissing of the dissatisfied crowd.

When Pole finally managed to get him up and slip the cover over his head the crowd was jeering so loudly that Kelly couldn't hear Pole's voice. He felt the mechanic's big hand inside the covering, guiding him, but he fell down climbing through the ropes and almost fell again on the steps. His legs were like rubber tubes. Stay up. His brain still murmured the words.

In the ready room he collapsed. Pole tried to get him up on the bench but he couldn't. Finally, he bunched up his blue coat under Kelly's head and, kneeling, he started patting with his handkerchief at the trickles of blood.

''You dumb bastard,'' he kept muttering in a thin, shaking voice. ''You dumb bastard.''

Kelly lifted his left hand and brushed away Pole's hand.

''Go—get the—money,'' he gasped hoarsely.

''What?''

''The money!'' gasped Kelly through his teeth.

''But—''

''*Now!*'' Kelly's voice was barely intelligible.

Pole straightened up and stood looking down at Kelly a moment. Then he turned and went out.

Kelly lay there drawing in breath and exhaling it with wheezing sounds. He couldn't move his right hand and he knew it was broken. He felt the blood trickling from his nose and mouth. His body throbbed with pain.

After a few moments he struggled up on his left elbow and turned his head, pain crackling along his neck muscles. When he saw that Maxo was all right he put his head down again. A smile twisted up one corner of his lips.

When Pole came back, Kelly lifted his head painfully. Pole came over and knelt down. He started patting at the blood again.

''Ya get it?'' Kelly asked in a crusty whisper.

Pole blew out a slow breath.

''*Well?*''

Pole swallowed. ''Half of it,'' he said.

Kelly stared up at him blankly, his mouth fallen open. His eyes didn't believe it.

''He said he wouldn't pay five C's for a one rounder.''

''What d'ya mean?'' Kelly's voice cracked. He tried to get up and put down his right hand. With a strangled cry he fell back, his face white. His head thrashed on the coat pillow, his eyes shut tightly.

''He can't—he can't do that,'' he gasped.

Pole licked his dry lips.

''Steel, there—ain't a thing we can do. He's got a bunch o' toughs in the office with 'im. I can't . . .'' He lowered his head. "And if—you was t'go there he'd know what ya done. And—he might even take back the two and a half."

Kelly lay on his back staring up at the naked bulb without blinking. His chest labored and shuddered with breath.

"No," he murmured. "No."

He lay there for a long time without talking. Pole got some water and cleaned off his face and gave him a drink. He opened up his small suitcase and patched up Kelly's face. He put Kelly's right arm in a sling.

Fifteen minutes later Kelly spoke.

"We'll go back by bus," he said.

"What?" Pole asked.

"We'll go by bus," Kelly said slowly. "That'll only cost fifty-six bucks." He swallowed and shifted on his back. "That'll leave almost two C's. We can get 'im a—a new trigger spring and a—eye lens and—" He blinked his eyes and held them shut a moment as the room started fading again.

"And oil paste," he said then. "Loads of it. He'll be—good as new again."

Kelly looked up at Pole. "Then we'll be all set up," he said. "Maxo'll be in good shape again. And we can get us some decent bouts." He swallowed and breathed laboriously. "That's all he needs is a little work. New spring, a new eye lens. That'll shape 'im up. We'll show those bastards what a B-two can do. Old Maxo'll show 'em. *Right?*"

Pole looked down at the big Irishman and sighed.

"Sure, Steel," he said.

Nightmare at 20,000 Feet

Richard Matheson

TELEPLAY BY RICHARD MATHESON

AIRED OCTOBER 11, 1963

STARRING WILLIAM SHATNER AND NICK
CRAVAT

"SEAT BELT, PLEASE," SAID THE STEWARDESS CHEER-
fully as she passed him.

Almost as she spoke, the sign above the archway which led
to the forward compartment lit up—FASTEN SEAT BELT—with,
below, its attendant caution—NO SMOKING. Drawing in a
deep lungful, Wilson exhaled it in bursts, then pressed the
cigarette into the armrest tray with irritable stabbing motions.

Outside, one of the engines coughed monstrously, spewing out a cloud of fume which fragmented into the night air.
The fuselage began to shudder and Wilson, glancing through
the window, saw the exhaust of flame jetting whitely from
the engine's nacelle. The second engine coughed, then
roared, its propeller instantly a blur of revolution. With a
tense submissiveness, Wilson fastened the belt across his lap.

Now all the engines were running and Wilson's head
throbbed in unison with the fuselage. He sat rigidly, staring
at the seat ahead as the DC-7 taxied across the apron, heating
the night with the thundering blast of its exhausts.

At the edge of the runway, it halted. Wilson looked out through the window at the leviathan glitter of the terminal. By late morning, he thought, showered and cleanly dressed, he would be sitting in the office of one more contact discussing one more specious deal, the net result of which would not add one jot of meaning to the history of mankind. It was all so damned—

Wilson gasped as the engines began their warm-up race preparatory to takeoff. The sound, already loud, became deafening—waves of sound that crashed against Wilson's ears like club blows. He opened his mouth as if to let it drain. His eyes took on the glaze of a suffering man, his hands drew in like tensing claws.

He started, legs retracting, as he felt a touch on his arm. Jerking aside his head, he saw the stewardess who had met him at the door. She was smiling down at him.

"Are you all right?" he barely made out her words.

Wilson pressed his lips together and agitated his hand at her as if pushing her away. Her smile flared into excess brightness, then fell as she turned and moved away.

The plane began to move. At first lethargically, like some behemoth struggling to overthrow the pull of its own weight. Then with more speed, forcing off the drag of friction. Wilson, turning to the window, saw the dark runway rushing by faster and faster. On the wing edge, there was a mechanical whining as the flaps descended. Then, imperceptibly, the giant wheels lost contact with the ground, the earth began to fall away. Trees flashed underneath, buildings, the darting quicksilver of car lights. The DC-7 banked slowly to the right, pulling itself upward toward the frosty glitter of the stars.

Finally, it levelled off and the engines seemed to stop until Wilson's adjusting ear caught the murmur of their cruising speed. A moment of relief slackened his muscles, imparting a sense of well-being. Then it was gone. Wilson sat immobile, staring at the NO SMOKING sign until it winked out, then, quickly, lit a cigarette. Reaching into the seat-back pocket in front of him, he slid free his newspaper.

As usual, the world was in a state similar to his. Friction in diplomatic circles, earthquakes and gunfire, murder, rape, tornadoes and collisions, business conflicts, gangsterism. God's in his heaven, all's right with the world, thought Arthur Jeffrey Wilson.

Fifteen minutes later, he tossed the paper aside. His stomach felt awful. He glanced up at the signs beside the two lavatories. Both, illuminated, read OCCUPIED. He pressed out his third cigarette since takeoff and, turning off the overhead light, stared out through the window.

Along the cabin's length, people were already flicking out their lights and reclining their chairs for sleep. Wilson glanced at his watch. Eleven-twenty. He blew out tired breath. As he'd anticipated, the pills he'd taken before boarding hadn't done a bit of good.

He stood abruptly as the woman came out of the lavatory and, snatching up his bag, started down the aisle.

His system, as expected, gave no cooperation. Wilson stood with a tired moan and adjusted his clothing. Having washed his hands and face, he removed the toilet kit from the bag and squeezed a filament of paste across his toothbrush.

As he brushed, one hand braced for support against the cold bulkhead, he looked out through the port. Feet away was the pale blue of the inboard propeller. Wilson visualized what would happen if it were to tear loose and, like a tribladed cleaver, come slicing in at him.

There was a sudden depression in his stomach. Wilson swallowed instinctively and got some paste-stained saliva down his throat. Gagging, he turned and spat into the sink, then, hastily, washed out his mouth and took a drink. Dear God, if only he could have gone by train; had his own compartment, taken a casual stroll to the club car, settled down in an easy chair with a drink and a magazine. But there was no such time or fortune in this world.

He was about to put the toilet kit away when his gaze caught on the oilskin envelope in the bag. He hesitated, then, setting the small briefcase on the sink, drew out the envelope and undid it on his lap.

He sat staring at the oil-glossed symmetry of the pistol. He'd carried it around with him for almost a year now. Originally, when he'd thought about it, it was in terms of money carried, protection from holdup, safety from teenage gangs in the cities he had to attend. Yet, far beneath, he'd always known there was no valid reason except one. A reason he thought more of every day. How simple it would be—here, now—

Wilson shut his eyes and swallowed quickly. He could still taste the toothpaste in his mouth, a faint nettling of peppermint on the buds. He sat heavily in the throbbing chill of the lavatory, the oily gun resting in his hands. Until, quite suddenly, he began to shiver without control. God, let me go! his mind cried out abruptly.

"Let me go, *let me go.*" He barely recognized the whimpering in his ears.

Abruptly, Wilson sat erect. Lips pressed together, he rewrapped the pistol and thrust it into his bag, putting the briefcase on top of it, zipping the bag shut. Standing, he opened the door and stepped outside, hurrying to his seat and sitting down, sliding the overnight bag precisely into place. He indented the armrest button and pushed himself back. He was a business man and there was business to be conducted on the morrow. It was as simple as that. The body needed sleep, he would give it sleep.

Twenty minutes later, Wilson reached down slowly and depressed the button, sitting up with the chair, his face a mask of vanquished acceptance. Why fight it? he thought. It was obvious he was going to stay awake. So that was that.

He had finished half of the crossword puzzle before he let the paper drop to his lap. His eyes were too tired. Sitting up, he rotated his shoulders, stretching the muscles of his back. Now what? he thought. He didn't want to read, he couldn't sleep. And there were still—he checked his watch—seven to eight hours left before Los Angeles was reached. How was he to spend them? He looked along the cabin and saw that, except for a single passenger in the forward compartment, everyone was asleep.

A sudden, overwhelming fury filled him and he wanted to scream, to throw something, to hit somebody. Teeth jammed together so rabidly it hurt his jaws. Wilson shoved aside the curtains with a spastic hand and stared out murderously through the window.

Outside, he saw the wing lights blinking off and on, the lurid flashes of exhaust from the engine cowlings. Here he was, he thought; twenty thousand feet above the earth, trapped in a howling shell of death, moving through polar night toward—

Wilson twitched as lightning bleached the sky, washing its false daylight across the wing. He swallowed. Was there going to be a storm? The thought of rain and heavy winds, of the plane a chip in a sea of sky was not a pleasant one. Wilson was a bad flyer. Excess motion always made him ill. Maybe he should have taken another few Dramamine pills to be on the safe side. And, naturally, his seat was next to the emergency door. He thought about it opening accidentally; about himself sucked from the plane, falling, screaming.

Wilson blinked and shook his head. There was a faint tingling at the back of his neck as he pressed close to the window and stared out. He sat there motionless, squinting. He could have sworn—

Suddenly, his stomach muscles jerked in violently and he felt his eyes strain forward. There was something crawling on the wing.

Wilson felt a sudden, nauseous tremor in his stomach. Dear God, had some dog or cat crawled onto the plane before takeoff and, in some way, managed to hold on? It was a sickening thought. The poor animal would be deranged with terror. Yet, how, on the smooth, wind-blasted surface, could it possibly discover gripping places? Surely that was impossible. Perhaps, after all, it was only a bird or—

The lightning flared and Wilson saw that it was a man.

He couldn't move. Stupefied, he watched the black form crawling down the wing. *Impossible.* Somewhere, cased in layers of shock, a voice declared itself but Wilson did not hear. He was conscious of nothing but the titanic, almost muscle-tearing leap of his heart—and of the man outside.

Suddenly, like ice-filled water thrown across him, there was a reaction; his mind sprang for the shelter of explanation. A mechanic had, through some incredible oversight, been taken up with the ship and had managed to cling to it even though the wind had torn his clothes away, even though the air was thin and close to freezing.

Wilson gave himself no time for refutation. Jarring to his feet, he shouted: "Stewardess! Stewardess!" his voice a hollow, ringing sound in the cabin. He pushed the button for her with a jabbing finger.

"Stewardess!"

She came running down the aisle, her face tightened with alarm. When she saw the look on his face, she stiffened in her tracks.

"There's a man out there! A man!" cried Wilson.

"What?" Skin constricted on her cheeks, around her eyes.

"Look, *look!"* Hand shaking, Wilson dropped back into his seat and pointed out the window. "He's crawling on the—"

The words ended with a choking rattle in his throat. There was nothing on the wing.

Wilson sat there trembling. For a while, before he turned back, he looked at the reflection of the stewardess on the window. There was a blank expression on her face.

At last, he turned and looked up at her. He saw her red lips part as though she meant to speak but she said nothing, only placing the lips together again and swallowing. An attempted smile distended briefly at her features.

"I'm sorry," Wilson said. "It must have been a—"

He stopped as though the sentence were completed. Across the aisle a teenage girl was gaping at him with sleepy curiosity.

The stewardess cleared her throat. "Can I get you anything?" she asked.

"A glass of water," Wilson said.

The stewardess turned and moved back up the aisle.

Wilson sucked in a long breath of air and turned away from the young girl's scrutiny. He felt the same. That was the thing that shocked him most. Where were the visions, the cries, the pummelling of fists on temples, the tearing out of hair?

Abruptly he closed his eyes. There had been a man, he thought. There had, actually, been a man. That's why he felt the same. And yet, there couldn't have been. He knew that clearly.

Wilson sat with his eyes closed, wondering what Jacqueline would be doing now if she were in the seat beside him. Would she be silent, shocked beyond speaking? Or would she, in the more accepted manner, be fluttering around him, smiling, chattering, pretending that she hadn't seen? What would his sons think? Wilson felt a dry sob threatening in his chest. Oh, God—

"Here's your water, sir."

Twitching sharply, Wilson opened his eyes.

"Would you like a blanket?" inquired the stewardess.

"No." He shook his head. "Thank you," he added, wondering why he was being so polite.

"If you need anything, just ring," she said.

Wilson nodded.

Behind him, as he sat with the untouched cup of water in his hand, he heard the muted voices of the stewardess and one of the passengers. Wilson tightened with resentment. Abruptly, he reached down and, careful not to spill the water, pulled out the overnight bag. Unzipping it, he removed the box of sleeping capsules and washed two of them down. Crumpling the empty cup, he pushed it into the seat-pocket in front of him, then, not looking, slid the curtains shut. There—it was ended. One hallucination didn't make insanity.

Wilson turned onto his right side and tried to set himself against the fitful motion of the ship. He had to forget about this, that was the most important thing. He mustn't dwell on it. Unexpectedly, he found a wry smile forming on his lips. Well, by God, no one could accuse him of mundane hallucinations anyway. When he went at it, he did a royal job. A naked man crawling down a DC-7's wing at twenty thousand feet—there was a chimera worthy of the noblest lunatic.

The humor faded quickly. Wilson felt chilled. It had been so clear, so vivid. How could the eyes see such a thing when it did not exist? How could what was in his mind make the physical act of seeing work to its purpose so completely? He hadn't been groggy, in a daze—nor had it been a shapeless, gauzy vision. It had been sharply three-dimensional, fully a part of the things he saw which he *knew* were real. That was the frightening part of it. It had not been dreamlike in the least. He had looked at the wing and—

Impulsively, Wilson drew aside the curtain.

He did not know, immediately, if he would survive. It seemed as if all the contents of his chest and stomach were bloating horribly, the excess pushing up into his throat and head, choking away breath, pressing out his eyes. Imprisoned in this swollen mass, his heart pulsed strickenly, threatening to burst its case as Wilson sat, paralyzed.

Only inches away, separated from him by the thickness of a piece of glass, the man was staring at him.

It was a hideously malignant face, a face not human. Its skin was grimy, of a wide-pored coarseness; its nose a squat, discolored lump; its lips misshapen, cracked, forced apart by teeth of a grotesque size and crookedness; its eyes recessed and small—unblinking. All framed by shaggy, tangled hair which sprouted, too, in fury tufts from the man's ears and nose, in birdlike down across his cheeks.

Wilson sat riveted to his chair, incapable of response. Time stopped and lost its meaning. Function and analysis ceased. All were frozen in an ice of shock. Only the beat of heart went on—alone, a frantic leaping in the darkness. Wilson could not so much as blink. Dull-eyed, breathless, he returned the creature's vacant stare.

Abruptly then, he closed his eyes and his mind, rid of the sight, broke free. It isn't there, he thought. He pressed his teeth together, breath quavering in his nostrils. It isn't there, *it simply is not there.*

Clutching at the armrests with pale-knuckled fingers, Wilson braced himself. There is no man out there, he told himself. It was impossible that there should be a man out there crouching on the wing looking at him.

He opened his eyes—

—to shrink against the seat back with a gagging inhalation. Not only was the man still there but he was grinning. Wilson turned his fingers in and dug the nails into his palms until pain flared. He kept it there until there was no doubt in his mind that he was fully conscious.

Then, slowly, arm quivering and numb, Wilson reached up for the button which would summon the stewardess. He would not make the same mistake again—cry out, leap to his feet, alarm the creature into flight. He kept reaching upward, a tremor of aghast excitement in his muscles now because the man was watching him, the small eyes shifting with the movement of his arm.

He pressed the button carefully once, twice. Now come, he thought. Come with your objective eyes and see what I see— but *hurry.*

In the rear of the cabin, he heard a curtain being drawn aside and, suddenly, his body stiffened. The man had turned his caliban head to look in that direction. Paralyzed, Wilson stared at him. Hurry, he thought. For God's sake, hurry!

It was over in a second. The man's eyes shifted back to Wilson, across his lips a smile of monstrous cunning. Then with a leap, he was gone.

"Yes, sir?"

For a moment, Wilson suffered the fullest anguish of madness. His gaze kept jumping from the spot where the man had stood to the stewardess's questioning face, then back again. Back to the stewardess, to the wing, to the stewardess, his breath caught, his eyes stark with dismay.

"What *is* it?" asked the stewardess.

It was the look on her face that did it. Wilson closed a vise on his emotions. She couldn't possibly believe him. He realized it in an instant.

"I'm—I'm sorry," he faltered. He swallowed so dryly that it made a clicking noise in his throat. "It's nothing. I—apologize."

The stewardess obviously didn't know what to say. She kept leaning against the erratic yawing of the ship, one hand holding on to the back of the seat beside Wilson's, the other stirring limply along the seam of her skirt. Her lips were parted slightly as if she meant to speak but could not find the words.

"Well," she said finally and cleared her throat, "if you—need anything."

"Yes, yes. Thank you. Are we—going into a storm?"

The stewardess smiled hastily. "Just a small one," she said. "Nothing to worry about."

Wilson nodded with little twitching movements. Then, as the stewardess turned away, breathed in suddenly, his nostrils flaring. He felt certain that she already thought him mad but didn't know what to do about it because, in her course of training, there had been no instruction on the handling of passengers who thought they saw small men crouching on the wing.

Thought?

Wilson turned his head abruptly and looked outside. He stared at the dark rise of the wing, the spouting flare of the exhausts, the blinking light. He'd *seen* the man—to that he'd swear. How could he be completely aware of everything around him—be, in all ways, sane and still imagine such a thing? Was it logical that the mind, in giving way, should, instead of distorting all reality, insert within the still intact arrangement of details, one extraneous sight?

No, not logical at all.

Suddenly, Wilson thought about war, about the newspaper stories which recounted the alleged existence of creatures in the sky who plagued the Allied pilots in their duties. They called them gremlins, he remembered. Were there, actually, such beings? Did they, truly, exist up here, never falling, riding on the wind, apparently of bulk and weight, yet impervious to gravity?

He was thinking that when the man appeared again.

One second the wing was empty. The next, with an arcing descent, the man came jumping down to it. There seemed no impact. He landed almost fragilely, short, hairy arms outstretched as if for balance. Wilson tensed. Yes, there was knowledge in his look. The man—was he to think of it as a man?—somehow understood that he had tricked Wilson into calling the stewardess in vain. Wilson felt himself tremble with alarm. How could he prove the man's existence to others? He looked around desperately. That girl across the aisle. If he spoke to her softly, woke her up, would she be able to—

No, the man would jump away before she could see. Probably to the top of the fuselage where no one could see him, not even the pilots in their cockpit. Wilson felt a sudden burst of self-condemnation that he hadn't gotten that camera Walter had asked for. Dear Lord, he thought, to be able to take a picture of the man.

He leaned in close to the window. What was the man doing?

Abruptly, darkness seemed to leap away as the wing was chalked with lightning and Wilson saw. Like an inquisitive child, the man was squatted on the hitching wing edge, stretching out his right hand toward one of the whirling propellers.

As Wilson watched, fascinatedly appalled, the man's hand drew closer and closer to the blurring gyre until, suddenly, it jerked away and the man's lips twitched back in a soundless cry. He's lost a finger! Wilson thought, sickened. But, immediately, the man reached forward again, gnarled finger extended, the picture of some monstrous infant trying to capture the spin of a fan blade.

If it had not been so hideously out of place it would have been amusing for, objectively seen, the man, at that moment, was a comic sight—a fairy tale troll somehow come to life, wind whipping at the hair across his head and body, all of his attention centered on the turn of the propeller. How could this be madness? Wilson suddenly thought. What self-revelation could this farcical little horror possibly bestow on him?

Again and again, as Wilson watched, the man reached forward. Again and again jerked back his fingers, sometimes, actually, putting them in his mouth as if to cool them. And, always, apparently checking, he kept glancing back across at his shoulder looking at Wilson. *He knows*, thought Wilson. Knows that this is a game between us. If I am able to get someone else to see him, then he loses. If I am the only witness, then he wins. The sense of faint amusement was gone now. Wilson clenched his teeth. Why in hell didn't the pilots see!

Now the man, no longer interested in the propeller, was settling himself across the engine cowling like a man astride a bucking horse. Wilson stared at him. Abruptly a shudder plaited down his back. The little man was picking at the plates that sheathed the engine, trying to get his nails beneath them.

Impulsively, Wilson reached up and pushed the button for the stewardess. In the rear of the cabin, he heard her coming and, for a second, thought he'd fooled the man, who seemed absorbed with his efforts. At the last moment, however, just before the stewardess arrived, the man glanced over at Wilson. Then, like a marionette jerked upward from its stage by wires, he was flying up into the air.

"Yes?" She looked at him apprehensively.

"Will you—sit down, please?" he asked.

She hesitated. "Well, I—"

"Please."

She sat down gingerly on the seat beside his.

"What is it, Mr. Wilson?" she asked.

He braced himself.

"That man is still outside," he said.

The stewardess stared at him.

"The reason I'm telling you this," Wilson hurried on, "is that he's starting to tamper with one of the engines."

She turned her eyes instinctively toward the window.

"No, no, don't look," he told her. "He isn't there now." He cleared his throat viscidly. "He—jumps away whenever you come here."

A sudden nausea gripped him as he realized what she must be thinking. As he realized what he, himself, would think if someone told him such a story. A wave of dizziness seemed to pass across him and he thought—I *am* going mad!

"The point is this," he said, fighting off the thought. "If I'm not imagining this thing, the ship is in danger."

"Yes," she said.

"I know," he said. "You think I've lost my mind."

"Of course not," she said.

"All I ask is this," he said, struggling against the rise of anger. "Tell the pilots what I've said. Ask them to keep an eye on the wings. If they see nothing—all right. But if they do—"

The stewardess sat there quietly, looking at him. Wilson's hands curled into fists that trembled in his lap.

"*Well?*" he asked.

She pushed to her feet. "I'll tell them," she said.

Turning away, she moved along the aisle with a movement that was, to Wilson, poorly contrived—too fast to be normal yet, clearly, held back as if to reassure him that she wasn't fleeing. He felt his stomach churning as he looked out at the wing again.

Abruptly, the man appeared again, landing on the wing like some grotesque ballet dancer. Wilson watched him as he set to work again, straddling the engine casing with his thick, bare legs and picking at the plates.

Well, what was he so concerned about? thought Wilson.

That miserable creature couldn't pry up rivets with his fingernails. Actually, it didn't matter if the pilots saw him or not—at least so far as the safety of the plane was concerned. As for his own personal reasons—

It was at that moment that the man pried up one edge of a plate.

Wilson gasped. "Here, quickly!" he shouted, noticing, up ahead, the stewardess and the pilot coming through the cockpit doorway.

The pilot's eyes jerked up to look at Wilson, then abruptly, he was pushing past the stewardess and lurching up the aisle.

"*Hurry!*" Wilson cried. He glanced out the window in time to see the man go leaping upward. That didn't matter now. There would be evidence.

"What's going on?" the pilot asked, stopping breathlessly beside his seat.

"He's torn up one of the engine plates!" said Wilson in a shaking voice.

"He's what?"

"The man outside!" said Wilson. "I tell you he's—!"

"Mr. Wilson, keep your voice down!" ordered the pilot. Wilson's jaw went slack.

"I don't know what's going on here," said the pilot, "but—"

"Will you look?" shouted Wilson.

"Mr. Wilson, I'm warning you."

"For God's sake!" Wilson swallowed quickly, trying to repress the blinding rage he felt. Abruptly, he pushed back against his seat and pointed at the window with a palsied hand. "Will you, for God's sake, *look?*" he asked.

Drawing in an agitated breath, the pilot bent over. In a moment, his gaze shifted coldly to Wilson's. "Well?" he asked.

Wilson jerked his head around. The plates were in their normal position.

"Oh, now wait," he said before the dread could come. "I saw him pry that plate up."

"Mr. Wilson, if you don't—"

"*I said I saw him pry it up*," said Wilson.

The pilot stood there looking at him in the same withdrawn, almost aghast way as the stewardess had. Wilson shuddered violently.

"Listen, I *saw* him!" he cried. The sudden break in his voice appalled him.

In a second, the pilot was down beside him. "Mr. Wilson, please," he said. "All right, you saw him. But remember there are other people aboard. We mustn't alarm them."

Wilson was too shaken to understand at first.

"You—mean you've *seen* him then?" he asked.

"Of course," the pilot said, "but we don't want to frighten the passengers. You can understand that."

"Of course, of course. I don't want to—"

Wilson felt a spastic coiling in his groin and lower stomach. Suddenly, he pressed his lips together and looked at the pilot with malevolent eyes.

"I understand," he said.

"The thing we have to remember—" began the pilot

"You can stop now," Wilson said.

"Sir?"

Wilson shuddered. "Get out of here," he said.

"Mr. Wilson, what—?"

"*Will you stop?*" Face whitening, Wilson turned from the pilot and stared out at the wing, eyes like stone.

He glared back suddenly.

"Rest assured I'll not say another word!" he snapped.

"Mr. Wilson, try to understand our—"

Wilson twisted away and stared out venomously at the engine. From a corner of vision, he saw two passengers standing in the aisle looking at him. *Idiots!* his mind exploded. He felt his hands begin to tremble and, for a few seconds, was afraid that he was going to vomit. It's the motion, he told himself. The plane was bucking in the air now like a storm-tossed boat.

He realized that the pilot was still talking to him and,

refocusing his eyes, he looked at the man's reflection in the window. Beside him, mutely somber, stood the stewardess. Blind idiots, both of them, thought Wilson. He did not indicate his notice of their departure. Reflected on the window, he saw them heading toward the rear of the cabin. They'll be discussing me now, he thought. Setting up plans in case I grow violent.

He wished now that the man would reappear, pull off the cowling plate and ruin the engine. It gave him a sense of vengeful pleasure to know that only he stood between catastrophe and the more than thirty people aboard. If he chose, he could allow that catastrophe to take place. Wilson smiled without humor. There would be a royal suicide, he thought.

The little man dropped down again and Wilson saw that what he'd thought was correct—the man had pressed the plate back into place before jumping away. For, now, he was prying it up again and it was raising easily, peeling back like skin excised by some grotesque surgeon. The motion of the wing was very broken but the man seemed to have no difficulty staying balanced.

Once more Wilson felt panic. What was he to do? No one believed him. If he tried to convince them any more they'd probably restrain him by force. If he asked the stewardess to sit by him it would be, at best, only a momentary reprieve. The second she departed or, remaining, fell asleep, the man would return. Even if she stayed awake beside him, what was to keep the man from tampering with the engines on the other wing? Wilson shuddered, a coldness of dread misting along his bones.

Dear God, there was nothing to be done.

He twitched as, across the window through which he watched the little man, the pilot's reflection passed. The insanity of the moment almost broke him—the man and the pilot within feet of each other, both seen by him yet not aware of one another. No, that was wrong. The little man had glanced across his shoulder as the pilot passed. As if he knew there was no need to leap off any more, that Wilson's capac-

ity for interfering was at an end. Wilson suddenly trembled
with mind-searing rage. I'll kill you! he thought. You filthy
little animal, I'll *kill* you!

Outside, the engine faltered.

It lasted for a second, but, in that second, it seemed to Wilson as if his heart had also stopped. He pressed against the
window, staring. The man had bent the cowling plate far
back and now was on his knees, poking a curious hand into
the engine.

"Don't," Wilson heard the whimper of his own voice
begging. *"Don't . . ."*

Again, the engine failed. Wilson looked around in horror.
Was everyone deaf? He raised his hand to press the button
for the stewardess, then jerked it back. No, they'd lock him
up, restrain him somehow. And he was the only one who
knew what was happening, the only one who could help.

"God . . ." Wilson bit his lower lip until the pain made
him whimper. He twisted around again and jolted. The stewardess was hurrying down the rocking aisle. She'd heard it!
He watched her fixedly and saw her glance at him as she
passed his seat.

She stopped three seats down the aisle. Someone else had
heard! Wilson watched the stewardess as she leaned over,
talking to the unseen passenger. Outside, the engine coughed
again. Wilson jerked his head around and looked out with
horror-pinched eyes.

"Damn you!" he whined.

He turned again and saw the stewardess coming back up
the aisle. She didn't look alarmed. Wilson stared at her with
unbelieving eyes. It wasn't possible. He twisted around to
follow her swaying movement and saw her turn in at the
kitchen.

"No." Wilson was shaking so badly now he couldn't stop.
No one had heard.

No one knew.

Suddenly, Wilson bent over and slid his overnight bag out
from under the seat. Unzipping it, he jerked out his briefcase

and threw it on the carpeting. Then, reaching in again, he grabbed the oilskin envelope and straightened up. From the corners of his eyes, he saw the stewardess coming back and pushed the bag beneath the seat with his shoes, shoving the oilskin envelope beside himself. He sat there rigidly, breath quavering in his chest, as she went by.

Then he pulled the envelope into his lap and untied it. His movements were so feverish that he almost dropped the pistol. He caught it by the barrel, then clutched at the stock with white-knuckled fingers and pushed off the safety catch. He glanced outside and felt himself grow cold.

The man was looking at him.

Wilson pressed his shaking lips together. It was impossible that the man knew what he intended. He swallowed and tried to catch his breath. He shifted his gaze to where the stewardess was handing some pills to the passenger ahead, then looked back at the wing. The man was turning to the engine once again, reaching in. Wilson's grip tightened on the pistol. He began to raise it.

Suddenly, he lowered it. The window was too thick. The bullet might be deflected and kill one of the passengers. He shuddered and stared out at the little man. Again the engine failed and Wilson saw an eruption of sparks cast light across the man's animal features. He braced himself. There was only one answer.

He looked down at the handle of the emergency door. There was a transparent cover over it. Wilson pulled it free and dropped it. He looked outside. The man was still there, crouched and probing at the engine with his hand. Wilson sucked in trembling breath. He put his left hand on the door handle and tested. It wouldn't move downward. Upward there was play.

Abruptly, Wilson let go and put the pistol in his lap. No time for argument, he told himself. With shaking hands, he buckled the belt across his thighs. When the door was opened, there would be a tremendous rushing out of air. For the safety of the ship, he must not go with it.

Now. Wilson picked the pistol up again, his heartbeat staggering. He'd have to be sudden, accurate. If he missed, the man might jump onto the other wing—worse, onto the tail assembly where, inviolate, he could rupture wires, mangle flaps, destroy the balance of the ship. No, this was the only way. He'd fire low and try to hit the man in the chest or stomach. Wilson filled his lungs with air. Now, he thought. *Now.*

The stewardess came up the aisle as Wilson started pulling at the handle. For a moment, frozen in her steps, she couldn't speak. A look of stupefied horror distended her features and she raised one hand as if imploring him. Then, suddenly, her voice was shrilling above the noise of the engines.

"Mr. Wilson, no!"

"Get back!" cried Wilson, and he wrenched the handle up.

The door seemed to disappear. One second it was by him, in his grip. The next, with a hissing roar, it was gone.

In the same instant, Wilson felt himself enveloped by a monstrous suction which tried to tear him from his seat. His head and shoulders left the cabin and, suddenly, he was breathing tenuous, freezing air. For a moment, eardrums almost bursting from the thunder of the engines, eyes blinded by the arctic winds, he forgot the man. It seemed he heard a prick of screaming in the maelstrom that surrounded him, a distant shout.

Then Wilson saw the man.

He was walking across the wing, gnarled form leaning forward, talon-twisted hands outstretched in eagerness. Wilson flung his arm up, fired. The explosion was like a popping in the roaring violence of air. The man staggered, lashed out, and Wilson felt a streak of pain across his head. He fired again at immediate range and saw the man go flailing backward—then, suddenly, disappear with no more solidity than a paper doll swept in a gale. Wilson felt a bursting numbness in his brain. He felt the pistol torn from failing fingers.

Then all was lost in winter darkness.

He stirred and mumbled. There was a warmness trickling in his veins, his limbs felt wooden. In the darkness, he could hear a shuffling sound, a delicate swirl of voices. He lying, face up, on something—moving, joggling. A cold wind sprinkled on his face, he felt the surface tilt beneath him.

He sighed. The plane was landed and he was being carried off on a stretcher. His head wound, likely, plus an injection to quiet him.

"Nuttiest way of tryin' to commit suicide *I* ever heard of," said a voice somewhere.

Wilson felt the pleasure of amusement. Whoever spoke was wrong, of course. As would be established soon enough when the engine was examined and they checked his wound more closely. Then they'd realize that he'd saved them all.

Wilson slept without dreams.

The Old Man

Henry Slesar

Teleplay by Rod Serling

Aired November 8, 1963, as "The Old Man in the Cave"

Starring James Coburn, John Anderson, and John Marley

THERE HAD BEEN REVOLTS AGAINST THE RULE OF the old man before, but this time the Governors were worried enough to send Tango, their spy, to the insurrectionist meeting. Tango was a fair-haired laughing youth liked by the farmers and mechanics of the Village, who forgave his laziness and ineptness with tools because he lifted their spirits when crops were stubborn or engines failed to turn. None suspected his secret allegiance to the Governors who lived in the stone house on the great hill.

He arrived at the meeting place with his one-string guitar on his back, and squatted in the rear of the cave amid the grim-faced malcontents. They were young men; it was always the young who questioned the old man's sovereignty, and they nodded to Tango and murmured welcome. The meeting was captained by a dark-eyed farmer's son named Sierra, and his opening tirade was punctuated by the gestures of his withered, mutated right arm. His speech was effective, and Tango found his own loyalty wavering, until Sierra allowed others to be heard.

Tango stood up, smiled engagingly at the crowd, and said, "You speak of liberty, and the word is sweet. But tell me what the Village will do without the old man? Who will tell us when to plant our crops and where? Who will know which fields are safe for our seed, and which contaminated? Who will know when the storms will come, and when the rains will be radioactive? And how to make the machines work again?"

Sierra snarled his reply. "You speak like a Governor," he said. "This is the argument with which they have enslaved us since the end of the war. They say we are children in the wilderness with the old man to guide us, and I say they speak with the tongue of greed."

The crowd murmured approval of his words. The withered arm waved over their heads, and Sierra's voice rose to higher pitch.

"Greed!" he said. "Greed and the love of power! The old man tells us how to plant our crops, and taxes the best we raise for him and his Governors. For a generation we have worked to restore electric power to the Village, but every watt we can produce is employed to light the stone house while we and our families live in darkness."

"There has always been the old man," Tango said gently. "Who knows what our lives will be like without him?"

"Have you seen him, Tango?" Sierra said, bitterly. "Has he ever deigned to let you sing your foolish songs for him?"

"No," Tango said. "I have never seen the old man. My father saw him once; he was an old man even then, my father said, tall and thin with a flowing white beard, like Moses."

"My father remembers him, too," a young man said. "He saw him when he was a child, but he describes him as fat, like a Buddha, and very wise."

The crowd laughed, and Tango, responding to laughter, put his fists on his hips and laughed louder than all the rest. "No matter what he looks like, he is certainly wise. His wisdom has kept us all alive, Sierra, even you know that. Our scouts have ventured out time and again, and never yet found life. We are alone on Earth; our Village is the world; we alone have survived the blasts and the dusts and the many deaths of the atom. And why? Because of *him*. Is it so wrong, then, to honor the old man with food and drink and electric power?''

The crowd muttered sullenly at his speech. For a moment, Sierra was without response. Then, shrewdly gauging the mood Tango had inspired, he dropped his evangelical manner and became the voice of reason.

''Of course you're right,'' he said calmly. ''When the Village was new, when the War had just ended, the old man's wisdom was sorely needed.'' He came towards Tango, speaking as a friend. ''But if he was an old man then, Tango, old when your father and my father were children, how old must he be now? A hundred? A hundred and ten? I know not what miracle has kept him alive, but I do know this. With advancing years, the arteries harden and the blood grows sluggish. The brain, no longer given its full nourishment, grows soft and weak. A man becomes senile, doting like an infant, often even insane.'' He raised the withered arm. Softly: ''Must we be ruled by an insane old man?'' Louder: ''Must we be children forever?'' A cry: ''We don't need the old man, Tango!''

They took up the cry. ''Who needs the old man? Who needs the old man?''

They were on their feet.

''Who needs the old man?''

Quietly, without hurry, Tango edged his way towards the mouth of the cave. Then he was running, fleet-footed, towards the stone house on the hill.

Breathing hard with his exertion, he struggled up the steep path to the iron door, throwing away his one-string guitar when it impeded his progress. He seized the great knocker and made it boom like thunder, until the Senior Governor himself came to answer. When he saw Tango in the doorway, he pulled him inside and waited anxiously for his breath to return.

"This is no idle talk," Tango panted. "There are hundreds of them, Senior, and they are at fever pitch. You must warn the old man—"

"Fools!" the Governor said, wringing his hands. "If their quarrel is with us, let them face us alone. We will lay down our lives to protect *him*." He looked back, up the dark stairway to the second floor which Tango, and no other Villager, had ever seen. "They have never learned to trust him; their fathers never learned to understand his importance. We must save him, at all costs—"

"There may not be time," Tango said. "They're organized, and they have a leader. Protect yourself, Senior—"

From the upper floor, there was a cry. The Senior rushed to the foot of the stair, and a long-robed Governor came hurrying down the steps to meet him.

"From the window—" he gasped. "Marchers, coming here."

"Go, my son," the Senior said. "You mustn't be found here; their wrath will fall upon you as well. I must return to my duties."

He waited until Tango was on the other side of the iron door. The youth hesitated, and then turned down the steep path. He could see the line of marchers coming resolutely towards the building; he could see the leaders as they paused to deploy their forces about the stone house. Then he was spotted.

"There he is!" Sierra shouted. "He's a spy! A spy! We should have known he was a spy!"

Tango fled, but there were swifter runners among the rebels. They brought him down. A stone lifted in the air, gripped in a determined fist; his skull was crushed. Then the youths stormed the stone house itself, bringing up a pine log to batter at the iron door.

They burst into the house, a hundred of them in the small

room. Yet even this hundred were halted by the sight of the lean, bent figure of the Senior on the stairway.

"Go no further," he said. "You are on sacred ground."

Sierra pushed to the forefront. "Are you claiming Godhood now?" he sneered. "We want the old man!"

"The old man has saved us all, and will continue to guard us. Destroy him, and you destroy the race."

They killed the Senior Governor, and went stampeding up the stairs. At the door of the old man's room, the remaining three Governors erected a frail barricade of flesh. They, too, were slain. The door was shattered open, and they blinked at the light that flooded the old man's room.

Then they stopped, awe-struck, and stared at the strange, bewildering complexity, the thing in the room that winked with a thousand eyes and murmured in the mysterious voice of machinery. It was helpless now, its programmers dead.

Then they killed the old man, the computer. It didn't take the people long to die.

The Self-Improvement of Salvadore Ross

Henry Slesar

TELEPLAY BY JERRY MCNEELY

AIRED JANUARY 17, 1964

STARRING DON GORDON AND GAIL KOBE

SALVADORE ROSS, TOO POOR, TOO SCRAWNY, AND spurned by the only girl he had ever loved, ran into more of his usual luck on Friday afternoon at the bottling plant. He slipped in a sticky pool on a runway and dropped fifteen feet to the cement floor. His right leg was broken, and he went cursing in an ambulance to the city hospital. They put him in a ward next to a wheezing old man with pneumonia. When an interne began poking at him the next morning, he yelled, and he told interne, hospital, old man, and bottling plant to go to hell.

He was calmer the next day, his young, broken-nosed face graven against the pillow like some bushy-haired gargoyle. Then the old man began muttering complaints.

"Ah, you ain't so bad," Sal said. "You should only break a leg like me, pal, you'll know what trouble is."

"Broken leg!" The old man wiped his mouth contemptuously. "Listen, I'll trade you that broken leg anytime. You just ask me."

Sal grinned. "All right, so I'm asking. You give me that little cold of yours, you can have my broken leg. See how you like it, pop."

"You don't know what you're talking. A young horse like you, you could break both legs and next month you'll be dancing."

"What's the matter, pop, you don't want to do business? Trade me for the leg, go ahead. Is it a deal?"

The old man chuckled. "Yeah, sure, it's a deal."

The next morning Sal figured there must have been a window open near his bed, because he woke up with a hacking cough and a wheeze deep in his chest. The new symptoms took his mind off the pain in his leg, and when the interne came around to examine the splints and prepare the leg for setting, Sal laughed and coughed and told him that he thought the damned thing had healed itself.

The interne took one look and hurried out of the ward, returning five minutes later with a sour-mouthed stethoscoped man in a rumpled gray suit. They both did a survey on his leg and the sour-mouthed one muttered something about faulty diagnosis. Then he ordered a series of tests. It was only after they left him alone that the old man in the next bed started moaning and complaining about his leg. Sal watched with interest as the new huddle took place, but he knew the results even before the experts announced it. He laughed to himself, remembering the swap they had made, and the situation tickled him so much that he didn't even marvel over the mysterious transaction. He was too pleased. The old guy was bitching more than ever, and Sal had proved his point. A broken leg was a hell of a lot worse than a lousy cold.

It took another ten days for him to get rid of the congestion in his lungs, but in ten days he was fit enough to leave the hospital. His first thought on leaving was to see how much sympathy he could get from the girl he loved.

Leah Maitland was the prettiest girl in Sal's neighborhood, and Sal had been hopelessly stuck on her since high school.

She was too pretty for him; she had melted brown eyes and a figure that made cheap clothes look silky and expensive. She was too smart for him, too; she had a father who was a retired teacher, who wore a shawl like an old lady and clucked whenever he heard Sal's crude speech. When Sal knocked on Leah's door, he hoped her father wouldn't be home. But he was.

"Leah's not here," he said. "She's at school."

"School?" Sal blinked at the old man, looking stupidly at the tattered cloth around his bent shoulders.

"She's taking a teacher's course, didn't you know? She ought to be home in a little while, if you want to wait."

"Never mind," Sal said. "Just tell her I was here. Tell her—" He stopped. "Tell her I was sick, but I'm okay now. Tell her I'll call her up soon."

The old man frowned, and the wrinkled, disapproving face moved Sal to lies.

"Tell her I quit my job at the plant. Tell her I got a much better job, that everything's different with me now."

"Different? How different?"

"Just different," Sal said. "So long, Mr. Maitland." And he stuck his thumbs in his pants pockets and went down the stairs, feeling unaccountably better.

He made one lie come true. He telephoned the bottling plant and told them he was quitting. Then he celebrated.

"You paying for this?" the bartender said, holding back on the bottle. "You said you quit your job."

"Sure, Phil, I got money. Compensation from the plant."

Phil, a heavy bald man with a religious medal clanking on a chain around his sweaty neck, grunted and poured the drink. Then he took Sal's dollar and put it in the register. He made a ceremony out of punching the key and slipping in the bill. Sal watched him and licked his lips at the sight of the fat pile of green. "I wish I had your dough," he said.

"Be thankful for what you got," Phil said piously.

"Like what?"

The bartender considered the question. Then he smiled,

good-naturedly. "Well, you got hair. That's more than I got."

"You want the hair? Take it." Sal tugged at the curly crop. Phil laughed, but Sal didn't. "No, I mean it. You want the hair, it's yours. You know what happened in the hospital? I traded an old guy for his pneumonia. He got my broken leg, and I got his pneumonia. What do you think of that?"

"I hear lots of funny stories."

"What's the matter, Phil? You're big with the faith stuff. I'll tell you what. You give me the dough in your register, you can have my hair. Fair enough?"

"Sure, it's a deal," Phil laughed. He mopped around Sal's elbows, and went off to serve a beer. But he came back and repeated it. "You give me the hair, Sal, you can have it all."

"Count it," Sal said.

Phil counted it, laughing all the time. There was one hundred and eight dollars in the register. Before the evening was out, Sal upped the total by four dollars. He got back to his room drunk. In the morning, he woke up sick with a hangover. When he put his hand to his aching head, he touched smooth skin.

He went to a mirror, and saw the shiny clean dome exaggerating the thin features and the broken nose. He started to shake all over and wished he had a drink. That made him think of Phil. He telephoned the bar and nobody answered. He called Phil at home.

"Jesus, Sal, Jesus, how'd you do it? It's a miracle!" Phil said. "I never saw nothing like it. My wife thinks it's a toupee." He laughed hysterically. "Pull it, honey, go on, yank it, sweetheart. Ouch! Ouch!" he said hilariously, ecstatically. Sal slammed the receiver down and wept into his hands.

In the afternoon, a kid brought him an envelope crammed with money. He put the bills on the bed, and it seemed like a pitiful amount for what he had exchanged. He swore never to get so bad a bargain again.

That night, in a new hat, new suit, new shoes, he went into a strange bar, looking for something. There was a tramp, with thick black hair, half-closed eyes, and a dry mouth, cadging drinks in whispers. Sal bought him one, and said:

"You really got the shakes, huh, pop?" He looked at the hair. "That's a nice head of hair for a man your age, pop."

"Damn cold rotten month," the tramp whined.

"Have another," Sal said. "Look, what you need is a couple of bottles to last you. You know what I mean?"

"No."

"What's an old guy like you need hair for? Old guys like you, all they need is a warm place and some whiskey, am I right? Tell you what, pop. How'd you like to make a trade?"

Back in his room, Sal resolved to stay awake and watch the miracle take place. There was no sense of wonder involved; he had only a mechanical interest in the process. But at three o'clock, he got sleepy and dozed off in a chair, dreaming of Leah. His eyes snapped open at dawn, and his hand flew to his head. In his fingers: thick, coarse, dirty, beautiful hair. He went to a mirror and whooped in delight. Not just because of the hair, but because he knew for sure, for *sure*, that he could do it anytime he wanted, that he could swap his way to everything he wanted.

Then he remembered Jan. Jan was a big muscular kid with blond hair and the temperament of a cocker spaniel, and the worst pool player that ever came out of P.S. 19. Sal had cleaned up on Jan plenty of times; he was no shark, but he looked like Hoppe next to the big clumsy kid. Jan was a chauffeur now, for a guy named Halpert, reputed to be filthy rich. And Halpert was old. Rich and old, and approachable through Jan. The combination was right.

He found Jan at Grimski's, leaning on a cue stick and smiling with innocent pleasure as his opponent dropped four in a row into the pockets. Sal pulled him aside and put the proposition to him. Would Jan introduce him to his boss?

"Mr. Halpert?" Jan's face lengthened. "Gee, Sal, I can't do that. Mr. Halpert don't see people, you know how it is. He hardly ever leaves the apartment."

"But I got a deal for him," Sal said fiercely. "It's important!"

Jan laughed sweetly. "He won't talk any deal, Sal, don't kid yourself. He's a funny old guy, but not *that* funny." He looked up as his opponent missed a bank shot and stepped away from the table. Jan looked over the setup on the bright green felt, tucked his tongue in the corner of his mouth, and missed. He chuckled, and chalked his cue.

"Listen," Sal said desperately. "You get me in to see Halpert, I'll give you something for your trouble."

"Like what?"

"I got no money, but I'll give you something else. You can have my game, Jan."

"Your what?"

"You can play good as me. I'll swap my pool game for it. Is it a deal?"

"I don't get you. You mean you'll coach me?"

"I won't have to. You'll play good as me, that's all. I can do things like that. I can't explain how, but I can. Just say yes, Jan, that's all you gotta say. If you start shooting good, will you get me in to see Halpert?"

"Hey," his partner said. "Make your shot."

"It's a deal," Jan laughed. He picked up his stick, and muffed an easy layup.

Early the next afternoon, he got a phone call from Jan, direct from Grimski's. Jan was too excited to be coherent, so Sal went to the pool parlor and listened to the stuttered story of his sudden prowess. He had just beaten Grimski himself, and the owner, baffled, had paid off a three-to-one bet on the game. Jan offered to take on Sal himself, but Sal knew better. Instead, he talked about old man Halpert.

Two days later, the chauffeur picked Sal up in Halpert's shiny Bentley, and took him to the big apartment house on lower Fifth Avenue. The car's interior made Sal choke with emotion, and so did the first sight of Halpert's floor-through apartment. Halpert was in the library; there was a real fireplace in the room.

"This is the guy I told you about," Jan said.

"He doesn't look like any doctor to me." Halpert said it contemptuously. He was a small fat man with a pink mottled face. His dark gray suit had a vest with white piping. He wheezed when he talked, and Sal could see the tiny veins in his nose and cheeks contract and expand with every breath.

When Jan left, Sal cleared his throat. "Not a doctor exactly, Mr. Halpert, is that what Jan said?"

"What do you want, boy?"

"I want to make a deal. Only it's gonna sound crazy, so don't throw me out right away. You know how old I am?"

"What the hell is this?" Halpert growled.

"I'm twenty-six. How old are you, Mr. Halpert?"

"Listen—" Halpert said.

"No, wait a minute. I don't care how old, Mr. Halpert. What I mean is, it don't matter. What I want to know is, how much would you give to be like me? Twenty-six, I mean?"

Halpert's small eyes moved quickly, as if he was afraid.

"Don't think I'm crazy, Mr. Halpert. I want to make a swap. You don't have to believe me, not yet. But if the price is right, I'll trade you my twenty-six for whatever you are."

"Jan!" Halpert shouted.

"Please, give me the benefit of the doubt. How much would you give to be twenty-six again, just tell me that and I'll get out of here."

"Is that a promise?"

"How much, Mr. Halpert?"

The old man relaxed a little, and went so far as to smile a small smile. "I'd give a million bucks, that's what I'd give. What kind of pills you peddling, kid?"

"You got that much money?"

"And more. Now will you get the hell out of here?"

"Will you swap me, Mr. Halpert? Will you give me a million bucks for my twenty-six?"

"Just like that?"

"All you do is say yes, Mr. Halpert. The rest is easy. Only don't try double-crossing me, it won't work. Once we make

the swap, it's final. I get the million bucks, you get to be
twenty-six. What do you say, Mr. Halpert?''

Four days later, Halpert signed up a crew of four, two of
them strapping women, and went on a south sea cruise in a
small yacht. His disappearance sent the stock of his company
into a tailspin, but that did not affect the fortune that had
passed into the hands of Salvadore Ross.

The rental agent that placed Sal in the East Side penthouse
had a lot of laughs with his wife over the transaction. An ancient, shriveled runt like Ross, wanting that kind of bachelor
quarters, was an incongruity worthy of laughter. The building employees chuckled, too, but they hid their amusement
behind the old man's back. He was too rich to offend.

Albert, the kid who ran the night elevator, was especially
polite. The old guy had taken a fancy to him; his first tip had
financed a sharp, second-hand suit. Albert, who was nineteen, thought about clothes almost as much as he thought
about women.

One night, he brought the old guy upstairs, and found him
friendlier than usual—he'd even invited Albert in for a drink
when his shift ended. Then he asked him questions.

"How old are you, Albert?"

"Nineteen, last April."

"How much you make a year?"

Albert blushed. "I dunno. I get thirty-six bucks a week."

"How long do you think it'd take to save a thousand?"

"Never," Albert grinned. "I could never save it."

"What would you give for that money?"

"Huh?"

"You're only nineteen. What if you were twenty? Would
that bother you a lot?"

"Nah. Nineteen, twenty, what's the difference?"

"Would you make a deal like that? Swap one year, for a
thousand bucks?"

"Boy, would I!"

Ross smiled. His mouth was a black hole. He opened a

desk drawer and took out a checkbook. He wrote laboriously. Albert looked at the shaky script, and whistled.

"Wow! Is this for *me*, Mr. Ross?'

"Sure it is," the old man cackled. "You just made a deal for it, Albert, a very good deal. Anytime you want to sell any more years, you come see me. And you can tell your friends about it, too; I'm always good for ready cash."

A week later, Albert returned. There was no perceptible change in his appearance, except for the new suit he wore. By the time he left, there was a check for five grand in the pocket.

With his new fortune, Albert resigned his job and took a trip out west. The young man who replaced him on the elevator was named Russell, and he was only seventeen. He left a month later, claiming a severe illness. The building management could believe it, all right; Russell looked a good ten years older.

There were others.

Six months later, Salvadore Ross stepped before the full-length mirror in the thick-carpeted penthouse bedroom, and saw himself once more as a young man of twenty-six.

He paid his call on Leah Maitland on a cold afternoon in October. He found Leah's old man in a wheelchair, with the shawl over his knees instead of his shoulders. He had been sick; he had suffered a stroke since Sal had seen him last; from the looks of the shabby apartment, the past year had been grim. Even Leah looked gaunter, her melted eyes brighter and more desperate.

"Where've you been?" she said lightly. "It's almost a whole year, Sal."

"I've been busy," he smiled. "New job, new apartment, new everything. I'm doing pretty well now, Leah."

The old man grunted and said nothing. He turned his chalky face away from Sal, and wheeled off into the bedroom.

"I'm sorry about your old man," Sal said. "Sorry about his being sick. Things must have been tough for you."

"You look—different, Sal."

"I am different," he said proudly. "Look, you think you can come for a little while? Take a little ride?"

"Ride?"

"I got a car now," Sal said casually.

The car was waiting outside. It was a Silver Cloud Rolls, chauffeurless, because Sal wanted only his hands on the silken wheel. Leah gasped when she saw it. When they emerged under the canopy of the glittering apartment house on the East River, her face was almost stupid in her bewilderment. She thought he was joking, or worse, that he was involved in something profitable but nefarious. He laughed at every expression of her consternation. It was the best day of his life.

The next week, he took her to the season's most expensive restaurant, and after, on the furry white couch in his penthouse living room, began a crude attempt at love-making. She warded him off, but there was no final rejection in her manner. He lit a real fire in the real fireplace, and Leah hugged herself contentedly as she watched the dancing flames. Sal knew it was the right moment, the romantic moment Leah would expect, and he made the proper speech. She didn't reply for a long while.

"I just don't know, Sal," she said.

"What's there to know? I want to marry you, Leah. You know I was always nuts about you." He put his arm around her shoulder. "I can be anything you want, Leah. You want me to be smart, like your old man, I could be that, too." He saw the dark shift in her expression, and said: "It's the old man that bothers you, ain't it? He still don't like me, huh?"

"No," she whispered. "He doesn't, Sal."

"And you think a lot of him—"

"It's not just that he's smart. It's something more important, Sal, something—"

"Something I don't have?" He turned her about to face him. "What is it, Leah? You just tell me what it is?"

"I don't know the word for it—"

"Then make up a word!"

"Heart. Compassion. I don't know—"

"Compassion—"

"I guess that's it. All my life, ever since I can remember, he's had that quality. I don't ever want to live without it, Sal. Can you understand that?"

It was during Leah's morning school session that Sal paid a visit to her father. The old man didn't appear surprised to see him, but there was added hostility in his greeting.

"Since when do you come to see me?" Maitland grunted. "You know Leah's not home mornings."

"I wanted to talk, Mr. Maitland, just the two of us."

"I have nothing to say to you, Salvadore." His face reddened. "If it's about Leah, nothing at all. You know I'm a sick man; don't you? I don't have long on this earth, Salvadore, a few months, maybe only weeks. I wouldn't want to leave my Leah in the hands of someone like you . . ."

"But you're wrong. I didn't come to talk about Leah."

The old man seemed perplexed; he must have been dreading a formal bid for Leah's hand. "Then what is it?"

"It's about you, Mr. Maitland. Look, I know you never liked me, and I didn't come here to change your mind. I came to talk business. I want to make a deal. I want to buy something."

"What are you talking about?"

"You got something I want, Mr. Maitland. I'm willing to pay for it, any price you name. You could use money, Mr. Maitland, I know that. Not for yourself; I mean for Leah . . ."

"I've got nothing to sell you. I don't own anything."

"Yes, you do," Sal said eagerly. "You got something I need real bad, Mr. Maitland. I don't know what you'd call it, exactly—Leah, she says it's like, compassion."

"What kind of crazy talk is this? Do you even know what you're talking about?"

"I know, don't worry about that. A lot of people thought I was crazy when I offered 'em this kind of deal. But I've done all right. Take my word for it," he said proudly. "I've done great!"

"You think you can *buy* a thing like that? Pay for it, like a dozen eggs?"

"I know I can, Mr. Maitland. All you do is say yes, and I'll give you any amount of dough you name. Within reason," he added softly. "Within reason, Mr. Maitland."

"I think you'd better go," the old man said. "I don't think you feel well, Salvadore."

"A hundred thousand bucks, Mr. Maitland. How does that strike you? Would you make a deal for that?"

"You're really serious?"

"I'll bring you the check tomorrow; enough money to take care of you for the rest of your life."

The old man chuckled. "All right," he said. "I don't know what kind of madness you've got, Salvadore. But all right."

The next day, Salvadore Ross woke up with tears on his cheeks. He brushed at them with his hand and looked at his moist fingertips with wonder. What was he crying about? What kind of nutty dreams had he had the night before?

He shrugged, got out of bed, and dressed slowly. He had breakfast, and the strange, sad mood persisted. Was this the compassion he had bargained for? This aura of melancholy, these unwanted tears? He found himself looking at people on the street with strange feelings of sympathy for the emotions he read on their faces. A bum hit him for a handout, and he found himself pressing a five-dollar bill in the dirty hand. A child was being scolded on the street; he wanted to go over and comfort her. He thought of Leah, and his thoughts were more complex, and more wonderful, than any he had ever experienced; it was as if she were with him right then, near him, loving him.

He hailed a taxi, and went to Leah's apartment.

"Mr. Maitland?" He knocked forcefully on the door, wanting to see the old man's gentle face, wanting to touch the hand of Leah's father. The door opened. "Hello, Mr. Maitland," Sal grinned. "Gee, it's good to see you, Mr. Maitland."

"Come in," the old man said. "You brought the check?"

"I brought it," Sal said.

"Is it certified?"

"It's a bank check, good as cash."

"Put it on the table," Maitland said coldly.

Sal wanted to make a speech, say something that would make him understand what he was feeling, but his emotion was bigger than his vocabulary. He reached into his pocket, found the check, and placed it carefully on the cloth-covered table near the old man.

Then he turned to Leah's father with a smile enriching his face, and put out his hand.

The old man didn't take it. His features were stone. He pulled aside the blanket on his lap, and there was a shotgun gripped firmly in his hands. The smile was still on Salvadore Ross's face when the old man pulled the trigger and killed him, without hesitation, without mercy, without compassion.

The Beautiful People

Charles Beaumont

Teleplay by John Tomerlin

Aired January 24, 1964, as "Number Twelve Looks Just Like You"

Starring Collin Wilcox, Suzy Parker, and Pam Austin

MARY SAT QUIETLY AND WATCHED THE HANDSOME man's legs blown off, watched on further as the great ship began to crumple and break into small pieces in the middle of the blazing night. She fidgeted slightly as the men and the parts of the men came floating dreamily through the wreckage out into the awful silence. And when the meteorite shower came upon the men, flying in gouging holes through everything, tearing flesh and ripping bones, Mary closed her eyes.

"Mother."

Mrs. Cuberle glanced up from her magazine.

"Do we have to wait much longer?"

"I don't think so, why?"

Mary said nothing but looked at the moving wall.

"Oh, that." Mrs. Cuberle laughed and shook her head. "That tired old thing. Read a magazine, Mary, like I'm doing. We've all seen *that* a million times."

"Does it have to be on, Mother?"

"Well, nobody seems to be watching. I don't think the doctor would mind if I switched it off."

Mrs. Cuberle rose from the couch and walked to the wall. She depressed a little button and the life went from the wall, flickering and glowing.

Mary opened her eyes.

"Honestly," Mrs. Cuberle said to the woman beside her, "you'd think they'd try to get something else. We might all as well go to the museum and watch the first landing on Mars. The Mayorka Disaster—really!"

The woman replied without distracting her eyes from the magazine page. "It's the doctor's idea. Psychological."

Mrs. Cuberle opened her mouth and moved her head up and down, knowingly. "I should have known there was *some* reason. Still, who watches it?"

"The children do. Makes them think, makes them grateful or something."

"Oh. Of course, yes."

"Psychological."

Mary picked up a magazine and leafed through the pages. All photographs, of women and men. Women like Mother and like the others in the room; slender, tanned, shapely, beautiful women; and men with large muscles and shiny hair. Women and men, all looking alike, all perfect and beautiful. She folded the magazine and wondered how to answer the questions that would be asked.

"Mother—"

"Gracious, what is it now! Can't you sit still for a minute?"

"But we've been here three hours."

Mrs. Cuberle sniffed.

"Do I really have to?"

"Now, don't be silly, Mary. After those terrible things you told me, of *course* you do."

An olive-skinned woman in a transparent white uniform came into the reception room."

"Cuberle. Mrs. Zena Cuberle?"

"Yes."

"Doctor will see you now."

Mrs. Cuberle took Mary's hand and they walked behind the nurse down a long corridor.

A man who seemed in his middle twenties looked up from a desk. He smiled and gestured towards two adjoining chairs.

"Well, well."

"Doctor Hortel, I—"

The doctor snapped his fingers.

"Of course, I know. Your daughter. Well, I know your trouble. Get so many of them nowadays, takes up most of my time."

"You do?" asked Mrs. Cuberle. "Frankly, it had begun to to upset me."

"Upset? Hmm. Not good at all. But then—if people did not get upset, then we psychiatrists would be out of a job, eh? Go the way of the M.D. But I assure you, I need hear no more."

He turned his handsome face to Mary. "Little girl, how old are you?"

"Eighteen, sir."

"Oh, a real bit of impatience. It's just about time, of course. What might your name be?"

"Mary."

"Charming! and so unusual. Well, now, Mary, may I say that I understand your problem—understand it thoroughly."

Mrs. Cuberle smiled and smoothed the metalwork on her jerkin.

"Madam, you have no idea how many there are these days. Sometimes it preys on their minds so that it affects them physically, even mentally. Makes them act strange, say peculiar, unexpected things. One little girl I recall was so distraught she did nothing but brood all day long. Can you imagine!"

"That's what Mary does. When she finally told me, doctor, I thought she had gone—you know."

"That bad, eh? Afraid we'll have to start a re-education

programme, very soon, or they'll all be like this. I believe I'll suggest it to the Senator day after tomorrow.''

''I don't quite understand, doctor.''

''Simply, Mrs. Cuberle, that the children have got to be thoroughly instructed. Thoroughly. Too much is taken for granted and childish minds somehow refuse to accept things without definite reason. Children have become far too intellectual, which, as I trust I needn't remind you, is a dangerous thing.''

''Yes, but what has this to do with—''

''Mary, like half of the sixteen-, seventeen- and eighteen-year-olds today, has begun to feel acutely self-conscious. She feels that her body has developed sufficiently for the Transformation—which of course it has not, not quite yet—and she cannot understand the complex reasons which compel her to wait until some vague, though specific, date. Mary looks at you, at the women all about her, at the pictures, and then she looks into a mirror. From pure perfection of body, face, limbs, pigmentation, carriage, stance, she sees herself and is horrified. Isn't that so? Of course. She asks herself, 'Why must I be hideous, unbalanced, oversize, undersize, full of revolting skin eruption, badly schemed organic arrangements?'—in short, Mary is tired of being a monster and is overly anxious to achieve what almost everyone else has already achieved.''

''But—'' said Mrs. Cuberle.

''This much you understand, doubtless. Now, Mary, what you object to is that our society offers you, and the others like you, no convincing logic on the side of waiting until nineteen. It is all taken for granted and you want to know why! It is that simple. A non-technical explanation will not suffice. The modern child wants facts, solid technical data, to satisfy her every question. And that, as you can both see, will take a good deal of reorganizing.''

''But—'' said Mary.

''The child is upset, nervous, tense; she acts strange, peculiar, odd, worries you and makes herself ill because it is beyond our meagre powers to put it across. I tell you, what we need is a whole new basis for learning. And, that will take doing. It will take *doing*, Mrs. Cuberle. Now, don't you worry about Mary, and don't you worry, child. I'll prescribe some pills and—''

''No, no, doctor! You're all mixed up,'' cried Mrs. Cuberle.

''I *beg* your pardon, Madam?''

''What I mean is, you've got it wrong. Tell him, Mary, tell the doctor what you told me.''

Mary shifted uneasily in the chair.

''It's that—I don't want it.''

The doctor's well-proportioned jaw dropped.

''Would you please repeat that?''

''I said, I don't want the Transformation.''

''But that's impossible. I have never heard of such a thing. Little girl, you are playing a joke.''

Mary nodded negatively.

''See, doctor. What can it be?'' Mrs. Cuberle rose and began to pace.

The doctor clucked his tongue and took from a small cupboard a black box covered with buttons and dials and wire. He affixed black clamps to Mary's head.

''Oh no, you don't think—I mean, could it?''

''We shall soon see.'' The doctor revolved a number of dials and studied the single bulb in the centre of the box. It did not flicker. He removed the clamps.

''Dear me,'' the doctor said. ''Your daughter is perfectly sane, Mrs. Cuberle.''

''Well, then what is it?''

''Perhaps she is lying. We haven't completely eliminated that factor as yet, it slips into certain organisms.''

More tests. More machines, and more negative results.

Mary pushed her foot in a circle on the floor. When the doctor put his hands to her shoulders, she looked up pleasantly.

"Little girl," said the handsome man, "do you actually mean to tell us that you *prefer* that body?"

"I like it. It's—hard to explain, but it's me and that's what I like. Not the looks, maybe, but the *me.*"

"You can look in the mirror and see yourself, then look at—well, at your mother and be content?"

"Yes, sir." Mary thought of her reasons; fuzzy, vague, but very definitely there. Maybe she had said the reason. No. Only a part of it.

"Mrs. Cuberle," the doctor said, "I suggest that your husband have a long talk with Mary."

"My husband is dead. The Ganymede incident."

"Oh, splendid. Rocket man, eh? Very interesting organisms. Something always seems to happen to rocket men, in one way or another." The doctor scratched his cheek. "When did she first start talking this way?" he asked.

"Oh, for quite some time. I used to think it was because she was such a baby. But lately, the time getting so close and all, I thought I'd better see you."

"Of course, yes, very wise, uh—does she also do odd things?"

"Well, I found her on the second level one night. She was lying on the floor, and when I asked her what she was doing, she said she was trying to sleep."

Mary flinched. She was sorry, in a way, that Mother had found that out.

"Did you say 'sleep'?"

"That's right."

"Now where could she have picked that up?"

"No idea."

"Mary, don't you know nobody sleeps anymore. That we have an infinitely greater life-span than our poor ancestors now that that wasteful state of unconsciousness has been conquered? Child, have you actually *slept*? No one knows how anymore."

"No, sir, but I almost did."

The doctor breathed a long stream of air from his mouth.

"But, how could you begin to try to do something people have forgotten entirely about?"

"The way it was described in the book, it sounded nice, that's all."

"Book, book? Are there *books* at your Unit, Madam?"

"There could be. I haven't cleaned up in a while."

"That is certainly peculiar. I haven't seen a book for years. Not since '17."

Mary began to fidget and stare nervously.

"But with the Tapes, why should you try to read books . . . Where did you get them?"

"Daddy did. He got them from his father and so did Grandpa. He said they're better than the Tapes and he was right."

Mrs. Cuberle flushed.

"My husband was a little strange, Doctor Hortel. He kept these things despite anything I said. Finally hid them, as I see."

The muscular black-haired doctor walked to another cabinet and selected from the shelf a bottle. From the bottle he took two large pills and swallowed these.

"Sleep . . . books . . . doesn't want the Transformation . . . Mrs. Cuberle, my *dear* good woman, this is grave. I would appreciate it if you would change psychiatrists. I am very busy and, ah, this is somewhat specialized. I suggest Centraldome. Many fine doctors there. Goodbye."

The doctor turned and sat in a large chair and folded his hands. Mary watched him and wondered why the simple statements should have so changed things. But the doctor did not move from the chair.

"Well!" said Mrs. Cuberle and walked quickly from the room.

Mary considered the reflection in the mirrored wall. She sat on the floor and looked at different angles of herself: profile, full-face, full-length, naked, clothed. Then she took up the magazine and studied it. She sighed.

''Mirror, Mirror on the wall . . .'' The words came haltingly to her mind and from her lips. She hadn't read these, she recalled. Daddy had said them, 'quoted' them as he put it. But they too were lines from a book . . . ''who is the fairest of—''

A picture of Mother sat upon the dresser and Mary considered this now. She looked for a long time at the slender feminine neck, knotted in just the right places. The golden skin, smooth and without blemish, without wrinkles and without age. The dark brown eyes and the thin tapers of eyebrows, the long black lashes. Set evenly, so that the halves of the face corresponded precisely. The half-hearted mouth, a violet tint against the gold, the white, teeth, even, sparkling.

Mother. Beautiful, Transformed Mother. And back again to the mirror.

''—of them all . . .''

The image of a rather chubby young woman, without lines of rhythm or grace, without perfection. Splotchy skin full of little holes, puffs in the cheeks, red eruptions on the forehead. Perspiration, shapeless hair flowing onto shapeless shoulders down a shapeless body. Like all of them, before the Transformation . . .

Did they *all* look like this, before? Did Mother, even?

Mary thought hard, trying to sort out exactly what Daddy and Grandpa had said, why they said the Transformation was a bad thing, and why she believed and agreed with them so strongly. It made little sense, but they were right. They *were* right! And one day, she would understand completely.

Mrs. Cuberle slammed the door angrily and Mary jumped to her feet.

''Honestly, expenses aren't so high that you have to leave all the windows off. I went through the whole level and there isn't a single window left on. Don't you even want to see the people?''

''No. I was thinking.''

''Well, it's got to stop. It's simply got to stop. Mary, what in the world has gotten into you lately?''

"I—"

"The way you upset Doctor Hortel. He won't even see me anymore, and these traumas are getting horrible—*not* to mention the migraines. I'll have to get that awful Doctor Wagoner."

Mrs. Cuberle sat on the couch and crossed her legs carefully.

"And what in the world were you doing on the floor?"

"Trying to sleep."

"You've got to stop talking that way! Why should you want to do such a silly thing?"

"The books—"

"And you mustn't read those terrible things."

"Mother—"

"The Unit is full of Tapes, full! Anything you want!"

Mary stuck out her lower lip. "But I don't want to hear all about wars and colonizations and politics!"

"Now I know where you got this idiotic notion that you don't want the Transformation. Of *course.*"

Mrs. Cuberle rose quickly and took the books from the corner and from the closet and piled her arms with them. She looked everywhere in the room and gathered the old brittle volumes.

These she carried from the room and threw into the elevator. A button guided the doors shut.

"I thought you'd do that," Mary said, slowly, "that's why I hid most of the good ones. Where you'll never find them!" She breathed heavily and her heart thumped.

Mrs. Cuberle put a satin handkerchief to her eyes.

"I don't know what I ever did to deserve this!"

"Deserve *what*, Mother? What am I doing that's so wrong?" Mary's mind rippled in a little confused stream now.

"What?" Mrs. Cuberle wailed, *"What?* Do you think I want people to point at you and say I'm the mother of a mutant?" Her voice softened abruptly into a plea. "Or have you changed your mind, dear?"

"No." *The vague reasons, longing to be put into words.*

"It really doesn't hurt, you know. They just take off a little skin and put some on and give you pills and electronic treatment and things like that. It doesn't take more than a week."

"No." *The reasons.*

"Look at your friend Shala, she's getting her Transformation next month. And *she's* almost pretty now."

"Mother, I don't care—"

"If it's the bones you're worried about, well, that doesn't hurt. They give you a shot and when you wake up, everything's moulded right. Everything, to suit the personality."

"I don't care, I don't care."

"But *why?*"

"I like me the way I am." *Almost, almost exactly. But not quite. Part of it, though; part of what Daddy and Grandpa must have meant.*

Mrs. Cuberle switched on a window and then switched it off again. She sobbed. "But you're so ugly, dear! Like Doctor Hortel said. And Mr. Willmes, at the factory. He told some people he thought you were the ugliest girl he'd ever seen. He says he'll be thankful when you have your Transformation."

"Daddy said I was beautiful."

"Well, really, dear. You *do* have eyes."

"Daddy said that real beauty is more than skin deep. He said a lot of things like that and when I read the books I felt the same way. I guess I don't want to look like everybody else, that's all."

"You'll notice that your father had *his* Transformation, though!"

Mary stamped her foot angrily. "He told me that if he had to do it again he just wouldn't. He said I should be stronger than he was."

"You're not going to get away with this, young lady. After all, I *am* your mother."

A bulb flickered in the bathroom and Mrs. Cuberle walked uncertainly to the cabinet. She took out a little cardboard box.

"It's time for lunch."

Mary nodded. That was another thing the books talked about, which the Tapes did not. Lunch seemed to be something special long ago, or at least different . . . The books talked of strange ways of putting a load of things into the mouth and chewing these things. Enjoying them, somehow. Strange and wonderful . . .

"And you'd better get ready for work."

Mary let the greenish capsule slide down her throat.

"Yes, Mother."

The office was quiet and without shadows. The walls gave off a steady luminescence, distributing the light evenly upon all the desks and tables. It was neither hot nor cold.

Mary held the ruler firmly and allowed the pen to travel down the metal edge effortlessly. The new black lines were small and accurate. She tipped her head, compared the notes beside her to the plan she was working on. She noticed the beautiful people looking at her more furtively than before, and she wondered about this as she made her lines.

A tall man rose from his desk in the rear of the office and walked down the aisle to Mary's table. He surveyed her work, allowing his eyes to travel cautiously from her face to the draft.

Mary looked around.

"Nice job," said the man.

"Thank you, Mr. Willmes."

"Dralich shouldn't have anything to complain about. That crane should hold the whole damn city."

"It's very good alloy, sir."

"Yeah. Say, kid, you got a minute?"

"Yes, sir."

"Let's go into Mullinson's office."

The big handsome man led the way into a small cubbyhole of a room. He motioned to a chair and sat on the edge of one desk.

"Kid, I never was one to beat around the bush. Somebody

called in a little while ago, gave me some crazy story about you not wanting your Transformation."

Mary looked away, then quickly back into the man's eyes. "It's not a crazy story, Mr. Willmes," she said. "It's true. I want to stay this way."

The man stared, then coughed embarrassedly.

"What the hell—excuse me, kid, but—I don't exactly get it. You ain't a mutant, I know that. And you ain't—"

"Insane? No; Doctor Hortel can tell you."

The man laughed, nervously. "Well . . . Look, you're still a cub, but you do swell work. Lots of good results, lots of comments from the stations. But Mr. Poole won't like it."

"I know. I know what you mean, Mr. Willmes. But nothing can change my mind."

"You'll get old before you're half through life!"

Yes, she would. Old, like the Elders, wrinkled and brittle, unable to move correctly. Old.

"It's hard to make you understand. But I don't see why it should make any difference, as long as I do my work."

"Now don't go getting me wrong, kid. It ain't me. But you know, I don't run Interplan. I just work here. Mr. Poole, he likes things running smooth and it's my job to carry it out. And as soon as everybody finds out, things wouldn't run smooth. There'll be a big to-do, y'understand? The dames will start asking questions and talk. Be the same as a mutant in the office—no offense."

"Will you accept my resignation, then, Mr. Willmes?"

"Sure you won't change your mind?"

"No, sir. I decided that a long time ago."

"Well, then, I'm sorry, Mary. Couple ten, twenty years you could be centraled on one of the asteroids, the way you been working out. But . . . if you should change your mind, there'll always be a job for you here. Otherwise, you got till March. And between you and me, I hope by then you've decided the other way."

Mary walked back down the aisle, past the rows of desks. Past the men and women. The handsome model men and the beautiful, perfect women, perfect, all perfect, all looking alike. Looking exactly alike.

She sat down again and took up her ruler and pen.

Mary stepped into the elevator and descended several hundred feet. At the Second Level she pressed a button and the elevator stopped. The doors opened with another button and the doors to her Unit with still another.

Mrs. Cuberle sat on the floor by the TV, disconsolate and red-eyed. Her blonde hair had come slightly askew and a few strands hung over her forehead.

"You don't need to tell me. No one will hire you."

Mary sat down beside her mother.

"If only you hadn't told Mr. Willmes in the first place—"

"Well, I thought *he* could beat a little sense into you."

The sounds from the TV grew louder. Mrs. Cuberle changed channels a number of times and finally turned it off.

"What did you do today, Mother?" Mary smiled, hopefully.

"What *can* I do now? Nobody will even come over! Everyone thinks you're a mutant."

"*Mother!*"

"They say you should be in the Circuses."

Mary went into another room. Mrs. Cuberle followed, wringing her hands, and crying: "Mutant, mutant! How are we going to live? Where does the money come from now? Next thing they'll be firing *me!*"

"No one would do that."

"Nobody else on this planet has ever refused the Transformation. The mutants all wish they could have it. And you, given everything, you turn it down. You *want* to be ugly!"

Mary put her arms about her mother's shoulders.

"I wish I could explain; I've tried so hard to. It isn't that I want to bother anyone, or that Daddy or Grandpa wanted me to."

Mrs. Cuberle reached into the pocket of her jerkin and retrieved a purple pill. She swallowed the pill.

When the letter dropped from the chute, Mrs. Cuberle ran to snatch it up. She read it once silently, then smiled.

"Oh," she said, "I was so afraid they wouldn't answer. But we'll see about this *now!*"

She gave the letter to Mary, who read:

Mrs. Zena Cuberle
Unit 451-D
Levels II & III
City

Dear Madam:
   In re your letter of Dec. 3 36. We have carefully examined your complaint and consider that it requires stringent measures of some sort. Quite frankly, the possibility of such a complaint has never occurred to this Dept. and we therefore cannot issue positive directives at this present moment.

   However, due to the unusual qualities of the matter, we have arranged an audience at Centraldome 8th Level 16th Unit, Jan 3 37, 23 sharp. Dr. Hortel has been instructed to attend. You will bring the subject in question.

Yrs,
DEPT. F

Mary let the paper flutter to the floor. She walked quietly to the elevator and set it for Level III. When the elevator stopped, she ran from it, crying, into her room.

She thought and remembered and tried to sort out and put together. Daddy had said it, Grandpa had, the books did. Yes. The books did.

She read until her eyes burned and her eyes burned until she could read no more. Then Mary went to sleep, softly and without realizing it.

But the sleep was not a peaceful one.

"Ladies and gentlemen," said the young-looking, classic-featured man, "this problem does not resolve easily. Doctor

Hortel, here, testifies that Mary Cuberle is definitely not insane, Doctors Monagh, Prynn and Fedders all verify this judgement. Doctor Prynn asserts that the human organism is no longer so constructed as to create and sustain such an attitude as deliberate falsehood. Further, there is positively nothing in the structure of Mary Cuberle which might suggest difficulties in Transformation. There is qualified evidence for all these statements. And yet—'' the man sighed ''—while the Newstapes, the Foto services, while every news-carrying agency has circulated this problem throughout the universe, we are faced with this refusal. Further, the notoriety has become excessive to the point of vulgarity and has resultantly caused numerous persons, among them Mrs. Zena Cuberle, the child's mother, grievous emotional stress. What, may I ask, is to be done therefore?''

Mary looked at a metal table.

''We have been in session far too long, holding up far too many other pressing contingencies of a serious nature.''

Throughout the rows of beautiful people, the mumbling increased. Mrs. Cuberle sat nervously tapping her foot and running a comb through her hair.

''The world waits,'' continued the man. ''Mary Cuberle, you have been given innumerable chances to reconsider, you know.''

Mary said, ''I know. But I don't want to.''

The beautiful people looked at Mary and laughed. Some shook their heads.

The man in the robes threw up his hands.

''Little girl, can you realize what an issue you have caused? The unrest, the wasted time? Do you fully understand what you have done? We could send you to a Mutant Colony, I suppose you know . . .''

''How could you do that?'' inquired Mary.

''Well, I'm sure we could—it's a petty point. Intergalactic questions hang fire while you sit there saying the same thing over and over. And in judicial procedure I dare say there is some clause which forbids that. Come now, doesn't the happiness of your dear mother mean anything to you? Or your duty to the State, to the entire Solar System?''

A slender, supple woman in a back row stood and cried, loudly: ''*Do* something!''

The man on the high stool raised his arm.

''None of that, now. We must conform, even though the problem is out of the ordinary.''

The woman sat down, snorted; the man turned again to Mary.

''Child, I have here a petition, signed by two thousand individuals and representing all the Stations of the Earth. They have been made aware of all the facts and have submitted the petition voluntarily. It's all so unusual and I'd hoped we wouldn't have to—but, well, the petition urges drastic measures.''

The mumbling rose.

''The petition urges that you shall, upon final refusal, be forced by law to accept the Transformation. And that an act of legislature shall make this universal and binding in the future.''

Mary's eyes were open, wide; she stood and paused before speaking.

''*Why?*'' she asked.

The man in the robes passed a hand through his hair.

Another voice from the crowd: ''Sign the petition, Senator!''

All the voices: ''Sign it! Sign it!''

''But *why?*'' Mary began to cry. The voices stilled for a moment.

''Because—Because—What if others should get the same idea? What would happen to us then, little girl? We'd be right back to the ugly, thin, fat, unhealthy-looking race we were ages ago! There can't be any exceptions.''

''Maybe they didn't consider themselves so ugly!''

The mumbling began anew and broke into a wild clamour.

''That isn't the point,'' cried the man in the robes, ''you *must* conform!''

And the voices cried: "Yes!" loudly until the man took up a pen and signed the papers on his desk.

Cheers; applause; shouts.

Mrs. Cuberle patted Mary on the top of her head.

"There now!" she said happily, "everything will be all right now. You'll see, Mary, dear."

The Transformation Parlor covered the entire Level, sprawling with its department. It was always filled and there was nothing to sign and no money to pay and people were always waiting in line.

But today the people stood aside. And there were still more, looking in through doors, TV cameras placed throughout and Tape machines in every corner. It was filled, but not bustling as usual.

The Transformation Parlor was terribly quiet.

Mary walked past the people, Mother and the men in back of her, following. She looked at the people, too, as she did in her room through turned-on windows. It was no different. The people were beautiful, perfect, without a single flaw. Except the young ones, young like herself, seated on couches, looking embarrassed and ashamed and eager.

But, of course, the young ones did not count.

All the beautiful people. All the ugly people, staring out from bodies that were not theirs. Walking on legs that had been made for them, laughing with manufactured voices, gesturing with shaped and fashioned arms.

Mary walked slowly despite the prodding. In her eyes, in *her* eyes, was a mounting confusion; a wide, wide wonderment.

She looked down at her own body, then at the walls which reflected it. Flesh of her flesh, bone of her bone, all hers, made by no person, built by herself or Someone she did not know . . . Uneven kneecaps making two grinning cherubs when they straightened, and the old familiar rubbing together of fat inner thighs. Fat, unshapely, unsystematic Mary. But *Mary*.

Of course. Of course! This *was* what Daddy meant, what

Grandpa and the books meant. What *they* would know if they would read the books or hear the words, the good, unreasonable words, the words that signified more, so much more, than any of this . . .

"Where *are* these people?" Mary said, half to herself. "What has happened to *them* and don't they miss *themselves*, these manufactured things?"

She stopped, suddenly.

"Yes! That *is* the reason. They have all forgotten themselves!"

A curvacious woman stepped forward and took Mary's hand. The woman's skin was tinted dark. Chipped and sculptured bone into slender rhythmic lines, electrically created carriage, made, turned out . . .

"All right, young lady. Shall we begin?"

They guided Mary to a large, curved leather seat.

From the top of a long silver pole a machine lowered itself. Tiny bulbs glowed to life and cells began to click. The people stared. Slowly a picture formed upon the screen in the machine. Bulbs directed at Mary, then re-directed into themselves. Wheels turning, buttons ticking.

The picture was completed.

"Would you like to see it?"

Mary closed her eyes, tight.

"It's really very nice." The woman turned to the crowd. "Oh yes, there's a great deal to be salvaged; you'd be surprised. A great deal. We'll keep the nose and I don't believe the elbows will have to be altered at all."

Mrs. Cuberle looked at Mary and grinned.

"Now, it isn't so bad as you thought, is it?" she said.

The beautiful people looked. Cameras turned. Tapes wound.

"You'll have to excuse us now. Only the machines allowed."

Only the machines.

The people filed out, grumbling.

Mary saw the rooms in the mirror. Saw things in the

rooms, the faces and bodies that had left, the woman and the machines and the old young men standing about, adjusting, readying.

Then she looked at the picture in the screen.

A woman of medium height stared back at her. A woman with a curved body and thin legs; silver hair, pompadoured, cut short; full sensuous lips, small breasts, flat stomach, unblemished skin.

A strange woman no one had ever seen before.

The nurse began to take off Mary's clothes.

"Geoff," the woman said, "come look at this, will you. Not one so bad in years. Amazing that we can keep anything at all."

The handsome man put his hands into his pockets, and clucked his tongue.

"Pretty bad, all right."

"Be still, child, stop, stop making those noises. You know perfectly well nothing is going to hurt."

"But what will you do with me?"

"That was all explained to you."

"No, no—with *me, me!*"

"You mean the cast-offs? The usual. I don't know, exactly. Somebody takes care of it."

"I want me!" Mary cried. "Not that!" She pointed at the image in the screen.

Her chair was wheeled into a semi-dark room. She was naked now, and the men lifted her to a table. The surface was like glass, black filmed. A big machine hung above in shadows.

Straps. Clamps pulling, stretching limbs apart. The screen with the picture brought in. The men and the women, more women now. Doctor Hortel in a corner, sitting with his legs crossed, shaking his head.

Mary began to cry loudly, as hard as she could, above the hum of the mechanical things.

"Shhh. My gracious, such a racket! Just think about your

job waiting for you, and all the friends you'll have and how lovely everything will be. No more troubles now.''

The big machine groaned and descended from the darkness.

''Where will I find me?'' Mary screamed. ''What will happen to *me*?''

A long needle slid into rough flesh and the beautiful people gathered around the table.

And then they turned on the big machine.

Long Distance Call

Richard Matheson

TELEPLAY BY RICHARD MATHESON

AIRED FEBRUARY 7, 1964, AS "NIGHT CALL"

STARRING GLADYS COOPER

JUST BEFORE THE TELEPHONE RANG, STORM WINDS toppled the tree outside her window and jolted Miss Keene from her dreaming sleep. She flung herself up with a gasp, her frail hands crumpling twists of sheet in either palm. Beneath her fleshless chest the heart jerked taut, the sluggish blood spurted. She sat in rigid muteness, her eyes staring at the night.

In another second, the telephone rang.

Who on earth? The question shaped unwittingly in her brain. Her thin hand faltered in the darkness, the fingers searching a moment, and then Miss Elva Keene drew the cool receiver to her ear.

"Hello," she said.

Outside a cannon of thunder shook the night, twitching Miss Keene's crippled legs. *I've missed the voice*, she thought, *the thunder has blotted out the voice*.

"Hello," she said again.

There was no sound. Miss Keene waited in expectant lethargy. Then she repeated. "Hel-*lo*," in a cracking voice. Outside the thunder crashed again.

Still no voice spoke, not even the sound of a phone being disconnected met her ears. Her wavering hand reached out and thumped down the receiver with an angry motion.

"Inconsideration," she muttered, thudding back on her pillow. Already her infirm back ached from the effort of sitting.

She forced out a weary breath. Now she'd have to suffer through the whole tormenting process of going to sleep again—the composing of jaded muscles, the ignoring of abrasive pain in her legs, the endless, frustrating struggle to turn off the faucet in her brain and keep unwanted thoughts from dripping. Oh, well, it had to be done; Nurse Phillips insisted on proper rest. Elva Keene breathed slowly and deeply, drew the covers to her chin and labored hopefully for sleep.

In vain.

Her eyes opened and, turning her face to the window, she watched the storm move off on lightning legs. *Why can't I sleep*, she fretted, *why must I always lie here awake like this?*

She knew the answer without effort. When a life was dull, the smallest element added seemed unnaturally intriguing. And life for Miss Keene was the sorry pattern of lying flat or being propped on pillows, reading books which Nurse Phillips brought from the town library, getting nourishment, rest, medication, listening to her tiny radio—and waiting, *waiting* for something different to happen.

Like the telephone call that wasn't a call.

There hadn't even been the sound of a receiver replaced in its cradle. Miss Keene didn't understand that. Why would anyone call her exchange and then listen silently while she said, "Hello," over and over again? *Had* it actually been anyone calling?

What she should have done, she realized then, was to keep listening until the other person tired of the joke and put down the receiver. What she should have done was to speak out forcefully about the inconsideration of a prankish call to a crippled maiden lady, in the middle of a stormy night. Then,

if there *had* been someone listening, whoever it was woul
have been properly chastened by her angry words and . .

"Well, of course."

She said it aloud in the darkness, punctuating the sentenc
with a cluck of somewhat relieved disgust. Of course, th
telephone was out of order. Someone had tried to contac
her, perhaps Nurse Phillips to see if she was all right. But th
other end of the line had broken down in some way, allowin;
her phone to ring but no verbal communication to be made
Well, of course, that was the case.

Miss Keene nodded once and closed her eyes gently. *Not.
to sleep*, she thought. Far away, beyond the county, the storn
cleared its murky throat. *I hope no one is worrying*, Elva Keen(
thought, *that would be too bad.*

She was thinking that when the telephone rang again.

There, she thought, *they are trying to reach me again.* She
reached out hurriedly in the darkness, fumbled until she fel
the receiver, then pulled it to her ear.

"Hello," said Miss Keene.

Silence.

Her throat contracted. She knew what was wrong, of
course, but she didn't like it, no, not at all.

"Hello?" she said tentatively, not yet certain that she was
wasting breath.

There was no reply. She waited a moment, then spoke a
third time, a little impatiently now, loudly, her shrill voice
ringing in the dark bedroom. *"Hello!"*

Nothing. Miss Keene had the sudden urge to fling the receiver away. She forced down that curious instinct—no, she
must wait; wait and listen to hear if anyone hung up the
phone on the other end of the line.

So she waited.

The bedroom was very quiet now, but Elva Keene kept
straining to hear; either the sound of a receiver going down
or the buzz which usually follows. Her chest rose and fell in
delicate lurches, she closed her eyes in concentration, then
opened them again and blinked at the darkness. There was

no sound from the telephone; not a click, not a buzz, not a sound of someone putting down a receiver.

"Hello!" she cried suddenly, then pushed away the receiver.

She missed her target. The receiver dropped and thumped once on the rug. Miss Keene nervously clicked on the lamp, wincing as the leprous bulb light filled her eyes. Quickly, she lay on her side and tried to reach the silent, voiceless telephone.

But she couldn't stretch far enough and crippled legs prevented her from rising. Her throat tightened. My God, must she leave it there all night, silent and mystifying?

Remembering then, she reached out abruptly and pressed the cradle arm. On the floor, the receiver clicked, then began to buzz normally. Elva Keene swallowed and drew in a shaking breath as she slumped back on her pillow.

She threw out hooks of reason then and pulled herself back from panic. *This is ridiculous*, she thought, *getting upset over such a trivial and easily explained incident. It was the storm, the night, the way in which I'd been shocked from sleep. (What was it that had awakened me?) All these things piled on the mountain of teeth-grinding monotony that's my life. Yes, it was bad, very bad.* But it wasn't the incident that was bad. It was her reaction to it.

Miss Elva Keene numbed herself to further premonitions. *I shall sleep now*, she ordered her body with a petulant shake. She lay very still and relaxed. From the floor she could hear the telephone buzzing like the drone of far-off bees. She ignored it.

Early the next morning, after Nurse Phillips had taken away the breakfast dishes, Elva Keene called the telephone company.

"This is Miss Elva," she told the operator.

"Oh, yes, Miss Elva," said the operator, a Miss Finch. "Can I help you?"

"Last night my telephone rang twice," said Elva Keene.

''But when I answered it, no one spoke. And I didn't hear any receiver drop. I didn't even hear a dial tone—just silence.''

''Well, I'll tell you, Miss Elva,'' said the cheery voice of Miss Finch, ''that storm last night just about ruined half our service. We're being flooded with calls about knocked-down lines and bad connections. I'd say you're pretty lucky your phone is working at all.''

''Then you think it was probably a bad connection,'' prompted Miss Keene, ''caused by the storm?''

''Oh, yes, Miss Elva, that's all.''

''Do you think it will happen again?''

''Oh, it *may*,'' said Miss Finch. ''It *may*. I really couldn't tell you, Miss Elva. But if it does happen again, you just call me and then I'll have one of our men check on it.''

''All right,'' said Miss Elva. ''Thank you, dear.''

She lay on her pillows all morning in a relaxed torpor. *It gives one a satisfied feeling*, she thought, *to solve a mystery, slight as it is. It had been a terrible storm that caused the bad connection. And no wonder when it had even knocked down the ancient oak tree beside the house. That was the noise that had awakened me of course, and a pity it was that the dear tree had fallen. How it shaded the house in hot summer months. Oh, well, I suppose I should be grateful*, she thought, *that the tree fell across the road and not across the house.*

The day passed uneventfully, an amalgam of eating, reading Angela Thirkell and the mail (two throw-away advertisements and the light bill), plus brief chats with Nurse Phillips. Indeed, routine had set in so properly that when the telephone rang early that evening, she picked it up without even thinking.

''Hello,'' she said.

Silence.

It brought her back for a second. Then she called Nurse Phillips.

''What is it?'' asked the portly woman as she trudged across the bedroom rug.

"This is what I was telling you about," said Elva Keene, holding out the receiver. "Listen!"

Nurse Phillips took the receiver in her hand and pushed back gray locks with the earpiece. Her placid face remained placid. "There's nobody there," she observed.

"That's right," said Miss Keene. "That's right. Now you just listen and see if you can hear a receiver being put down. I'm sure you won't."

Nurse Phillips listened for a moment, then shook her head. "I don't hear anything," she said and hung up.

"Oh, wait!" Miss Keene said hurriedly. "Oh, well, it doesn't matter," she added, seeing it was already down. "If it happens too often, I'll just call Miss Finch and they'll have a repairman check on it."

"I see," Nurse Phillips said, and went back to the living room and Faith Baldwin.

Nurse Phillips left the house at eight, leaving on the bedside table, as usual, an apple, a cookie, a glass of water and the bottle of pills. She puffed up the pillows behind Miss Keene's fragile back, moved the radio and telephone a little closer to the bed, looked around complacently, then turned for the door, saying, "I'll see you tomorrow."

It was fifteen minutes later when the telephone rang. Miss Keene picked up the receiver quickly. She didn't bother saying hello this time—she just listened.

At first it was the same—an absolute silence. She listened a moment more, impatiently. Then, on the verge of replacing the receiver, she heard the sound. Her cheek twitched, she jerked the telephone back to her ear.

"Hello?" she asked tensely.

A murmuring, a dull humming, a rustling sound—what was it? Miss Keene shut her eyes tightly, listening hard, but she couldn't identify the sound; it was too soft, too undefined. It deviated from a sort of whining vibration . . . to an escape of air . . . to a bubbling sibilance. *It must be the sound of the connection*, she thought, *it must be the telephone itself making the noise. Perhaps a wire blowing in the wind somewhere, perhaps . . .*

She stopped thinking then. She stopped breathing. The sound had ceased. Once more, silence rang in her ears. She could feel the heartbeats stumbling in her chest again, the walls of her throat closing in. *Oh, this is ridiculous,* she told herself. *I've already been through this—it was the storm, the storm!*

She lay back on her pillows, the receiver pressed to her ear, nervous breaths faltering from her nostrils. She could feel unreasoning dread rise like a tide within her, despite all attempts at sane deduction. Her mind kept slipping off the glassy perch of reason; she kept falling deeper and deeper.

Now she shuddered violently as the sounds began again. They couldn't *possibly* be human sounds, she knew, and yet there was something about them, some inflection, some almost identifiable arrangement of . . .

Her lips shook and a whine began to hover in her throat. But she couldn't put down the telephone, she simply couldn't. The sounds held her hypnotized. Whether they were the rise and fall of the wind or the muttering of faulty mechanisms, she didn't know, but they would not let her go.

"Hello?" she murmured, shakily.

The sounds rose in volume. They rattled and shook in her brain.

"Hello!" she screamed.

"H-e-l-l-o," answered a voice on the telephone. Then Miss Keene fainted dead away.

"Are you certain it was someone saying *hello?*" Miss Finch asked Miss Elva over the telephone. "It might have been the connection, you know."

"I tell you it was a *man!*" a shaking Elva Keene screeched. "It was the same man who kept listening to me say hello over and over and over again without answering me back. The same one who made terrible noises over the telephone!"

Miss Finch cleared her throat politely. "Well, I'll have a

man check your line, Miss Elva, as soon as he can. Of course, the men are very busy now with all the repairs on storm wreckage, but as soon as it's possible . . ."

"And what am I going to do if this—this *person* calls again?"

"You just hang up on him, Miss Elva."

"But he keeps calling!"

"Well." Miss Finch's affability wavered. "Why don't you find out who he is, Miss Elva? If you can do that, why, we can take immediate action, you see, and . . ."

After she'd hung up, Miss Keene lay against the pillows tensely, listening to Nurse Phillips sing husky love songs over the breakfast dishes. Miss Finch didn't believe her story, that was apparent. Miss Finch thought she was a nervous old woman falling prey to imagination. Well, Miss Finch would find out differently.

"I'll just keep calling her and calling her until she *does*," she said irritably to Nurse Phillips just before afternoon nap.

"You just do that," said Nurse Phillips. "Now take your pill and lie down."

Miss Keene lay in grumpy silence, her vein-rutted hands knotted at her sides. It was ten after two and, except for the bubbling of Nurse Phillip's front room snores, the house was silent in the October afternoon. *It makes me angry*, thought Elva Keene, *that no one will take this seriously. Well*—her thin lips pressed together—*the next time the telephone rings I'll make sure that Nurse Phillips listens until she does hear something.*

Exactly then the phone rang.

Miss Keene felt a cold tremor lace down her body. Even in the daylight with sunbeams speckling her flowered coverlet, the strident ringing frightened her. She dug porcelain teeth into her lower lip to steady it. *Shall I answer it?* the question came and then, before she could even think to answer, her hand picked up the receiver. A deep ragged breath; she drew the phone slowly to her ear. She said, "Hello?"

The voice answered back, "Hello?"—hollow and inanimate.

"Who is this?" Miss Keene asked, trying to keep her throat clear.

"Hello?"

"Who's calling, please?"

"Hello?"

"Is anyone there!"

"Hello?"

"*Please . . . !*"

"Hello?"

Miss Keene jammed down the receiver and lay on her bed trembling violently, unable to catch her breath. *What is it,* begged her mind, *what in God's name is it?*

"Margaret!" she cried. "*Margaret!*"

In the front room she heard Nurse Phillips grunt abruptly and then start coughing.

"Margaret, please . . . !"

Elva Keene heard the large-bodied woman rise to her feet and trudge across the living room floor. *I must compose myself,* she told herself, fluttering hands to her fevered cheeks. *I must tell her exactly what happened, exactly.*

"What is it?" grumbled the nurse. "Does your stomach ache?"

Miss Keene's throat drew in tautly as she swallowed. "He just called again," she whispered.

"Who?"

"That man!"

"What man?"

"The one who keeps calling!" Miss Keene cried. "He keeps saying hello over and over again. That's all he says— hello, hello, hel . . ."

"Now stop this," Nurse Phillips scolded stolidly. "Lie back and . . ."

"I don't *want* to lie back!" she said frenziedly. "I want to know who this terrible person is who keeps frightening me!"

"Now don't work yourself into a state," warned Nurse Phillips. "You know how upset your stomach gets."

Miss Keene began to sob bitterly. ''I'm afraid. I'm afraid of him. Why does he keep calling me?''

Nurse Phillips stood by the bed looking down in bovine inertia. ''Now, what did Miss Finch tell you?'' she said softly.

Miss Keene's shaking lips could not frame the answer.

''Did she tell you it was the connection?'' the nurse soothed. ''Did she?''

''But it isn't! It's a man, a *man!*''

Nurse Phillips expelled a patient breath. ''If it's a man,'' she said, ''then just hang up. You don't have to talk to him. Just hang up. Is that so hard to do?''

Miss Keene shut tear-bright eyes and forced her lips into a twitching line. In her mind the man's subdued and listless voice kept echoing. Over and over, the inflection never altering, the question never deferring to her replies—just repeating itself endlessly in doleful apathy. *Hello? Hello?* Making her shudder to the heart.

''Look,'' Nurse Phillips spoke.

She opened her eyes and saw the blurred image of the nurse putting the receiver down on the table.

''There,'' Nurse Phillips said, ''nobody can call you now. You leave it that way. If you need anything all you have to do is dial. Now isn't that all right? Isn't it?''

Miss Keene looked bleakly at her nurse. Then, after a moment, she nodded once. Grudgingly.

She lay in the dark bedroom, the sound of the dial tone humming in her ear; keeping her awake. *Or am I just telling myself that?* she thought. *Is it really keeping me awake? Didn't I sleep that first night with the receiver off the hook? No, it wasn't the sound, it was something else.*

She closed her eyes obdurately. *I won't listen*, she told herself, *I just won't listen to it.* She drew in trembling breaths of the night. But the darkness would not fill her brain and blot away the sound.

Miss Keene felt around on the bed until she found her bed

jacket. She draped it over the receiver, swathing its black smoothness in woolly turns. Then she sank back again, stern breathed and taut. *I will sleep,* she demanded, *I will sleep.*

She heard it still.

Her body grew rigid and, abruptly, she unfolded the receiver from its thick wrappings and slammed it down angrily on the cradle. Silence filled the room with delicious peace. Miss Keene fell back on the pillow with a feeble groan. *Now to sleep,* she thought.

And the telephone rang.

Her breath snuffed off. The ringing seemed to permeate the darkness, surrounding her in a cloud of ear-lancing vibration. She reached out to put the receiver on the table again, then jerked her hand back with a gasp, realizing she would hear the man's voice again.

Her throat pulsed nervously. *What I'll do,* she planned, *what I'll do is take off the receiver very quickly—very quickly—and put it down, then push down on the arm and cut off the line. Yes, that's what I'll do!*

She tensed herself and spread her hand out cautiously until the ringing phone was under it. Then, breath held, she followed her plan, slashed off the ring, reached quickly for the cradle arm . . .

And stopped, frozen, as the man's voice reached out through darkness to her ears. "Where are you?" he asked. "I want to talk to you."

Claws of ice clamped down on Miss Keene's shuddering chest. She lay petrified, unable to cut off the sound of the man's dull, expressionless voice, asking, "Where are you? I want to talk to you."

A sound from Miss Keene's throat, thin and fluttering.

And the man said, "Where are you? I want to talk to you."

"No, no," sobbed Miss Keene.

"Where are you? I want to . . ."

She pressed the cradle arm with taut white fingers. She held it down for fifteen minutes before letting it go.

* * *

"I tell you I won't have it!"

Miss Keene's voice was a frayed ribbon of sound. She sat inflexibly on the bed, straining her frightened anger through the mouthpiece vents.

"You say you hang up on this man and he still calls?" Miss Finch inquired.

"I've *explained* all that!" Elva Keene burst out. "I had to leave the receiver off the phone all night so he wouldn't call. And the buzzing kept me awake. I didn't get a *wink* of sleep! Now, I want this line checked, do you hear me? I want you to stop this terrible thing!"

Her eyes were like hard, dark beads. The phone almost slipped from her palsied fingers.

"All right, Miss Elva," said the operator. "I'll send a man out today."

"Thank you, dear, thank you," Miss Keene said. "Will you call me when . . ."

Her voice stopped abruptly as a clicking sound started on the telephone.

"The line is busy," she announced.

The clicking stopped and she went on. "To repeat, will you let me know when you find out who this terrible person is?"

"Surely, Miss Elva, surely. And I'll have a man check your telephone this afternoon. You're at 127 Mill Lane, aren't you?"

"That's right, dear. You will see to it, won't you?"

"I promise faithfully, Miss Elva. First thing today."

"Thank you, dear," Miss Keene said, drawing in relieved breath.

There were no calls from the man all that morning, none that afternoon. Her tightness slowly began to loosen. She played a game of cribbage with Nurse Phillips and even managed a little laughter. It was comforting to know that the telephone company was working on it now. They'd soon catch that awful man and bring back her peace of mind.

But when two o'clock came, then three o'clock—and still

no repairman at her house—Miss Keene began worrying again.

"What's the *matter* with that girl?" she said pettishly. "She promised me faithfully that a man would come this afternoon."

"He'll be here," Nurse Phillips said. "Be patient."

Four o'clock arrived and no man. Miss Keene would not play cribbage, read her book or listen to her radio. What had begun to loosen was tightening again, increasing minute by minute until at five o'clock, when the telephone rang, her hand spurted out rigidly from the flaring sleeve of her bed jacket and clamped down like a claw on the receiver. *If the man speaks,* raced her mind, *if he speaks I'll scream until my heart stops.*

She pulled the receiver to her ear. "Hello?"

"Miss Elva, this is Miss Finch."

Her eyes closed and breath fluttered through her lips. "Yes?" she said.

"About those calls you say you've been receiving."

"Yes?" In her mind, Miss Finch's words cutting—"those calls you *say* you've been receiving."

"We sent a man out to trace them," continued Miss Finch. "I have his report here."

Miss Keene caught her breath. "Yes?"

"He couldn't find anything."

Elva Keene didn't speak. Her gray head lay motionless on the pillow, the receiver pressed to her ear.

"He says he traced the—the difficulty to a fallen wire on the edge of town."

"Fallen—wire?"

"Yes, Miss Elva." Miss Finch did not sound happy.

"You're telling me I didn't hear anything?"

Miss Finch's voice was firm. "There's no way anyone could have phoned you from that location," she said.

"I tell you a *man* called me!"

Miss Finch was silent and Miss Keene's fingers tightened convulsively on the receiver.

"There must be a phone there," she insisted. "There must be *some* way that man was able to call me."

"Miss Elva, the wire is lying on the ground." She paused. "Tomorrow, our crew will put it back up and you won't be . . ."

"There *has* to be a way he could call me!"

"Miss Elva, there's no one out there."

"Out where, *where*?"

The operator said, "Miss Elva, it's the cemetery."

In the black silence of her bedroom, a crippled maiden lady lay waiting. Her nurse would not remain for the night; her nurse had patted her and scolded her and ignored her.

She was waiting for a telephone call.

She could have disconnected the phone, but she had not the will. She lay there waiting, waiting, thinking.

Of the silence—of ears that had not heard, seeking to hear again. Of sounds bubbling and muttering—the first stumbling attempts at speech by one who had not spoken—how long? Of—*hello? hello?*—first greeting by one long silent. Of—*where are you?* Of (that which made her lie so rigidly) the clicking and the operator speaking her address. Of—

The telephone ringing.

A pause. Ringing. The rustle of a nightgown in the dark.

The ringing stopped.

Listening.

And the telephone slipping from white fingers, the eyes staring, the thin heartbeats slowly pulsing.

Outside, the cricket-rattling night.

Inside, the words still sounding in her brain—giving terrible meaning to the heavy, choking silence.

"Hello, Miss Elva. I'll be right over."

An Occurrence at Owl Creek Bridge

Ambrose Bierce

TELEPLAY BY ROBERT ENRICO

AIRED FEBRUARY 28, 1964

STARRING ROGER JACQUET

A MAN STOOD UPON A RAILROAD BRIDGE IN NORTH-
ern Alabama, looking down into the swift water twenty feet
below. The man's hands were behind his back, the wrists
bound with a cord. A rope closely encircled his neck. It was
attached to a stout cross-timber above his head and the slack
fell to the level of his knees. Some loose boards laid upon the
sleepers supporting the metals of the railway supplied a footing for him and his executioners—two private soldiers of the
Federal army, directed by a sergeant who in civil life may
have been a deputy sheriff. At a short remove upon the same
temporary platform was an officer in the uniform of his rank,
armed. He was a captain. A sentinel at each end of the bridge
stood with his rifle in the position known as ''support,'' that
is to say, vertical in front of the left shoulder, the hammer
resting on the forearm thrown straight across the chest—a
formal and unnatural position, enforcing an erect carriage of
the body. It did not appear to be the duty of these two men to
know what was occurring at the center of the bridge; they

merely blockaded the two ends of the foot planking that traversed it.

Beyond one of the sentinels nobody was in sight; the railroad ran straight away into a forest for a hundred yards, then curving, was lost to view. Doubtless there was an outpost farther along. The other bank of the stream was open ground —a gentle acclivity topped with a stockade of vertical tree trunks, loopholed for rifles, with a single embrasure through which protruded the muzzle of a brass cannon commanding the bridge. Midway on the slope between bridge and fort were the spectators—a single company of infantry in line, at "parade rest," the butts of the rifles on the ground, the barrels inclining slightly backward against the right shoulder, the hands crossed upon the stock. A lieutenant stood at the right of the line, the point of his sword upon the ground, his left hand resting upon his right. Excepting the group of four at the center of the bridge, not a man moved. The company faced the bridge, staring stonily, motionless. The sentinels, facing the banks of the stream, might have been statues to adorn the bridge. The captain stood with folded arms, silent, observing the work of his subordinates, but making no sign. Death is a dignitary who when he comes announced is to be received with formal manifestations of respect, even by those most familiar with him. In the code of military etiquette silence and fixity are forms of deference.

The man who was engaged in being hanged was apparently about thirty-five years of age. He was a civilian, if one might judge from his habit, which was that of a planter. His features were good—a straight nose, firm mouth, broad forehead, from which his long, dark hair was combed straight back, falling behind his ears to the collar of his well-fitting frock coat. He wore a mustache and pointed beard, but no whiskers; his eyes were large and dark gray, and had a kindly expression which one would hardly have expected in one whose neck was in the hemp. Evidently this was no vulgar assassin. The liberal military code makes provision for hanging many kinds of persons, and gentlemen are not excluded.

The preparations being complete, the two private soldiers stepped aside and each drew away the plank upon which he had been standing. The sergeant turned to the captain, saluted and placed himself immediately behind that officer, who in turn moved apart one pace. These movements left the condemned man and the sergeant standing on the two ends of the same plank, which spanned three of the crossties of the bridge. The end upon which the civilian stood almost, but not quite, reached a fourth. This plank had been held in place by the weight of the captain; it was now held by that of the sergeant. At a signal from the former the latter would step aside, the plank would tilt and the condemned man go down between two ties. The arrangement commended itself to his judgment as simple and effective. His face had not been covered nor his eyes bandaged. He looked a moment at his "unsteadfast footing," then let his gaze wander to the swirling water of the stream racing madly beneath his feet. A piece of dancing driftwood caught his attention and his eyes followed it down the current. How slowly it appeared to move! What a sluggish stream!

He closed his eyes in order to fix his last thoughts upon his wife and children. The water, touched to gold by the early sun, the brooding mists under the banks at some distance down the stream, the fort, the soldiers, the piece of drift—all had distracted him. And now he became conscious of a new disturbance. Striking through the thought of his dear ones was a sound which he could neither ignore nor understand, a sharp, distinct, metallic percussion like the stroke of a blacksmith's hammer upon the anvil; it had the same ringing quality. He wondered what it was, and whether immeasurably distant or nearby—it seemed both. Its recurrence was regular, but as slow as the tolling of a death knell. He awaited each stroke with impatience and—he knew not why—apprehension. The intervals of silence grew progressively longer; the delays became maddening. With their great infrequency the sounds increased in strength and sharpness. They hurt his ear like the thrust of a knife; he feared he would shriek. What he heard was the ticking of his watch.

He unclosed his eyes and saw again the water below him. "If I could free my hands," he thought, "I might throw off the noose and spring into the stream. By diving I could evade the bullets and, swimming vigorously, reach the bank, take to the woods and get away home. My home, thank God, is as yet outside their lines; my wife and little ones are still beyond the invader's farthest advance."

As these thoughts, which have here to be set down in words, were flashed into the doomed man's brain rather than evolved from it, the captain nodded to the sergeant. The sergeant stepped aside.

II

Peyton Farquhar was a well-to-do planter, of an old and highly respected Alabama family. Being a slave owner and like other slave owners a politician he was naturally an original secessionist and ardently devoted to the Southern cause. Circumstances of an imperious nature, which it is unnecessary to relate here, had prevented him from taking service with the gallant army that had fought the disastrous campaigns ending with the fall of Corinth, and he chafed under the inglorious restraint, longing for the release of his energies, the larger life of the soldier, the opportunity for distinction. That opportunity, he felt, would come, as it comes to all in war time. Meanwhile he did what he could. No service was too humble for him to perform in aid of the South, no adventure too perilous for him to undertake if consistent with the character of a civilian who was at heart a soldier, and who in good faith and without too much qualification assented to at least a part of the frankly villainous dictum that all is fair in love and war.

One evening while Farquhar and his wife were sitting on a rustic bench near the entrance to his grounds, a gray-clad soldier rode up to the gate and asked for a drink of water. Mrs. Farquhar was only too happy to serve him with her own white hands. While she was fetching the water her husband approached the dusty horseman and inquired eagerly for news from the front.

"The Yanks are repairing the railroads," said the man, "and are getting ready for another advance. They have reached the Owl Creek bridge, put it in order and built a stockade on the north bank. The commandant has issued an order, which is posted everywhere, declaring that any civilian caught interfering with the railroad, its bridges, tunnels or trains will be summarily hanged. I saw the order."

"How far is it to the Owl Creek bridge?" Farquhar asked.

"About thirty miles."

"Is there no force on this side the creek?"

"Only a picket post half a mile out, on the railroad, and a single sentinel at this end of the bridge."

"Suppose a man—a civilian and student of hanging—should elude the picket post and perhaps get the better of the sentinel," said Farquhar, smiling, "what could he accomplish?"

The soldier reflected. "I was there a month ago," he replied. "I observed that the flood of last winter had lodged a great quantity of driftwood against the wooden pier at this end of the bridge. It is now dry and would burn like tow."

The lady had now brought the water, which the soldier drank. He thanked her ceremoniously, bowed to her husband and rode away. An hour later, after nightfall, he repassed the plantation, going northward in the direction from which he had come. He was a Federal scout.

III

As Peyton Farquhar fell straight downward through the bridge he lost consciousness and was as one already dead. From this state he was awakened—ages later, it seemed to him—by the pain of a sharp pressure upon his throat, followed by a sense of suffocation. Keen, poignant agonies seemed to shoot from his neck downward through every fiber of his body and limbs. These pains appeared to flash along well-defined lines of ramification and to beat with an inconceivably rapid periodicity. They seemed like streams of pulsating fire heating him to an intolerable temperature. As to his head, he was conscious of nothing but a feeling of fulness—of congestion. These sensations were unaccompanied by thought. The intellectual part of his nature was already effaced; he had power only to feel, and feeling was torment. He was conscious of motion, encompassed in a luminous cloud, of which he was now merely the fiery heart, without material substance, he swung through unthinkable arcs of oscillation, like a vast pendulum. Then all at once, with terrible suddenness, the light about him shot upward with the noise of a loud splash; a frightful roaring was in his ears, and all was cold and dark. The power of thought was restored; he knew that the rope had broken and he had fallen into the stream. There was no additional strangulation; the noose about his neck was already suffocating him and kept the water from his lungs. To die of hanging at the bottom of a river!—the idea seemed to him ludicrous. He opened his eyes in the darkness and saw about him a gleam of light, but how distant, how inaccessible! He was still sinking, for the light became fainter and fainter until it was a mere glimmer. Then it began to grow and brighten, and he knew that he was rising toward the surface—knew it with reluctance, for he was now very comfortable. "To be hanged and drowned," he thought, "that is not so bad; but I do not wish to be shot. No; I will not be shot; that is not fair."

He was not conscious of an effort, but a sharp pain in his wrist apprised him that he was trying to free his hands. He gave the struggle his attention, as an idler might observe the feat of a juggler, without interest in the outcome. What splendid effort!—what magnificent, what superhuman strength! Ah, that was a fine endeavor! Bravo! The cord fell away, his arms parted and floated upward, the hands dimly seen on each side in the growing light. He watched them with a new interest as first one and then the other pounced upon the noose at his neck. They tore it away and thrust it fiercely aside, its undulations resembling those of a water-snake. "Put it back, put it back!" He thought he shouted these words to his hands, for the undoing of the noose had been succeeded by the direst pang that he had yet experienced. His neck ached horribly; his brain was on fire; his heart, which had been fluttering faintly, gave a great leap, trying to force itself out at his mouth. His whole body was racked and wrenched with an insupportable anguish! But his disobedient hands gave no heed to the command. They beat the water vigorously with quick, downward strokes, forcing him to the surface. He felt his head emerge; his eyes were blinded by the sunlight; his chest expanded convulsively, and with a supreme and crowning agony his lungs engulfed a great draught of air, which instantly he expelled in a shriek!

He was now in full possession of his physical senses. They were, indeed, preternaturally keen and alert. Something in the awful disturbance of his organic system had so exalted and refined them that they made record of things never before perceived. He felt the ripples upon his face and heard their separate sounds as they struck. He looked at the forest on the bank of the stream, saw the individual trees, the leaves and the veining of each leaf—saw the very insects upon them: the locusts, the brilliant-bodied flies, the gray spiders stretching their webs from twig to twig. He noted the prismatic colors in all the dewdrops upon a million blades of grass. The humming of the gnats that danced above the eddies of the stream, the beating of the dragonflies' wings, the strokes of the water spiders' legs, like oars which had lifted their boat—all these made audible music. A fish slid along beneath his eyes and he heard the rush of its body parting the water.

He had come to the surface facing down the stream; in a moment the visible world seemed to wheel slowly round, himself the pivotal point, and he saw the bridge, the fort, the soldiers upon the bridge, the captain, the sergeant, the two privates, his executioners. They were in silhouette against the blue sky. They shouted and gesticulated, pointing at him. The captain had drawn his pistol, but did not fire; the others were unarmed. Their movements were grotesque and horrible, their forms gigantic.

Suddenly he heard a sharp report and something struck the water smartly within a few inches of his head, spattering his face with spray. He heard a second report, and saw one of the sentinels with his rifle at his shoulder, a light cloud of blue smoke rising from the muzzle. The man in the water saw the eye of the man on the bridge gazing into his own through the sights of the rifle. He observed that it was a gray eye and remembered having read that gray eyes were keenest, and that all famous marksmen had them. Nevertheless, this one had missed.

A counterswirl had caught Farquhar and turned him half round; he was again looking into the forest on the bank opposite the fort. The sound of a clear, high voice in a monotonous singsong now rang out behind him and came across the water with a distinctness that pierced and subdued all other sounds, even the beating of the ripples in his ears. Although no soldier, he had frequented camps enough to know the dread significance of that deliberate, drawling, aspirated chant; the lieutenant on shore was taking a part in the morning's work. How coldly and pitilessly—with what an even, calm intonation, presaging, and enforcing tranquility in the men—with what accurately measured intervals fell those cruel words:

"Attention, company! . . . Shoulder arms! . . . Ready! . . . Aim! . . . Fire!"

Farquhar dived—dived as deeply as he could. The water roared in his ears like the voice of Niagara, yet he heard the dulled thunder of the volley and, rising again toward the surface, met shining bits of metal, singularly flattened, oscillating slowly downward. Some of them touched him on the face and hands, then fell away, continuing their descent.

One lodged between his collar and neck; it was uncomfortably warm and he snatched it out.

As he rose to the surface, gasping for breath, he saw that he had been a long time under water; he was perceptibly farther down stream—nearer to safety. The soldiers had almost finished reloading; the metal ramrods flashed all at once in the sunshine as they were drawn from the barrels, turned in the air, and thrust into their sockets. The two sentinels fired again, independently and ineffectually.

The hunted man saw all this over his shoulder; he was now swimming vigorously with the current. His brain was as energetic as his arms and legs; he thought with the rapidity of lightning.

"The officer," he reasoned, "will not make that martinet's error a second time. It is as easy to dodge a volley as a single shot. He has probably already given the command to fire at will. God help me, I cannot dodge them all!"

An appalling plash within two yards of him was followed by a loud, rushing sound, *diminuendo*, which seemed to travel back through the air to the fort and died in an explosion which stirred the very river to its deeps! A rising sheet of water curved over him, fell down upon him, blinded him, strangled him! The cannon had taken a hand in the game. As he shook his head free from the commotion of the smitten water he heard the deflected shot humming through the air ahead, and in an instant it was cracking and smashing the branches in the forest beyond.

"They will not do that again," he thought; "the next time they will use a charge of grape. I must keep my eye upon the gun; the smoke will apprise me—the report arrives too late; it lags behind the missile. That is a good gun."

Suddenly, he felt himself whirled round and round—spinning like a top. The water, the banks, the forests, the now distant bridge, fort and men—all were commingled and blurred. Objects were represented by their colors only; circular horizontal streaks of color—that was all he saw. He had been caught in a vortex and was being whirled on with a velocity of advance and gyration that made him giddy and sick. In a few moments he was flung upon the gravel at the foot of the left bank of the stream—the southern bank—and behind a projecting point which concealed him from his enemies. The sudden arrest of his motion, the abrasion of one of his hands on the gravel, restored him, and he wept with delight. He dug his fingers into the sand, threw it over himself in handfuls and audibly blessed it. It looked like diamonds, rubies, emeralds; he could think of nothing beautiful which it did not resemble. The trees upon the bank were giant garden plants; he noted a definite order in their arrangement, inhaled the fragrance of their blooms. A strange, roseate light shone through the spaces among their trunks and the wind made in their branches the music of aeolian harps. He had no wish to perfect his escape—was content to remain in that enchanting spot until retaken.

A whiz and rattle of grapeshot among the branches high above his head roused him from his dream. The baffled cannoneer had fired him a random farewell. He sprang to his feet, rushed up the sloping bank, and plunged into the forest.

All that day he traveled, laying his course by the rounding sun. The forest seemed interminable; nowhere did he discover a break in it, not even a woodman's road. He had not known that he lived in so wild a region. There was something uncanny in the revelation.

By nightfall he was fatigued, footsore, famishing. The thought of his wife and children urged him on. At last he found a road which led him in what he knew to be the right direction. It was as wide and straight as a city street, yet it seemed untraveled. No fields bordered it, no dwelling anywhere. Not so much as the barking of a dog suggested human habitation. The black bodies of the trees formed a straight wall on both sides, terminating on the horizon in a point, like a diagram in a lesson in perspective. Overhead, as he looked up through this rift in the wood, shone great golden stars looking unfamiliar and grouped in strange constellations. He was sure they were arranged in some order which had a secret and malign significance. The wood on either side was full of singular noises, among which—once, twice, and again—he distinctly heard whispers in an unknown tongue.

His neck was in pain and lifting his hand to it he found it horribly swollen. He knew that it had a circle of black where the rope had bruised it. His eyes felt congested; he could no longer close them. His tongue was swollen with thirst; he relieved its fever by thrusting it forward from between his teeth into the cold air. How softly the turf had carpeted the untraveled avenue—he could no longer feel the roadway beneath his feet!

Doubtless, despite his suffering, he had fallen asleep while walking for now he sees another scene—perhaps he has merely recovered from a delirium. He stands at the gate of his own home. All is as he left it, and all bright and beautiful in the morning sunshine. He must have traveled the entire night. As he pushes open the gate and passes up the wide white walk, he sees a flutter of female garments; his wife, looking fresh and cool and sweet, steps down from the veranda to meet him. At the bottom of the steps she stands waiting, with a smile of ineffable joy, an attitude of matchless grace and dignity. Ah, how beautiful she is! He springs forward with extended arms. As he is about to clasp her he feels a stunning blow upon the back of the neck; a blinding white light blazes all about him with a sound like the shock of a cannon—then all is darkness and silence!

Peyton Farquhar was dead; his body, with a broken neck, swung gently from side to side beneath the timbers of the Owl Creek bridge.